COASTAL CONFESSIONS

COASTAL
CONFESSIONS

- A NOVEL -

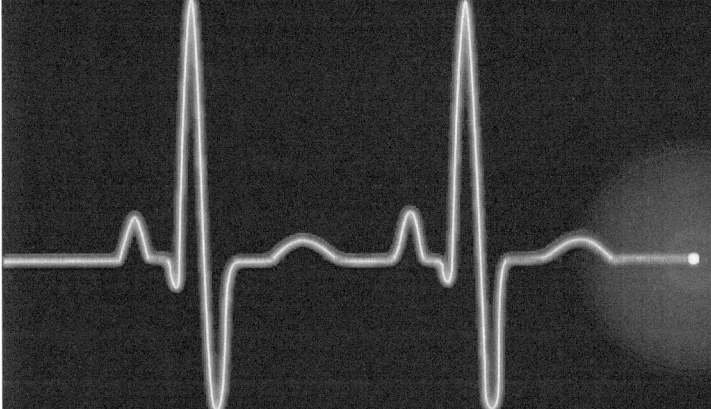

DENNIS CARR

Published by MedEcon Analytics, LLC

THIRD EDITION

Cover design by Kristin Webster

Special thanks to Bill Thompson Editing

Additional assistance by Cheryl Carr and Griffin Carr

ISBN 978-0-9881-8640-8

This is a work of fiction. Characters, corporations, institutions and organizations in this novel are the product of the author's imagination, or if real, are used fictitiously without any intent to describe their actual conduct. However, references that are documented in footnotes are accurate.

If you wish peace, prepare for war.

—*VEGETIUS*

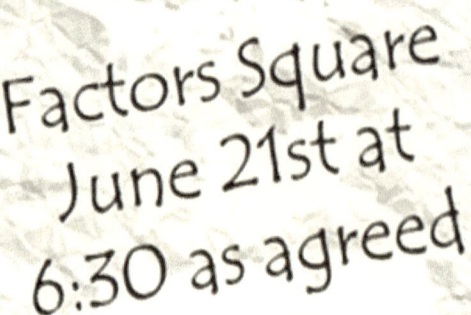

Factors Square
June 21st at
6:30 as agreed

Chapter 1
Monday, June 20th
8:00 P.M.

Jonathon Browning climbed down into the ditch wearing an Armani tuxedo and found himself standing waist-deep in marsh grass. The stakeout had been a bust, and even though he didn't have a clue as to what had gone wrong, he had no one to blame but himself. As he plodded through the mud in his best oxfords, a carload of teenagers blew by on the Tybee Island Causeway, honking and yelling out of the windows. He kneeled down and picked up a small brown package, tearing it open. A cassette tape dropped out into his hand, affixed to a note that was barely legible. It contained only a date, time, and location.

He climbed out of the ditch and lifted his Oakleys, scanning a ribbon of highway that divided the salt marsh like a well-worn bookmark. In the distance a bridge arched high over Lazaretto Creek, Tybee Island's only lifeline to the mainland. Turning toward the sunset he dropped the sunglasses back onto his nose, noticing how the telephone lines sparkled like strands of Christmas lights in the fading light.

He hopped into a gray Z4 Roadster and popped the tape into a portable cassette player sitting on the passenger seat. The recording crackled at first, producing little more than sound bites of irregular breathing before lapsing into silence.

He started the car and cranked up the stereo to drown out the revving engine. *Soak Up The Sun* blasted into the evening air as the convertible's top disappeared into a bay behind the seats. Palm trees swayed in the breeze overhead as a smile emerged, playing with his dimples like a game of connect-the-dots. Without warning the cassette suddenly came to life and shattered his reality, instantly confirming his worst suspicions. This was no longer a game.

A moaning filled the Z4's cabin and scattered his thoughts like fingernails on a chalkboard. He floored the accelerator and a cloud of sand and seashells rained down on the grassy shoulder. The Pirellis struggled for traction, fishtailing until they found the hot sticky asphalt and the car leaped forward.

Salt air whipped at his face as the wind teased his hair into that twist and shout look. When he finally looked into the rear-view mirror, a mistress of blacktop, yellow lines, and palm trees converged against the horizon. Releasing the shifter, he noticed his hand was shaking as he ejected the tape and tweaked the volume on the stereo.

Crossing the Thunderbolt Bridge into Savannah, he navigated through a maze of brick-lined avenues and worked his way over to the historic district. A block off of Johnson Square, he nosed the Roadster into a spot on the curb, drawing the attention of a pair of state troopers leaning against a stretch limousine. They locked onto his every move as he slid out of the driver's seat, brushing off his tux. He buttoned his jacket and stepped up onto the sidewalk, stopping next to a sign that read: *Telfair Hall.* Combing his fingers through a tangle of dark hair, he caught a glimpse of a mansion as he passed through the wrought-iron gates and continued up a driveway. Ahead, two centuries of moss clung to the brick facade, producing an eerie gray-green glow in the scant lighting. The drive yielded to a walkway that brought him to the front steps, where he paused to take in the sounds of a cocktail party underway inside.

"Good evening, sir," a man announced from a portico up top. He held open a door with his chin elevated.

Jon climbed the steps and entered, where a greeter in tails stood behind a lighted stand. Next to him, an officer looked on as Jon reached into his jacket.

"The invitation won't be necessary, Dr. Browning. It's nice to see you this evening."

Jon leaned to one side, taking in the crowd.

"I'm afraid cocktails have already been served," the greeter continued. He leaned forward and lowered his voice. "And there seems to be a gentleman in the library who has requested a moment with you."

"Thank you," Jon said stepping into the foyer.

A throng was collecting beneath a crystal chandelier as he edged past a winding staircase. Down a hallway he came to a door bearing a *Do Not Disturb* sign and slipped inside.

It was dark except for the glow of a Tiffany lamp. He knew the library well, but the lighting made it difficult to see the floor-to-ceiling bookshelves. On the far wall a table sat between two windows. The sheers from one fluttered, revealing a raised sash.

"I trust you're alone," a man said, his voice rising from a chair in the corner. As he stood the shadows masked his true dimensions.

"Charles Rhodes," Jon said. "You're the last person I expected to see tonight."

Rhodes remained silent, and Jon noticed there was a week's growth of beard on his face. The clothes looked slept-in.

"You've got five minutes to explain yourself," Jon said, glancing back at the door.

"I tracked your man as far as the Fort Pulaski entrance. Any closer and he would have spotted me."

"Who is he?"

"Apparently just a lowlife in an old van with out-of-state plates," Rhodes said.

"Ten grand and that's all you can tell me?"

"He threw a package out the window."

"Which you were supposed to retrieve." Jon checked his watch. "Tell me something I don't know."

"We're done."

Jon cut his eyes up at Rhodes, who stood a head taller.

"You're a smart man, so trust me on this one," Rhodes said. "Whatever you're thinking, forget about it."

"I'd say you know more than you're letting on."

"Believe what you want to believe."

"I hired you for answers."

"Listen, I don't know how you got mixed up in all this—"

"All of what?" Jon interrupted.

Rhodes pulled out a stack of bills and dropped them on a table. "There's your money. Don't call me again." He drew back the sheers and stepped out of the window and was gone.

Jon returned to the foyer and climbed the staircase, where couples in formal wear were lingering outside a ballroom. As he stopped to speak to a councilman, a man with an earplug walked by, sporting a visible bulge beneath the lapel of his dinner jacket. Jon excused himself and headed inside, shaking hands along the way until something caught his eye.

Across the room, the glitter of sequins on the fitted black dress beaconed like a city set on a hill, a show-stopper even in the sea of beautiful people. Jon crooked his neck for a better look at the lines of her trim figure, finally settling his gaze upon a tempest of red hair. A pair of diamond earrings dangled loosely about her neck, accentuating the tanned complexion. Fixated, he worked his way closer, noticing that the woman was talking to a man whose back was toward him. Just as their eyes met, the man dipped into the crowd, and Jon slipped in and kissed her on the cheek.

"You look divine," Jon said. "Was that Sam Hallworth?"

"Cut the horseshit," Beth said, her lips barely separating. She raised an empty champagne flute to shield her expression. "You think you can just waltz in here and . . . Where have you been?"

Jon surveyed the room, momentarily returning to her stare.

"So this is how it's going to be?"

"You tell me."

"My conscience is clear. How about yours?"

Beth hitched a hand on her hip.

"Let's just say I had to take care of something," Jon said.

Beth's eyes dropped. "How dare you stand me up."

"Let's not mischaracterize the situation."

"You know how these people are."

"Is this about the new car?"

"A whore, if you ask me."

"Good one," Jon said, smiling. "My best secret until a few minutes ago."

Beth turned to make sure no one was within earshot. "What in God's name are you babbling about now?"

"Fallen angels, my dear," Jon said.

"Well, I'll just call Dr. Phil and maybe he can explain what the hell that means."

"Somehow I thought you'd be a bit more understanding. After all it's been . . . what . . . three days?"

"In case you haven't noticed, everything's not about you."

Jon cut his eyes over her shoulder.

"Look at me when I'm talking to you," Beth said.

"Jonathon, there you are," a voice interrupted.

Beth bristled at the sound of Richard Stone's voice. He was standing next to the guest of honor.

"Jonathon," Richard said. "I believe you know the governor."

Chapter 2
Monday, June 20th
9:30 P.M.

John Edward Callahan offered Jon his hand.

"A pleasure to see you again, sir," Jon said.

"Wonderful to be back in Savannah, Jonathon," the governor replied, stepping past him. "And I remember this pair of lovely blue eyes."

"Of course," Jon said. "My wife, Beth."

She pasted a smile on her ruby-red lips, her eyes flitting nervously between Jon and the governor.

"A delight to see you both," the governor said.

"Did Mrs. Callahan make the trip down with you?"

"I'm afraid not," the governor said somewhat amused. "She's back home keeping the jackasses out of the garden." He tipped his champagne, giving Beth a wink.

"Governor, as I mentioned, Jon was responsible for the bond offering we were discussing earlier," Richard said.

"Music to my ears, Jonathon," the governor said.

"That's very kind of you. Perhaps I could interest you in an update."

The governor held up a finger. "One moment." He turned and interrupted an adjoining conversation.

A man in tortoise-rimmed glasses squeezed in next to the governor, taking in the faces. "A good evening to you all . . . I'm Lawrence Tate, Press Secretary."

"Jonathon has offered to brief us on the Chatham Medical Devices financing. Are you familiar with their story?" As the governor paused for a response, Lawrence's expression went blank.

"Allow me," Jon said, clearing his throat. "The governor is referring to Chatham's bond offering earlier this year. Stone & Associates structured the financing under the state's new tax law."

Lawrence took the cue, suddenly animated. "That's right—the one announced a few months ago at the Business Summit. Chatham's the one doing all the acquisitions. Some type of medical services, if memory serves me correctly."

"Medical technology," Jon added. "They're creating hundreds of new jobs."

"Which is precisely the goal of the governor's tax reform," Lawrence said. "But forgive me, please continue."

"Chatham is currently eyeing another opportunity. The details are confidential, but the tax policy remains critical to the company's expansion plans."

"Let's see, I believe Bob Stein is their CEO," Lawrence said, toying with his glasses. "We should figure out how to generate a little publicity for Chatham."

"My sentiments exactly," the governor said. "Stein has a lot of influence in the business community. Is he here tonight?"

"I'm afraid not, Governor," Richard said. "But he asked me to convey his best wishes on your upcoming reelection bid."

"Gentlemen, this is marvelous news," Lawrence said. "I'll have someone from my office contact him. Don't be surprised if you read about Stein in the weekend edition."

"Thank you, Lawrence," the governor said.

"Now if you'll excuse us, I'm afraid I need a moment with the governor," Lawrence said to the others.

After a parting toast, the two men headed for an exit.

"What can you tell me about Michael Johnson?" Richard said, turning to Jon.

"I dropped his bio on your desk this morning. Michael's one of those MIT prodigies with dual majors in biomedical engineering and computer science. He went on to earn his MD at Harvard."

"He seems to be a good fit for Bob, given they both have medical backgrounds."

"That's true, but Michael never practiced medicine," Jon said. "He headed out to Silicon Valley after medical school, working for a couple of venture-backed startups before striking out on his own. Since founding Johnson-Medisys, he has developed some remarkable technology."

"I understand he's been living hand-to-mouth," Richard said. "Does he have outside funding?"

"Only a few angel investors. He's not one to invite public scrutiny over his work. You might say he's a control freak of sorts."

"Well, it's clear Bob is smitten with his new patient monitor."

"That's just the tip of the iceberg. The real value is in the microchip technology. It's going to revolutionize health management," Jon said.

"I believe you mentioned that to Bob. Are you referring to the hospital market?"

"I'm talking about total health care delivery."

"Really?" Richard said, rather impressed. "How did you convince Michael to entertain the offer from Chatham?"

"Just let me handle Michael."

"As you wish. But you know how Bob can be."

"Tell him not to play games with Michael."

"Easier said than done," Richard said. "By the way, the governor read your article in the *Atlanta Business Chronicle*. It seems he's smitten with the idea that you're the right person to spearhead his next campaign. Think about it." He patted Jon's shoulder. "If you'll pardon me, I have to go mingle." He turned and kissed Beth on the cheek, then stepped away.

"Well-well, Chatham Medical Devices," Beth said, suddenly intrigued. "Aren't you Mr. Tight Lips?"

"A word of advice," Jon said. "Don't go there."

"Did I touch a nerve?"

"Leave it alone, Beth." Jon looked around the room. "I could use a beer."

"It's a champagne reception." She rolled her eyes. "Don't be silly."

"You just don't get it, do you?"

"As you said earlier, you know how these people are," Jon said. "I have to go now."

As Jon turned and walked away a steward entered the ballroom and rang a bell, announcing the governor's speech. He directed the guests downstairs, while Richard and Jon joined a group of dignitaries on a landing at the top of the staircase.

Beth headed down to the foyer and settled in next to Donna Stone, as the crowd awaited the governor's appearance.

"So Beth, how are the children?" Donna said.

"Growing faster than kudzu," she quipped. "I might as well be clothing half of Savannah with all of the donations I'm making to the Junior League this year."

"Enjoy it while you can. William's heading off to college this fall."

"An empty nester?" Beth's eyes widened. "Say it isn't so."

"He'll be attending the University."

"And you as young as a schoolgirl."

"Please. I've raised three boys."

"When you and Richard walked in tonight, I was taken back by how you looked like a true princess in that dress."

"That's sweet of you," Donna said, stealing a glance at Beth's outfit. "I can't remember the last time I squeezed into a gown like you're wearing. What is that—Versace?" Her eyes drifted lower, settling on a pair of strappy heels. "It makes me wonder whose husband owns the firm."

The crowd pressed in around them, applauding as the governor appeared up on the landing.

"I heard an adoring story about how you and Jon first met at a dinner here at Telfair Hall?" Donna said. "Is it true?"

"Actually, it was Factors Square. But he did reserve the library for our first date."

"How romantic."

"Would you excuse me?" Beth said, touching Donna's arm. She turned and pressed through the crowd, disappearing into a hallway beneath the stairs. At the far end, she entered the ladies room.

"Mayor, distinguished guests, ladies and gentlemen—it is with utmost pride that I join you as governor of the great state of Georgia this evening. My heart is warmed once again to enter our wonderful port city, to celebrate not only the history, but the tremendous progress we have ushered in these past few . . ."

Beth stepped in front of the bathroom mirror, primping in her dress. As she freshened up her lipstick, a man in a black tuxedo pushed open the door and startled her. He flipped the latch behind him, forcing her into one of the stalls before she had time to react. Wedging the marble door shut with his back, he pulled her close and pressed his mouth to hers. As she struggled under his grasp, she finally managed to pry her arms free, punching wildly at his face. In the split-second he pulled back, she shoved him and his head snapped back in a thunderclap against the door.

Chapter 3
Monday, June 20th
11:15 P.M.

Jon loosened his bowtie as the governor's limousine sped off behind a procession of flashing lights. He headed over to the curb and hopped in the Z4, starting the engine.

"Would you care to explain what you're doing here?" Jon said, glancing over in the passenger seat.

"It's a beautiful night and the top was down—"

"I'm referring to the reception," Jon interrupted. "You had no right."

"Darling, surely you know better."

He raised an eyebrow, noticing a bruise on her shoulder. "What's this? You're looking a bit frazzled."

"What every woman loves to hear," Beth said, flipping down the visor for a look in the mirror.

Jon noticed the cassette player sitting on the console and ejected the tape, slipping it in his jacket. "Better buckle up," he said, slamming the car into gear.

Beth ignored him and raised her arms into the rushing wind instead.

"Suit yourself." Jon shifted, hugging the curb as they turned onto Abercorn. A parade of stately homes clipped by, looming through the trees.

Beth plucked Jon's sunglasses off the dash.

"What do you think?" she said.

He cut his eyes at her.

"Come on. It's just you and me now. What do you say we go and do something crazy?" Beth reached over and poked him.

Jon didn't bite. "I've got to work tomorrow."

"Oh yeah, I forgot. It wouldn't do for little Jonny to miss his bedtime."

"Keep pretending, Beth."

"And it's such a wonderful day in the neighborhood, la-de-dah," she said, flipping on the stereo.

"Beth, we need to talk."

"Says the man with the, I'm not really into you look."

"What's that supposed to mean?"

"It means—*dear husband*—I could use a little attention over here."

Jon ran a hand through his hair.

"Just get over it," Beth said.

He drove on in silence, leaving the groomed lawns of Ardsley Park behind. A few miles further, he turned and zipped past Oglethorpe Mall. As the traffic thinned Beth leaned closer, her eyes hidden behind the sunglasses.

"A-ttennnnn-tion," she sang out.

"Beth—"

"I need attention . . . a-ttennnnn-tion," she repeated, cheerleader-like. When it didn't get a rise, she kicked off her shoes and climbed up in the seat. A champagne flute rolled from her lap into the floorboard.

"What are you doing?"

She stood up and grabbed the windshield to steady herself.

"Attention . . . can anybody hear me out there?" she shouted into the night. Her hips began to sway to the music as she stared down at Jon, fingering the straps of her dress.

"You're going to get us—"

"A-ttennnnn-tion," she yelled louder, spreading her arms wide.

"Sit down."

Beth flopped down in the seat, laughing.

"Loosen up, Darling."

Jon checked the rearview mirror.

"You can always count on the good old boys from Stone & Associates. Wouldn't you agree?" Beth said.

"That's enough."

"Hey, you're no Boy Scout."

The trees gave way to a sea of floating marsh grass as they crossed a bridge onto the Diamond Causeway. A full moon sparkled in the golden tidal creeks wandering down the sides of the road.

"Why do they think you're so wonderful?" Beth said, breaking the silence.

"We've already been through this."

"You didn't have to sit through Richard carrying on with those pricks about your Stanford PhD and how you impressed the Nobel Laureates at Hoover's last—"

"Beth—"

"Or how brilliantly you advised Buffett or some other ass on a deal while jetting off to Carmel in a Gulfstream."

"Will you—"

"I was waiting to hear the one about how the queen served you tea and crumpets. They're all a bunch of—"

"That wasn't me. It was Richard. And for the last time, nobody thinks I'm wonderful. Okay?"

"Nice try. Did you hear what the governor said?"

"He wouldn't even have recognized me if it hadn't been for Richard."

"You made him look good, and you weren't even trying."

"I was simply doing my job."

"And you'll wind up on the front page of the newspaper, at least according to Sir Lawrence Olivier, or whatever his name is."

"He was talking about Bob Stein." Jon reached for the gearshift.

"Another fine prick. What are you doing?"

"They're raising the drawbridge." Jon pulled the car to a stop at a flashing gate, and a sweeping view of the Intracoastal Waterway unfolded before them. He felt a breeze kick up off the water, offering a hint of saltiness. A section of the bridge lifted into the sky, and across the water Skidaway Island basked in the moonlight.

"Do you think I'm wonderful?"

"Yes, you're wonderful."

She tucked her legs underneath her, twisting toward him. "You know, this is my first ride in the new Beemer." She planted her chin on his shoulder and pulled off the sunglasses.

"How many glasses of champagne did you have tonight?"

She didn't answer, but instead reached for his lap.

"Whoa." Jon grabbed her wrists, checking the mirror. A string of headlights dotted the causeway.

Beth pulled free and hiked up her dress, straddling the console facing backwards. Clutching the headrests, she threw back her head as the pulsing lights from the bridge flashed crimson against her shoulders. Her body seemed to defy gravity, floating on air for a magic moment.

"First runner-up," she said, plunging back to earth. Tears suddenly glistened in her eyes. Her chin dropped as she looked down at the approaching headlights. "Right behind—"

"Beth, that was a long time ago."

"You're no different from the rest of them, are you dear Jonathon?" Her expression was dramatic, like a chorus singer. A pair of headlights lit up her face. "A princess . . ." she said in a soft whisper. Her aura faded as she let go of the headrests and collapsed into the seat, sobbing.

Jon took a breath, fighting the queasiness in his stomach. The gates arched upward and a horn blew behind him. He put the car in gear and drove on.

Chapter 4
Tuesday, June 21st
6:30 A.M.

The townhouses surrounding the park were asleep, their wrought-iron fences invisible in the first rays of sunup. A nearby bishop's crook street lantern flickered, offering only the faintest semblance of light willowing through a thick canopy of oaks. The park, better known to locals as a square, was bordered on four sides by brick-paved streets. It was similar to the dozens that had been designed by James Oglethorpe in the seventeen hundreds. No traffic had passed by since the pre-dawn paper deliveries an hour earlier.

The heat had already begun to transform the early morning mist into a sauna by the time Jon stepped off of Bull Street and started down the sidewalk. His stride fell into a steady rhythm as his footsteps echoed off the townhouses, intensifying as he zeroed in on Factors Square. He crossed the street and paused near an entrance, scanning for any signs of the blue van. When he saw none, he turned his attention to the interior of the square.

His eyes traced a brick walkway to an open area, where he could just make out a man lying on a bench. Continuing his search in the near-darkness, he saw no one else around. He took another look at the homeless man, a familiar sight in the city, particularly in the early morning hours. The scene hit a nerve, reminding him of stories he had heard at the Mission, how the metal benches cut into the shoulder blades and the Lowcountry humidity penetrated deep into the bones. He pulled a handkerchief out of his jacket and wiped perspiration from his forehead.

Jon entered the square, with the click of his heels on the walkway not even fazing the man on the bench. Moving deeper into the shadows, he continued to scan the square. As he approached the bench, he detected movement for the first time. The man slowly creased his forehead, and then pumped his brows to draw a stocking cap down onto the bridge of his nose. He sniffled a time or two before his body stiffened, turning to iron.

Jon stepped closer to the bench, but the man's eyes were hidden beneath the rim of the cap. Now that they were in close proximity, the park's tranquility took on a tension. An Eden only moments ago, the silence felt threatening. Upon closer inspection, he noted a twitch in the man's right arm. The light wasn't helping, but he seemed to be clinging to something inside the sleeve of his corduroy jacket. As he considered his next move, the seconds lapsed into an eternity.

"Are you here to see me?" Jon finally said. His voice pierced the silence, but was absorbed by the trees. He turned to a granite cross only a few feet away. The blue-gray stone rose out of the shadows like an apparition. He was captivated by its size, the movement of light flickering across the rough surface.

The man's breath suddenly crackled as he pivoted toward Jon. A trickle of sweat ran down his neck.

"I'm here about the tapes," Jon said.

The man seemed dazed as his head inched off the bench, staring from the fringes of the cap.

"What do you know about this?" Jon leaned over and pulled out a cassette.

A sliver of eye took a peek, carefully sizing Jon up. He scanned all six feet of him before glancing down at the shoes.

"This is public property," the man said, his words raspy.

"I'm not here to—"

"Then what the hell do you want?" The man raised up on an elbow, and then sat upright, never taking his eyes off of Jon.

"Talk to me," Jon said.

The man tugged at the sleeve of his jacket. "Rich man—huh? That's what I thought." Maintaining eye contact, he squeezed the pipe inside his sleeve.

"You have me here, so let's talk."

"Show me the cash," the man said. "And when we're done, do yourself a favor and forget you were here."

"Fair enough." Jon looked down the street, slipping the cassette into his jacket. "I brought the money."

"Smart move. That tape ain't something you want out on the street, now is it? And the others are just like it."

"Two hundred dollars a tape, right?" Jon checked his watch. "The police will be making their rounds soon, but take all the time you need." He looked over his shoulder, like he was expecting someone.

"What did you do, anyway?"

Jon smiled as he turned back to him. "Oh, you're good."

"How's that?"

"It's a compliment."

"I think you're toying with me."

"It's your meeting, so if you're here to accuse me of something, let's have it. Otherwise, why don't you tell me who put you up to this?"

"Listen, mister—"

"What's your name?" Jon interrupted.

The man snickered. "Like I'd—"

"I'll give you an extra hundred."

"It's none of your damn business."

"You made it my business," Jon said, taking the opposite end of the bench. He looked up at the granite cross, studying it in silence before speaking again. "Are you a spiritual man?"

"Right," the man said. "Like I see the hand of the Almighty in my line of work." His arm stiffened as he fingered the pipe. "You one of those preachers?"

"Not even close. Investment banking."

"I might have known from the shoes."

"Excuse me?" Jon said. When there was no response, he added, "Five hundred a tape and you tell me everything."

"Damn if you couldn't raise a good mutiny."

"Rumor has it that this square was one of Oglethorpe's original twenty-four, but that's all we know about it. History doesn't get more beautiful than this." He raised a hand to the cross. "Nobody knows who put that here. It's more or less an orphan— the way I feel sometimes."

The man took a peek, and then looked away like it hurt his eyes. "Why did you pick this spot?"

"Like you said, it's public property." Jon pulled out his wallet and thumbed through some bills.

"The tapes are strictly between you and me," the man said, easing the pipe out.

Jon counted without looking up.

"I'm afraid the rest of our business comes courtesy of a new client," the man added.

He gripped the pipe and swung it high over Jon's head. As it arched toward its mark, a sliver of sunlight caught it for a split second, triggering Jon's reflexes. He never saw what was coming, but he dove for the ground. The weapon grazed off of his side and rang solid against the metal bench. Jon's wallet slipped from his hand and spiraled through the air, landing on a patch of grass. Rolling out of harm's way, he gasped for breath as the world around him blurred and the pipe bounced across the brick walkway in slow motion. He blinked to clear the moisture from his eyes, refocusing on his attacker. The homeless man snapped up the wallet and ran out of the park.

Chapter 5
Tuesday, June 21ˢᵗ
7:15 A.M.

Charles Rhodes didn't answer his phone. Instead of voicemail, the line went dead after three rings. As the gold dome of City Hall disappeared behind a row of townhouses, Jon hung up and dialed again. When Captain didn't answer, he left a message on his machine, glancing up as a mist began to fall from the sky. He stopped at the Z4 parked on the street, popping open the trunk and dropping the pipe inside. To his left and right, the rear entrances of refurbished row houses lined the alley, with an occasional oak overhanging the sidewalks from the small grassy courtyards along the way. He crossed the alley to a door with a brass *Stone & Associates, LLC* plaque and inserted a key, slipping inside.

"Great, you're here."

Jon fell back against the door, squaring his shoulders against the solid mahogany millwork. He hung his head, letting out a breath. A woman in a shapely navy suit stood in the rear foyer, staring at him.

"Don't do that," Jon said.

"Richard's been trying to reach you on your cell . . ." Brenda's eyes widened as her mouth fell open mid-sentence. Her dark hair brushed against her shoulders as she stepped toward him. She paused under a brass chandelier, taking inventory. "Jon, what on earth happened to you?"

"It's nothing."

"Your suit is torn," she said, looking down at his jacket. "Did something attack you out on the island?"

"Brenda, we're not going to debate this again. Skidaway is a golf community—"

"Yeah, but you're out there isolated from civilization."

"We're connected to the mainland by a drawbridge."

"And then there's the fence and gates."

"They're security gates."

"And wild animals," Brenda said.

"Yes, it's a wildlife preserve. I live on a barrier island, not an episode of *Survivor*."

"Then what mauled you?"

Jon shook his head. "I'm fine—really." He stepped across the foyer and started down a hallway. Brenda turned and followed along behind him.

"Let's see—I've known you for, what, five years? And this is definitely not your look."

"Brenda, you're in-house legal counsel, not the designated fashion critic."

"Tell that to Richard. He's put me in charge of everything from HR to security.

"Thanks for reminding me."

"As I was saying, Richard's having breakfast with the governor at the Hyatt and wants you to handle a conference call he set up. Not to add stress to your morning, but he said Johnson-Medisys is your deal and he's counting on you to talk sense into your buddy, Michael Johnson. He wants you to wrap up the first round of negotiations. Here's a fax with late-breaking details. Richard says this could eighty-six the acquisition."

Jon stopped and scanned the fax, then cut his eyes at Brenda. "What time is the call?"

"It started twenty minutes ago. Charlie had to get the ball rolling since you were missing in action."

"Charlie—at this hour?"

"When Richard couldn't reach you, he told me to improvise, so I called Charlie. I also brought in Terri and Steve for backup."

"Never let Charlie screw with one of my deals."

"Then answer your phone. They're in the boardroom. I told Charlie I'd send you in as soon as you arrived."

"Who's negotiating on the other end?" Jon checked his watch and started walking again.

"Michael Johnson, himself. And I'd say he's got at least two lawyers on the line with him."

"Michael's definitely on a rampage over this one." Jon raised the fax over his shoulder. "It's four-thirty in San Diego."

"That's why you're here," Brenda said. "If you're hungry, there's coffee and Danish inside."

Jon came to a stop in front of a cherry-paneled door, reaching for the doorknob. His hand missed as Brenda squeezed in between, facing him.

"Could I trouble you to get my Johnson-Medisys file?" Jon bent over and hiked up a pants leg, retrieving a leather wallet from his sock. Brenda held her ground as he straightened up, a mere breath separating them. He flipped through the wallet.

"It's on the conference table," Brenda said, reaching for his jacket. She stuck a finger through a tear, eyeing the wallet as he had slipped it in his pocket.

"Remember what I said about Charlie." Jon sidestepped Brenda and turned the knob, heading inside as the jacket slipped through her fingers. He paused, and then looked back at her. Brenda's eyes were alert, yet inquisitive. "It was a wild boar," he said, and then closed the door.

Chapter 6
Tuesday, June 21st
7:30 A.M.

Two hundred feet above the Savannah River, the Talmadge Memorial Bridge seemed to float on thin air. The white concrete and cable silhouette glowed in the early morning light, riding high above the water as graceful as a swan. The bridge beckoned to the throngs of tourists drawn to the nearby historic district, but offered little evidence of the no man's land that lay in its shadows. Only a short stroll from Factors Walk, the area had been left for abandoned, a blight between Savannah's River Street and the bustling seaport a short distance away.

As the sun took its first peek over the Atlantic downriver, a warehouse sat shrouded in mist, hovering on a narrow strip of riverbank. The stone foundation bordered the water's edge, clinging to a collapsed wharf where cotton and rice had once been loaded aboard ships. A series of arches crowned the cargo-sized doors that ran the building's length, which had been nailed shut decades ago and remained sealed tighter than a powder keg. Above them, light escaped through a row of smoked-glass windows.

On the inland side of the warehouse, a brick alley ran parallel to the river. Foul smelling and wet, it was invaded daily by a collection of outcasts that typically snaked-on for half a city block. A landing at one corner provided access to the building, where a line presently stretched across the pine flooring to a cafeteria-style serving area in the back corner. The gymnasium-sized room opened up to a raised roofline, with its exposed beams reeking of creosote. On the far wall, a wooden staircase climbed to a closed doorway on the second floor.

In the serving area, grits plopped onto plastic plates with the precision of a military air strike. Captain Louis Beecher, Jr., proprietor of the Seafarer Mission, stood next to a stainless steel pot barking orders to a volunteer crew. Steam rose into the rafters, swirling around like contrails until it was sucked out a flapping gable fan. Just enough buttery aromas hung in the air to induce the smacking of lips up and down the line. In better times the sizzle of eggs and pork had greeted the hungry clientele at sunup, but complaints were few as of late, even though the offering had been little more than watered down grist.

Although highly regarded around the Mission, Captain Beecher's salt-and-pepper reputation garnered little appeal to pure-bred Savannahians. Friends called him "Captain", while those less enamored with the old seaman referred to him as "LBJ". A man of few platitudes, his mannerisms invited a groundswell of contempt among the blue bloods. He had long since determined to define life on his own terms, an attitude he found necessary in his mission to lift Savannah's destitute.

"Sanky, you're supposed to be on detail," Captain said, raising his voice above the clatter of pots and pans.

Sanky stood in line with a plate in his hand, staring down at the floor. His clothes were straight out of *Oliver Twist*.

Captain stepped back from the counter and walked around, whistling as he caught a glimpse of the shoes. "What do we have here?"

"Dr. Browning asked me to pick up his tux yesterday. I told him I liked the shoes, and he gave 'em to me, just like that," Sanky said. The gray stubble on his face gave way to a smile. He looked up just long enough to hand his plate to a server.

Captain squinted. "You're not likely to be 'a needing those anytime soon, at least not for employment purposes. There's talk that the Port Authority is hiring down at the docks this morning."

Sanky spun toward the door.

"Hold on. You've got time for breakfast," Captain said, re-treating behind the counter. "But don't go messing up them shoes. I'll never hear the end of it if Jonathon Browning finds out I sent you to unload cargo in patent leather." Captain took the plate from the server and handed it across to Sanky.

"Blessings to you, Captain," Sanky said with a head bow. He hurried over to a wooden table in the seating area.

As the line advanced, the next man stepped up and Captain took his plate and scooped a ladle of grits. A stocking cap sat low across the man's nose. "Hello mate," he said, passing the plate back. The man didn't respond, only turned and disappeared into the crowd. Captain frowned, and then called after him, "Nice cap."

When the last patron had been served Captain banged on a pot for silence, and then announced, "Distinguished ladies and gentlemen, as we have entered into a new day, a day the Almighty has so graciously blessed, let us pause to give thanks."

Every utensil idled.

"Our father, admiral of this earthly fleet of humanity, use these grits to nourish our bodies, but more importantly this Mission to feed our souls. May we experience life not in these earthly rags, but in the bounty of your eternal promise. Amen."

"Amen" echoed across the warehouse, followed by the scrap-ing of forks.

* * *

Terri and Steve stood like statues in their tailored suits next to a polished conference table, praying for the silence to linger until cooler attitudes could prevail. A rustling of paper emerged from a speakerphone in the center of the table, and they collectively tensed, fearing the sound might trigger a reaction. Avoiding eye contact with anyone, they remained safely out of the line of fire, each holding their breath. Leather chairs were scattered around the boardroom, sitting empty for the past forty-five minutes as Jon and Charlie paced the white wool carpet on the opposite side of the table, clearly at odds over the most recent exchange.

The eye of the storm passed.

"Michael, you've drawn yourself into a corner. I'm truly disappointed in your response," Jon said, turning to focus outside the window. "I assume you still want to do a deal?"

Michael's tone rattled the speaker. "That's easy for you to say, Jonathon. You haven't labored with the business for the past seven years. And furthermore, you've known my position from the start."

"That's beside the point."

"No, that is the point."

"Focus on the facts, Michael," Jon countered.

"And what are the facts?"

"Chatham Medical Devices is not responsible for your underfunded pension liability. And correct me if I'm wrong, but your board appointed the current trustees. A lot of investment portfolios have tanked in this market, so I'd advise you to be flexible at this stage in the negotiations."

"You don't understand—"

"Here's the bottom line. Unless your position changes immediately, you'd better be prepared to walk away." Jon paused as more rustling crackled through the speaker. "You're demanding commitments even you can't fulfill if Chatham decides to push back from the table. The West Coast karma is fading fast, my friend. We're talking seven figures, here. You've got to fund the deficit."

"I'll take whatever position I choose. Maybe you've forgotten—the company bears my name."

"Michael, the banks are about to force you into liquidation. We're talking about flesh-eating vultures swooping in to auction off the furniture. How does that sound after seven years?"

Charlie slapped a hand to his forehead, and then reached over and hit the mute button. "Jon, what the hell are you doing? He's on the verge of killing this thing." The veins in Charlie's neck stuck out, giving him a flush complexion.

"Settle down, Charlie."

"Bob Stein is going to blow a fuse."

"Charlie, back off."

"Richard, where are you when we need you?" Charlie said, raising his hands in the air.

"We're on strategy."

"Meaning what? . . . On course? Chatham's making a play for this company and you just threatened the owner. Are you kidding?"

"I proposed the Johnson-Medisys deal to Bob, so Michael had better wake up and thank his lucky stars. He's got nowhere else to turn." Jon looked across the table at Terri and Steve, who stood frozen in place. He glared back at Charlie. "If Michael walks, I'll give him two months before he's forced to sell. Bob will pick up the company for a song and pocket another five million on the transaction."

"All hell can break loose in two months. You know that," Charlie said. "Besides, Bob swears he won't last another thirty days."

"Bob changed the terms, not Michael," Jon said.

"Jon, maybe you should counsel with Richard?" Terri said, breaking her silence. She walked over and handed Charlie a Pellegrino.

Charlie took out a handkerchief and dabbed at his bald spot. "That's just it, Terri. Richard left Jon in charge. But he'll have all of our heads if this thing tanks."

"Michael knows the downside. Sooner or later he'll have to negotiate," Steve chimed in.

The room grew silent as all eyes drifted over to Jon, who was now staring out the window. The cool hazel tones in his eyes sparkled in the sunlight. Jon let a smile slip, like the telling of a secret.

"What?" Charlie said, looking around the room to see if the others were following.

"How about this—"

Terri shot Steve a look, cutting him off mid-sentence.

"Are you just going to stand there with that smirk on your face, or are you going to tell us?" Charlie said.

"Jonathon." It was Michael on the speakerphone. Everyone tensed up. "Are you there?"

Jon motioned for Charlie to release the mute.

"Listen, Michael. Bob has already lined up a hospital to beta-test your technology. I'm working on another one that has national recognition. Do you understand the implications? If the technology is validated, your shares will be worth a fortune. You'll be a rich man."

Michael cleared his throat, but didn't respond.

"Michael?" Jon said.

"This is going to cost you."

"I need an answer."

"Are you positive Bob is inflexible on his position?"

"One hundred percent."

"Then let's move forward," Michael said.

Chapter 7
Tuesday, June 21st
9:00 P.M.

With round one of the Johnson-Medisys negotiations wrapped up, Jon headed over to the Moon River Brewing Company on Bay Street with Terri and Steve for a well-earned celebration. Inside they found Charlie seated at a table in the bar, next to a boulder-sized fermenting tank that sat on display behind a glass wall. A waitress nudged through the crowd and started clearing glasses from the table as a steady stream of customers passed by on their way to the dining area.

Charlie was busy eyeing a tourist at the bar as they walked, spouting off at Jon in the process. "Well, if it isn't the former first mate of the USS Merrill Lynch." He turned and hefted a beer mug.

"We'll have a round for the table," Jon said to the waitress before turning to face Charlie. "Is there a problem?"

"Uh-oh," Terri said, rolling her eyes. "I think I hear the beer speaking."

"You worked for Merrill?" Steve said.

"Are you new around here?" Charlie quipped.

"Four months and two days." Steve smiled.

"Jon's somewhat of a legend at Merrill. Of course, they nearly belly-flopped before Bank of America bailed them out," Charlie said.

"Definitely the beer," Terri said, turning to Steve. "Jon was in charge of biotech investments in San Francisco and has quite the reputation around Silicon Valley. If the rest of Merrill had been run like his division, they'd still be independent."

"A real swashbuckling hero," Charlie said.

"He does have that tall, dark, and handsome persona," Terri added.

"So what lured you to Stone & Associates?" Steve said.

"Smaller companies with bigger upside potential. Deals that never appear on Merrill's radar."

"And he's a Southern boy at heart," Terri said.

"What is he—like your secret lover or something?" Steve reached over and grabbed a mug as the waitress returned with the beer.

"It's kind of nauseating, isn't it?" Charlie said. "Beth Browning would rip out Terri's eyelashes if she so much as sniffed his aftershave."

"Whoa," Steve said.

"Give it a rest, Charlie," Jon said. "Let's keep this civilized."

"Watch him boys. If you're not careful, he'll make you walk the plank. You saw, firsthand, what he did to Michael Johnson today."

"Charlie, you've had enough to drink." Jon flipped open his cell phone. "Now, if you'll excuse me, I need to make a call." He slipped away through the crowd.

The sidewalk out front was dark and brimming with pedestrians. Jon had to sidestep the foot traffic as he dialed. Across Bay Street he could see gray tuxedoed attendants busy greeting guests at the Hyatt. Half a block down tourists swarmed the crosswalk, and a familiar profile appeared among the faces. He strained for a better look, but then someone crashed into him and knocked the phone out of his hand. Snapping it up, he said, "Beth?" He heard her voicemail greeting on the other end of the line as he took another look down Bay. The crosswalk was clear. Hanging up, he headed back inside.

". . . anyway, when Jon was in junior high he had this strict English teacher," Charlie said. "You know the kind—pointed glasses, tight bun, and everything—"

"Sorry guys, I've got to take care of some things at the office," Jon interrupted. "And for the record, only two people in Savannah think that story is funny—Charlie and my wife."

"Bummer man," Steve said.

"My sentiments exactly," Jon said. "The drinks are on me."

Jon sat down and turned on a lamp, dialing from his desk phone. "Bob—Jonathon Browning. Sorry to call so late, but it's been a long day. Michael is on board with your changes, so we're ready to draft an agreement. My only concern is how the patents may impact the valuations. They're worth nearly as much as Chatham, so I've got an analyst reviewing the filings. I'm praying this doesn't turn into a merger of equals." He paused to listen, and then continued, "Well, you're talking about a cash flow matter. It's possible he'll run out of funds before the patents issue, but that's a gamble. Listen, I contacted a venture capital firm out in California. They agree we should—"

Jon stopped mid-sentence as Stein cut him off.

"That's a drop in the bucket. I'm talking about—" Jon paused again. "Okay, I've got to run . . . I understand . . . Call me anytime."

Jon held back an urge to give Stein a piece of his mind as he hung up and turned to his computer, scrolling through a string of e-mails.

"Great job today, Jon."

"Terri," Jon said, surprised to hear her voice as she stepped into his office. "That's kind of you."

"By the way, you seriously impressed Steve tonight. He had no idea Richard hired you to refocus the firm on technology companies."

"Steve was a good hire. Let's get him up to speed fast. So how's the beast?"

"Charlie? Last I saw of him, he was offering to take a blonde bar-hopping on River Street."

"Why am I not surprised?" Jon said. "Anyway, thanks for your efforts on the due diligence. We've got a nice head of steam now, so I wouldn't be surprised if this deal closes over the summer."

"How about a wager? Let's say—dinner at the Chart House?"

"Winner selects the wine?"

"You're on," Terri said. "Anyway, I won't keep you. Congratulations and don't forget to go home."

"That's next on my list."

As Terri disappeared, Jon looked at the clock and exhaled. He typed a response to an e-mail from Michael, and then logged off. Locking his office, he walked down the hall and exited out the back entrance. Crossing the alley, perspiration had beaded on his forehead by the time he reached the car. He opened the door and felt a sauna-like wave spill out.

Starting the engine his mind shifted into gear, prioritizing the tasks for the coming day. He flipped on the air conditioner and pulled out his cell phone, but then realized it was past business hours, even on the West Coast. He wiped his forehead with a handkerchief as he turned onto Bull Street, remembering he had tried to call Beth around nine-thirty. A horn blew behind him and he sped up. His thoughts shifted to Bob Stein, marveling that the man was like a bull in a china shop. *He never listens,* he thought. At the next intersection, the fatigue from the day finally caught up with him. He yawned, never realizing he had run a red light.

Chapter 8
Tuesday, June 21ˢᵗ
11:30 P.M.

The moon was sparkling on a tidal creek behind the house when Jon turned into the brick-lined driveway. A row of palms cast shadows across the gray cedar siding as he pulled into the garage. Moments later he was relieved to find peace and quiet inside, dropping off his briefcase in the study. He remembered the tear in his jacket and took it off, tossing it into a chair. For the first time all day, he felt the tension beginning to lift. A pass through the kitchen turned up no leftovers, so he headed upstairs and slipped through a dark bedroom into the master bath. Doing his best not to wake Beth, he closed the bathroom door and switched on the lights, yawning as he turned on the shower and making a mental note to check on the children. Afterwards he would microwave a pizza, and then bunk in the guest room for the night.

Minutes later, Jon stepped out of the shower and dipped into an adjoining walk-in closet. Exchanging his towel for a pair of shorts and t-shirt he turned to leave, stopping just short of a collision with Beth. He recoiled, stepping back as the vanity lights captured her expression, warning him that trouble was ahead.

"You startled me," Jon said, nudging past her. "Are the kids in bed?"

"Jonathon, I need to talk to you."

"Where were you earlier—"

"Listen to me." Beth grabbed an arm. "Jonathon!"

The tone in her voice hastened his pace for the bedroom. "I can't do this now," Jon said, suddenly freezing, as if slamming into an invisible wall.

"Do I have your attention now?"

"Okay—I'm listening," Jon said, speaking slowly.

In the glow of the bathroom lights, Jon looked out into the bedroom where picture frames hung unevenly on the walls—two others lay on the floor in shards. He noticed knickknacks and perfume bottles strewn across the dresser, dripping on the carpet. A crystal lamp had been knocked over, the pleated shade crushed. Draped over the foot of the bed, a mass of covers collected on the floor, with the matching pillows scattered in every direction. Stepping back into the bathroom, he turned to her.

"When did this happen?"

"Will you just . . ."

"Have you called nine-one-one?"

"I'm trying to tell you."

"Okay, okay. Just take your time."

Beth closed her eyes. "I already called the police," she said.

"Give me a minute, here." Jon took another look at the room and ran a hand through his hair. "I was hoping you hadn't."

"They filed a report."

Jon reached out to touch her, but she pulled back.

"The officer said they would keep an eye on the situation," she continued.

"The media's going to have a field day with this."

"Jonathon, forget about that and listen to me." Beth moved toward him and grabbed his forearm.

"Are the kids all right?"

"You need help," she said, clinging to him.

"Let me handle this."

"You need someone to help you deal with . . . us."

"Beth, the confession has to wait."

"Get help," she repeated. "I know someone—"

"Where are the kids?"

"Doctor—"

"Answer me," Jon said, pulling free and disappearing down the hall.

Beth dropped to the floor and kept her eyes trained on him as he slipped into Bailey's room. Then she spoke softly to herself, a mere whisper. "Why don't you love me?"

Chapter 9
Wednesday, June 22nd
6:15 A.M.

Captain sat in his office on the second floor of the Mission, squinting out a window at the Talmadge Bridge. He studied the currents swirling around a concrete stanchion as he pressed the telephone to his ear.

"Where have you been, Boy? I've been trying to reach you since yesterday."

On the other end, Jon checked his cell phone and switched on the ringer. "Sorry, my mistake."

"Everything okay in that bloody corporate minefield of yours?"

"It couldn't be better. And for the record, the good guys are winning. How's business at the Mission?"

"Maybe you should come down and see for yourself. I like it when my board members stop by for a dose of reality," Captain said. "You didn't quite sound like yourself when you left the message. It might be me, but I sense a hint of it now?"

"The call—right. I had a run-in with a street guy over at Factors Square."

"Still frequenting that park, are you?"

"What can I say? I go there to be alone."

"You and that cross are like Moses and the burning bush. But I don't blame a man for staking out some holy ground."

"Let's not get carried away. The Good Book doesn't say anything about *X* marking the spot."

"If you're referring to meeting your bride-to-be in a bloody park, I'd definitely say someone predestined that one."

"Anyway, I didn't want to get the police involved," Jon said, ignoring the comment. "I thought you might be able to ID him. One minute we were having a conversation, the next he decided to crack me over the head with a metal pipe."

"Did he hit you?"

"It was only a flesh wound, but he messed up a perfectly good bench before making off with my wallet."

"You're familiar with most of the regulars. What did he look like?"

"He was wearing a corduroy jacket, with all the buttons missing, and a red-striped stocking cap."

"You don't say," Captain said. "Was it a lot of money?"

"Not much, but I'd like to get my wallet back."

"The Lord just may be with you. I'm pretty sure this mate of yours stopped by for breakfast yesterday," Captain said. "But I can't say I've ever seen him before."

"Just to be clear, he's no mate of mine."

"Boy, when will you learn? The ways of the street are like one of your hostile takeovers."

"I let down my guard, but I was on holy ground, remember?"

"I'm heading down to prepare breakfast," Captain said. "If I spot your man, I'll see what I can do."

"If you don't mind, I'd prefer you let me talk to him."

"Why? So you can give him a reward? I saw those shoes you gave to Sanky. You're turning all of my clientele into Rockefellers.

I guess they'll be erecting a Jonathon Browning monument down at that park of yours pretty soon."

"You'd probably like me better if I was a pillar of stone, wouldn't you?"

"The Lord makes us all special . . . You're sure you're all right?"

"Nothing a hard day's work won't cure."

"Don't be a stranger. Blessings to you, Boy."

Chapter 10
Thursday, June 23rd
9:30 P.M.

Breaking the ice after two days—Jon knew it was going to be a challenge as he entered the house, dropping off his briefcase in the study. He headed into the family room, where Mozart was playing on the stereo. No one seemed to be at home, but then he noticed a magazine lying open on the sofa. At the far end of the room, candles were flickering on the fireplace hearth. He followed the stacked-stones up to a vaulted ceiling and turned to check out the second-story landing. Beth was standing at the rail in a flowered halter top and capris.

"I'm coming up to say goodnight to Carver and Bailey," Jon said.

"About that . . ." Beth said, looking away.

"What have you done?"

"You said you wanted to talk."

"Beth, I'm getting pretty tired of coming home and finding that the children have been sent to your mother's."

She stood stoic, hitching a hand on her hip. When she didn't respond, Jon made a detour into the kitchen and grabbed a beer. He stepped out the back door and pulled up a chair at an umbrella table on the pool deck.

As he sipped his beer, he heard the door slam, followed by the drumbeat of Beth's heels approaching. Yanking out a chair, she slapped the magazine on the table and sat down, giving him a fake smile.

Jon looked off into the marsh, taking another sip before breaking the silence. "Carver left a message at the office this afternoon. He's pretty excited about the boat show this weekend. For a six-year-old, he seems to have life figured out—he wants to be a professional jet-ski racer." Jon shook his head. "He said he had a picture to show me when I got home."

"That's all he's been talking about," Beth said, her tone a bit edgy.

"He's like a fish, when he's in the water. I guess that explains why he watches the Discovery Channel so much."

"Well, if you spent a little more time with him and Bailey, I wouldn't have to depend on my mother so much."

Jon turned and raised an eyebrow, but let the comment pass.

"Beth, I'll get straight to the point. I'm not wired to live like this. The living arrangements are strained, and I'm practically living out of a suitcase. My only refuge is at the office."

"The understatement of the century," Beth said, rolling her eyes.

"Regardless of how you feel, if this is going to work, you're going to have to explain the confession," Jon said, pausing for a response.

She brushed back her hair.

"Tonight would be a good start," he added.

"How's this? I stopped by a clinic this week and had my blood tested . . . According to the results, there's nothing to worry about."

Jon hesitated. "That wasn't exactly on my radar, but okay."

"Jonathon, you know what I want."

"That's not true. I don't even know what to call this." Jon gave her his look. "Five men, Beth . . . *five*. That borders on promiscuity. No, nymphomania."

"Five?" She came out of the chair. "I never said such a thing."

A sense of relief surfaced, but quickly disappeared as Jon realized what had just happened. "I'm afraid you did . . . And I constantly play the words over in my mind, even in my sleep."

"Then you misunderstood."

"That's a little hard to swallow at this point."

"There were two," Beth said, staring directly into Jon's eyes.

"I realize you were upset that night, but that's not what you said."

"Why do I bother?"

"Okay," Jon said, raising a hand. "Let's just keep this rational." He looked over at the pool. The underwater lights sparkled like topaz against the night sky. "Maybe I'm the one who is going crazy."

"Jonathon, regardless of what you think you may have heard, I said there were two. Read my lips. T-W-O."

"But you distinctly mentioned there were others—three to be exact. How do you account for them?"

Beth shifted in her seat. "If we agree there were three, can we get past this?"

"This isn't a negotiation."

"There were actually two . . . But since you're analyzing this to death, the other was just a one-off. Are you happy now?" She folded her arms and turned her back to him.

"A one-off? . . . Are you serious?" Jon said. "So you're now claiming there were three?"

"We're here because you said you had questions, but this feels more like an interrogation. I forgot about one incident, so don't go making it into something else."

"So far, I've heard five . . . two . . . and three? Which is it? I can't deal with this if you can't tell me the truth."

"Why do you take everything so literally? For once in your life don't get so hung up on the words."

"You've violated our marriage vows, and now you're going to sit there and tell me how I should react?"

"You're not doing this to me. And just so you know, it all happened before we met. I didn't violate anything."

"Beth, you asked me to forgive you for your indiscretions, and that's putting it nicely." Jon loosened his tie.

"Those aren't my words, and you know it."

"Then why did you confess to these so-called incidents, if they all happened before we were married?"

"You need help," Beth said, ignoring the question.

"Okay, then let's try this. Give me their names."

"That's insane. I told you before, you don't—"

"I want the truth."

"The names won't help."

"That's for me to decide," Jon said. When she didn't budge, he stood up and started for the house.

"What do I have to do to convince you?" Beth shouted.

"You can start by telling the truth."

Over his shoulder Jon heard metal scraping, and then a splash. As he turned, Beth was standing at the edge of the pool, and the umbrella table bobbed in the water.

"You're freaking out over nothing," Beth protested, looking over a shoulder at him. "Jonathon, you need to—"

"Five affairs, Beth."

"Three men . . . And it was a long time ago," she said, starting toward Jon.

"I'm not doing this any longer," Jon said. "We both know what this is about."

Beth stopped in her tracks, opening her eyes wide. "God told me to confess," she said, now speaking softly.

"This just keeps getting better . . . You expect me to believe that?"

"How dare you."

"Don't try to blame God for our marriage problems. We've done quite enough on our own."

When Beth looked up, her face had hardened.

"Why are you dragging God into this now?" Jon said.

"You don't know everything."

"Is there anything else you haven't told me?"

"I'm not playing your game."

"Beth, we have to face the facts, or I'm afraid this isn't going to end well." Jon turned and walked inside.

Chapter 11
Friday, June 24ᵗʰ
7:30 A.M.

Captain stirred two oversized steel pots as a head of steam rose into the rafters. A collection of misfits busied themselves stacking plates, while others filled coffee dispensers perched at the end of the serving line.

"Sanky, more water," Captain yelled, eyeing a line that extended out the front door. He looked up into the steam. "Lord, I've read about how you fed thousands with a tiny bit of bread and a couple of fish. I'm hoping for that kind of grace this morning." Sanky interrupted the prayer, nudging by to refill the pots. Captain finished up, with his eyes still uplifted. "Just don't send 'em away hungry."

"You're going to need more mouths to feed if that one gets answered," Jon said, stepping through the line.

"Amen to that," Captain said, his spirit suddenly lifting. "Five more minutes, and I was kicking you off of the board of directors."

"That's quite an attitude for a bustling Friday morning."

"I suspect there'll be standing room only on this day the Lord has so mysteriously blessed," Captain said.

"I'm reporting for duty," Jon said, reaching for an apron.

"Grab one of those ladles and serve to your heart's desire."

"Aye, Captain," Jon said.

By eight-fifteen, they had fed three hundred and forty-seven mouths. The crowd seemed satisfied, despite another morning of runny grits. It had taken barely forty-five minutes for the coffee towers to drip dry, officially ending breakfast service for the morning. Afterwards there was cleanup duty, and Jon hung around for a visit with Captain.

"Did you spot your assailant this morning, Boy?" Captain said, topping the stairs to his second floor office. He carried a coffee tin in his hand, with Jon in tow. "'Cause I sure didn't."

"I'm afraid not."

"Step inside, and we'll size up the situation." Captain slid behind a desk in the corner as Jon pulled up a chair.

Jon settled in, taking in the scenery outside the window. The glass was as thick as a Coke bottle, but offered a generous view of the Talmadge Bridge. He sat in silence as Captain rummaged through a desk drawer.

"I haven't seen your attacker since Tuesday morning. It seems he's a curious fellow, though," Captain said.

"What are the chances he'll reappear?"

"Well, I only saw him the once. And I didn't know about the wallet at the time." Captain blew into a mug before filling it with coffee and setting it in front of Jon. He poured a second cup for himself. "I fed him a bellyful, like the others. But then he skipped out on me before we could have a talk." He raised his cup and looked up at Jon, who was still gazing outside. "You seem someplace far way. What's on your mind, Boy?"

Jon looked into his mug, studying the eyes of grease.

"Captain, what prompted you to start the Mission?"

Captain gave him a wayward look. "You might say, I'm one of those who puts his faith in that which cannot be easily explained."

"That sounds like something from the Bible."

"No, it's actually a line from an episode of *Northern Exposure*," Captain said, quickly realizing the humor was lost on him.

"What's your take on these people who claim God has spoken to them?"

"You lost me," Captain said.

"It's a simple question."

Captain leaned back, stumped for a moment. "I can't honestly say the Almighty has ever communicated verbally to me, if that's what you're getting at. But the Good Book does say we've been given a sound mind."

"A calling?"

"I guess some people might refer to it that way."

"Which may account for some of the mysteries of the faith, but I have to tell you, my antenna goes up every time someone tells me God told them to do something."

"If you don't mind my saying, you're confusing the hell out of me." Captain grabbed the tin and refilled his cup. "I'm sensing that tone in your voice again."

Jon swirled the dregs in his cup. "You were warning me about the street a few days ago. I'd say it's life, itself, that's a hostile takeover—for all of us."

Captain chuckled. "Next, I suspect you'll be a wanting to calculate how many angels can dance on the head of a pin." He reached out and brushed Jon's knee. "What's eating you, Boy?"

Jon shook his head.

"We're mates," Captain said. "Talk to me."

"When the time is right."

"This hostile takeover of yours, I take it that chunk of granite down at the square isn't offering any answers?"

Jon looked up, meeting Captain's gaze. "Two days ago you said it was my burning bush."

"I just don't want you to confuse this insanity called life with her Creator."

"I'll be sure to write that down."

"That oversized rock of yours isn't some genie in a bottle, you know? The Almighty never promised us three wishes."

"No arguments there," Jon said.

"This can't be about the wallet."

"Forget the wallet."

Captain's chair squeaked as he leaned back. "Seeing how we're caught in irons at the moment, maybe you won't mind if I change the subject," he said. "Does anything seem odd to you about meeting up with this scoundrel in the square?"

"You know the story," Jon said. "He was a homeless guy sleeping on a bench."

"But you go to that park every morning, don't you?"

"Tuesdays and Thursdays."

"What time?"

"Around six-thirty," Jon said. "What's your point?"

"Ever been there—say—two hours earlier?"

Jon squinted. "Four-thirty—are you kidding?"

"That's what I thought. I got curious after hearing your story, so I called down to one of my buddies at the police station. Did you know they patrol that square every two hours?"

"Come on, Captain. All I asked was if you'd ever seen the guy."

"What if I told you your assailant wasn't on that bench two hours before the attack?"

"Then he must have arrived between rounds. The guy lives on the street—you can't predict what he's going to do."

A freighter's horn blasted, echoing across the river. Both men turned to the window where a ship's bridge passed in the distance.

"It could be nothing, but you're right about one thing. I've worked these streets for years, and the Savannah police run their operations tighter than a jib around those squares. I don't see any way for this guy to have slipped by. And mind you, it happened on a Tuesday when Mr. Investment Banker frequents Factors Square. For someone new to these parts, I'd say he sure figured things out in hurry," Captain said. "As you're fond of saying, *X* marks the spot."

"Better known as street smarts."

"Exactly. But how did he know you were going to show up with your big fat wallet at six-thirty? How did he figure that out after just pulling into town?"

"A stroke of luck? Maybe it's simply misfortune on my part."

"You think?" Captain said. He studied Jon's face.

"What's gotten into you? I've never seen you get so worked up over a few bucks."

"You come to notice things in my line of work. From the little I know, this fellow didn't quite fit in at the Mission," Captain said. "I mean, he had the clothes and rough appearance, but I noticed he didn't have the hands."

"The hands?"

"That's right—street hands. They're rough and dirty, especially the fingernails. No, something was off. The hands didn't go with the outfit, but the eyes now . . . if I could have gotten a look into his eyes. Street eyes have this loneliness in them, like a bottomless black hole. Things go in, but nothing comes out."

"You're overthinking this, so give it a rest. I'm done with it, okay?"

"Maybe you shouldn't be. There's one thing I haven't mentioned. Remember how I told you I hadn't seen the guy since Tuesday? Well, an interesting thing happened the next day. After I spoke to you I went down to serve breakfast, and your corduroy jacket and stocking cap came waltzing right into the Mission."

Jon leaned forward, gripping his mug with both hands. "But you just said you haven't seen him since Tuesday."

"For sure. But it seems Sanky was practicing his cha-cha-cha on top of the dumpster out behind the Mission on Tuesday evening. Music was drifting up from River Street, so he says the mood struck him."

"Wait a minute. Sanky was dancing?"

"We've got a gal who drops by once a week to give lessons. I told you about it."

"Yeah, but Sanky has trouble stirring a pot."

"You're sidetracking me, Boy. The moment struck him, and Sanky forgot where he was. He slipped and fell headfirst into the dumpster. When he climbed out, he had these." Captain opened a drawer, tossing a jacket and cap on the desk. "He came to breakfast Wednesday morning wearing them."

"You've just given me another good reason to cut my losses," Jon said.

"Since there haven't been any reports of a streaker loose on the streets of Savannah, I'd say our attacker changed out of these into a different outfit, just like Sanky."

"That may explain what he did with the money."

"There's one more thing. My police buddy lit up when I mentioned your name. It seems there was a domestic incident reported at your house on Tuesday night, the same day you were attacked. He said someone ransacked the place. It seems you were involved in two crimes that day. What's that all about?"

Jon gave Captain his look. "I mentioned earlier that I didn't want to involve the police. I'm working on a sensitive acquisition, and the press could wreak havoc if I'm not careful. Clients tend to get nervous when they're about to invest millions with someone who's involved in a crime, even a victim.

"Beth filed a police report."

"I want to keep it out of—"

"But she decided not to press charges," Captain said.

"Charges? What are you talking about?"

"Boy, she told the police it was you."

Chapter 12
Friday, June 24th
8:15 P.M.

Bob Stein dropped a folder on the conference table and his lawyer scooped it up, depositing it in a leather satchel. Stein rubbed his eyes, and then checked his Rolex.

"The governor's office called this afternoon and wants me to do an interview for a piece in the newspaper," Stein said to Jon.

"That kind of publicity is priceless. Just remember, Michael has you under a nondisclosure agreement."

"What is he going to do—sue me? He needs this worse than I do."

"We've just spent ten hours hammering out a draft contract, so do yourself a favor and don't muddy the waters," Jon said.

"Can you believe the arrogance of that SOB? He's going down, and you can be sure of that."

"Bob, you're the one who violated the original terms. Let me give you some advice—"

"Just do as I say, and you'll be rewarded."

"A breach in the nondisclosure or any interim provision is a deal breaker. You're looking at a two-and-a-half million dollar breakup fee, plus legal expenses," Jon continued. "Take a look at the draft and give me your comments by Monday. Now if you'll excuse me, it's late and I have to go."

Jon ushered the men out of the boardroom, and then retreated to his office. He sat back in his chair and picked up a stack of faxes from a syndication of investors interested in the acquisition. He reviewed the signed confirmations and spun around to drop them on a credenza. A sudden movement in the window startled him, but then he noticed it was his own image staring back in the glass. He rubbed his eyes and pushed a button on his desk phone to check voicemail. As he listened, he turned again to the credenza for his day planner. A pair of brass-frames caught his attention. He could easily see how much the kids had changed since the photos had been taken. Even though both still had freckled tans, Carver's sun-streaked hair highlighted his baby features in the picture. Most of them were but a memory, now that he had hit a growth spurt. Bailey's golden curls were a different story, and he hoped they would stay that way for at least a few more years.

He swiveled back to the desk and picked up a folder, tossing it to one side. A puff of air sent a slip of paper fluttering to the carpet, and Jon leaned down to pick up a telephone message in Brenda's handwriting. David Stephens, the caller, was a pastor at South Coast Church. Actually, he was now CEO of a new venture the church had started up called South Coast Ministries, Inc.— SCMI for short. Jon had worked with Stephens on several occasions, mostly on committees, prior to his role at SCMI. But he rarely called him at the office.

"Good, you're still here," Brenda said, popping her head in Jon's office. "I have Richard on the phone. He's calling from San Diego and needs to speak with you. Line one."

"Why did we send him out there?" Jon said.

"PR."

"Public relations—that sounds like trouble," Jon said, waving her off. "Go home, but close my door first."

"You're one to be talking—like a man without a country." Brenda pulled the door shut before he could respond.

"Richard," Jon said, answering the call on speakerphone. He continued to flip through paperwork.

"Jon, do you mind taking me off the speaker?"

"I'm here alone, Richard. What's on your mind?"

"We need to discuss your call with Michael on Tuesday. And before you say anything, I'll be the first to admit these sorts of things are routine in negotiations. Heaven knows I've had my share of confrontations over the years, but discipline is crucial in sensitive matters. Michael was kind enough to print a copy of last night's e-mail, and I have to admit it caught me totally off guard. I'm in Michael's office now, but he's stepped out for a moment. He's pretty livid about your attitude."

"Richard, my actions were completely justified. If you have any doubts, take a look at the results of the call. And what's this about an e-mail?"

"Apparently, it's a follow-up to your argument over the pension matter."

"From last night?"

"Early this morning."

"You'll have to be more specific."

"Let me refresh your memory. It says: 'Michael, I appreciate your negotiating position in representing the interests of your shareholders. However, if you continue to violate disclosure requirements, I will have no recourse but to report your actions to the appropriate authorities. Stone & Associates will take any and all necessary actions to exercise diligence on behalf of our client.' And it's signed, Jonathon."

"Richard, I didn't send that."

"Listen, you have been putting tremendous pressure on yourself. I want to close this transaction as much as you do, and Bob Stein is counting on both of us. But you can't use this kind of language, especially in writing."

"Michael's not the problem—"

"I'm looking at the e-mail right now," Richard said. "It's from your corporate account."

"When was it sent, exactly?"

"This morning—let's see—twelve-forty-seven."

"I was in bed at eleven last night."

"What do you say we just call it a truce?" Richard said. "I've already apologized and assured him the terms are final. The pension issue was merely an oversight."

"Richard—"

"Jon, take me off the speaker." Richard paused for the click. "There's something else on my mind, and I wanted you to hear it directly from me. Randall Phipps called earlier today about a board matter at South Coast. Purely out of pastoral concern, he confided in me about some problems between you and Beth. From what I understand, Beth has been upset with you for the past few days over a personal matter. He really didn't elaborate on the details—"

"Richard, you've got it wrong."

"No, Randall was quite clear. And frankly, you have been a bit stressed lately. In my opinion, you should follow their advice and get this thing behind you."

Jon picked up Stephens's message, and then flipped through the stacks on his desk.

"Jon, I know this deal means a lot to you, but with mounting marital problems, even the best of us can lash out in moments like this."

"Richard, you said *their* suggestions. Did Randall happen to mention that David Stephens was involved?"

"More or less."

"Did he imply, in any way, that I had refused to meet with David Stephens?"

"Not directly, but I assumed as much."

"What does Stephens have to do with Beth and me? He's off launching SCMI—book stores, fitness centers, eco-ministries. He's turning the church into a retail mall."

"You saw the strategic plan at the latest finance meeting. Stephens has taken responsibility for all of the non-traditional ministries, and family counseling falls under his domain."

"Then why is Randall involved?" Jon said.

"As executive pastor, he has oversight duties— you know that. But you need to calm down and accept the fact that it's okay to admit you need help. The good news is the heavy lifting on Johnson-Medisys is practically done. It's mostly paperwork from here, and I can have Charlie wrap things up so you can take time to get your personal priorities in order. I can't afford to have you on the sidelines when we land our next client. Whatever your opinion of David Stephens, he is merely a facilitator. If he doesn't suit you, then find a professional who does. In fact, knowing you as I do, I highly recommend it—and the sooner the better."

Chapter 13
Friday, June 24th
9:10 P.M.

Jon hung up the telephone and turned to his computer, opening his e-mail. He checked the *Sent Items* folder to verify that the document Richard had read over the telephone only moments ago wasn't there. He parsed through a string of messages from Michael Johnson, but none had the reported date and time. Closing the program, he had an urge to call Richard back and set the record straight, but then he backed off, realizing it would be impossible to overcome his doubts without hard evidence.

Jon clicked on the computer's recycle bin as his cell phone began to ring, glancing at the display. The originating telephone number had been blocked. He flipped the phone open.

"This is Jonathon Browning."

"Agree to nothing," a voice said, almost in a whisper.

"Excuse me?" Jon replied.

"Sign nothing."

There was only silence.

"Who is this? . . . Sign what?" The line went dead and Jon came out of his chair.

He hung up and paced across the office, his mind retreating to the e-mail. Brenda had access to his computer, but she had no reason to be in the office at one in the morning, much less using his e-mail account.

A call to her office confirmed Brenda had gone for the evening, so Jon sat down and picked up where he had left off. There were seven documents in the recycle bin, and as expected, the missing e-mail wasn't among them. Hitting a brick wall, he grabbed the telephone memo and dialed Stephens's number. Voicemail picked up, and Jon checked his watch. The greeting provided a cell phone number, so he hung up and dialed again.

"Hello, this is David Stephens."

"David, Jonathon Browning."

"Jonathon, thanks for calling back. I wasn't sure I would hear from you."

Jon rocked back in his chair. "Just exactly, what is that supposed—"

"Hold on there, cowboy," Stephens interrupted. "I wasn't trying to—"

"Question my character?"

"Listen, I'm not exactly up to dealing with this sort of thing on a Friday night."

"That makes two of us," Jon said. "But maybe you can clear up one thing. Why does Randall think I have refused to meet with you?"

"Now let's not take what I said out of context. Beth simply indicated that you had declined outside assistance. If I have misinterpreted the situation, please accept my apologies."

"You have my attention, so let's talk," Jon said.

"Then how about breakfast in the morning, say seven-thirty?"

* * *

Saturday, June 25th
7:30 A.M.

Jon sat at a table in the Hilton with his first cup of coffee, studying the Saturday morning diners. The DeSoto Grille had a touristy flare—mostly retirement-age couples sitting at linen-draped tables, clanking silverware between trips to the buffet line.

"Jonathon," David Stephens said, slipping up behind him in a blazer and khakis. "Thanks for meeting on such short notice."

"I thought it best to clear the air as soon as possible," Jon said, rising out of his chair.

"Please, don't get up," Stephens said, turning as a waitress approached. "Sanka, my dear."

"Will you gentlemen be having the buffet?"

"Just coffee for me," Jon said.

"Let's see . . . I'm working out at the gym later," Stephens said, debating with himself. He sat down and looked up at the waitress. "Why not?"

"Sure you wouldn't like a biscuit and gravy, hon?"

Jon shook his head. "Thank you."

"Gotta love a man with willpower." She tapped a pencil on Stephens's shoulder. "Help yourself to the buffet whenever you like."

"So Jonathon, you guys are burning the midnight oil down at the office. I hear there's a big deal in the works, from the sound of things."

"It's nothing out of the ordinary."

"That's got to be one stressful profession. Buyers, sellers, and lawyers—with millions of dollars changing hands. It seems like a minefield to me."

"That's not quite how I would describe it, but we have our days," Jon said.

"When you think about it, we're both in the business of help-ing people—you in medical technology, and me with innovative ministries. I could use a man like you at SCMI."

"You can't afford me."

"Then maybe you could offer some investment advice."

"Richard is probably better equipped to handle your type of needs."

"Fine man, that Richard. Randall swears by him." Stephens took a sip of coffee.

"David, forgive my forwardness, but would you mind if we address the matter at hand?"

"I've heard you're a bottom line sort of guy," Stephens said, smiling. "I'm not sure what Beth has told you, but she has sched-uled several meetings with me recently."

"She hasn't mentioned them to me."

"That's not surprising. She's terribly upset over your argu-ment a few days ago."

"It wasn't exactly an argument, but please continue."

"She called to ask the church for assistance. Perhaps you've noticed she's been out of sorts lately." Stephens raised his hands in a "that explains it all" gesture. Then he added, "Jonathon, she really wants to work things out."

"Then we're on the same page. But you can appreciate how confusing the situation is at the moment. And I agree. Beth hasn't been herself."

"Acknowledging your confusion, to use your words, is a defin-ing first step," Stephens said. "But I distinctly sense you're still in shock."

"So you have experience with this sort of thing?"

"Similar circumstances," Stephens said, nodding.

"Then you won't mind if I ask your batting average?"

"I get it . . . You're a numbers guy. I'm afraid statistics don't always predict outcomes when you're dealing with human emotions. In your particular case, a willingness to cooperate can be an excellent indicator." Stephens glanced over at Jon, somewhat pleased.

"And how exactly would you describe our case?"

"A rocky prelude, but improving."

"Can you expand on that?"

"We're sitting here having a conversation, aren't we?" The waitress slipped in to top off their coffee before Stephens continued. "I recommend that we focus on how to move forward."

"David, every effort I've made to communicate with Beth hasn't gone well. And I have to admit, I'm not accustomed to having outsiders so intimately involved in family matters."

"Trust me. It's normal for you to feel this way."

"So if I agree to move forward, as you call it, what's the next step?"

"I would like to refer you to a therapist who specializes in marital issues. I can appreciate the fact that you're skeptical at this stage, but many people react similarly in the beginning."

"I take it you have a counselor in mind?"

"With the progress we've made, I believe we should continue with the psychologist Beth is currently seeing."

"Has she agreed to the arrangement?"

"She wants to forgive you, Jonathon."

Jon lowered his coffee cup. "She wants to forgive *me*?"

"It's very clear from the reports I've received from Dr. Lowe—"she still loves you very much."

"Lowe is her psychologist?"

"That's right—Dr. Tim Lowe."

"Is there anything else he has told you?"

"I can assure you, Tim has a solid grasp of the case. And that's half the battle when it comes to dealing with any psychosis."

"I suppose that makes me the other half of the battle," Jon said.

"It's true you'll have to open yourself up to the process. Ultimately, that means changing the unhealthy behaviors that created the situation."

"Given she's already under Dr. Lowe's care, why did she ask you to contact me?"

"People frequently turn to their pastor in a moment of need. I'm only here to help."

"And you believe we're in good hands?"

"With God, all things are possible. But I really must defer to Dr. Lowe for the prognosis."

Chapter 14
Sunday, June 26th
12:25 P.M.

Bells chimed from the campanile, as David Stephens preferred to refer to the structure, rising high above South Coast's pristine campus. Four stories beneath the tower's red-tiled roof, a contemporary building of stucco and glass blended into the coastal landscape with an artistic flare fit for a watercolor. What it lacked in terms of old school charm was more than offset by the cathedral-like grandeur, owing to its sheer dimensions. A palm-lined median greeted visitors down at the main gate, where a fountain spewed water into a man-made lake that had been manicured like a national monument. Orange-vested attendants roamed the massive parking lots, preparing for the tsunami of souls that was about to be unleashed following the eleven o'clock service.

Inside, worshippers filled the building to capacity, overflowing into the aisles on both levels of the main auditorium like a springtime flood. For the duration of the ninety minute production, latecomers had squeezed in and lined the walls, joining an outpouring of applause as the service began to wind down. Reverend Randall Phipps stepped away from a Lucite podium in a blazer and polo shirt and dashed off the stage, waving to the crowd as he disappeared down front. A chorus of cheers broke out as a band bounced up onto center stage with their instruments blaring at full throttle. A verse of encouragement flashed up on a theatre-sized screen, with images of smiling faces scrolling by in the background. The rhythm fell into a reverberating anthem as the audience sang out, their passion bouncing off the walls in surround sound. As the final note was sounded, the flock suddenly burst into the aisles, their bodies shuffling elbow-to-elbow as if wandering through a laboratory maze. Worshippers, dressed like tourists, charged for the exits that were now springing open all around the auditorium. The scene invoked images of floodgates releasing torrents of water.

"Reverend Phipps," Beth called out, pitching her voice high above the mayhem. Her red outfit was turning heads as she defied the crowd in a quest to rouse Phipps's attention. When he didn't respond, she made a final lunge and snagged him by the arm. "What a beautiful message this morning," she sang out. "My heart has been lifted by an unquenchable spirit."

"Give thanks to the Author of life," Phipps said, turning at the sound of her voice. He pressed his hands together, prayer-like.

"I've got chill bumps," Beth said, rubbing the sleeves of her jacket.

"Be faithful, my child—a doer of the word and not one who simply hears." Phipps smiled and grasped her hands. "And where is Jonathon this fine morning?"

Beth's countenance sank as she pulled Phipps aside. "I'm afraid he desperately needs your prayers." She gave a wide-eyed glance over at Carver and Bailey, who were fidgeting in their seats a few rows back.

"Still no progress?" Phipps said.

"David finally managed to reach out to Jonathon, but we're both concerned about his intentions."

"Give the matter a little more time. I have every confidence Brother Stephens will be able to work this out."

"I . . ." Tears welled up in Beth's eyes. "Forgive me, if I'm not myself today. It's been heartbreaking to see how he's slipping away, a day at a time."

"With everything that's happened, you mustn't blame yourself," Phipps said. "As we've discussed, the elder board stands behind you during this difficult period."

"But what if he turns away from the church?" Beth opened her purse and pulled out a tissue. "Who will I turn to then?"

"The church watches after the flock, so never doubt our unwavering support."

"But there must be something I can do?"

"For the moment, you must have faith and act upon Brother Stephens's advice. We speak regularly, so he'll let me know if I need to be involved."

"Thank you, Reverend Phipps." Beth closed her eyes and wrapped her arms around his neck.

"You're in good hands," Phipps said.

Beth dabbed the tissue under an eye, and then looked over and smiled at her children.

* * *

Jon and Captain settled in next to a window at The Lady & Sons. The first of the churchgoers had already begun to form a line on the sidewalk outside, where a red-striped awning adorned West Congress Street.

"You're quite the man of mystery showing up at the Mission this morning," Captain said. "I should think you'd be hobnobbing with the brass out at South Coast."

"Ouch," Jon said. "I suppose I should turn the other cheek." He scooted his chair back from the table so he was under a ceiling fan.

"All I'm saying is it's not your habit."

"If you must know," Jon said, "I came down for a reality check."

"Reality? What're they preaching out at South Coast these days?"

"Are we going to argue about this?"

"Of course not, but I know for a fact you're acting peculiar."

Jon gave Captain his look, and then starred out the window.

"It's clear you didn't bring me here just to stuff me with fried chicken," Captain quipped.

"Do you realize that ever since you heard about the break-in at the house, you've looked at me suspiciously? You don't actually think I did it, do you?"

"What do the police say?"

"Nothing so far, but you didn't answer my question," Jon said. "I'm still waiting for Beth to come clean with the truth."

"Now that's a side of you I've never seen before."

A waitress swung in next to the table with a tray of drinks. She paused for Captain to grab a couple of iced teas, and then moved on.

"Listen, this started long before the break-in," Jon said. "A week ago Friday I got home late from work, and Beth was quite upset and said we needed to talk. As it turns out, she wanted to make a confession. It seems like a dream now, but she told me she had an affair." He cut his eyes at Captain. "In fact, she informed me she had been with five men. For the first time in my life, I didn't know what to say. When she finished her story, she could clearly see I was stunned—and I was. But it was almost as if she was telling me out of duress, like she thought I already knew.

Afterwards, she fell apart and started screaming and crying, 'Oh my God, you didn't know.'"

Jon leaned forward, collecting his thoughts. "By this point, I had concluded that I needed more to go on. But all she could say was she wanted my forgiveness. When she refused to discuss it any further, I gave up and have been wrestling with it ever since. As you know, the break-in happened on Tuesday. Two days later we talked, and she swore there were only two men, an entirely different story. But after a lengthy argument, she threw me again by admitting there were three. When she realized I wasn't buying it, she started saying all sorts of crazy things.

"Once she managed to settle down I pressed some more, telling her I needed to know names. And as you can probably guess by now, she resisted. But I couldn't let it pass, especially since she wanted my forgiveness. From that moment on, she has refused to talk. She won't listen to anything I have to say."

"That was Thursday night?" Captain said.

"Right, but get this. Not only did she change the number of affairs, she now claims they all happened before we were married. When I questioned why she had decided to confess after all these years, she said God told her to do it."

Jon leaned back in his chair and ran a hand through his hair, looking around. The dining area was now bustling with the after-church crowd, helping themselves to the buffet.

"So who have you talked to about this?" Captain said.

"Richard was the first. He suggested I take a leave of absence from work. How's that for confidence? And then David Stephens from the church contacted me. I believe you've met him. Beth somehow got him involved, and now he's suggesting I meet with a psychologist."

"He's the one that's turning South Coast into Disneyland. A friend of mine told me Stephens made a bid to purchase Oglethorpe Mall." Captain pointed a finger at Jon. "You didn't hear that from me."

"He's in charge of SCMI, a church spin-off that's expanding into new ministries."

"Boy, you weren't kidding about that reality check," Captain said. "What's your next move?"

"I'm working on a plan, but I'd rather not involve the police— at least for now."

"Then maybe you should give this Stephens fellow a chance. After all, he's a man of faith."

"So am I," Jon said. "Only I don't act on blind faith."

"Well, if you ask me, you should take your time. Don't fire all your torpedoes at once."

"You're right about that," Jon said. "Nothing makes sense when I talk to Beth."

"Have no doubt . . . The Almighty can see you through—"

"I didn't come here for a sermon," Jon interrupted.

"Okay, reality it is. You know where to find me." Captain waited for Jon to look him in the eyes. "Now how about that bloody buffet you promised me?"

After lunch, Jon and Captain crossed Bay Street and slipped down an alley that wound its way to the Mission. When they arrived, they stopped at Jon's car.

"You know, I've been studying that incident of yours in the square," Captain said. "Did I understand you to say you retrieved the weapon?"

"That's right."

"And what became of it?"

"It's here in the trunk." Jon inserted a key and popped the lid.

Captain reached in, whistling. "Now that'd put a nice crack in your skull." He lifted the pipe and rolled it in his hands. "You'd be singing with the angels if he'd smacked you with this."

"Tell me about it. I just buried a Brooks Brothers suit," Jon said, slamming the trunk. "Just keep it."

"Believe I will," Captain said. He rested a hand on Jon's shoulder.

"My number's not up, Captain. So don't waste your time trying to protect me." Jon opened the car door. "And no police."

"Blessings to you, Boy" Captain said.

Chapter 15
Monday, June 27th
7:05 A.M.

Jon was the first to arrive at the office, settling into his chair as he dialed Captain's number.

"I wanted you to be the first to know I took a shot across the bow last night," Jon said, skipping formalities.

"A fine morning to you as well," Captain said. "At least you're in the battle."

"That's debatable. Beth argued with me for hours. She now claims I'm using the confession to manipulate her. I thought we'd bottomed out, but then she threatened a restraining order."

"Sounds more like a shot to the stern," Captain said.

"It's aggressive language for sure, but she's not going to separate me from my children."

"Did you talk to Stephens?"

Jon looked up and spotted Brenda in his doorway. "Captain, can I call you later? I've got to run."

"I'm not interrupting, am I?" Brenda said, stepping inside.

"Actually, you're a sight for sore eyes—a smiling face on Monday morning," Jon said, hanging up the telephone.

"The first pot of coffee is on the launching pad. Can I interest you in a cup?"

"Make mine a double," Jon said.

Moments later, Brenda returned with two steaming mugs. "Java de Brenda. It's good for what ails you, especially Monday mornings."

"Before I forget, do you remember sending an e-mail to Michael Johnson after hours on Thursday?"

"I don't think so, but I'll check." Brenda set down her cup and started for the door.

"It was sent from my e-mail account."

Brenda stopped in the doorway and turned. "I don't send e-mail on your account."

"Does anyone else have access to it?"

"Why do you ask?"

"It seems Michael received a flaming e-mail from me. Only problem is, I didn't send it."

"And you think I did?" Brenda said with a laugh. "Besides, I didn't work late on Thursday."

"Where do you keep my password?"

"Right here," she said, tapping the side of her head.

"So you're certain you never gave it to anyone?"

"Positive. And you've known me long enough—"

"It doesn't make sense," Jon said, setting down his cup.

"I'll just go clear out my desk," Brenda said, popping out into the hallway. She stuck her head back, smiling.

"Is there something else?" Jon said, laughing.

Brenda stuck out her tongue and disappeared.

Jon spun around to his computer and logged on to the company network. Navigating through the menus, he leaned back in his chair, searching for clues. When he was unable to come up with anything, he found the number for the computer help desk and dialed. The call went directly into a queue, so he left a message.

"Excuse me, Jon," Brenda said, reappearing. "I have an idea. Richard had me install a security system last year. We haven't really broadcasted it to the associates, but it keeps a record of everyone entering and exiting the building."

"How does it work?"

"Each office key has a chip. When an associate passes through the doorway, the monitoring system captures the movement."

"Can it identify each individual?"

"The chips have unique signatures—no two are alike. I suppose it could be fooled if someone borrowed your key."

"Do you think you could check the system for last Thursday night?"

"I'll call the security company and have a report sent over." Brenda headed for the door, and then stopped. "This is sort of creepy, isn't it?"

* * *

A walk in Factors Square had Jon looking sideways at a few of the homeless people loitering in the area. One passed by pushing a shopping cart, and he found himself eyeing the contents for anything suspicious. He took a detour to the Port City Deli for coffee before returning to the office and placing a call to Dr. Lowe. As the receptionist put him on hold, his mind flashed back to an hour earlier in the square. He had been sitting in front of the granite cross, when he had experienced what he would later come to think of as a defining moment. The receptionist interrupted his thoughts and announced she was transferring him to the doctor.

"Hello, Jonathon," Dr. Lowe said. "David Stephens told me to expect your call."

"He moves in mysterious ways," Jon said.

"Listen, I won't waste your time on the telephone. I'd like to schedule a consultation as soon as possible. Beth has already filled me in on the basics, but it's important that we sit down and get acquainted," Lowe said. "From there, we can assess next steps."

Jon was surprised at how fast the conversation progressed, hanging up with a four o'clock appointment. There was a knock at his door, and Brenda poked her head in.

"I picked up a call from the help desk while you were out. Here's an extension—ask for Chase. And Richard wants to see you when you're available."

"Is there any news from the security company?"

"They promised to fax over a report this afternoon." Brenda cut her eyes and frowned. "Is there anything you'd like to tell me?"

Jon picked up his day planner. "Now that you mention it, I'm taking the afternoon off." He grabbed a folder and tossed it across the desk. "Those are my comments on the Johnson-Medisys contract. Take a look and let me know if they raise any legal issues. If not, pass them along to Charlie. He's pulling together the next draft."

Brenda raised her eyebrows. "Are you sure you're okay?"

"I'll be fine. We'll catch up later."

"You think I'm being nosey, don't you?"

Jon smiled and shook his head as he pressed the speaker-phone and dialed.

"This is Chase," a voice answered. "Name and e-mail account, please."

"Hi Chase, this is Jonathon Browning." He gave him the account.

"Thank you, Jonathon. How can I help you?"

Jon stepped Chase through the events of the previous week.

"Well, it's only possible for someone to send e-mail from your address if they're logged on to your account," Chase said.

"So you're saying no one can trick the system into using my address."

"It's only possible if they're logged on using your personal account. The software automatically attaches the address of the sender. I've never seen security breached on this particular system."

"I hate to break it to you, but some genius hacked into my account."

"Does anyone else have your password?"

"The company security officer."

"Do you trust him?" Chase said.

"*Her*—and yes—I trust her."

"Then I'm afraid—wait a second—let me check the server status for last Thursday night. Nope. All systems were normal. You know, your company should invest in a system upgrade."

"What do you mean?" Jon said.

"You're running an old release. If you had the latest version, e-mail would be stored on a central server, and I could access all of your transactions. With the older software, you have to sign on to each computer to search for the e-mail in question."

"So you're saying if someone used my e-mail account, a copy may still be on their computer?"

"That's right, but only if they haven't deleted it."

"Chase, you've been great. Can I give you my mobile number in case you think of anything else?"

"Sure," Chase said. "I don't know about you, but these kinds of things drive me crazy, at least until I figure them out."

Jon hung up and headed down to Richard's office.

"Jon, please come in," Richard said, waving him inside. He got up and closed the door. "I wanted to follow up on how you're doing." He walked over and joined Jon at a conference table. "I dropped two bombs on you at once on Friday. I apologize if I seemed overly direct, but in my book they're both critical issues."

"And I intend to prove you wrong on both accounts."

"Come now, Jon. Let's be professional about—"

"You'd be well advised to keep Bob Stein on a short leash. After all, he is your friend," Jon said. "You'll have a revised draft of the contract tomorrow."

"At which time, you will step out of the negotiations until further notice."

Jon stood up. "I met with David Stephens's over the weekend, and I've agreed to talk to a psychologist this afternoon."

"That's all I'm asking."

"And I'll thank you to back off and let me do this my way."

"Fair enough," Richard said. "I'm counting on a speedy recovery, especially after my latest conversation with the governor about the re-election campaign. I don't have to tell you what the exposure can do for the firm."

Chapter 16
Monday, June 27th
4:15 P.M.

Jon tossed the *Family Assistance Program* brochure on a coffee table and took another look around the waiting room. He couldn't quite pinpoint the problem, but something seemed all wrong. For the past fifteen minutes, the room had been as quiet as a library, with a half-dozen patients sitting glassy-eyed and curled up in their own little worlds. *This doesn't feel like a place of healing*, he thought.

"Dr. Browning," a receptionist announced. She ushered him down a hallway, and then into a spacious office. "If you'll have a seat, Dr. Lowe will be with you shortly." She smiled and closed the door behind her.

Jon noticed that the space reminded him of a lawyer's office. A heavy wooden desk and bookcases sat at one end of the room, complete with plump leather chairs. On the far side, a floral sofa and two armchairs sat clustered around a glass coffee table. Heavy drapes covered a picture window just beyond them.

Jon slipped over and peeked out of the drapes before taking a seat in one of the chairs. After a few minutes of solitude, he found himself gripping the armrests and loosened up, waiting another ten minutes for Lowe to arrive.

When the door opened, the doctor puffed into the office with an extended hand. "Jonathon, so nice to see you. I'm Dr. Timothy Lowe."

"Please, call me Jon," he said, standing up.

Lowe waved him back into the chair. "Make yourself comfortable, while I grab a pad."

As the doctor turned, Jon caught a snapshot of his profile. Clothed in an oxford shirt and wool slacks, Lowe had flushed cheeks and sported a belly that sagged just enough to conceal his belt buckle.

"So Jonathon, I am indeed encouraged by your sense of priority," Lowe said as he plopped down in the adjoining chair.

"Were you expecting a different response?"

"It's a compliment," Lowe said. "David Stephens briefed me about your meeting over the weekend."

"I wasn't aware you worked weekends," Jon said.

"Actually, I bumped into him at church."

"South Coast Church?"

"My family has been there for years. And since David oversees the church's counseling services, we talk frequently."

"I think I'm beginning to get the picture," Jon said. His eyes drifted over to the bookcases.

"If you don't mind, I would like to start by having you share your perspective on the marital situation."

Jon spent the next thirty minutes describing the night Beth had made her confession. He explained the transformation that had taken place during their subsequent discussions. "From my vantage point," Jon concluded, "the entire sequence of events has grown more confusing over time."

"Interesting . . . and how do you feel about her right now?" Lowe asked.

"After eight years of marriage, I feel betrayed."

"Are you willing to sit down and work through this confusion, as you describe it?"

Jon shifted in his seat. "Do you mind telling me how far along you are with Beth in the process?"

"And why does that interest you?" Lowe said, jotting on the pad.

"Since you've been meeting with her for some time now, I would like your assurances that you can approach the situation objectively, given what you may have already heard."

"Is there reason to think otherwise, Jonathon?"

"How straight do you want it?"

"You can tell me anything."

"I find it revealing that I haven't noticed any improvements in Beth's behavior after weeks of counseling."

"Since you've been completely open with my questions, I can assure you that you have a relationship worth saving, not only for your sake, but for the children as well." Lowe set down his pen. "I suggest we press on and fight the good fight. At any point you feel we're off track, raise the flag and I'll hear you out. How does that sound?"

"Like a politician, but I understand your position," Jon said. "Let's move forward."

Lowe made another notation on his pad.

"All I ask is that you commit yourself to the sessions."

"I'm in . . . Close the bag, doctor."

"Excellent. So that will be all for today." Lowe stood up. "On your way out, ask the receptionist for a personal information questionnaire and a release form. Also, have her schedule you for an MMPI."

"MMPI?" Jon said.

"Minnesota Multiphasic Personality Inventory. Don't let the name scare you. It's simply a tool to jumpstart the counseling. Be sure to fill out all the paperwork before you come back in."

"Then what?"

"My staff will compile the results and forward them to me for assessment. Then you and I will sit down to discuss my findings."

It was five-fifteen when Jon left Lowe's office. He hopped into the car and dialed Brenda.

"Hi, Jon. Where are you?" Brenda said.

"Just leaving an appointment. Any luck with the security report?"

"Hot off the press. When would you like to go over it?"

"Now's perfect."

"It looks like they ran it for two full days, Thursday and Friday."

"Let's start by confirming when everyone left on Thursday evening," Jon said. "And I also want to check to see if anyone came in later that night."

"I'm looking at Thursday's report. I left at five-thirty-seven, and you knocked off around nine. Terri left a little before you at eight-fifty-four. Steve, six-fourteen."

"What about Charlie?"

"Oh yeah, he took off before I did, and Richard was in San Diego. Everyone's accounted for."

"And no one entered the office later that evening?"

"Let's see . . . The cleaning service arrived at nine-fifteen and left at ten-twenty, but that's it."

"Then let's take a look at Friday."

"Charlie was the first to arrive at six-thirty. What time did you say the e-mail was sent?"

"Twelve-forty-seven."

"Did the help desk offer any suggestions?" Brenda said.

"They confirmed that the person signed on using my account."

"So where do we go from here?" Brenda said, pausing. "Hmm . . . That doesn't sound good coming from the security officer, does it?"

"Brenda, first thing tomorrow morning I want you to log on to my account at every computer in the office. Chase says the e-mail may still be on the computer that sent it. And before you leave today, drop the security report on my desk. Do I have any messages?"

"Just one—Captain called."

Chapter 17
Monday, June 27th
6:00 P.M.

Tim Lowe kicked back in his chair, hefting a pair of size twelve loafers onto the desktop. He started pounding a fist on one of the armrests as he balanced a telephone receiver on his shoulder.

"Listen, I can't just manufacture the information. I've got to conduct a few sessions. You know, piece together the sequence of events."

"Who's going to know the difference? It's your word against his," Hallworth countered on the other end of the line.

"Sam, you may have heard of the American Psychological Association? They have a code of ethics that we professionals operate by."

"My dear marital counselor, how long have we been working together with these lost souls?" Hallworth said.

There was silence. "What's your point?" Lowe finally said.

"Since we agreed to this little arrangement, how many times have you been convicted of violating your so-called code of ethics?"

"It doesn't matter. There have been complaints, not to mention inquiries. That Blackman fellow came a little too close."

"Yeah, yeah. The records are sealed."

"It's not your neck," Lowe said. He pulled a set of keys out of his desk drawer.

"I've told you, once you're exonerated from a complaint the state forgets. Nothing's in the file."

"Even this conversation is illegal, but you already know that." Lowe dropped his feet to the floor and tossed the keys on the desk.

"Only if it can be proven in a court of law," Hallworth said.

"Are we sure Browning is worth the risk?"

"I did an Internet search—eleven hundred hits. He's been tracked by the business press since he graduated from Stanford. He was a financial hotshot on the West Coast before signing on with Stone & Associates. Boutique investment banking they call it. The guy's got money, an up-and-comer."

"And maybe too smart to be handled," Lowe said.

"You know, I heard an interesting story from Stephens. It seems he's under the impression that you told Beth Browning to confess. The way I hear it, he caught wind of it and had to step in and put things back on track. I think the term he used was, 'pulled Lowe's ass out of the fire'. You want to piss him off again? With the economy the way it is, tell me where you're going to find this caliber of clientele on your own."

"I'll warn you like I did David. He's confided too much in her, and she's a loose cannon. This isn't how we typically mange these cases," Lowe snapped back. "Now here's the deal. You guys stand down so I can do a complete evaluation. Otherwise, I'm out. The authorities know these things take time. It lends credibility to the outcome."

"And to the size of your bank account."

"Hey, you're no stranger to the feeding frenzy."

"So we work together, as always," Hallworth said. "What're you getting so worked up for?"

"I'll get the signature on the release, and we do this my way. Then you'll have access to my records and the leverage you need."

"You're forgetting. I'm waiting on my cut."

"You're cut? You've done nothing, so far," Lowe said.

"I practically dictated that thesis she wrote, which alone could send the guy to the nut house. I'm doing your work."

"It's called a case history. Anyway, I've got to spend time with him. Both of them."

"You greedy bastard."

"We're just getting started, and there's nothing to report."

"Just don't take too long. I'm dying to see Browning dance, especially when the wheels of justice start nipping at his heels," Hallworth said, striking a match.

"That's your concern. I don't want to know about it," Lowe said. "And by the way, I'm sick and tired of those cigars you smoke."

"It's all in your mind, counselor. Of course, you realize the day's coming when we're going to put you up on the witness stand. I get all hot and bothered just thinking about it." A telephone rang in the background. "I've got to take the other line."

"I'll get the paperwork together. You follow protocol." Rocking back in his chair, Lowe let the receiver roll off his shoulder, and then slammed it into a trash can.

* * *

Tuesday, June 28th
6:50 A.M.

The morning mist surrendered to the encroaching rays of sunshine filtering through the oaks. As Jon sat self-absorbed on the bench in Factors Square, he didn't notice that someone was approaching.

"Morning to you."

"Captain?" Jon said, turning. "This is unexpected."

"I've heard so much about this place, I thought I'd come down and experience it for myself."

"Your timing's off."

"I don't know about that," Captain said. He surveyed the landscape, stopping for a look at the granite cross. "I can see why you come here."

"I've already unloaded on your boss, so watch yourself." Jon said, rolling his eyes skyward.

"You have to respect a man who's in pursuit of reality. Isn't that what you called it on Sunday?"

"I feel better grounded when I start the day here."

"Fair enough," Captain said, still staring at the rock. "It kind of reminds me of the Garden of Eden."

"Speak for yourself."

"That's not the attitude you intend to leave with, is it?"

"The jury's still out."

"Do you mind if I share some reality with you, while you're waiting for inspiration to strike?"

"It's public property."

"Slide over," Captain said, sitting down.

"Who's serving down at the Mission?"

"Never you mind that. I've got a fine crew on deck."

"I've never known you to skip breakfast." Jon looked over at Captain, forcing a smile.

"So this is where you were attacked?" Captain rubbed a hand across the bench until he felt the indentation. He paused for a moment, as if in thought.

"Ah, you skipped breakfast for a reason," Jon said.

"You know you're dealing with a stubborn old mule, don't you? If it isn't too much to ask, I'd like to figure out what happened here."

Jon slid off the bench. "Like I told you, he surprised me, and I had to dive for the ground, but the pipe glazed me and struck the bench. In the process the wallet came out of my hand, and the pipe bounced across the walkway. Then the guy ran away."

"And what did he say to you before it all happened?" Captain said.

"Very little."

"I'll give you one thing. There's more to this attack than a stroke of bad luck. It's something special all right, just like your little Eden here."

"You still don't believe me, do you?"

"Settle down. I'm just saying there's more than meets the eye here—predestination they call it in the Bible."

"Come on, you're not suggesting God was involved?" Jon said, returning to the bench.

"I'm merely suggesting there was intent."

"And you also said something about reality."

"Sorry, I get carried away sometimes." Captain glimpsed over at Jon, and then slapped a knee. "The pipe—I took it over to the Home Hardware on Abercorn."

"You took the pipe to a hardware store?"

"Well, I couldn't very well take it to the police, could I?"

"Good answer."

"Funny thing about this piece of iron," Captain said. He reached over and pulled the pipe out of a canvas bag next to the bench, holding it up for Jon to see. "If you look down at one end, you'll notice a sliver of barcode. I spoke to the manager in the plumbing department. He identified it as one of theirs."

"Not exactly a shocker. It came from Home Hardware."

"Apparently, the length of pipe intended for your skull was cut from a longer section."

"What are you talking about?"

Captain pointed. "See where this barcode is cut off. Well, it's cut because the pipe was scored from a twenty-four inch piece." He pulled a second pipe out and aligned it with the weapon.

"They fit," Jon said with a puzzled look on his face. He leaned over to see if anything else was in the bag. "Where did you get that?"

"That's what I'm trying to explain, Boy. The Home Hardware man identified the barcode as one of theirs. He explained how these pipes don't come in short lengths, like your weapon. They have to be cut from a standard size."

"Twenty-four inches," Jon said, taking a closer look.

"Now you're talking. The manager took me over to a saw, right there in the store where customers custom fit pipes to their own specifications."

"Why are you telling me all this?"

"We were looking at the saw when I noticed a scrap pile next to it. I dug a little and found the matching piece." Captain held up the longer pipe.

"So you're saying the other half of the pipe was at Home Hardware."

"Don't know about you, but I find it interesting that someone living on the street would walk into Home Hardware and engineer a weapon for the purpose of whacking Mr. Investment Banker in the square on a Tuesday morning."

"Wait a minute," Jon said. "The guy probably stole the pipe from whoever bought it."

"Could be. But you're forgetting what I told you about the attacker's hands. Are you sure you don't recall anything else?"

"Only that someone broke into my house that night. Maybe it's the same guy?"

"Not according to your wife."

Jon shrugged off the comment.

"Does the Home Hardware manager remember who bought the pipe?"

Captain shook his head. "Afraid not, but get this. The scraps are hauled off from the store every Monday." He raised the weapon again. "That means this little number was cut less than twenty-four hours before you were attacked."

Chapter 18
Tuesday, July 5th
4:45 P.M.

Dr. Lowe cleared his throat as he sat poised with pen in hand.

"Perhaps we can start with an update," Lowe said. He looked up from his notepad at the ceiling. "How would you describe the environment at home over the past week?"

"In mergers and acquisitions, we would call it hostile," Jon said. "Everything has deteriorated since I last saw you."

"Can you elaborate?"

"There's been a total breakdown in communication." Jon hesitated. "For example, last night she told me she had confessed everything to God and doesn't intend to discuss the matter any further. She continuously accuses me of manipulating her."

"Who typically initiates the conversation?"

Jon shot Lowe a look. "I do. But it doesn't matter. She's mostly nonresponsive and our home feels like solitary confinement."

"Sex life?"

"Uh—no."

"When would you say was the last time?"

"I don't recall."

"Days—weeks—months?"

"Weeks."

"And if you could change anything about the situation, what would that be?" Lowe scribbled furiously.

"The confession remains a mystery. I want the facts."

"And how does that make you feel?"

"Betrayed."

"Angry—anxious—hostile?"

"No," Jon said, giving the doctor another look.

"Interesting." Lowe tapped his pen on the pad. "Is there anything else?"

"You've got the overall picture. What can you tell me about the MMPI?"

Lowe flipped open a pink folder in his lap. From where Jon sat, he could see a scattergram on the inside cover. Lowe lifted a sheet and studied it in silence before responding.

"How would you say you were feeling the day you completed the MMPI?"

"I would describe it as a normal afternoon." Jon shrugged.

"That's interesting."

"How should I have felt?"

"Well, you're going through a period of marital discord. I find it curious that you would choose to marginalize what must have been very powerful emotions at the time."

"I work in a stressful profession, so I probably don't react to conflict the way most people do."

Lowe shifted in his chair, clearly uncomfortable with the answer. "So if I understand correctly . . . your marriage is failing and you come to see a psychologist, but you're feeling fine?"

"That's not what I said, but I'm not an emotional person," Jon said. "Are you going to give me the results?"

"The results are inconclusive."

"Inconclusive? What does that mean?"

"You know. They raise additional questions."

"Such as . . ." Jon rolled his hand.

"Did you accurately represent yourself?"

"I don't follow you. I thought that was the idea—to advance the counseling at a faster pace."

"The results don't line up with the circumstances," Lowe said. He shuffled the papers, continuing to study them with a troubled expression.

"Then perhaps you'd better clarify. I spent two hours filling out forms." Jon leaned forward. "And I paid hundreds for the privilege. I scheduled today's appointment as you instructed—another one hundred and fifty bucks—"

"And now you seem to be growing anxious, maybe even angry," Lowe said. He made a note in the folder.

"I'm here for your expertise, and all you have offered is inconclusive."

"Jonathon, stop and think about your present reality. Think about what has happened. Think about your childhood. You can't possibly be fine."

"Once again, I didn't say fine," Jon said, standing up. He immediately sat back down. "And what about my childhood?"

"Your situation is anything but normative."

"The extreme marital discord, as you call it, has nothing to do with my childhood. This is about a confession Beth made two weeks ago."

"Under severe stress," Lowe added, writing in the folder again.

"Are we talking about me or Beth?"

"I have reviewed your family history," Lowe said. "And I understand your story very well."

"Meaning what?"

"There's a reason why you're incapable of expressing love to your wife."

Jon stood up and ran a hand through his hair.

"I have no idea what you're talking about. And for the record, if Beth has told you things about my background, she doesn't even know most of my family."

Lowe stared for a moment, and then spoke slowly. "Let's just say, I've had a recent discussion with someone who cares for you very much . . . someone who has your best interest at heart. I've been able to confirm many of Beth's details through another source."

"And who is this person?"

"I'm afraid the individual has requested to remain anonymous."

Jon raised his hands in the air. "This is supposed to help?"

"Jonathon, you have a problem with trusting people, don't you?"

"At the moment, I have an issue with anonymous informants."

"That's not exactly the situation."

"Then let's stick with the facts. To begin with, you're lending credibility to second-hand information. When I provide you with specifics about my life, you describe it as inconclusive." Jon moved toward the window. "Next you tell me an anonymous source has confirmed accusations that Beth has leveled against me. Then you conclude I have a trust issue. Am I understanding you correctly, doctor?"

"We need to explore your childhood further. It will be the focus of our next session."

"I have a better idea. Why don't we invite my entire family and get straight to the truth?"

"That won't be necessary."

"Then I'm not talking about my childhood, at least until we get the vagaries straightened out."

Lowe ignored Jon's comment, positioning his pen again. "Tell me about your relationship with Brenda Simpson."

"She is our in-house attorney at Stone & Associates."

"Has she accompanied you on any recent business trips?"

"All of the associates travel, when it's required."

"You've never traveled alone with her?"

"What are you insinuating?"

"I'm just trying to explore certain possibilities."

"Then perhaps you can explain what Brenda Simpson has to do with my childhood."

Lowe checked his watch. "I'm afraid our time is up. Did you sign the release?"

"I reviewed it, but I don't see a need for it."

"David Stephens has requested a weekly briefing on our sessions." Lowe rose from his chair and walked over to the desk.

"Then maybe I should be his informant."

"Spare me, Jonathon. David frequently confers with me as a professional courtesy."

"So let's schedule a time for us all to get together."

"You don't make the rules. This is a condition he has established in working with you and Beth."

"I believe David delegated the matter to you," Jon said. "He said so himself."

"Listen, I feel it's in everyone's interest to maintain open communication. The church only wants what's best."

"And I'll agree, as long as I'm present."

"Beth won't consent to it."

"Why not?" Jon said.

"Without the release, she'll take legal action. At least, that's my professional opinion."

"But the counseling is for us. Why would she—"

"I'm afraid, this isn't open for debate," Lowe interrupted.

"Tim, your methods are beginning to bother me."

"So now you're an expert in psychology?"

"That's not what I meant."

"Here's the situation, Jonathon," Lowe said. "I'm the doctor, you're the patient. I will determine the course of treatment and you will sign the release."

"And if I don't?"

"Then don't come back."

* * *

"Now I lay me down to sleep, I pray the Lord my soul to keep. Help me sleep throughout the night and wake me with the morning light. God bless my turtle, Shelly. Help my cut finger to be all better, and please feed those who are hungry. Amen."

"Good night, Sweet Pea," Jon said.

"Good night, Daddy. I love you." A small pair of arms squeezed tightly around Jon's neck.

"I love you more."

"No way. I love you to the top of the Tybee Lighthouse," Bailey's little voice squeaked.

"Uh-huh, and I love you to Disney World and back."

"That's a lot."

"And don't you forget it."

"Daddy, can you sleep in my room tonight?"

"That wouldn't be fair to Carver."

"But you sleep in there, all alone. Aren't you scared without a night light?" Bailey said.

"I'm not scared because I know you're close by. And I can hear you every time you roll over in bed."

"I can hear you, too." Bailey giggled. "Especially, when you're snoring."

"Snoring? That's not snoring, it's just breathing loud."

"No, Daddy, it's snoring."

"Go to sleep," Jon said, trying not to laugh. He pulled the covers up so that only Bailey's head and her teddy bear's ears stuck out.

"I love you, Daddy."

Chapter 19
Wednesday, July 6th
7:30 A.M.

Jon slipped into the office early for a cup of coffee with Brenda to get an update on the Johnson-Medisys contract. Afterwards, she expressed concerns over his recent absence, prompting him to explain his marital situation and abbreviated work schedule. Despite the momentary discomfort, Jon felt better once everything was out in the open, realizing Brenda would be an ally during his time away from the office.

Just as he thought his workday was over, one of Dr. Lowe's predictions materialized in the form of a telephone call as he stuffed papers into a briefcase. "Jonathon Browning," he said, stretching the receiver over to his computer.

"Jonathon, Sam Hallworth here. Did I catch you at a good time?"

"I'm on my way out of the office," Jon said.

"This should only take a minute—"

"Sam, I already told you, Brenda handles our outside legal relationships," Jon interrupted.

"We can do this the easy way—or your way."

"Listen, I don't have time—"

"I've been retained by your wife as legal counsel."

Jon stood up and reached over, closing the door. "In what capacity?"

"Section nineteen filings. In laymen's terms, you might say Mrs. Browning has grown tired of your lack of responsiveness to her good faith efforts to resolve certain marital issues. Consequently, she has chosen to take the high road and pursue the matter in a court of law." He paused.

Jon returned to his desk. "Tell her we'll discuss section nineteen when I get home tonight."

"You're an intelligent man, so let me make this simple. Everyone knows you're a big investment banking executive, and aggressive as hell from what I understand. Mrs. Browning is intimidated by you. Her emotional state is no match for your tactics."

Jon swiveled in his chair and focused on the pictures of his children. "Sam, what gives?"

"Psychologists have a name for it. They call it inferior tendencies of codependence. I intend to produce expert witnesses who will testify that your behavior borders on abuse."

"Now I've got the picture. When did she retain you?"

"Not germane to the conversation, Dr. Browning." Hallworth allowed a few strategic seconds to tick by.

"So now, it's Dr. Browning?"

"She's determined to regain control of her life and dignity."

Jon grabbed his day planner and jotted a few notes. "What if I told you, you've got the story wrong, Sam?"

"On the record, I would say your feelings are unfounded."

"I didn't say anything about feelings. But as far as that goes, I'm the one who's been traumatized."

"And you can appreciate the fact that my call is not intended to entertain your accusations," Hallworth said. "My client wants relief from your abusive behavior."

"Nice try, but this isn't about abuse. Tell me how much she owes you, and I'll take care of the bill. Beth and I will discuss the truth tonight."

"The truth is useful, but only if it can be proven in a court of law."

"And that is exactly what's going to happen, if you're not careful. Why don't we get to the real purpose of your call? I assume your client wants something from me."

"Dr. Browning, are you aware that the majority of your marital estate are held exclusively in your name?"

"Yes, I am. And they've been that way for the past eight years."

"Your wife wants access to the investment accounts—today."

"Why the sudden interest?"

A match struck on Hallworth's end of the line.

"The court frowns upon individuals who hoard control of marital assets. A judge will order you to provide equal access to Mrs. Browning."

"How much does she want?" Jon traced a dollar sign in his planner.

"I appreciate the offer, but she intends to petition the court for access to all of the funds. And I'd love to debate this by the hour, but I have another call."

"I'll take it up with Beth tonight."

"Consider yourself served, Dr. Browning."

"I suggest you step aside."

"One other thing. Mrs. Browning feels threatened by your presence in the marital residence."

"Sam, you already know my position. And in case you're interested, the house is our largest marital asset."

"These photos are quite disturbing," Hallworth said, hanging on the last word. "Personally, I'd be an emotional wreck living with someone who could destroy such an elegant home."

"Listen, you're wasting my time."

"The truth ultimately rests with a court of law," Hallworth said.

"So what's the bottom line on this scam?"

"Vacate the marital residence by the end of the week. And I don't care for your choice of words."

"That's not going to happen."

"Then I'll petition the court for a restraining order to insure the safety of my client."

"Be sensible, Sam. We've got children in the house."

"Take the matter under advisement, if you wish. But I wouldn't labor under the pretense that this is a negotiation. While I'm filing the restraining order, I'll have the judge freeze the investment accounts."

"The assets are safe."

"I'm sure you can appreciate my position. I'm only acting in the interest of my client," Hallworth said. "Now if you'll excuse me, I have a call on the other line. Drop by my office. I've drafted an agreement for your signature."

"Fax it over, and I'll review it."

"Don't try my patience, Dr. Browning. And by the way, you're entitled to counsel."

As Jon hung up, there was a knock at his office door.

"Jon?" Richard said, stepping in. "I thought we had an understanding."

"Save it, Richard. I'm leaving." Jon stood up, fighting hard not to show his irritation. "Did you need to see me?"

"Since you're here, how did it go with the psychologist?"

"I'm handling it, okay?"

"Randall indicated there was a positive step. At least, that's the word from David Stephens."

"Then let's leave it at that."

"What would you say to dinner with Donna and me over at the club tomorrow night?"

"Tomorrow isn't good." Jon reached for his briefcase.

"Very well," Richard said. "I'll see you at the South Coast board meeting tonight."

Chapter 20
Wednesday, July 6th
8:45 P.M.

It was dark when Jon pulled into the parking lot at South Coast Church. The bell tower glowed above the campus like a beckoning lighthouse. Down by the entrance, the fountainhead had been illuminated and sprayed a fine mist into the air, casting a rainbow of colors over the lake. He headed into the administrative wing, where he waited in a hallway until Richard stepped out to invite him in. Jon followed him into an impressive suite that had all of the character of a Fortune 500 boardroom. Recessed lighting warmed an oversized cherry conference table, where eleven of Savannah's finest businessmen reclined in their leather chairs, with Reverend Randall Phipps sitting at the head. Dark paneling covered the walls, each of them adorned with an impressive array of oil paintings. Across the room, a slide glowed on a multimedia screen, reading: "Capital Expansion Program, Phase III".

"Jonathon, so nice to see you," Phipps said, rising from his chair. The rest of the men followed suit and greeted Jon, all familiar faces.

"If you'll take your seats, we'll get started on the project update," Richard said. He offered Jon a chair, and then sat down next to him. "As you all know, Jonathon works with me at Stone

& Associates and is a valued member of the church. He has periodically advised David Stephens on the building committee, so we'll hear from him momentarily."

"Richard, would now be a good time to brief the new members on why Stephens has left the board?" someone said.

Randall Phipps rose out of his chair, glancing at Richard. "Allow me to do the honors." He clasped his hands together. "Six months ago the board determined that the time had come to develop a strategic plan for South Coast. We made this prayerful decision based on a survey given to our members late last year. As a result of a thorough process conducted by our appointed steering committee, their analysis revealed that there were two very different, yet important paths the church was pursuing. The first, I will call traditional ministries. These are functions offered by every mainline denomination: worship services, education, fellowship, and outreach into the community. Our loyal members have long supported these core competencies."

"You're referring to the people who contribute the lion's-share of funding to the church," someone commented.

"About eighty percent, if I'm not mistaken," Randall said. "But at the same time, we discovered that the future of South Coast has more to do with what goes on outside the walls of our exquisite facility, here, than has traditionally been the case. In fact, David Stephens, who headed up the steering committee, deserves credit for helping us to understand this new trend. I thank God that he has had the vision to champion this need for change. I believe we have reached a defining moment in the life of our church, even though we face significant challenges, and I appreciate the earlier reference to this point. According to the surveys, the older members of our congregation oppose the use of their contributions to support these outside ventures."

"That's not surprising," one of the new board member remarked. "But they did agree to drop the denominational reference on the sign out front."

"Yes, another of David Stephens's proposals," Randall said.

"I haven't heard anyone complaining about these new ministries. How did you manage to defuse the objections?" someone said.

Randall smiled. "To avoid division among the ranks, we decided to divest the church of the new initiatives. To be specific, we spun the ministries out into a separate corporation. David became chief executive officer of SCMI and has tapped the steering committee to help out until he sets up his own board of directors."

"How is he financing the ministry, given the sentiments of our key contributors?" someone asked.

"We started by setting aside what Richard calls seed money to get things off the ground. David has also managed to raise additional funds from individuals who I thought would never approve of the idea. He has been under significant pressure to become self-sufficient, but ultimately his success depends on a unique structure we've put in place. Richard, do you mind explaining?" Randall sat down.

"What we have done is quite common in the business world. We started by setting up a legal entity called South Coast Ministries, or SCMI for short," Richard said. "In return for their initial investment, SCMI has granted South Coast Church forty-nine percent of the stock in the company."

"A company . . . I thought they were a ministry?" someone said. "And why does the church want to own stock?"

"These new ministries have the potential of producing substantial returns," Richard said.

"Can you summarize what SCMI will be doing?" someone asked.

"As Randall indicated, David and his team are focusing on areas where the church has never operated, such as mass media, fitness centers, family counseling, legal aid, daycare, and eco-ministries," Richard said.

"And these all stand to make money?"

"Very easily," Richard said.

"The return on our investment will actually generate additional funding for our traditional ministries," Randall added.

"Who owns the other fifty-one percent?" Jon said. He swiveled in his chair to face Richard.

All eyes turned to Jon, then back to Richard.

"That's an excellent question," Richard said. "We believe SCMI has the best chance of succeeding if we provide the key executives with equity in the business."

"But you said it was a ministry," someone challenged.

"Legally, it's a business, but we all know it's a ministry," Richard said. "But to answer the original question, the steering committee granted fifteen percent of the shares to David and authorized him to distribute the remaining thirty-six percent to his staff and board members, once hired."

"So as you can see, we're entering an exciting period in the life of the church, which brings us to the purpose of tonight's presentation," Randall said, gesturing to the screen. "Richard, shall we?"

Richard remained in his seat as he introduced the first slide. "As most of you are aware, the church completed the initial building program about ten years ago. The layout of the facility was designed so that the auditorium could be used for Sunday services, as well as for social and recreational events. We quickly outgrew the space, and Phase II was completed three years later.

This expansion included the current auditorium, an education wing, and administrative offices. We converted the old auditorium into a gymnasium for sporting events."

"How much did we spend on the original building and Phase and II?" someone asked.

Richard paused to advance the slide. "Our first building was completed at a cost of three-point-five million. As you will recall, Phase II represented a substantial expansion, given we had grown to around fifteen hundred attendees. It came in at around seven-and-a-half million."

"How much do we currently owe on the existing structures?" someone asked.

"The original project has been fully paid off. But we got creative for Phase II and floated a bond offering to secure the funding for more favorable terms."

"And how much of that debt is currently outstanding?"

"Technically—all of it. But we're three years into the program and have set aside three-point-six million in contributions for repayment so far."

"That's what I thought." The board member who had asked the question was busy jotting on a notepad. "According to my calculations, we're short of where we need to be."

"We are behind, but only by a nose," Richard said. "The repayment projections are based on substantial growth in attendance and donations for the final two years of the program. I should also point out that our charter members have purchased half of the bonds. The experts have advised us that twenty-five to forty percent of these bondholders will forego repayment, essentially treating it as an additional contribution to the church."

"But only if they don't catch wind of the SCMI investment," someone said.

"I think they'll be pleased with the arrangement once they see the results," Richard said.

"Let's give them the good news," Randall chimed in.

Richard advanced the slide. "Gentlemen, as of last quarter, we have reached ninety percent of capacity in the current facilities, averaging sixty-two hundred on Sunday mornings. Based on these latest figures, we should begin Phase III immediately."

"I'm not sure this is good news," someone commented. "Can we afford another expansion?"

Randall sprang to his feet. "I not only appreciate the question, but also your sense of responsibility in asking." He walked the length of the room and stepped in front of the screen. "We must cast our ministry in a new light. For example, we are investing, not spending," he said, his tone increasingly passionate. "This is about the community—people who need to hear South Coast's message. We have been called for a purpose, to reach the lost and hurting souls of Savannah. And need I remind you, what God has so commissioned, he will see to fruition. We must stand firm in our faith and trust him for the outcome."

"Randall, we're all businessmen, well aware of the concept of investing versus expense," someone said. "Nobody's questioning our purpose. The real question is whether we can work out the finances. As of today, we're almost four million in the hole. Are you confident we can handle the additional risk?"

"That's an excellent question, and the perfect lead into why I've asked Jon to join us tonight," Richard interjected. He stood up and extended an arm, drawing everyone's attention to Jon.

Jon rose from his seat and took a position next to the screen, a few feet from where Randall remained standing.

"The figure under consideration for Phase III is fourteen million dollars," Jon began.

A collective murmur broke out around the table.

"Unfortunately, in preparing for tonight's presentation, I discovered an oversight in the figures—a material one."

"What do you mean?" Randall said.

"In order to begin Phase III, we need to acquire the property adjacent to our campus. Based on my analysis, the current estimates don't account for the purchase."

"Let me assure you. That's all been handled."

"We have to include the purchase in the estimates, Randall. As you know, it's a sizeable outlay."

"We have already signed the option to purchase the property."

"And that's well-and-good," Jon said. "But the price has to be in the millions, and we have to account for it."

"Well, I guess that's why you guys pay us the big bucks," Randall said, beaming at the board members. "David Stephens took a leave of absence several years ago for a fellowship at the lieutenant governor's office. As the time, Governor Callahan served in the position, and David had the foresight to discuss South Coast's future expansion needs with him. To our good fortune, David was able to secure an option on the property through a state land program." He beamed, like a salesman about to close a deal. "As providence would have it, David recently executed the option and has agreed to fund the transaction out of his SCMI operating budget. So gentlemen, the fourteen million dollar estimate is correct."

"Why haven't you mentioned this before?" someone said.

"And where's the contract?" another protested.

"Gentlemen, the deal was struck years ago," Randall said. "We should bow our heads at this very moment and give thanks."

"If you don't mind, I think we should hear Jon's presentation first," someone said. He checked his watch. "Can we move on?"

All eyes turned to Jon.

"I've done an analysis of membership trends, attendance, and contributions over the past three years. Basically, the figures suggest an additional thirteen million in financing is feasible."

"That can't be right," Randall said.

"I based the projections on the most recent data, but if you have reasons to accelerate the growth, then I'll certainly build the assumptions into my model."

"I don't think we should be gambling with these kinds of numbers," someone said. "We have an obligation to our bondholders. How would it look if we defaulted?"

"Gentlemen, I have one simple question . . . Do you have the faith necessary to secure the funds that are required to support this ministry?" Randall said.

"Jon, you've been through the package. Tell us what you think," Richard said.

"Quite frankly, I wouldn't raise the entire amount. A better strategy is to reduce the scope of the project."

"And how would you do that?" someone asked.

"By cutting the facilities earmarked for the indigent population."

"You can't be serious," Randall said.

"Randall, let Jon explain his reasoning," Richard said.

"The indigent facilities include a kitchen, dining hall, and bathrooms. The construction, alone, is seven hundred and fifty thousand."

"That's only five percent of the project," Randall said. "More importantly, we have a biblical mandate to reach out to the less fortunate in our community."

"I tend to agree, but why compete with established services?" Jon said.

"You have something better in mind?"

"The Seafarer Mission."

"Hold on," Randall said, raising his hands in the air. "You're talking about an itinerant operation."

"I'm referring to the Mission, which happens to be reaching the very population you're targeting," Jon said. "Captain Louis Beecher has adequate space to meet these needs for the next three years."

Randall dropped his hands as the room grew silent. "Old LBJ—now I've heard it all. Believe me. South Coast doesn't associate with his type."

"What's wrong with Captain Beecher?" someone asked.

"He's a glutton and a drunk. No doubt, you're familiar with the term, 'a girl in every port'. Well, he's the poster child. The man's reputation will jeopardize our standing in the community."

"I sit on the Mission's board and can assure you, not only is he having a positive impact in the community, but he's also operating at a fraction of the cost you're proposing for this project," Jon said.

"I'm not buying it. He's downtown crawling around with the riffraff and whores," Randall said. "These people need to be cleaned up and removed from the inner city."

"The riffraff and whores, as you call them, are the indigent. We fine people should do everything we can to help them," Jon said. "I've seen the results, firsthand: meals, job counseling, drug rehabilitation, spiritual help, bathrooms, showers, and clean beds. I admit the facility needs a few upgrades, but we're talking about less than a hundred thousand dollars. If South Coast funds the renovations and operating costs over the next three years, you'll deliver much better outcomes than this proposal."

"How does he do it?" someone asked.

"By spending the money directly on people's needs," Jon said, holding a document in the air. "This plan invests money in bricks and mortar, not the poor. And the seven hundred and fifty thousand dollars doesn't address the ongoing expenses to run the facility."

Randall stepped between Jon and the others. "I believe that will do, Jonathon."

"Wait. What's the estimate for the operating costs?" someone asked.

"We'll discuss that momentarily," Randall said, shuttering the discussion.

Richard stood up. "Jon, thank you for your time. Do you have a report to leave behind?"

"Yes, of course," Jon said, setting a folder on the table. "Thank you and good night, gentlemen."

Richard ushered Jon out into the hallway. "Excellent work, Jon. The board will review your proposal and get back to you with any questions. And don't worry about Randall. He always gets worked up over these sorts of things."

Richard gave Jon a pat on the shoulder and headed back inside. As the door closed, Jon heard a board member say, "What has gotten into you, Randall?"

Randall paced the room, with his hands tucked behind his back. "I have to apologize for what you have just witnessed. I can see now that Jonathon is no state of mind to be advising the board. Wouldn't you agree, Richard?"

"His proposal has its merits, Randall." Everyone's eyes shifted from Randall to Richard. "I would like to give it some thought. Perhaps we should bring Captain in for a presentation."

"That old man has no place in this church," Randall said.

"Randall, there's plenty of people in the community who respect Beecher," someone said.

"It is irresponsible to cast our pearls before swine. Turning that pirate loose at South Coast would be a mistake."

"No one's turning him loose. We're merely looking into the possibility of investing in the Mission," someone said.

"And I'm telling you, it's unacceptable to delegate this type of responsibility outside the church body."

"Perhaps we should continue this discussion at our next meeting." Richard pressed a remote and the presentation went dark. "By then, we'll all have had time to think about Jon's suggestion."

"Listen to me. Jonathon Browning has no business offering advice to this board," Randall repeated. "Richard, tell them about his leave of absence."

"Randall," Richard said, silencing him with a look.

"Gentlemen, you'd better explain yourselves," someone said.

Chapter 21
Thursday, July 7th
9:25 A.M.

A telephone call to Stewart and Claire Baines was all it took for Jon to secure a lease on the second floor of their Tybee Island beach house. The elderly live-in owners of the vintage oceanfront property had rented out the upper half of their home to a dwindling base of vacationers for over two decades. In the past Jon had booked the property for weekend getaways, but the Baineses were delighted when he committed to taking it for the entire summer.

Jon spent the morning arranging for a U-Haul on Saturday and scheduling to have Internet service installed. Around noon, he dropped by the post office to fill out change of address forms. Afterwards, he swung by the office to handle a distress call he had received while out running his errands.

When he arrived, a red-faced Charlie waved him into his office as he barked at some poor soul on the other end of a phone call. Jon removed a stack of folders from the guest chair and took a seat in front of the desk. Without warning, Charlie's temper flared and a backhand sent papers flying off the desktop.

"Then never mind," he yelled into the phone. "No, send the damn paperwork ... right ... right. We'll have the Chatham legal team comment, and I'll get back to you . . . Don't mention it." He slammed down the receiver.

"A Johnson-Medisys lawyer, I take it?" Jon said.

"Frigging idiot," Charlie said. "Take a look at this." He passed a document to him. "Jon, about last week—"

"Forget about it," Jon interrupted, looking down at the fax.

"So Richard tells me you're taking a backseat from here on out."

"The deal is ninety percent done, so don't blow it," Jon said, holding up the fax. "What prompted this?"

"That is Michael Johnson's response to newly hatched overtures from Bob."

"Has Richard seen it?"

"I was hoping you'd like to do the honors."

"Did Bob actually say this in public?"

"It sure sounds like him, but you know him better than I do."

Jon stuffed the fax in his pocket and climbed out of the chair. "I'll handle it."

"So what gives? Everyone thought this deal was your fast track to the big *P* when you landed it."

"Partner—is that what you think?"

"Damn straight. At least, until now."

"Richard thought I needed a breather before the next big thing."

"Come on. We all know there's not another deal brewing at the moment," Charlie said. "The rumor around the office is—problems at home."

"Everything's fine, Charlie."

"Anything you need, just say the word. Hey, remember when you moved into that mansion out on Skidaway. Who manhandled the sleeper sofa, huh? Charlie walked around and plopped down on a corner of the desk.

"I thought that tweed boat anchor was going to take you down, right there on the stairway. I envisioned a plaque in the foyer, 'Here lies Charlie Porter'."

"You still can't admit I'm the better man."

"A better sofa mover, I'll give you that." Jon pointed a finger.

"All seriousness aside, I owe you one, Buddy. Just say the word."

"Count on it," Jon said. "Are we done here?"

"Maybe you could put a contract on that weasel I just hung up on."

"Nice try," Jon said as he stepped into the hallway.

As he passed Brenda's office she called out to him, and he made a detour. "Richard wants to speak to you," she said, handing Jon a telephone. She frowned and mouthed, "Sorry."

"Yes, Richard."

"Jon, Brenda tells me Charlie called you in for assistance. He'll learn nothing if you don't stand down and let him handle things. Now, I want you out of there."

"Before or after I diffuse Bob's latest bombshell?"

"What seems to be the problem?"

"He's screwing everything up. Michael's lawyer has put Bob on notice about breaches in confidentiality. And I'd say he's got a point. If this acquisition goes public, and then falls through during negotiations, Michael's out of business."

"I'll take care of Bob, but maybe it would be a good idea for you to talk to Michael."

"That's why I'm here, Richard."

"After that, your job is limited to signing paperwork, at least until you resolve your personal matter. While I have you on the phone, what's the news on that front?"

Jon ran a hand through his hair and glanced over at Brenda. "Round one goes to Beth. I have agreed to move out of the house, but she's going to allow access to the kids."

"That's unfortunate."

"I offered her a large check to keep the lawyers at bay. She has agreed to cash it only if there's an emergency. For some reason, she's worried about money, if something were to happen to me."

"I had no idea lawyers were involved," Richard said.

"I've also committed to paying for all of her living expenses until things are settled."

"That was fast. How did she get all that?"

"Let's just call it a lapse in judgment. The agreement is verbal, so it's nonbinding."

"Jon, I spoke to one of the elders at the church—"

"Richard, the church isn't involved. It was all brokered through her lawyer."

There was an awkward silence.

"Well then, just keep your wits about you," Richard said. "Listen, I've got to be off. Call me with any updates."

"I guess I should have excused myself," Brenda said, scrunching her nose as Jon handed her the telephone. "Are you okay?"

"Nothing a summer at the beach won't cure. Do you have anything else before I leave?"

"One quick thing," Brenda said. "Evidently, you registered for something called the Executive Leadership Program in Colorado Springs. The meeting materials arrived in the morning mail, and they are requesting that you confirm your attendance."

"I'd almost forgotten about that."

"Richard's been asking if you're attending." Brenda shuffled a stack of paper. "Here it is, July eleventh through the fifteenth."

"Colorado . . . it may be just what the doctor ordered," Jon said.

* * *

Saturday, July 9ᵗʰ
1:20 P.M.

Even with Tybee Island sitting a short fifteen miles east of Savannah on the Atlantic, the change in scenery could not have been more pronounced. Jon and Charlie managed to transport all of Jon's necessities in a single round-trip up and down Highway 80 with the rented U-Haul. Charlie commandeered the van while Jon drove his vintage Land Cruiser, a vehicle he planned to use to shuttle the kids back and forth on their island visits. With the apartment already furnished, the contents of the U-Haul consisted mostly of clothes and personal effects. Charlie complained about the countless boxes, but welcomed a rematch with the sleeper sofa. This time the challenge took him up a graying flight of steps attached to the outside of the beach house.

"What in the John Brown do you need this thing for anyway?" Charlie said. "You've already got a bed."

"This fine piece of furniture doubles as a guest suite."

"I take it the crowd you're running with isn't very discriminating."

"It's for the kids."

"When are we taking a break? I've been going at this all morning. I'm beginning to think you're running a sweatshop here?"

"Slide the sofa against the wall," Jon said. "How does pizza sound?"

"Screw that. I need a beer."

Lunch arrived as they were emptying the remnants from the U-Haul. Collapsing on a screen porch that overlooked the Atlantic, they dug into the pizza and sipped beer.

"You know the house isn't much to write home about, but the view is off the charts," Charlie said. He spilled his drink as he used it to point out at the ocean.

"That's the magic of this place."

"I noticed the paint is flaking off the clapboards outside. Why didn't you spring for something fancier?"

"It's simple, and this is where I belong."

"Give me a break. Nobody's going to believe you've gone bonsai."

"It doesn't matter what they think."

"Jon, what exactly are you doing?" Charlie pulled another slice of pizza out of the box.

"I've always loved it out here."

"No. Why exactly are you in this situation?"

Jon stared at a shrimp boat tossing about in the waves beyond the surf. "It's complicated. Let's just say things aren't making sense at home and leave it at that."

"Well get some help, man. You're both intelligent people. Go see a shrink, if you have to."

Jon gave Charlie his look. "We're trying, okay?"

"Clearly, not hard enough."

"I'm doing what I think is best."

"You know how to work it out. Show Beth you're committed. You're a negotiator. Use some of that crap on her."

"It's a two-way process, Charlie."

"You've always said negotiations have to be a win-win proposition, so listen to her and give her the benefit of the doubt. Whatever she wants, just do it, and get past this."

"Do you have any idea of what you're talking about?" Jon said.

"As a matter of fact, I do. Give her a reason to reciprocate."

"She wanted me out of the house."

Charlie hesitated. "Okay . . . That's a start. I've known Beth for a long time, so there's a point to all of this."

"That's right, a sharp point. And there were other things I wouldn't agree to—"

"Don't shoot the messenger, Buddy. All I'm saying is you should work with her, so you can move back home. If not for her, do it for the kids."

"See that shrimp boat?" Jon said, standing up and grabbing the pizza box. "Take a close look at how it's fighting the current out there. That's the situation."

"Well, do what you do best—calm the waters."

Chapter 22
Saturday, July 9th
11:00 P.M.

Around eleven on Saturday, Jon ventured out for his first walk on the beach, returning to the apartment to settle into a Pawleys Island Hammock on the porch. With a bottle of Gonzo in hand, he stretched out as the rising tide played a dirge for him. In the distance, he saw the flickering lights of ships waiting to enter the Savannah River. A stone's throw away, sea oats danced in the soothing ocean breeze as the night cast its spell.

Jon retrieved another microbrew from the refrigerator, suddenly feeling guilty about the tension with Charlie earlier in the day. Checking the time, he decided it was too late to call to clear things up and returned to the porch. Dropping into the hammock, he breathed in the intoxicating scent of the ocean as his mind began to wander.

Beth's confession—that was the issue—and it made less sense every time they talked. Even the chronicle of events didn't seem to fit. Everything had evolved in sound bites. She had lost control of her emotions on multiple occasions, possibly due to stress, and it had completely shut down her ability to communicate. But the chameleon-like transformation over the past few days bothered him most. Within seventy-two hours her attitude had changed, and in a short period of time she had somehow evolved from transgressor to victim, resulting in his eviction from the house. He had challenged himself repeatedly, questioning if he had heard correctly that first night. The words . . . The look on her face . . . And then the destroyed bedroom only days later.

He shifted in the hammock, unable to get comfortable. His mind wouldn't let go, so he slipped on his Topsiders and descended the stairs to 7th Street. The Baineses' house sat at the end of the street next to an arched boardwalk connecting to the beach. Looking first toward the ocean, he turned and headed inland until he reached Butler Avenue, and then hung a left. Power lines stretched overhead as far as he could see into the darkness, with little traffic to speak of, only the samba of the katydids.

When he came to the Tybrisa Street intersection, Jon turned back toward the beach. He stopped to gaze into the window at Doc's Bar, noticing upturned chairs on the tabletops. Continuing down the stretch of empty sidewalk, he climbed a ramp onto the Tybee Pier. Once he reached the end, he turned and looked back at the crescent moon. It had already peaked and was sinking inland. A young couple cuddled next to a wooden rail, so intertwined they didn't even register his arrival.

As Jon inhaled the night air, his thoughts went adrift and a question surfaced, and then lingered. Why did everyone think he was the problem? He got the sense that there was some type of common knowledge about an issue between him and Beth, one that people had already come to accept. Only he was arriving late to the party. And it seemed like Charlie had been pushing him earlier, possibly the reason he had snapped at him. Did Charlie see something he couldn't see, or was he simply playing him? Of course, given the circumstances, the situation was probably as awkward for Charlie as it was for him.

He wondered if it was possible for others to recognize behaviors that he couldn't see in himself. No question, Richard had concerns or he wouldn't have told him to take time off from work. And what if Hallworth was right—what if Jon had destroyed the bedroom? On top of that, was it conceivable that Lowe actually did know something about his childhood? He had read how people under certain conditions had tendencies to block out bad experiences.

But he remembered his youth and could play back countless stories of growing up. Naturally, they were far from perfect, but there was nothing violent or abusive in them. He liked to reflect on his small town upbringing. He breezed through high school and had great memories of Stanford. He worked hard all his life, secured a job, and advanced quickly in his profession. What was there to suppress?

Charlie was right about one thing—the olive branch. He even remembered a childhood story about how to treat others, even if they harbored ill feelings toward you. But what if he was unable to understand how those feelings originated? Was the *Golden Rule* the answer? If he was behaving irrationally and couldn't perceive it, how was he going to change?

Jon felt as if his head was going to explode as he contemplated a potential blind spot within himself. Lowe was a PhD, and a member of South Coast Church. The guy was experienced. He knew what he was doing. Even Captain said he deserved a chance.

But there was a tougher reality. Accepting Lowe's counsel meant he would have to concede on a major front. He had to be willing to accept that the problem was him, not Beth. And he had to come to grips with the fact he was responsible for the entire situation: the affairs, the destroyed bedroom, and the confession. If his ability to reason was flawed, what he considered to be his greatest strength was actually a weakness. His mind couldn't grasp the possibility of a condition so severe that he didn't know what he was doing—a mental mirage. But how could he have gotten so far in life? Jon ran a hand through his hair and turned to the ocean.

He looked over the rail and down into the churning waters fifteen feet below. Waves sent spray into the air as they slapped the concrete pylons. The tide was moving out. He watched the currents swirl and struggle to find their way out to sea, suddenly feeling a peace. The ocean knew nothing of the problems of life. It was accepting, it was constant, and it knew no fears. He heard music and thought he recognized the tune, and then turned to see the couple laughing and heading for the shoreline.

Jon turned back to the open Atlantic. He knew why he was drawn to the sea. It was limitless, larger than life, stretching farther than he could see. There were mysteries his mind couldn't fathom. The ocean connected with his longing to trust in something bigger than himself, and it was like a song entreating him to a place far removed from his problems.

Jon sensed a stirring and suddenly felt all alone on the pier. Climbing up on the railing, he spread his legs, and then raised his hands into the wind. Fanning his palms outward, he felt the breeze enveloping his body. The aroma of salt air filled his head as he closed his eyes and raised his chin heavenward. The couple's music played on in his mind, for the moment vaporizing all other thoughts into the night.

Memories washed over him, like silt-covered waves clouding his vision. He remembered a time in his teens when he had plunged into the jetties of the St. Mary's River, shoulder-deep in the salty currents and drifting along as if nothing else mattered. He could almost feel the swells of a simpler time as he longed to live that way again.

The wind swirled, and Jon imagined himself floating on celestial constellations, leaving the confusion behind. A gust caught him by surprise, and he lost his balance, falling backwards. As his feet pounded onto the pier he collapsed to his knees, exhausted. Grasping for breath, he pulled himself up by the rail, and then leaned over, staring into the waves below. He felt pain, wrestling with a stream of doubt until the tape somehow found its way into his consciousness.

It came from deep within him, and Jon suddenly couldn't reconcile the conflict. He shouted, "Hell no," and looked out at the ocean. He knew exactly what he had to do.

Chapter 23
Sunday, July 10th
7:00 A.M.

The SCMI steering committee sat in a conference room with sweat beading on their foreheads. By the time the air conditioner whirred to life, tempers had already begun to flare. They had been waiting for over half an hour for the meeting to begin and David Stephens was nowhere in sight.

"This is his meeting," someone complained. "Why is it so hot in here?"

"When I was on the facility team, we programmed the cooling system to turn on precisely two hours before the first service," another answered. "This place is a well-oiled machine."

"Are you serious?"

"I've had enough," someone said, taking out his phone. "I'll try his cell phone."

"Randall Phipps is a stickler for results. I've heard him go on and on about how every leader should look for ways to eliminate deterrents to worship. We did our part and computerized the HVAC system to factor out human error, a pretty ingenious idea, if you ask me."

"How is Stephens going to lead SCMI, if he can't be on time for his own meetings?"

"He's not answering his cell."

The conference room door swung open, and Stephens huffed in with a Starbucks cup in hand. "Good morning, gentlemen." He dropped a briefcase on the table.

"If you intended to keep us waiting, at least you could have brought us all coffee."

"Let's get on with it," someone snipped.

"I apologize for the delay," Stephens said. "I had an issue with my two-year old this morning."

"I seem to recall a lecture you once gave us about how wives are to take care of that department."

"Her parents aren't doing well, so she had to fly down to Florida. But I believe I've made a breakthrough and discovered a way to tame the terrible twos."

There was a snicker. "Yeah, wait till he's a teenager."

Stephens took a seat and offered a drive-by prayer, and then handed out an agenda, checking off each item as they went. When they reached the end of the list, he began repacking his briefcase. "I have a final matter related to our counseling ministry that I have intentionally left off of the agenda—a quick update on the Browning case and a recommendation for next steps." He cut his eyes at the meeting's secretary.

"So you want me to stop taking minutes?"

"Typically, SCMI meetings will follow church decorum," Stephens said with a wink. "But when it comes to sensitive matters, we must take every precaution."

"I missed the last meeting. What are we discussing here?" someone said.

"The secretary can fill you in once we're done," Stephens said. "As we discussed previously, I arranged for a meeting with Jonathon Browning two weeks ago. As a result, he made appointments for the initial marital counseling with Dr. Tim Lowe.

Now that we have succeeded in putting the wheels in motion, I have asked Beth Browning to provide regular updates on our plans to reconcile the marriage."

"What plans?"

"The ones previously delegated to this committee," Stephens said. "Dr. Lowe has met twice with Jonathon and conducted a preliminary evaluation based on a battery of psychological instruments. But I'm afraid we've already reached an impasse. He refuses to comply with our directive to provide access to Dr. Lowe's files."

"I can't speak for the others, but I don't have a clue what you mean by a battery of instruments," someone said. "And may I ask how we know all of this, since he hasn't agreed to whatever it is you're talking about?"

"As an upstanding member of the church, Dr. Lowe is doing everything possible to support the efforts of this committee," Stephens said.

"But can he legally do that?"

"First of all, let me remind you that our discussions are confidential," Stephens said. "Secondly, our work is spiritual work. SCMI is not technically constrained by the US legal system, an institution created by man."

"Correct me if I'm wrong, but I believe we are supposed to respect government authorities."

"Gentlemen, you are church elders, and as such you represent South Coast Church, a church ordained by heaven above. I don't need to remind you . . . The world continues to drift from our standards on marriage. God hates divorce. When our legal system conflicts with what we believe, we have a responsibility to act upon our ordained duties."

"Then what's the point of Jonathon signing a legal document?"

"I'm not an attorney, but we have been advised that it's necessary."

"David, I'm really uncomfortable with all of this. Are you saying SCMI's lawyer wants a signed document from Dr. Browning?"

"We are following a much broader principle, here. Your actions must be grounded in truth, not manmade social norms. It's your God-ordained responsibility."

"Okay, enough with the ordained rhetoric. We're dealing with human lives, so let's be reasonable."

"In my opinion, we should let the Browning's know we are here for them, if they need help. We can't force them to do anything against their will."

"Gentlemen," Stephens said, rising out of his chair. "We have taken an oath to fulfill our divine duties. Otherwise, we're as depraved as Jonathon Browning, who at this very moment is harboring a sinful nature."

"That's easy for you to say. I think we should meet with him and hear his side of the story. Beyond that, I'm not even sure why we are involved. When is Dr. Lowe taking over this case, permanently?"

"I have counseled Jonathon, and I'm telling you, he has strayed. For any of you who doubt my words, you'll find your evidence at the eleven o'clock service." Stephens raised a hand and pointed at the far wall. "Mark my words. Beth Browning will once again be worshipping alone with her precious little children."

"So let's meet with Jonathon. Maybe we can take him to lunch."

"How long have you been an elder?" Stephens said.

"Eight months."

"I've been doing this for over twenty years. I can assure you, now is the time for decisive action."

"But it seems like we're doing it in a sneaky way—"

"In a discreet way," Stephens interrupted.

"If it's true we operate above the system, then this discussion is pointless."

"Okay, let's step back for a moment," Stephens said. "It has recently been reported that Jonathon is having an affair." He paused for effect. "I'm sure each of you can appreciate the fact that a man in such a position doesn't have his family's best interest at heart. It is a behavior that impairs a man's judgment. Our inaction merely relinquishes this family to the forces of the world."

The elders exchanged looks, shaking their heads in silence.

Confident he had closed the argument, Stephens turned his back to the elders, clinching his hand into a fist. Then he pumped it, Tiger Woods-like.

Chapter 24
Sunday, July 10th
9:00 A.M.

Flight 653 set down in the crisp Colorado Springs morning, leaving plenty of time for Jon to drop off his luggage at the Broadmoor Hotel and grab a shower before playing a round of golf. Afterwards, he headed over to the Golden Bee where a throng of tourists had huddled around a ragtime piano, singing and consuming yards of European beer. It didn't take much for the sing-a-longs to wear thin, so he headed back to the hotel for an appointment.

Inside the lobby, Jon slipped into the West Bar to find a much tamer crowd sitting around the well-stocked bar. As he descended a short flight of stairs a lower-level seating area, the entire back wall opened up onto a patio overlooking a lake. He searched the faces before proceeding outside to find Michael Johnson kicked back at a table.

Michael rose with a smile, his blond hair fluttering in the evening breeze as Jon approached. He was dressed in a pair of loose-fitting chinos and an untucked woven shirt. When he stepped out from the teak table, Jon noticed he was wearing a pair of Birkenstocks.

"I see you've made the right decision and accepted my invitation," Jon said.

Michael offered his hand. "The jury's still out, but as you can see, I'm here."

A waiter slipped over and took Jon's drink order, and then departed as the men settled into their chairs at the table. Michael poured red wine from a bottle, setting it down next to a flickering candle. Jon breathed in the fresh air and looked out across the lake, where lights were beginning to glow in the dusk.

"Did you fly out here just to see me?" Michael said.

"I have other business in the area."

They made small talk until Jon's beer arrived.

"Nothing else for me," Jon said to the waiter.

"Tell me something," Michael said. "What exactly were you thinking when you sent that crazy e-mail?"

Jon gave him his look. "It wasn't me."

"I passed it on to Richard, thinking it was part of the plan."

"Forget about it." Jon took a sip of beer.

"So what are we doing here?"

"That depends. Are you asking as a businessman or a friend?"

"You tell me."

"This is the deal—the one you've been waiting for." Jon leaned back in his chair. "Are you familiar with Chatham's market?"

"Why would I waste my time?" Michael said. "Bob Stein has pissed me off for the last time, so I filed the legal notice, just like we discussed."

"Are you familiar with their market?" Jon repeated.

"I haven't specifically analyzed their numbers, but yes, more or less."

"Chatham Medical Devices is a regional player. They've amassed a diversified portfolio from a series of acquisitions—

everything from blood pressure monitors to electrocardiograms. But they're a minor player due to their me-too technology and limited geographic reach."

"Then why am I interested?"

"For one thing, you're broke."

Michael snapped up his wine glass and looked away. "I didn't fly twelve hundred miles to hear that again."

"Nor I," Jon said. "Chatham's product line is weak, but well-rounded. They've crushed the competition in the Southeast because they offer a well-rounded suite of equipment to their customers. In the health care world, that simplifies the administrative burden, meaning less paperwork. It's an important distinction when you're dealing with hospital bureaucracies."

"I'm still waiting for the pony," Michael quipped.

"Their customers rave about them. Once Chatham gets a foot in the door, they snap up the lion's share of monitoring business. The problem is the hospitals they deal with are relatively small."

"So if my devices broaden their portfolio, that can't be a big win for either of us."

"Hear me out. It's the big medical centers that can afford the latest technology. I've been looking into your patents, and the microcircuits you've developed have broader applications in emergency rooms and surgical suites. Placing your chips into Chatham's equipment will reduce the overall footprint. With space at a premium, doing away with much of the clutter in the OR is a big win for physicians. While we're doing that, we can also upgrade most of the current technology. But more importantly, you've engineered secure broadband into your design. That means we can network images, vital signs, data—even hospital electronic records."

"So you want to capture live data?" Michael said.

"I want to deliver real-time information to doctors. And not just from the monitors, but from MRIs, lab reports, and patient records as well. High speed. High Definition. A medical GPS at the physician's fingertips."

"What's the market potential?"

"One hundred times bigger than Chatham's current strategy. On the consumer side, we'll be able to revolutionize the current offering of wearable devices, allowing physicians to monitor vital signs twenty-four-seven, a major benefit for chronic medical conditions or patients recently released from the hospital. We're looking at breakout technology with global reach," Jon said.

"And a major investment. How are you going to secure the financing?"

"Venture capital. The patents open the door to an equity round, which also gives us time to redeploy the technology."

"How much are we talking?"

"Whatever you need."

"Like I said before, it's going to cost you."

"Let me worry about that. Are you in?"

"I was never out," Michael said.

* * *

Monday, July 11th – Friday, July 15th

On Monday morning, Jon left the hotel for a kickoff meeting at the Center for Dynamic Leadership. The organization operated primarily from executive referrals and was housed only a few miles away in a glass and stone building surrounded by the Rockies. Even though Richard had recommended the program months earlier, Jon had only a limited knowledge of the agenda he was walking into. The week started with four days of intense psychological testing, role playing, and situation analysis. And despite being warned from the first day that there would be surveillance conducted during all activities, the participants were later surprised to discover they had not only been evaluated at official sessions, but at meals and cocktail hours as well. Jon was intrigued, yet invigorated by the challenges put before him.

On Friday morning he reported to a conference room, where he was scheduled to meet with Dr. James Rodwin. The one-on-one debriefing represented the final step in the program.

"Please have a seat," Dr. Rodwin said, closing the door. "Congratulations. You're a survivor." The doctor shook Jon's hand, and then walked over and sat down across the table. "Not everyone makes it to this point. You may have noticed that several of your colleagues departed after Tuesday's role-playing exercise."

"If memory serves me correctly, that was the blizzard encounter," Jon said with amusement. "We don't see many of those in Savannah."

"Indeed. But you've just validated one of our key findings. Statistics indicate that a sense of humor can be critical in stressful situations."

"Getting away from the real world for a time of reflection has been really good for me."

"And as you can see, we have the perfect setting." Dr. Rodwin gestured to the mountains outside the window. "After a week here, you may appreciate why I left my corporate job for this line of work."

"So this is how it ends—with you rubbing it in? Maybe you're onto something."

"Not so fast. I don't advise a change of that nature, at least not in your situation. Jon, I think you're going to find what I'm about to share with you interesting. Seldom does a psychologist have an opportunity to see a profile that converges as distinctly as yours."

"That sounds encouraging."

"As you are aware, trained professionals have been observing you throughout the week. In fact, I was one of those observers. In your case, my own assessment lined up beautifully with the other staff."

"I take it, that's good?"

"Good is a relative term, but yes. The self-assessment you completed a few weeks ago maps succinctly with our live observations. Even the three-sixty surveys from your manager, peers, and subordinates aligned very nicely. One submission was an outlier, but we consider it irrelevant."

"Irrelevant?"

"Any time multiple sets of information correlate conclusively to a certain profile, a lone outlier is discounted. To be more precise, we exclude it from our analysis since the person's opinion may be biased," Dr. Rodwin said.

"I've known all of these people for years."

"Don't even go there. The assessment is for you, not about the others. You're probably tired of them by now, but we've administered a dozen psychological instruments during the week. And they all converge beautifully with the human data points."

"Can you translate that for me?"

"You enjoy your work and feel professionally challenged."

"That's true."

"And how about the owner of your firm—what is his name?"

"Richard. We typically work well together, with a healthy dose of conflict, of course."

"That's not surprising. You've managed to align your personal values and strengths with the right career opportunity. You'd be surprised how many of your peers are searching for that purpose in life. They're looking for the right career situation, and even for a new start in their personal lives."

"So am I what you professionals call well adjusted?"

"You have an uncanny self-awareness, something rarely seen in the profession, Jon."

"Perhaps you could elaborate on that a bit?"

"You are transparent. Whatever you think about yourself is a good indicator of how others perceive you."

"That's interesting," Jon said, stirring in his chair. "So if someone were to suggest I was unaware of certain personal behaviors, would that be cause for suspicion?"

"Is this a hypothetical question?"

Jon shook his head.

"Then perhaps you can be more specific," Dr. Rodwin said.

"A psychologist in Savannah has suggested that I may be suppressing childhood memories."

"Was this recently?" Dr. Rodwin picked up a pen. "It sounds as if you have a concern."

"Suppressing memories isn't exactly a warm and fuzzy for me."

"What type of memories?"

"For starters, abuse," Jon said.

"I can't imagine. There was nothing of this nature reflected in the instruments or observations." Dr. Rodwin opened a folder on the table, flipping pages and nodding as he went.

"Dr. Rodwin, are you familiar with something called an MMPI?"

"Why do you ask?" Dr. Rodwin stopped reading and cut his eyes up at Jon.

"I recently completed an MMPI as a part of marital counseling."

"How long have you been in this counseling?"

"A couple of weeks. But I wanted to ask you about the results. The psychologist said they were inconclusive."

"Are you certain that's what he said?" Dr. Rodwin didn't wait for a response. "Did he administer additional instruments?"

"A background questionnaire."

"Were there any additional sources of information he may have used?"

"To my knowledge, only what my wife told him."

"Which may suggest he's drawn certain conclusions from her point of view."

"But there's one other thing. He claimed that someone else had confirmed what she told him, but they asked to remain anonymous."

"Jon, how about some water?" Dr. Rodwin stood up and walked over to a sideboard. He brought back two bottles of water.

"Whatever you have to say, I'd prefer you give it to me straight, Dr. Rodwin." Jon got up to stretch his legs, allowing Rodwin a few moments of thought before returning to his seat.

"My guess is you've already considered what I'm about to advise, so here it is. My counsel is to stop seeing this psychologist."

"I may have failed to mention it, but I'm a Protestant and this psychologist happens to be a member of my church."

"Jon, not everyone who calls himself a Christian means you well."

"Are you suggesting he's intentionally misleading me?"

"That, or the possibility he has never been properly trained."

"He came at the recommendation of our pastor. In fact, he's adamant we counsel with this guy."

"Let me make myself perfectly clear. In my opinion, you should get out," Dr. Rodwin said. He stood up and walked to the window.

Jon cocked his head. "Of the counseling . . ."

"The psychotherapy and the church, possibly even the relationships," Dr. Rodwin said.

"What about my marriage?"

"Give me the background on your marital situation." Dr. Rodwin listened intently as Jon explained Beth's activities over the previous weeks. Afterwards, he said, "First, if you and your wife need marital advice, and it sounds like you do, find a reputable counselor and try working things out. You don't need a psychologist."

"I'm confused. Isn't that what you guys do?" Jon stood and ran a hand through his hair.

"We deal with psychological problems. I've just given you a clean bill of health. Any psychologist worth his salt will draw the same conclusions."

"But the marriage is failing."

"Jon, sit down. Do you have any idea about how the MMPI is designed to be used?"

"Only what Dr. Lowe has told me."

"MMPI stands for Minnesota Multiphasic Personality Inventory. It was developed to diagnose specific types of problems. No one with even an elementary clinical understanding would begin their evaluation by giving you this instrument."

"Could it be about the money? You know, inconclusive means years of therapy."

"Jon, listen to me carefully. When I say the MMPI was developed for detecting problems, I mean severe psychosis. Do you follow?"

"You'd better spell it out for me."

"Gross mental illness. Conditions like schizophrenia, hallucinations, sexual orientation, and these sorts of issues." Dr. Rodwin watched as Jon got out of his chair again. "So you see why I'm concerned. You sought advice regarding the indiscretions of your spouse, and in return were administered a psychological instrument that may appear relatively benign to you. But on a professional level, he suspects mental problems."

"Could he be going through a process of elimination?"

"It doesn't work that way. A skilled psychologist will only administer the instrument after he has observed behaviors warranting further assessment. In your case, there was no basis for the concern. Even if he were acting on statements from your wife, he should have gotten to know you, possibly used the instruments I gave you this week."

"This sounds serious," Jon said.

"That's an understatement."

"But what about the church? They want a signed legal—"

"Not a chance," Dr. Rodwin interrupted.

"Her lawyer says it's a good faith gesture."

"It's dangerous territory. The lack of ethics is inexcusable."

"I haven't agreed to anything."

"Jon, I don't mean to alarm you, but it is common practice for attorneys to use MMPI results in the courtroom. Divorce and child custody cases are fairly typical. Have the two of you met for a joint session with Dr. Lowe?"

"We're scheduled to begin when I return." Jon paused. "Do you have any thoughts on why the church is pressing for the legal release?"

"I'm afraid I can't advise you on that point."

"Beth has hinted at a lawsuit, if I don't comply with their request."

"The best counsel I can give you is to set a course that puts you at peace with your own internal compass. Do you know if Dr. Lowe has given your wife the MMPI?"

Jon stood in silence for a moment. "I haven't thought about that. But I don't know the answer."

"If he isn't evaluating the two of you similarly, it opens the door to bias." Dr. Rodwin straightened up and placed both hands on the table. "If she believes you're the problem and has found a professional to affirm the notion, then there may be little motivation to seek out common ground. It also means you'll be at a disadvantage in attempting to reason with her."

"Do you have any thoughts on why they're doing this?"

"Jon, I honestly don't know. But you must also think of your children. An adult with these tendencies often finds it expedient to manipulate them into believing that the other parent is at fault or unfaithful. The children become a weapon."

"How do I determine if this is what I'm dealing with?"

"Unfortunately, it's very difficult."

Jon glanced down at his watch. "I have a flight to catch."

"I'm not sure we've addressed all of your concerns. Was there anything else you wanted to discuss?"

"There is the matter of a tape."

"And it's related to the marital matter?"

"It adds additional perspective, especially after what you've just told me," Jon said.

"Leave me your contact information, and we'll talk."

Chapter 25
Saturday, July 16th
10:00 A.M.

The three bedroom townhouse sat in a sprawling community along Highway 204 on the outskirts of town. The neutral colors, tiled roofs, and splashy shutters were all symbols of Savannah's urban renewal, washing over the Southside like a spring tide. As the humidity turned to haze, air conditioners buzzed to life, initiating the first rights of a muggy morning.

"When are you going to do something about this bedroom?" Charlie said. He slipped a hand beneath the covers and poked a woman lying next to him.

"I–don't–know," she said, her words muffled by a pillow.

"You said you were going to class this place up."

"I meant with my presence."

"So?" Charlie said.

"So that's the last time I go clubbing with you on Hilton Head," she groaned.

"It was Bluffton."

"That's even worse."

"So we'll do River Street next time."

"Don't be an idiot, Charlie."

The covers rustled as Charlie patted her on the rear. "Your enthusiasm sucks, in more ways than one at the moment."

"Sell it . . . and move downtown."

"Sell what?"

"The condo," she said.

"It's a townhouse."

"Have I taught you nothing?"

"It's an up-and-coming neighborhood. My next door neighbor is a pediatrician."

"Mine owns five percent of UPS," she said.

"The real estate agent said it was a good investment."

"It's a halfway house for middle class losers." The tangle of red hair flopped onto the pillow as Beth rolled onto her back and pushed up on her elbows.

"You've always had a better eye than me for this sort of thing," Charlies said.

"That's because I follow Martha Stewart's blog." Beth's leg snaked from beneath the sheets as she rolled onto her side, digging her toenails into Charlie's half-exposed torso. "So you really think I'm better?"

"No only better, you're the best. And just in case you missed it, Martha Stewart did time."

"You don't have enough moxie to pull it off, so don't be a prick."

"We're yin and yang, baby."

"And the reason my mother calls you the prodigal son."

"She's always liked me, and you know it," Charlie said. "Especially, after the homecoming rescue."

Beth's face hardened.

"I like to think of it as the night of my salvation," Charlie said.

"Tom was so full of himself. That football game meant more to him than my homecoming title. And I was his girlfriend."

"You know how it is. Senior year. Team captain. Quarter-back."

"Who cares? I'm talking about me."

"I still care," Charlie said.

"And you were rewarded, so shut up."

"Oh, yeah . . . the Camaro." Charlie touched her nose, and then brushed a hand through her hair.

"The stupid jock didn't even see it coming."

"Maybe he didn't," Charlie said, resisting a smile.

"That car is a pile of scrap and half as old as you are. Why do you still own it?"

"It's a classic. And besides, it reminds me of your coming out party."

"More like—your coming out, wouldn't you say?" Beth said.

"We could take her out for a spin. Déjà–you," Charlie said, pumping his eyebrows.

"I'll never set foot in that car again."

"Took-my-Chevy-to-the-levy," Charlie sang out.

"Keep croaking and you can spend the rest of the morning alone."

"So what's the latest on Jon?"

"Based on your drunken stupor last night, he's Mr. Deal-Making-Wonderful," Beth said.

"No, what's our next move?"

"I swear, if you screw this up for me—"

"I'm your yang, baby."

Beth smiled. "He's been in Colorado all week."

"That's right," Charlie said, smacking himself on the fore-head. "What are we doing here? We could be lounging out by your pool."

"Charlie, are you forgetting about the children? Is it me, or do I have to do all the thinking?" Beth ran a finger across his lips.

"The children are staying with your mother. I ran into them at the mall, yesterday, while you were reportedly at an appointment with your ministers." Charlie snapped at her finger, playful-like.

"Ow!" Beth said, snatching the finger loose. "And keep your nose where it belongs. No one put you in charge of my calendar."

"Jon adores those kids. And he's always trusted you, so you had better watch your step."

Beth snickered. "Remember when Jon set up the Chatham financing last year?"

"How could I forget? Richard wouldn't shut up about it," Charlie said. "You would have thought he walked on water."

"I never told you about the celebration aboard Bob Stein's yacht."

"You're mistaken. Bob reserved the Chart House for the evening. It was a private dinner."

"That was for the stiffs. The real event took place on Bob's sixty-foot cruiser. My daddy's friend was out fishing on the Wilmington River that day and almost caught us."

"Caught who?"

"A boatload of executives and ladies, young enough to be their daughters. You can do the math."

"Why would Bob . . . What were you doing there?"

"My daddy's friend spotted some females dancing up on the deck, but he was too blind to recognize anyone."

"I have to tell you," Charlie said. "I don't like the sound of that."

Beth rose up, allowing the sheet to slip free, piling up around her knees. "You don't think I got this tan by being a prude, do you?"

"So now you're telling me you were on Bob's cruiser sunbathing?"

"Are we getting upset?"

"Hell no," Charlie said, looking away.

"While we're having true confessions, here, you never told me who else happened into the back seat of that Camaro." Beth grabbed Charlie's chin and forced him to look at her.

"That was over twenty years ago."

"Charlie?"

"Beth, I—"

"Don't play games with me."

"Come on, you know what I mean."

Beth leaned in close, nose to nose. "I've never heard you complain about my baked-on finish before."

"I—it's just—we've known each other for so long."

"And don't ever you forget it," Beth said, biting Charlie's bottom lip.

"Beth, you are wonderful, you know?"

"Charlie, give it a rest. And dump the condo."

Chapter 26
Sunday, July 17th
2:00 P.M.

On Sunday, Jon introduced Carver and Bailey to his new front yard, a medley of sand, sea oats, sun and sky, magnified by the beauty of the Atlantic Ocean. The afternoon tide had retreated, leaving behind an expanse of packed, wet sand. With the perfect setting for a game of high speed chase, they started their outing by renting bicycles. Carver held an early advantage as Jon had to pump extra hard on his bike, sporting a rusty chain and Bailey on the back, to boot. Repeatedly attempting to sneak up on his dad, Carver's red Schwinn gave him away every time he circled back on him, betrayed by a kickstand that rapped against the pedal. Cycling set the stage for Frisbee, followed by the less strenuous art of sand castle building. No sooner had the outer defenses of the structure been completed than an encroaching wave hastened an end to the castle's brief Tybee history.

"How about a swim?" Jon said, watching the intensity of Bailey's little hands working to save the castle. The question seemed to be lost on her as she continued to labor without looking up.

"She's not going in, Dad," Carver said. He emptied a bucket of sand.

"Sure she will. She loves the ocean."

"Dad, she's not gonna do it," Carver said, as Bailey continued in silence.

"What's the deal, guys?" Jon patted the sand with a plastic shovel.

"She saw the shark special on Discovery Channel," Carver said, shaking his head.

"Do you want to tell me about it?"

"Great whites, Dad. They were gobbling up seals. You could see the blood and guts."

"But that wasn't around here."

"Washington DC," Carver said, businesslike.

"No, that's not right."

"Daddy, is that where the President lives?" Bailey said, breaking free from her trance.

"Yes, Bailey, but not great whites—"

"Is too—we saw it on TV," Carver said.

"Carver, they don't live in that area. At least not enough to film a television special," Jon said, mumbling the last part to himself.

"Then why did they say so?"

"I'm pretty sure they were referring to Washington State. And that's a long way from here. It's all the way across the country, on the Pacific Ocean."

"Is that the Pacific Ocean?" Bailey pointed without looking up.

"No dummy, that's the *Atlantis* Ocean," Carver said.

"What do you say the two of us hit the waves?" Jon said to Carver.

"Dad, we have a castle to build."

"I guess someone has to save the queen."

"Besides, Mommy told us not to get in the water," Bailey said.

Jon grabbed a bucket and scooped up some sand, emptying it in front of Bailey. Carver worked on a breach in one of the walls.

"Stupid ocean," Carver grumbled.

"Daddy, why did you move to the beach?" Bailey said. The question popped out casually, as if she were asking the time.

"Well—"

"He wanted to," Carver interrupted.

"But I want Daddy to live with me," Bailey said.

"And I like being at home with you."

"Can you come back with us?"

"That's Mommy's house, and she's the boss of it," Carver said.

"Hey guys, listen. For now, I need to live at the beach."

"Can we spend the night?" Bailey said.

"Next visit, you get to spend the entire weekend."

"Can I sleep in the hammock?" Carver asked.

"You're not afraid the sharks will get you?"

"Don't be silly. They live in the ocean."

"Then the hammock's all yours."

"What about me?" Bailey got up and walked over to her dad.

"You get the foldout and cartoons on Saturday morning."

"And chocolate chip pancakes?" Bailey said.

"And chocolate chip—"

"Can we get a dog?" Carver said.

"Whoa, just a minute, cowboy. Let's test the hammock arrangement, first."

"If Carver gets a dog, then I want one too."

"Hey guys, do you know what I'm thinking?" Jon squinted and looked out to sea.

"What?" they said in unison. Two pairs of eyes followed his gaze.

"I'm wondering what really lives in that ocean." Jon rubbed his chin.

"Probably, lots of fish and crabs," Carver said.

"Eeww—crabs," Bailey said.

"And jellyfish and whales."

"And the Little Mermaid."

"And don't forget—sharks."

"Sharks," Jon said. "I'm not afraid of any sharks." He got up without looking back and marched into the surf.

"No, Daddy—no!" they both screamed, dancing in place.

Jon looked over his shoulder and yelled, "Those sharks will head for the Pacific, if they know what's good for them." The waves lapped at the bottom of his swimsuit.

"Daddy, he'll eat you," Bailey shouted.

"They'll think you're a seal," Carver screamed.

Jon stopped and turned with his eyes wide, then started running toward the beach, yelling, "Ahhhh!"

"Ahhh!" Carver and Bailey screamed.

Three pairs of feet bolted for the house.

Chapter 27
Sunday, July 17th
7:30 P.M.

When Jon returned from dropping the children off at Beth's, Captain's ragged Toyota was parked on the street next to the Baineses' house. Getting out of his car, Jon looked around and spotted him atop the arched 7th Street boardwalk. He was leaning on a rail, looking out across the sand dunes that separated the oceanfront houses from the beach. Jon climbed halfway up before he stirred.

"Hey, no loitering," Jon called out.

"It's what I do best."

"Then maybe I'll join you," Jon said, reaching the top.

"When I stand here and look seaward, I see the very face of God," Captain said.

"I could spend hours out here."

Captain reached out and squeezed Jon's shoulder. "You and me both," he said. "How are you, Boy?"

"I've been better. How did you find me?"

"Street preacher's a man of many callings—part minister, part intelligence officer. Otherwise, he loses half of his clientele."

"I've never been much for hiding."

"Mind if we take advantage of this beautiful sunset?" Captain said. They walked down the wooden planks and onto the beach. "Why did you run off and disappear on me?"

"I planned to call you in another day or two." Jon stopped to take off his shoes.

"Perhaps I'm jumping the gun, coming here like this?"

"Don't worry about it. I had the kids out earlier."

"How're they taking it?"

"They were begging to spend the night. It looks like I'll have to brush up on my parenting skills before their next visit," Jon said.

Reaching the wet sand, they turned north toward the Savannah River. As they walked, Jon gave Captain a condensed version of the move and his visit to Colorado Springs.

"I won't meddle in what's not rightly my business, but you know what us mariners say about going to sea alone."

They walked in silence for a while, and upon reaching the jetties, they stopped to watch a sailboat in the mouth of the river.

"There's nothing like a sunset on the beach," Jon said. He stuffed his hands in his pockets and waded into the water.

Captain basked in the serenity as the sun painted the clouds pink over the Atlantic. "By the way, I got a phone call from Richard Stone. It seems he wants a tour of the Mission. From the sound of things, the man just might be an angel."

Jon turned to start the journey home. "I didn't figure you'd mind if I put in a word for you." He looked over at Captain with a smile. "Randall has it in his mind to start a ministry for Savannah's indigent. He wants to build a facility on the Southside, only it makes no sense. I suggested the Mission would be a better investment."

"Now you're quite the mate, aren't you? But let's not go and stir up that hornet's nest. The Lord will look after the Mission."

"Didn't I just hear you mention something about an angel?"

"Richard's a fair man, but South Coast—I don't know," Captain said. "It's not my way to make trouble, especially when it comes to the church."

"Captain, that sounds a bit like hypocrisy. Corporate boards clash over donating money to the Mission all the time, and you don't give it a second thought. In fact, you're usually in the middle of it."

"That's different."

"So you're saying South Coast shouldn't support the Mission?" Jon said.

"Now, I didn't say that." Captain raised a finger. "The church has her purpose, just like the Mission."

"If I didn't know better, I'd say you were acting like they're competitors. I see it more as a synergy."

"You know what I mean. You're no stranger to dueling egos."

"Sooner or later, the saints have to lay down their swords. Otherwise, everybody's going to lose interest in what you're offering," Jon said.

"Peace among the saints, they call it. The Mission's not into mergers and acquisitions, like some people I know."

Jon walked in the edge of the surf, letting it wash over his feet. "Need I remind you, you're the one who told me to trust South Coast? And besides, I've never seen you back down from anything. Not Randall. Not the church. No one."

"My situation is different. You're a member at South Coast. You're committed."

"It's not a game, Captain."

"And I'm not the Lord, Boy."

"Then meet with Richard."

"I'll study it," Captain said. The house came into sight, and they turned inland.

"That's the spirit." Jon placed an arm around Captain's shoulder, crossing the beach in silence until they reached the sand dunes. "I meant to ask you. Did you find out anything new on my attacker?"

"I thought you were done with all of that."

"I'm just curious."

"The ocean does crazy things to a man," Captain said. "But no—nothing."

The two men climbed the boardwalk and stopped at Captain's car.

"How about joining me for dinner?" Jon said.

"I'm afraid I've got to be back in town. The boys will be needing me, but you drop by anytime." Captain reached for the car door. "Blessings to you, Boy."

Jon climbed the stairs and watched as Captain drove away. The telephone rang, and he headed inside.

Chapter 28
Monday, July 18th
7:40 A.M.

Rising at sunup, Jon put in a three mile jog on the beach and showered before venturing over to the Breakfast Club, first stopping off at the Tybee Market for a copy of *The Savannah Press*. Midway through the headlines and a second cup of coffee, his appointment arrived.

"I was afraid you were lost," Jon said, folding up the paper.

"What is this place? There's a line forming on the sidewalk," Stephens said with a thumb over his shoulder.

"It's a Tybee landmark. You have to get in early to be seated."

Stephens stuck his nose in the air and sniffed. "Is that grease I smell?"

"It's not tofu."

"So, I see your humor's intact." Stephens sat down and unrolled his silverware for an inspection.

"Prepare yourself for the best breakfast in town," Jon said. "That's the mayor and a couple of councilmen over there."

Stephens looked over at the booths lining the Butler Avenue side of the restaurant. The light streaming from the windows cast a patina on the Formica tabletops. Some were partially hidden by an exposed kitchen jutting out into the center of the restaurant.

"Lifestyles of the rich and famous," Stephens said. "Jon, just so I don't waste anyone's time, I'll get right to the point. I was hoping for an update on where you stand since our last meeting. I could be wrong, but it seems we're losing momentum."

"Perhaps you'd like to start the conversation by explaining why Dr. Lowe is pressing for a legal release."

Stephens shifted in his seat, apparently still uncomfortable with the surroundings. "It's more or less standard operating procedure."

"That doesn't tell me anything."

"Jonathon, I sense distrust in your voice. Is there a problem with Dr. Lowe?" Stephens picked up his coffee cup, inspecting the rim.

"Given that it's my marriage we're discussing, I'd appreciate a response about the release." Jon paused as the waitress stepped up to the table. "I'll have the special."

"Just coffee," Stephens said. The waitress scribbled on a pad, and then hurried off. "Fair enough—both you and Beth are members of South Coast. Beth came to us requesting assistance with your marital situation. Ordinarily, I sit down with you to provide prayer support and counseling, but as you can understand, SCMI has run out of bandwidth for handling all of the cases. Since you can afford a professional, you were natural candidates to refer to a psychologist."

Jon looked over the top of his coffee cup, directly into Stephens's eyes. "That explains why we're seeing Dr. Lowe, but it doesn't explain the legal document—"

"You didn't allow me to finish. The church has turned you over to Tim for counseling." Stephens held up his fingers, making a double-quote sign. "But the church would like to continue monitoring your progress."

"Forgive me, but isn't that now Dr. Lowe's job?"

"That would be true if you weren't members of the church. As you may recall, your membership vows enjoined you to a covenant relationship at South Coast. This means you've agreed to submit yourself to the church."

"And this includes signing legal documents—"

"I'll tell you what it states," Stephens interrupted, "if you'll allow me a moment. You have agreed to support the fellowship of believers and respect those in authority over the congregation."

"Meaning who?"

"For starters, Randall and myself. But more importantly, the ruling elders."

"Is Randall aware of what is going on?"

"I've briefed him on the situation, but there's no need for his direct involvement. He has much greater responsibilities on his plate."

"I see."

"Jonathon, I don't quite get your attitude."

"I have this thing about people who aren't accountable."

"I can assure you, I report to a much higher authority."

"I've offered a compromise, David."

"If you're referring to your proposal to attend the review meetings with Tim, I'm afraid that's logistically impossible. If we open that door, the business of the church will bog down in scheduling conflicts."

"I'm not talking about everyone else. I am referring to Beth and me. What do you intend to do with the information?"

"We'll use it to help you. It's that simple. You have to trust us," Stephens quipped.

"I'm uneasy with other members of the congregation being so closely involved in church business, as you call it."

"Tim is a professional," Stephens said.

"And he's ordered me to sign a legal document."

Stephens snapped his head around and stared at Jon. "Extenuating circumstances require—"

"There you go again. What exactly does that mean?"

"For one thing, aggressive behavior." Stephens exhaled. "Beth is afraid of you. She fears for the safety of your children."

"This kind of talk is only proving my point."

"She sends them to her parent's house for their own protection," Stephens said. "Do you own a handgun?"

"David—"

"She's uncomfortable with a gun in the house."

"For the record, I don't live in the house any longer. But you already know that."

"Why are you refusing to cooperate? You continue to mock me and show no respect for the church."

Jon looked away, motionless for a spell. The Tybee Pier experience flashed through his mind as he studied the crowd outside on the sidewalk.

Sensing an opening, Stephens reached over and placed a hand on Jon's arm. "Fight for your marriage. Do what any good Christian would do. Sign the form, and let Tim help."

Stephens's words hung in the air as a conversation at the next table caught Jon's attention. He listened as two men debated. "I tell you, don't sign anything," one said to the other. Jon turned to them, but neither man paid him any attention.

Jon looked up at Stephens. "How about Sam Hallworth? He is another interesting member of the church."

Stephens fidgeted with his napkin for a moment, finally pressing it flat. "What's your point?"

"He recently threatened legal action against me."

"Given the circumstances, I'm not surprised."

"He and Beth are suing a fellow church member. In Beth's case, a husband."

Stephens shook his head, holding back a smile that was forming at the corners of his mouth. "Yet another reason to work with me. I'd like to help."

"But doesn't that break the so-called covenant? What do your operating procedures have to say about lawsuits? This entire arrangement seems a bit incestuous," Jon said.

Stephens stood up and tossed his napkin on the table. He leaned over and thrust a finger in Jon's face. "God's ordained are charged with caring for your soul. This situation is of your own making, so don't threaten me."

Stephens turned and marched out of the restaurant.

Chapter 29
Monday, July 18th
9:20 A.M.

After the explosive meeting with Stephens on Tybee, Jon left the island and drove into downtown Savannah. En route he dialed Charles Rhodes's cell, only this time the line didn't ring at all. He considered dropping in at the Hyatt, where he and Rhodes had typically met before his disappearance, to see if there were any signs of him. Instead, he decided to carry on with his plans for the morning.

Circling the block twice, he found a spot near the Bull Street Library and headed inside to the front desk, where a librarian directed him to a computer containing the card catalogue. As he sat down, he pulled out a sheet of paper that Dr. Rodwin had given him in Colorado Springs. Typing in the title of a book, he got a hit and located it on an aisle in the rear of the building.

Jon lugged the volume over to a table, sat down, and went to work. The spine crackled as he flipped through the pages. Then, he read:

> **The Minnesota Multiphasic Personality Inventory:** The Individual Form (MMPI) Adolescent, adult
> – Ages 16 and older

Purpose: Assesses individual personality. Used for clinical diagnosis and research on psychopathology. **Description:** 550-item true-false test of 10 clinical variables or factors of personality: hypochondriasis, depression, hysteria, psychopathic-deviate, masculinity-femininity, paranoia, psychasthenia, schizophrenia, hypomania, and social introversion.[*]

After studying the page carefully, Jon backtracked to a shelf where he had spotted a medical dictionary minutes earlier. He thumbed the pages until he found what he was looking for:

psychopathology 1. the medical discipline that deals with mental disease. 2. the study of mental disorders. 3. mental activity associated with abnormal behavior.

Fifteen minutes later, Jon climbed the stairs at the Mission, skipping every other step on his way up to Captain's office.

"Oh it's you," Captain said, looking somewhat surprised when Jon appeared in the doorway.

Jon leaned against the doorjamb, out of breath.

"Since you're here, there's someone I'd like you to meet," Captain said. "Jon, this is Aaron Talbot, editor of *The Savannah Press* religion section." A grey-bearded man rose from a chair to greet him. "Aaron's planning to run another piece on the Mission."

---

[*] Adapted from *Tests - Sixth Edition: A Comprehensive Reference for Assessments in Psychology, Education, and Business* (p. 123), by T. Maddox, 2008, Austin, TX: PRO-ED. Copyright 2008 by PRO-ED, Inc. Adapted with permission.

The men exchanged pleasantries before Talbot excused himself and slipped over to the door.

"Louis, I'll send you a draft," Talbot said.

"Blessings to you," Captain said.

Jon walked over and handed Captain a stack of photocopies from the library before plopping down in a chair. "Take a look at those."

"Help yourself to some water from the fridge." Captain put on his glasses and scanned the documents. "This looks like a bunch of psychobabble."

"Do you remember our discussion about David Stephens from a few weeks ago?"

"Something tells me I may regret it," Captain said.

"I gave you a rundown on our meeting at the DeSoto."

"If memory serves me correctly, he advised you to seek professional counseling."

"The psychologist turned out to be a church member, Dr. Tim Lowe. He also happens to be the person Beth has been seeing for some time."

"I'm with you so far." Captain set down the papers and got up, walking over to the door. "Keep talking." He slipped into the next room.

"After our first appointment, Lowe had me complete a psychological assessment called the MMPI, Minnesota Multiphasic Personality Inventory. He told me it was designed to provide background information and a way to accelerate the counseling process."

Captain reappeared with a bottle of water and handed it to Jon, returning to his desk. He picked up the papers. "Where did you get these?"

"At the library," Jon said. "When I was in Colorado, I spent time with a psychologist, who gave me a full psychological assessment. He's the one I told you about on Sunday. As it turns out, he was deeply concerned that I had taken the MMPI and counseled against seeing Lowe again." Jon gestured toward the desk. "I pulled this information from a psychology reference manual, and it confirms his advice."

Captain skimmed the papers, scratching his head. "Am I missing something or does this suggest Lowe thinks you're crazy?"

"Bingo," Jon said. "But get this. When I asked him for the MMPI results, he told me they were inconclusive."

"What does that mean?"

"According to Dr. Rodwin, nothing."

"So do you believe Lowe is up to something, or just doesn't know what he's doing?"

"Dr. Rodwin put me through a battery of tests that all turned out normal. In the process, he gave me a clean mental bill of health, but raised a number of questions about Lowe's approach to marital counseling."

"Have you spoken to Stephens about—"

"One more thing," Jon interrupted. "The night Lowe side-stepped the MMPI results, he asked me to sign a legal release, authorizing him to provide information to the church."

"South Coast?"

"According to Stephens, it's standard operating procedure at SCMI," Jon said.

"And what's Stephens's take on all of this?" Captain gestured at the photocopies.

"When I attempted to confront him with my concerns this morning, he stormed out of the meeting. But that was after he read me my rights."

By the time they had wrapped up the discussion, Captain was speechless, and Jon packed up and headed out to Tybee. When he arrived at the beach house, the drive-under garage was empty, so he parked on the side of the driveway. The last time he had blocked access to the garage, Claire Baines had given him a scolding that he would never forget.

Chapter 30
Tuesday, July 19th
6:38 A.M.

Jon rose at six and slipped outside to the screen porch, where the sun was already splashing pinkish hues across the eastern horizon. Puffs of clouds partially veiled the emerging ball of light that was rising out of the Atlantic. The low tide had left behind a gray expanse of sand for early morning joggers, who were gearing up for their workouts. A school of dolphins broke the water's surface just beyond the surf, trailing in the wake of a shrimp boat that was chugging along the shoreline. He stirred, suddenly remembering that he had promised to stop by the office to sign paperwork.

Jon heard voices downstairs and walked across the porch, opening the screen door. He spotted Stewart Baines coming up the staircase. Claire stood at the bottom, lecturing to him. When Stewart noticed Jon at the door, he stopped and yelled up, "Blocked us in Jonny-boy."

Looking down at the yard, Jon spotted the Z4 sitting in the driveway, only it was now blocking the garage. He glanced out at the street, noticing that the Land Cruiser remained parked on the curb as he had left it. Scratching his head, he cut his eyes back to Stewart.

"Someone's going to get our table," Claire called out, as if Stewart was hard of hearing.

A troubled expression formed on Stewart's face as he looked over a shoulder at his wife before turning to Jon. "We're late for the breakfast buffet down at Captain Chris's. She gets this way if we're not there when the doors open."

Jon started down the steps as Stewart did an about-face, leading the way. When they reached the bottom, Jon circled his car, as if looking for something. "I don't understand . . . I parked so you could get in the garage last night."

"It's that damn Walker again," Claire said.

"Don't get her started, Jon," Stewart said.

"You know who did this?" Jon said. "How did they get my keys?"

"Walker doesn't need keys," Claire said.

Stewart leaned in close to Jon and whispered, "I warned you."

"The butt scum's been mocking us like this for twenty-five years. Last time, he flooded the entire downstairs and ruined a full load of laundry—"

"The pipe busted, Woman," Stewart said, raising his hands over his head.

Claire shuffled over to Jon's side, straightening a wrinkle in her dress. Then she looked up. "He's been doing this for twenty-five years," she repeated. "They found him buried over by the Cockspur Island Lighthouse in nineteen hundred and fifty-two. He was murdered. That was before Stewart and I moved in, but I know all about it. They say he came from down around Brunswick, but that doesn't matter."

"Claire, why did he move my car?" Jon said, fighting back a smile.

"Why does a ghost do anything? Because that's what they do. He broke the back window a few years ago. Then he blew up a new RCA television—"

"Claire, lightning struck the power pole. The EMC man told you so."

"Listen, I'll move the car so you two can get off to breakfast," Jon said.

Claire turned to Stewart and snorted, and then headed for the garage.

* * *

There were no cars in the parking area when Jon arrived at the office, leaving time for a quick visit to Factors Square. When he returned, he noticed Brenda's car near the back entrance. As he unlocked the door he paused to examine the frame, running a hand down the surface. If the security system was there, it was well-hidden.

When he entered the foyer, Brenda's head peeked out from Jon's office. "Jon, you scared me. I didn't expect you this early." She headed down the hall to give him a hug. "Charlie told me you were coming in this morning. So how was Colorado?"

"The Broadmoor Hotel was terrific. You have got to see this place. It's completely surrounded by the Rockies. And the leadership program was excellent."

"How about sightseeing?"

"Just a round of golf."

"You went to Colorado, and that's all you did?" Brenda said, scrunching her nose.

"You won't believe this, but Pike's Peak was closed due to heavy snowfall."

"In July? Weird. Well, Charlie's waiting in his office."

"You don't know about weird until you hear about my morning," Jon said, shaking his head. "I didn't see Charlie's car outside."

"He dropped it off at the car wash, so I gave him a ride in. You'd think he went for a drive on the beach. It was a mess. By the way, he's blaming you for having to come in early."

"He called the meeting."

"Better grab a cup of coffee. He's going to talk your ear off."

Jon stopped off at the breakroom, and then continued down the hallway. As he walked into Charlie's office, he held up a hand and gestured to his watch. "I charge by the hour."

"You blood-sucking scoundrel. And I thought you were on our team," Charlie said.

"Brenda was just telling me how you've turned your Porsche into a beach buggy."

Charlie coughed, and then cleared his throat. "Sorry."

"So when is the closing?" Jon said.

"If Michael gets off the dime—soon." Charlie walked around the desk with papers in his hand. "He's complaining about Bob again, but that's Richard's problem."

"I told Richard to call me."

"Yeah, well a little psychology and a cattle prod may be what it takes to get this thing done."

"So let's have a look," Jon said, holding out a hand.

They sat down at a conference table, where Charlie rattled on about Michael as Jon signed the documents. Charlie cracked a joke, and they both laughed.

Brenda poked her head in. "There must be drinking going on in here. Contracts are never this much fun."

Charlie's telephone rang, and he got up and answered. "Okay . . . Hold on."

"You will observe how he choreographed the telephone call for just the precise moment. Now that he has my signature, he's done with me," Jon said.

"Treat me like a tuna, and I cut you off," Charlie said to Jon, pressing the receiver to his chest. "But seriously guys, I've got to take this call."

Brenda closed Charlie's door as she and Jon stepped out into the hall.

"I thought I heard your voice," Richard said. Jon turned to see him heading toward them. He stopped and put a hand on Jon's shoulder. "Brenda, would you call Bob Stein and confirm our lunch reservations at the Oglethorpe Club?" He eyed Jon. "I spoke to Captain Beecher, and he's agreed to give me a tour of the Mission."

"You'll be impressed," Jon said. "Let me know if I can help."

Richard lowered his voice. "I heard a rumor that you visited the Mayo Clinic down in Jacksonville over the weekend?"

"Where did you hear that?"

"Bob knows the head of the ER down there."

"I took a detour on the way back from Colorado. It was personal business."

"Fair enough, but I don't have to warn you about meddling in Bob's plans. He's pretty set on doing this deal his way."

"Believe me, I know," Jon said. "I trust you've convinced him to back off of Michael?"

"Did Michael say something?"

"I was hoping you'd tell me."

"Bob knows what he's doing."

"Good to hear."

"So how are you, personally?"

"Do you know this psychologist David Stephens has recommended?"

"Only in passing. Randall mentioned him, in confidence of course." Richard leaned closer. "You don't look so well."

"It's nothing," Jon said.

"That's the spirit." Richard's eyes delved deep into Jon's. "You know, due diligence is your best suit. If you ask me, that's your path to success."

"Richard," Brenda called down the hall. "Bob wants to speak to you on line two."

"Wrap this thing up with Stephens, and do it fast. I need you back in the office." Richard winked and turned, marching away.

Jon followed him until he reached Brenda's door.

"I almost forgot," Brenda said. "I finished checking the computers for our mystery e-mail . . . I found absolutely nothing."

"Wait," Jon said with a puzzled look on his face. His eyes drifted down to Richard's office, and then back to Brenda. "That means someone must have deleted it."

"I'm glad you brought that up. Chase gave me a crash course on that sort of thing. As it turns out, they aren't actually deleted. He stepped me through the recovery process, but it didn't turn up anything. Weird, huh?"

Chapter 31
Tuesday, July 19th
9:50 P.M.

Locals frequented the Back Porch for its laid-back atmosphere and generous portions of Southern-fried seafood. Jon slipped into the Tybee establishment at the end of serving hours and dined on a platter of beer-battered shrimp before wandering over to Doc's Bar. There he ran into a trio of GI's and joined them for a round of pool, intrigued by their back-and-forth discussion about an overzealous commissioned officer. It took only a few beers for their stories to spiral into a tar-and-feathering, cascading into a medley of far-fetched indiscretions. As the night wore on, the banter eased him into a sense of detachment, a welcome escape from his own state of affairs.

After two rounds of pool, Jon hung up his cue and paid the bar tab, heading down the sidewalk toward the ocean as he took in the storefronts along Tybrisa Street. He decided to skip the pier and descended a set of steps to the beach, which for the most part was deserted at the hour. The moon flickered between puffs of windswept clouds as he neared the 7th Street beach access. He lingered for a half hour in the edge of the surf before turning for the house.

Approaching the sand dunes, Jon noticed movement in the bushes in front of the Baineses' house. At first he thought he was seeing trash blown in from the beach, but as he moved in for a better view, he noticed how the shrubs were whipping about in the wind, but there was something bulky behind them.

Without thinking, he lowered his head and eased to the top of boardwalk, observing how the object didn't budge as the ocean gusts continued to rattle the bushes. He dropped to a knee and focused on the spot, waiting for a break in the clouds. The moment came and went quickly, offering only the faintest clue as to what he was seeing.

Initially he didn't get it, but then like a flashbulb he suddenly realized what it was he was seeing. The image was poor in the sparse moonlight, only now he was pretty sure it was the profile of a hat in front of the white clapboard siding. But from his angle, the bushes were concealing whoever was wearing it.

Careful not to be noticed, Jon inched down the boardwalk in a crouched position, staying below the height of the handrail. Thankfully, the sea oats were rattling in the wind atop the dunes, offering an additional buffer between him and the intruder. When he reached the street, Jon sprinted to the far end of the house to distance himself from a buzzing light pole. With the prowler on the ocean side, he decided it would be better to circle around the back and approach him from the darkness. Clinging close to the foundation, he moved in short steps to a downstairs window, peeking inside. The Baineses were asleep on a couch, with a twenty-four hour news program blaring on the TV. Claire was still wearing the flowered dress from earlier that morning.

Jon passed the drive-under garage, and then turned to cross the backyard. Once he reached the far corner, he stuck his head out to check for signs of life, but saw no one. He continued up the side yard on the balls of his feet, hoping to make as little noise as possible. As he closed in on the ocean side once again, the pounding of the surf obstructed his hearing. Using the darkness to his advantage, he slipped behind a palm tree, figuring the prowler was probably only feet away. Doing his best to control his breathing, Jon looked up into the sky at the thick cloud cover. *Move now or lose the element of surprise*, he thought.

Stretching for a glimpse, Jon peered around the palm and had trouble seeing in the washed-out light. At first glance, no one was behind the bushes. Waiting for his eyes to adjust, he took a second look, this time certain the cap was not there. A thought suddenly hit him, and he turned to make sure no one had doubled back on him. The side yard was quiet.

Easing away from the palm, Jon parted the bushes where he had first seen the cap and leaned down for a closer look. As he stepped forward, his shoulder bumped an iron pipe that ran up the side of the clapboards. Dropping to a knee, he noticed footprints in the sand. A gust rustled the bushes, and he quickly rose to his feet as moonlight engulfed the house. He turned to study the pipe, tracing it upward.

As his eyes made contact, a man dropped from the sky and knocked him backwards into the bushes. Branches snapped as the attacker plunged down on his chest, riding him to the ground. Jon felt the air explode from his lungs, but the assailant seemed unfazed as he rolled to his feet and bolted for the beach. A mental fog began to set in and Jon struggled for breath as he caught a final glimpse of the assailant disappearing over a sand dune. Then he blacked out.

When he came to, Jon made an effort to get up, and waves of pain shot up his back like an electric shock, forcing him to sit in place. He checked his watch and figured he had been unconscious for at least twenty minutes. That meant the attacker could be off of the island by now. Making another effort to get to his feet, he hunched over and placed his hands on his knees for balance. As he did so, a white object came into focus on the ground. Reaching down, he picked up a business card, but was unable to make out the print in the poor lighting. He brushed off his clothes and limped over to the stairs.

Chapter 32
Wednesday, July 20th
8:18 A.M.

Jon was waiting for Captain in his office at the Mission, when he topped the staircase after serving breakfast.

"You're getting to be a regular these days. Why didn't you drop in earlier for grits?" Captain gave Jon a curious look and headed behind his desk.

"I was attacked again last night, so I'm moving a little slow this morning," Jon said. He took a few minutes to fill Captain in on the details.

"I trust you were smart enough to call the police this time."

"They filled out a report. But I was unconscious for a while, so they weren't able to pursue the suspect."

"Did you have a doctor check you out?"

"It wasn't that bad."

"Well, you don't look so good, but I don't see any permanent damage," Captain said. "Were you able to give the police a good description of your assailant?"

"He was wearing a hat, so I didn't get a look at this face. Before I blacked out, he took off for the beach on foot. And we don't know what type of car, if any, he might have been driving."

"It's not likely he walked all the way out to Tybee. If it's the same fellow as before, he's sure got it in for you." Captain leaned back for a look out the window. "So what are you thinking?"

"At the moment—how did he find my house?"

"That's easy," Captain said. "He's got your driver's license."

"True, but it has my Savannah address, not the beach house."

"Guess you're right about that." Captain put his feet up on the desk. "Then he must have followed you out to the island yesterday."

"That's highly unlikely," Jon said. "I was putting the Z4 through the paces on the way home, so it would have been obvious if someone had been tailing me." He slipped the business card out of his pocket. "I have something to show you, but I want you to keep it between the two of us. And no more nonsense about angels dancing on pins."

Captain frowned. "I'll do my best."

Jon slid the business card across the desk as Captain dropped his feet to the floor.

"I'm pretty sure my attacker left that behind last night," Jon said.

Captain put on his glasses. "A private investigator?" he said, flipping the card over. "What's this? A telephone number?"

Jon's cell phone rang, and he paused to answer. "Jonathon Browning . . . Yes, Cliff . . . Are you sure? . . . I'll be right over."

Cliff Sherman unlocked the front door at First Savannah Bank and greeted Jon and Captain as they climbed the steps.

"Cliff, do you know Captain Beecher?"

"Only by name. It's nice to meet you, sir."

"What can you tell me about the transactions?" Jon said as the three men crossed the lobby to his office.

"I was reviewing yesterday's activity log and noticed some unusual activity on your account, so I decided to call you before taking any action. Have a seat, and I'll get the drafts." Cliff disappeared for a moment and returned with copies. "There are three checks," he said, laying them on his desktop. "Do you recognize any of them?"

Jon came out of his chair.

"Keep calm, Boy," Captain said, reaching out to him.

"They were drawn on your investment account, the one we set up through our brokerage division. The checks on this account have to clear our New York office before we receive copies here in Savannah." Cliff pointed to an inscription near the top of one. "You've made a steady stream of deposits over the past few years, and I remember you once told me you were using the account for long-term investments. Then out-of-the-blue, these three cleared yesterday."

"Everything you said is true, but I wrote this one, here." Jon sat down and picked up the check. "As you may have noticed, it's made out to my wife."

"Okay, my mistake," Cliff said. "But I wanted to be sure."

"Actually, it wasn't supposed to be cashed. The check was attached to a letter. You can see the staple holes from the original."

"What about these?" Cliff repositioned the other two.

"They . . . look like my signatures."

"But are they your signatures?"

Jon shook his head.

"So you agree these are forgeries?"

"Twenty-five thousand each . . . I'm pretty sure I would remember."

"That's a lot of grits," Captain said, whistling.

"My sentiments exactly," Cliff said. "Fortunately, any expert would tell you these are highly suspicious. The first one is made out to Elizabeth Browning, check number 6103."

"And to think, I trusted her," Jon said.

"But look at 6137 and 6148," Cliff said, pointing. "There hasn't been a single check processed between 6103 and 6137, or 6137 and 6148."

Jon pulled a check book out of his satchel and flipped through the register. "Checks 6137 and 6148 are missing, just as you said. But the others are here."

"It sure looks like someone stole from you," Captain said.

"Cliff, what's the process for cashing a twenty-five thousand dollar check?" Jon said.

"I'll step you through it. First, take a look at 6103 made out to Elizabeth Browning for fifty-thousand dollars." Cliff flipped it over. "Right here . . . You can see it was deposited into an account at the Bank of Effingham County."

"So you're saying she has an account there?"

"Possibly, but I'm not certain. Once it was endorsed, it could have been deposited into anyone's account at Effingham."

"Wouldn't the depositor have to show some form of identification?" Captain said.

"You bring up an interesting point, but it relates to 6137 and 6148. Both are made out to Savannah First," Cliff said.

"So they were cashed here at the bank?" Jon said.

"Actually, they were brought into two separate branches. As you can see, a bank teller coded the account number on the back of each." Cliff pointed. "Do you recognize it, Jon?"

"That's definitely our checking account. But who owns the account at Effingham?"

"I don't know at this point, but I called the bank manager to try to find out," Cliff said.

"Can we freeze the funds?"

"The manager wouldn't divulge the particulars over the phone, but she was able to verify a balance of only ten dollars."

"Where did the money go?" Captain said.

"The fifty-thousand cleared the bank by wire transfer," Cliff said.

"I think it's pretty clear who owns the account," Jon said.

"Since the first check was made out to your wife, she is the only person who could have legally endorsed it. It may take a subpoena to get the rest of the details," Cliff said. "But you're wasting your time. If she cashed it, she's done nothing illegal, given it was made out to her. So if you're thinking about going after the funds, I'd hire a good lawyer."

"Call it what you want, but the money's bloody well gone," Captain said.

"Actually, you didn't let me get to the interesting part about 6137 and 6148." Cliff aligned them on his desk. "You identified your First Savannah account on these, but I noticed that the funds were withdrawn within hours of each other at different branches. They look suspicious, even though both tellers verified the person's identification. I took the liberty of checking the branch security cameras this morning, and here's what I discovered." Cliff turned his monitor around.

"That can't be," Jon said. "See that emblem, there. It's my sailing hat."

"Do you know who it is?" Cliff said.

"Are you kidding? With the hat and sunglasses, it could be anybody."

"Despite the signatures, the gaps in the check register suggest they're forgeries," Cliff said.

"Why would you let someone dressed like that come into a bank and cash a check for twenty-five thousand dollars, much less two checks for that amount?"

"This will probably come as a surprise to you, but your wife recently set up a line of credit to guarantee large transactions of this nature. And then there's this little piece of information." Cliff reached across the desk and tapped each check.

Jon looked up at the ceiling.

"What is it, Boy?" Captain said.

"He cashed the checks using my driver's license."

Chapter 33
Wednesday, July 20th
11:42 A.M.

As soon as he turned onto 7th Street, Jon spotted a patrol car sitting in the Baineses' driveway. He spotted a young officer leaning against the trunk and pulled up behind him and stepped out. Despite overcast conditions, the officer's was wearing a pair of mirrored sunglasses. He tipped his hat and approached Jon, clutching an oversized envelope in one hand.

"Dr. Browning, I'm sorry to meet up with you like this."

"Is there something wrong?"

"As an agent of Tybee Island and Chatham County, I'm afraid I have to serve you these papers. The officer raised the envelope.

Jon didn't blink, only took the documents.

"They didn't exactly tell me what's inside, but the word is they're from the Superior Court. I'll need to get your signature." He handed Jon a pen. "How's the Beemer running?"

Jon signed a slip and tore it loose, handing it over. Without saying a word, he turned and walked over to the staircase and looked back. The officer was standing next to the car with his head down, like he was ashamed of himself.

"Do you have any contacts at the Savannah Police Department?" Jon said.

"Can't say I have, but I can ask the chief."

"Forget about it," Jon said, waving him off with the envelope. He started to turn, but stopped. "I hit one-ten on the causeway last week, with no traffic. She handled beautifully."

The officer wiggled his sunglasses and smiled. "Yeah, well don't give me a reason to come back."

* * *

Thursday, July 21st
9:58 A.M.

Foregoing his Thursday morning ritual in the park, Jon pulled into a parking spot next to a tabby building on Gaston Street. Entering an ornate stained-glass door, he walked up to a mahogany desk centered in a cathedral-like rotunda with his heels clicking on the polished marble tiles. The receptionist placed a call upstairs before directing him to a staircase at the rear.

An assistant greeted him on the second floor landing. "Good morning, Dr. Browning. If you will follow me," she said, leading him down a hallway. Her pin-striped suit blended well with the guilt-framed oil paintings they passed along the way. She tapped on a door and stepped inside. "Dr. Browning is here to see you."

"Jonathon, it's a pleasure," Bill Davenport said, rising from his desk. "I've been keeping abreast of this big merger deal you're working on in the *Chronicle*. It sounds quite impressive." He waved the assistant out.

"That's very kind of you," Jon said. He noticed there were more oil paintings on the office walls, surrounded by mahogany bookcases. Davenport sat behind a stately desk.

"Please," Davenport said, shaking Jon's hand before ushering him over to a conference table. "Did you study law?" He waited for Jon to sit, then he followed suit.

"I'm afraid not. I have a PhD in economics from Stanford University."

"Well, that explains a lot." Davenport picked up a folder that was sitting on the table. "At the moment I'm not taking on new clients, but in your case I'd say a little goodwill never hurt anyone." He opened the folder. "I received your fax, so let's take a look."

"I brought along the original, if you need it." Jon lifted his satchel and sat it in his lap. "The Sheriff's Office served me at home yesterday."

Davenport situated a pair of half-rimmed glasses on his nose, skimming the first document. "Do you recall the name of your wife's attorney?"

"Sam Hallworth." Jon pulled a folder out of the satchel and set it on the table.

Davenport looked up from the fax and peered over his glasses, exhaling rather dramatically. "Do you mind if I cuss?"

"Bad news?" Jon said, surprised by the sudden changeup.

"I've dealt with the son-of-a-bitch on more occasions than I care to admit. But I can tell you this. I won the last one." Davenport swung over to a credenza and removed a file, flipping through it. "It was a high-profile divorce case—two years ago." He returned to the table and picked up the fax.

"Would it be helpful for me to give you an overview of the situation?" Jon said.

Davenport didn't answer, only hunched over the table as he read. Every few seconds he uttered, "Uh-huh." He skimmed through the last few pages before removing his glasses. "Well, what we've got here is pretty standard language. I don't like the arrangement for the children. Any judge in his right mind will give you joint custody. And I don't care for the financial demands, either. We can do better, if you can document any premarital assets. Based on what I'm seeing here, I'd say a settlement should be in the cards. These things typically get settled out of court."

"What if I want to pursue custody of the children?"

"Then you'd better pull a rabbit out of your hat," Davenport said. "You'll have to prove she isn't fit to care for the children. I don't mind telling you, that's a tough row to hoe in Georgia. How old are the children?"

"Bailey is four, and Carver, six. I've worked out interim arrangements for them to spend time with me at Tybee."

"So you've moved out of the marital residence?" Davenport said, grimacing. "That gives them a little more leverage, but it's water over the dam. You've got the ability to care for the children?" He didn't pause for a response. "Does your wife work outside the home?"

"Not currently," Jon said. "But she did, prior to the children."

"Primary custody for a man means you'd better have an iron-clad plan . . . one-two-three, zippo. And be prepared to duke it out in court. I'd say they're not likely to agree to your custody proposal, that is, if she's worth her salt." Davenport flipped through the fax again. "You'll have to pardon me . . . I get carried away every now and then, Jon. Now, first we need to gather documents for the discovery request."

"Isn't five—"

"Five years of bank statements, tax returns, and other pertinent documents—that's not unreasonable. Is that what you were about to ask?" Davenport barely breathed. "If you have them, produce them. Take the list at the back, here, and put everything into a box and bring it to my office. Sam wants them delivered, but he can forget about that. Don't put anything in the box that's not on the list, you hear me?" Davenport shook his glasses at Jon. "And if you don't have ready access to something, don't go out of the way to produce it." Davenport tossed the list on the table and leaned back in his chair. "Any questions?"

"Next steps. There's a notice to appear for a deposition," Jon said. "It's the last page."

"You're a stickler for details, aren't you? I'll notify Sam when the discovery documents are ready. He can send someone over to pick them up, but I'll charge him for my paralegal's services. By the way, she goes for seventy-five an hour. Now, the deposition." He folded back a page in the fax. "Let's see. They want to depose you next Friday. That's pretty quick—wait a minute." Davenport returned to the discovery request. "The bastard was sloppy." Jon stretched for a look. "Sam requested the discovery documents a week after the deposition."

Jon settled back in the chair, easing his satchel to the floor. "I don't understand."

"Here's the new plan. Hold on to the box until after next Friday. If he asks for the documents at the deposition, tell him you haven't had time to pull them together yet."

Jon looked at Davenport. "Is that legal?"

Davenport raised an eyebrow. "You should've been a lawyer, Jon. Let me rephrase. Don't put the documents in the box until after next Friday. Now, have you ever done a deposition?"

"Only in corporate lawsuits. Nothing personal."

"Then you know the routine. Answer only what's asked—nothing more, nothing less. When responding to a yes-or-no question, answer appropriately. Don't pontificate or knit a flag. If you're unclear about something, have Sam clarify. At any point it's needed, I'll be there to give you guidance."

"There have been some crazy things that have happened. Do you want to hear about them?"

"Only if they're pertinent to the case."

Jon filled him in on Beth's confession. He also explained the stolen checks.

"I want copies of those checks before you leave, if you have them with you," Davenport said. "The rest is circumstantial."

"What if Hallworth tries to contact me again?"

"I'll call and let him know I'm representing you. From this point forward, he'll deal directly with me. I'll also confirm the date and time of the deposition. Your schedule's clear next week?"

"Whatever you need."

"Good. I'm in court most of the week, so we'll get together on Friday before the deposition. I'll drive you over to Sam's office in case we have last minute issues." Davenport took a couple of breaths, his face flush from the discussion. "Do you think there's any chance she'll agree to give you custody? Think about it and get back to me."

"I feel better already," Jon said.

"Then now's as good a time as any to drop this on you. My rate is five hundred dollars an hour. And I'll need a check for ten grand to get the wheels off the ground."

Chapter 34
Thursday, July 21st
5:50 P.M.

Charlie polished off a pint of Swamp Fox and flagged a waitress as Jon came walking into the Moon River. Terri, Steve, and Brenda were sitting with Charlie in the bar area at his favorite table next to the stainless steel brewing tank.

"It must be nice to clock in at happy hour," Charlie said, mostly to rouse Jon. The others looked up from their conversation as Jon approached the table. "Especially, after putting in a hard day at the beach."

"You will notice, the glass isn't half full or half empty," Jon said, pointing to Charlie's mug. He sat down between Terri and Steve. "Did anyone inquire about the bar tab arrangement?"

"Well, it's the least you could do," Charlie said. "Hefting that sleeper sofa of yours up a flight of stairs constitutes hazardous duty."

"I thought the sofa was about being there for me?"

"Jonathon—Jon, my boy. Let's not split hairs, here," Charlie said. "Besides, happy hour's not about compensation."

"I'm afraid to ask." Jon cut his eyes over to Brenda and smiled.

"Happy hour is about being there for you," Charlie said. A waitress tapped him on the shoulder, and he reached out, wrapping an arm around her. "Julie, we'll have five pints."

"What are we drinking?" Jon said.

Julie lowered an empty serving tray, tapping a drumbeat with her fingernails.

"Swamp Fox IPA. It's nothing but the best for this group," Charlie said. "Jon, I'd like you to meet Julie. She'll be serving us this evening."

There was snickering as the others detected an ambush.

"Julie, a pleasure," Jon said.

"And if you wouldn't mind, she needs your credit card," Charlie said.

"It's house policy for running a tab." Julie held out a hand.

"You'd be asking for cash in advance, if you knew this guy," Jon said. He handed over his American Express. "Now, who's here for whom?"

"Such disrespect, even after I strained my back carrying that bloody couch."

"What have I told you guys?" Jon said, looking around the table.

"We attempted to sneak out of the office." Terri pointed at Charlie. "But he was guarding the door."

"I thought Charlie was buying," Brenda said.

"Brenda—so talented and innocent, yet so trusting," Jon said. "When American Express says, 'don't leave home without it', they aren't talking about Charlie."

"There you go nitpicking again. It's not the money, it's the experience."

"Charlie, enough with the Zen," Terri said.

"Yes, young grasshopper."

"What are you talking about?" Brenda asked.

"Brenda, don't encourage him," Jon said.

"No bloody way," Charlie said.

"I'll wager you ten dollars she doesn't remember the name of the television show," Jon said.

"You're on," Charlie said, turning to Brenda. "For a free beer, what famous TV show made the phrase, young grasshopper, popular?"

"Famous?" Terri and Steve chimed in unison.

"It's a classic," Charlie said.

"It would scare the hell out of us all, if we knew his definition of classic," Jon said.

"Classic show?" Brenda said. "Let's see. Was it a comedy?"

"Oh darling, you're ripping my heart out!"

"You're toast, Charlie," Steve said.

"I become one with the universe every time I watch an episode," Charlie said.

"*NOVA*?" Brenda said, scrunching her nose.

"PBS . . . Charlie . . . please. There's not enough beer in Georgia," Terri said.

"*Pinky and the Brain*."

Everyone turned to Jon.

"*Pinky and the Brain*?" Terri repeated. She dropped her head on Jon's shoulder and started laughing.

Julie returned to the table with the beer.

"Give that man all five of those," Jon said to Julie.

"Very funny," Charlie said. "Who'd think you were in investment banking?"

"I'm not getting in the middle of this." Julie set the pints in front of Charlie.

"Let's make it double or nothing. I'll bet Julie doesn't know the answer, either," Jon said.

"Know what?" Julie handed Jon his card. "Never mind, I don't want to know." She spun around to leave.

"Wait, I want in. This is easy money," Terri said.

"What's it going to be, Charlie?" Jon grabbed Julie's hand to keep her from walking off.

Charlie took a slug from one of the pints. "It can't get any worse." He lowered the mug. "Julie, what classic show made the phrase, young grasshopper, famous?"

Julie rolled her eyes up at the ceiling. "If this is a pickup line, it ain't going to work, boys," she said, slipping the tray under an arm.

"I was wrong," Charlie said. "I throw myself at the mercy of the court."

"Are you conceding?" Jon said.

"What I meant to say is, it can get worse. I recant. I'm a reformed man now."

Everyone in the group laughed as Julie planted a hand on her hip. "No more beer for you two," she said. "And I'm doubling my tip."

"So you don't know?" Jon said. Julie stuck her tongue out and marched away. "That's twenty bucks, Charlie. You want to go again?"

"Hold on," Brenda said. "I want to know the answer."

"Brenda, I'm getting rich," Jon said. "Work with me, here. I'll buy you dinner, maybe a yacht."

The group lost it as Charlie covered his face.

Brenda leaned in to Jon as the others continued to razz Charlie. "So how are you doing, Jon? The office isn't the same when you're not there."

"Well, as of yesterday, I'm legally separated."

"Do you think you'll be able to work things out, amicably?" Terri said, leaning into the conversation.

"It doesn't look good."

"Sorry to hear that," Terri said. "Even if you can't count on Charlie, we're here for you." She patted Jon's hand.

"When will you be back in the office?" Brenda said.

"Don't pressure him. He'll know when he's ready," Charlie broke in. "I'm here for you, Jon."

"Translated—he wants my office," Jon said.

"He'll tangle with me if he tries to pull that off," Brenda said.

"Hey, missy. You report to me now," Charlie said.

"Big deal . . . I have a slush file on you this thick, so watch yourself." Brenda lifted a hand above her head.

"I'll give you twenty bucks for it," Jon said.

Everyone at the table roared.

"It's not for sale," Brenda said, looking around at Jon. "But you can have a copy for free."

"Bloody vultures." Charlie raised his mug and drained it.

"So who's up for dinner?"

"Thanks, Jon, but I've got to get home," Terri said, standing up.

"I'm with you," Steve said.

"Well, I'm not hanging around for more abuse," Charlie said. "I'll walk you both back to the office."

Terri leaned over and whispered in Brenda's ear, "*Kung Fu*."

"What's *Kung Fu*?" Brenda said so everyone could hear.

"The name of the show," Terri said.

"You mean, like karate?"

"Blasphemy!" Charlie slid out of his chair and wedged in next to Brenda. "*Kung Fu* is no more karate than a Yugo's a luxury car."

"Yugo, what's that?"

"Keep your mouth shut before you lose another twenty bucks," Terri said, pushing Charlie toward the door. "Enjoy your dinner."

"Good night, young grasshoppers," Charlie said.

Chapter 35
Thursday, July 21st
10:35 P.M.

A crescent moon floated high above the muggy night, the stickiness clinging to anyone unfortunate enough to be out at the hour. Darkness enveloped the inner sanctum of South Coast Church, with the exception of David Stephens's office, where light spilled underneath the door into an empty reception area.

"Is this what we've come to? You said the process was untouchable. We're like a den of thieves, only worse," Tim Lowe said. "Aren't either of you concerned?"

Sam Hallworth sat cocked, ready to attack. "Get a hold of yourself, for Pete's sake—"

"Enough of the bickering," Stephens said. "Tim, I need an update on your efforts since our last meeting."

"It's pretty cut-and-dry. I'm waiting for Jonathon to return the legal release. I issued an ultimatum, just like we discussed. The ball's in his court." Lowe jotted on a pad.

"What are you doing?" Stephens said.

"I'm making a note for his file."

"Do not—I repeat—do not put anything about this meeting in writing. I thought I made that clear." Stephens leveled a finger at Lowe.

"It's my responsibility to maintain a clinical record of the diagnosis and treatment. We've been through this before. There's a matter of ethical standards, and my state license," Lowe said, tossing his pen down. "How did I ever—"

"You'll screw us all with your protocol—counseling Beth Browning to confess her indiscretions. What's gotten into you? If anyone knows how to make this thing work, it should be you." Stephens gestured to Hallworth. "What have you got?"

"By the way, that photo idea was brilliant," Hallworth said. "I thought for sure it would bring him running to my office to sign the papers. I even buried some legalese to help Dr. Freud, here, out of his predicament." He looked up at Stephens and changed his expression. "And then one of the South Coast elders somehow got involved. Next thing I know, Beth Browning agreed to an interim settlement. You're the Holy Roller. How do you account for that?"

"I'll look into the matter," Stephens said, turning back to Lowe. "If you had control of your patients, we wouldn't be dealing with this, now would we?" Lowe shifted in his seat, not responding. "What did she agree to Sam?"

"For starters she booted him out of the house, but gave him rights to see the children. Unfortunately, he talked her into accepting the temporary financial arrangement I called you about." Hallworth turned to Lowe. "I don't understand why you can't deliver a knockout with the case history we concocted. You've got everything you need—"

"I'm only going to repeat this one more time." Lowe's cheeks turned beet-colored. "I've already stuck my neck out, and I don't intend to risk anything more." He looked to Stephens, and then stood up to pace. "He's smart and doesn't take the emotional bait, like most patients. I can't change his personality. He's questioned the treatment protocol, even the psychological assessment. It makes me nervous."

"Sit down," Stephens said to Lowe, cutting his eyes to Hallworth. "You mentioned he gave her a check. Where is it?"

"You tell me. I'm still waiting for my retainer. She owes me fifteen grand. You're getting the tithe, and Freud is collecting for services rendered. She seems to be coming up short, even with the fifty grand and monthly support he's agreed to."

"Let's not lose sight of the big picture," Stephens said. "Once Randall agrees to the counseling center, there'll be plenty of new opportunities for all of us."

"What's the hold up?" Lowe said.

"He doesn't think the timing is right for another real estate investment. As it turns out, space may be available in Phase III of the church expansion. Thanks to our dear, Jonathon."

"For the record, none of us makes any real money until we secure enough incriminating information to force a payoff." Lowe wiped perspiration off his forehead.

"Tim, why don't you run down to the kitchen and get us all some water? We've got to figure out how to get things back on track." Stephens waited for Lowe to leave, then walked over and closed the door. He circled the table, studying his footsteps, as if deep in thought. Then he looked up at Sam. "Tim's holding back on us."

"What do you mean?"

"He doesn't have enough skin in the game." Stephens sat down. "I say we give him the ball and let him run with it. Otherwise, he'll sit back and let us do all the work."

Hallworth smiled. "So what's the—"

Lowe barreled through the door with three water bottles, setting them on the table. "So where do we go from here?"

"We're reviewing the strategy," Stephens said. "It's clear the plan needs to be fine-tuned." He stood up again. "Sam, I want you to look into every possible angle for leveraging the full weight of the law."

"Then you've got to deal with the elder issue—"

"I'll get to that. Do whatever it takes to make Jonathon realize that Tim is his only salvation from a divorce suit. And do it quickly," Stephens said.

"Given we're all in this together, I need to see a little cash," Hallworth said, rubbing his fingers together.

"SCMI's reserves are tied up at the moment, but I'll see what I can do."

"The doctor's worried about risk . . . I've got paralegal costs and the expense of a deposition on Friday."

"That's a good point. We can use the deposition to raise the ante," Stephens said, pausing. "I've got an idea, but we'll talk later. Tim, we've got a change in plan. I want you to call Beth and tell her you're doing everything in your power to arrange a joint session. Then contact Jonathon, and tell him Beth has conceded to one appointment without the legal release."

"What if she doesn't agree?"

"Just do it. And make sure you convince her charming husband that you're the only thing standing between him and Sam-the-Ripper, here. Spin it so he believes the release is his key to the kingdom. Document your ongoing treatment protocol, write down every instance he refuses to work with you, and strengthen the case for your diagnosis."

"And if he doesn't bite?"

"Pull him aside and explain the legal frenzy that's about to erupt. Then call Sam and let him take it from there," Stephens said. "In the meantime, Sam, contact Tim if you come up with anything he can use."

"What about the elder?"

"I'll handle it," Stephens said, holding up his hands. "Let's all remember, Beth's outbursts can be an asset in this case. Sam, we'll get together on Thursday to prepare for the deposition." He sat down. "Is there anything else?" The men sat in silence. "Okay then, let's close in prayer."

Chapter 36
Friday, July 22nd
1:30 P.M.

A car door slammed, and Jon walked out of his bedroom onto the porch. No sooner had he spotted the car parked on the street, than he heard footsteps climbing the outside stairs. Brenda's face appeared at the screen door, wearing a delicate smile and a pair of sunglasses. Jon hurried over, his eyes drawn to the stack of folders in her arms and a canvas bag slung over a shoulder. He unlatched the door.

"A pleasant surprise," Jon said, reaching for the files.

"Please tell me Charlie called." She followed Jon inside.

"There's nothing quite like starting the morning with Charlie complaining about being overworked, underpaid, and underappreciated. Afterwards, he dropped the bomb about a new round of contract revisions, how he knew I must be busy and didn't want to impose, but he could bring them out to me, if I could do him a favor. After an earful, he explained he was sending you instead."

"That about covers it. Although he didn't tell me how charming your place is." Brenda crossed the porch, looking out at the Atlantic. "There's nothing like a room with a view. I've always dreamed about living in a place like this. It's awesome, Jon."

"So Charlie gave you the afternoon off to sample the good life. He said you were going to take a little R&R for your troubles. Of course, that's code for delaying you long enough so I can finish the work. That way, he won't have to drive out and pick it up. How about a wager?" Jon stepped through a set of double French doors and set the folders on a makeshift desk.

Brenda poked her head inside and looked around. "Not on your life. I'm still freaked out over that grasshopper fiasco," she said, laughing. "This is perfect—desk, antique bed, master bath."

"Make that, the only bath."

"But it works," she said. "Can I have the tour?"

"Well, here you have the master suite," Jon said, holding out a hand and walking her back out. "And this porch is a feature found only on the finer homes on the island. It performs double-duty, since it's the only way to get from the bedroom into the living room and kitchen." He pointed to a set of doors she had walked past when she arrived.

"What do you do in winter?" Brenda glanced back at the bedroom doors.

"That's a very good question. My landlords tell me the upstairs used to be two apartments in the Seventies. When they remodeled, and I use the term loosely, they decided to spare the interior by not cutting a doorway through the wall." Jon led her through the second set of doors into the living room.

"And this . . . could this be the infamous sleeper sofa?" Brenda dropped onto one of the tweed cushions, patting it with her hands.

"Officially, it's known as the guest suite. But more importantly, it's Bailey's home away from home on weekends. Carver claimed the hammock on the porch, but I'm thinking that arrangement is going to fizzle about thirty minutes after bedtime. And over here's the kitchen—"

"Wow. Avocado appliances. I've been reading about how the retro colors are making a comeback," Brenda said. She gave the kitchen the once-over.

"You're mistaken, my dear. That's not retro. It's original equipment. Nothing but the nostalgic for this beach shack. Fortunately, I do have cable and Internet service."

"I think you're going to be okay, Jonathon Browning. And by the way, dinner at the Moon River was simply divine last night." Brenda rose up on her toes and gave him a hug.

Jon patted her on the back, and then stepped away. "So here's the routine. I'm going to work on the contract while you kick back on the beach. If you need anything, there are drinks and snacks in the kitchen." He turned and walked out onto the porch with Brenda in tow.

"I brought a change of clothes for the beach." She slipped the bag off her shoulder.

"Then just pop into the bedroom, and I'll be on the porch when you're done." As Brenda stepped inside, he closed the French doors behind her.

Jon was studying a sailboat out on the water, when the bedroom doors opened and Brenda reappeared, barefoot and wearing a cover-up. She sneaked into the kitchen and returned with her bag, dropping a bottle of water inside.

"The signal is, one if by land, two if by sea," she said, untangling a pair of sunglasses from her hair.

"You may need this." Jon handed her a folding chair. As she opened the screen door, he added, "And watch out for sharks—great whites."

"Are you saying it's not safe to go in the water?" She lifted the sunglasses.

"I saw it on Discovery Channel," he said, looking away to keep from laughing.

Brenda dropped the glasses back onto her nose and disappeared down the steps. Jon waited until she reappeared on the beach in front of the house, watching as she unfolded the chair and applied suntan lotion. When she was done, she stretched out with a book.

Jon went inside to retrieve the files, and after grabbing a cup of coffee, carried the work out onto the porch. He lost track of time, remaining focused on the task until he had finished. When he closed the last folder, he got up and carried his cup into the kitchen, returning to the porch in time to spot Brenda trudging across the sand toward the house. He waited until he heard footsteps, and then met her at the top of the stairs.

"Did you see the guy that drove up to me on the Segway?" Brenda said as she came in. "I don't know if he was checking me out or just putting on a show, but I swear there wasn't enough Spandex on the man to make a decent slingshot." She made a face. "You didn't warn me about the land sharks."

"I would have saved you, but as you know, I had all of this work," Jon said, raising a folder. "Which reminds me . . . I'm done. So Charlie's spared. When you return to the office, have him initial the contract changes. Michael's going to blow a gasket when he sees this."

"That doesn't surprise me," Brenda said, removing her sunglasses. "Now, I have something for you. Charlie told me if you finished the amendments this afternoon, he was buying dinner."

"Charlie's driving out for dinner?"

"Actually, he's busy, but he gave me this." Brenda reached into her bag and pulled out cash. "He suggested the outdoorsy restaurant down by the pier."

"You can't be serious. Charlie Porter gave you money?" Jon scratched his head.

"Yeah, he made me sign for it," she said, laughing. "You must be famished, working all afternoon like that."

"Now that you mention it, I could use something to eat. Let's see." Jon stared into the kitchen. "I've got a perfectly good bottle of Yellow Tail, arguably well-suited for such an occasion. And I'll run down to the market for cheese and crackers. Do you prefer Gouda, Swiss, or Cheese Whiz?" Brenda started giggling. "We'll enjoy a sunset on the porch, and then head down for dinner afterwards."

"That sounds perfect. Charlie wants me to call him with a status, so I'll do that while you're out. Then I'll freshen up for dinner and a sunset."

When Jon returned, there was no sign of Brenda. He put away the groceries and returned to the porch, calling out to her. The bedroom doors were open, but there was no reply. When he leaned around the doorway, he noticed that the bathroom door was ajar and a blanket of steam covered the visible half of the mirror. Then a hairdryer flipped on, and Brenda's hand reached out, holding a washcloth. As she stretched to wipe away the steam, he suddenly realized she wasn't dressed. She moved again, exposing a bare back, and he caught himself staring.

Stepping back, Jon felt like a school kid. Unsure if she'd seen him, he headed for the kitchen and grabbed a beer from the refrigerator. Afterwards, he settled into a chair on the porch.

A few minutes later, Brenda leaned out of the bedroom doorway. "Charlie kept me on the phone forever," she said, as Jon turned in his chair. "He wasn't at the office, so I had to call his cell phone. By the way, he insisted we try the coconut-battered shrimp. I'll be ready in a few." She started inside, and then stopped. "I thought we were having wine."

Jon held up the beer. "It's just a little something to cool off. I'll go pop the cork."

Brenda closed the doors.

"Ready," Brenda said.

Jon heard a pair of heels step out on the wooden floor behind him and a chill ran up his spine. He sat looking out at the water, waiting for her to circle around into his line of sight. When she stopped, he couldn't help but stand up. His arm went limp, nearly dropping the beer in his hand as she stood between him and the Atlantic, hovering in a way he'd never seen her before. Her blue dress dipped in front, fashionably fitted with spaghetti straps that tied around her neck. A pair of earrings sparkled in the late afternoon sunlight, playing against her silky dark hair that brushed her bare shoulders.

Jon ran a hand through his hair. "Wow," he said. "I think . . . I should put on something more appropriate. Give me a minute."

After a brief absence, he returned in a white oxford button-down, khaki shorts, and loafers, to find Brenda seated in his chair. Gazing down the length of her tan legs to a set of color-coordinated toenails, he noticed how perfectly the outfit had been accessorized with a pair of white heels.

"I bought them at the mall yesterday. Do you like them?" She extended a leg, looking up from the chair.

"Uh . . . How about some wine?" Jon gave her the cow eyes and hurried into the kitchen, returning with the wine and crackers before pulling up a chair next to her.

"You're so adorable in your beach house," Brenda said. "With the time you put in at the office, who'd ever guess you had time for a private life?"

Jon sliced the Gouda, and then laid out crackers on a small tray. "That particular question is up for debate, especially under current circumstances. But the way I figure it, if you take the ocean, beach, and fresh air—bask around in it for a while—sooner or later life will make sense."

Brenda watched as he sampled a cracker, and then took a sip of her wine. "If I didn't know better, I'd think you were a closet romantic. And maybe this is some kind of trick. Doesn't the sun set on the other side of the island?" She looked into his eyes, smiling.

Jon kicked back in his chair, returning the smile. "That is true, but if you will be patient, I do have a defense. At sunset, the colors over the Atlantic will be absolutely spectacular."

After dinner at Fannies on the Beach, Brenda persuaded Jon to check out a Caribbean-style band on the upper deck. They grabbed a corner table and ordered drinks just in time for her to charm Jon into getting out on the dance floor.

"Charlie said you're a good dancer."

"He knows better than that. Are you sure he gave you the C-note?"

"You're messing up this exotic island scene I've got going on in my head. There has to be dancing." Brenda rested her hands on his shoulders. "Sunsets, dinner, wine—candlelight."

"This place is somewhat of a tourist trap," Jon said. "But I do like the palm tree lights on the railing over there."

"Now you're getting the hang of it. I can't remember when I've seen you so relaxed. I think you're going to be just fine, once you get all of this behind you."

"I'll have my people get back to your people," Jon said as he looked down at a blue van parked on the street. It resembled one that had been sitting next to the house all day. "I'm working through the issues, but it's nice to have friends like you around for support."

"That's funny. I don't feel like I'm helping," Brenda said as the band finished the song. "Would you mind asking them to play another one . . . something slow?" She slipped a bill from her top.

"Not in public," Jon said, grabbing her hand and laughing. He walked over and spoke to the band leader, and a Jimmy Buffett tune crooned off the steel drums.

"Add Buffett to that thing in your head," he said.

Brenda looped her arms around his neck as he took another look at the van. It was headed down the street. When the song ended, Jon paid the tab, and they left.

Pulling into the Baineses' driveway, Jon checked the street before taking Brenda upstairs for her bag. He carried the files down to the car, helping her with the door.

"Tonight's been really fun. I hate to admit it, but you're exactly as I pictured away from the office."

"I'll take that as a compliment."

Inching closer, she pecked him on the cheek.

"Thanks for helping out with the contract," Jon said. "We'd better call it a night."

"Oh, I just thought . . ." She looked up at Jon, puzzled.

"It's okay."

"But—"

"It was a perfect night, so let's leave it at that." He hugged her, and then closed the door. Standing in the driveway, he waved as she pulled away.

When he started inside, Jon heard a rustling across the street and stopped. The moonlight reflected off something in the darkness, drawing him into the street. Before he could get a bearing, the hedges parted, and a man jumped out and ran around the corner of the neighboring house. Without thinking, Jon darted into the yard, making a direct path toward the spot where the prowler had disappeared. He sprinted across the lawn, only to be hampered by a privacy fence before working his way around to 6th Street, just a block over. Stepping out onto the curb, he heard screeching tires and looked up ahead to see the blue van fishtail out onto Butler Avenue and speed away.

Chapter 37
Friday, July 29th
10:05 A.M.

The conference room at Sam Hallworth's office reeked of cheap cigars. There were stacks of Bankers Boxes in all four corners, each bearing the name of an unfortunate client: Bennett, Chatsworth, Blackman, and of course, Smith. The meeting table resembled a battlefield on the morning after, the chairs somewhat dingy from an assortment of infectious-looking stains. English hunt scenes adorned the walls, illuminated by buzzing overhead lighting. Near the entrance, a lady was busy setting up a piece of equipment she had rolled in like a piece of Samsonite. Jon and Beth sat on opposite sides of the table.

Hallworth entered the room with Bill Davenport trailing behind him. The two men made no effort at pleasantries as Hallworth introduced Jon to the lady, a court reporter who would be documenting the deposition. He suggested lunch at noon and breaks only as needed. With formalities out of the way, he excused himself and settled into a private conversation with Beth, who had remained silent in the interim.

To kick things off, the court reporter had each person identify themselves for the record. Afterwards, Hallworth read down a laundry list of questions for Jon, confirming his identity.

Following a short break, Hallworth spent the next grueling hour drilling him on financial disclosures. "Dr. Browning, were you aware that you would be asked questions about your personal finances today?"

"Yes."

"Then please explain why you have failed to bring the necessary documents to the deposition."

"I am merely complying with your request to appear here today," Jon said.

"Did you spend time with Mr. Davenport in preparing for these proceedings?"

"Yes."

Hallworth curled his upper lip as he leveled a double-barreled stare directly between Jon's eyes. "Did you not also receive a request for discovery, ordering you to bring such documents to this proceeding?"

Jon didn't respond.

"Sam," Davenport said, clearing his throat. "The discovery documents are due next week."

Hallworth snorted, and then paused to rustle through a folder. Beth leaned in for a look, just as his lip curled once again. "So do you have any of the documents with you today?"

"No."

"Is this some kind of game to you, Dr. Browning?"

"I believe I already explained my position."

"Are you telling me that you've had time to pull together nothing?"

"Objection, Sam. My client answered the question, so let's move on," Davenport said.

"Fifteen minute break," Hallworth snapped.

Davenport checked his watch and raised an eyebrow as Hallworth grabbed some papers and hurried outside with Beth. He complimented Jon on his performance, warning him that retaliation was just over the horizon.

"What are we doing here?" Jon said to Davenport. "I've been in pawn shops that are cleaner than this place. Mother Justice is getting—"

"Stay focused, Jon," Davenport said. "And take your time with each question."

Beth and Hallworth reentered the room with additional folders and gathered in their seats.

"Dr. Browning, what is the current balance in your First Savannah investment account?" Hallworth said, poising his pen above a legal pad.

"I don't know."

"Seriously? You're a financial professional and don't know your account balance?"

"No, not specifically."

"Okay, then . . . Approximately how much?" Hallworth said.

Jon cut his eyes over at Davenport.

"Sam, you can't expect my client to speculate on critical details, like this. As you know, the court isn't going to accept approximations when it's time to carve the baby."

"Dr. Browning, are you and Mrs. Browning currently seeing a psychologist for marital counseling?" Hallworth pushed aside a folder, and then flipped open another.

"Yes."

"Please tell us about the diagnosis and any treatment recommendations. And for the record, state the doctor's name," Hallworth said.

"I believe you know his name. And as far as the diagnosis goes, I can't say."

"You can't say, or you won't say, Dr. Browning?"

Jon didn't respond.

"He's already given you an answer," Davenport said.

"Strike the question," Hallworth said, moving on to another folder. "I would like to mark this as Exhibit 1." He waved a photo in front of the court reporter, and then slid it across the table. "Dr. Browning, can you describe what you see in this picture?"

"It's the master bedroom in our home."

"Would you care to comment on the damage presented in this photo?"

Beth shifted in her seat.

"I came home from work a few weeks ago and found the room, as you see it here. I can't—"

"You can't say, or you won't say, Dr. Browning?" Hallworth said, cutting him off.

"Perhaps I should start from the beginning—"

"Strike the question," Hallworth interrupted. "Dr. Browning, are you a member of South Coast Church?"

"Yes."

"And is it true you have refused to cooperate with Reverend David Stephens, who is presently counseling you and Mrs. Browning on your marital issues?"

"No."

Hallworth came out of his chair. "Your answer is no? This isn't the report Mrs. Browning received from Mr. Stephens." He turned his back to the table, studying one of the English prints before resuming the questioning. "Have you followed Reverend Stephens's counsel in seeking to reconcile the marriage, as my client has?"

"No, but—"

"Thank you, Dr. Browning." Hallworth sat down, exchanging whispers with Beth.

Davenport leaned in next to Jon. "What's the story?"

"David Stephens is a pastor at our church. Beth got him involved in the aftermath of the confession. He's the one who recommended Dr. Lowe, who also happens to be Stephens's friend and a member of the church."

"You're not comfortable following the advice of your pastor?" Davenport said.

"Not when he's demanding that I sign a legal release as a condition for counseling," Jon said. "Did I mention Hallworth is a member of the church?"

"Sam's a spiritual man?" Davenport snickered, quickly regaining his composure. "If I were you, I'd get the hell out of that church."

Clearing his throat, Hallworth continued. "I'd like to enter Exhibit 2 into the proceedings." He held up a second photo and slid it across the table. "Dr. Browning, would you please identify the automobile in the picture?"

"It's my car."

"Let the record show that Dr. Browning has identified the gray BMW in the exhibit as his personal vehicle." Hallworth reached into the folder and produced another photograph. "Exhibit 3." He slid it across, smiling. "Dr. Browning, I'll ask you to identify the location of your personal vehicle in this exhibit."

Jon fingered a corner of the photo as Davenport looked on. The Z4 was sitting in a parking lot in front of a row of townhouses. A sign out front read: *2735 Marsh Point Place*. Jon gave Davenport a puzzled look, and then stared across the table. "It appears to be a townhouse where one of my associates lives."

"It appears to be, or perhaps is the residence of Miss Brenda Simpson?" Hallworth said.

"I don't understand."

"Allow me to repeat the question. Is that your car?"

"It is, but—"

"Thank you, Dr. Browning." Hallworth reached into the folder once again. "Now, I have a few more exhibits. So bear with me. This will be Exhibit 4. Please identify the automobile in this picture and describe the location."

Davenport studied the photo with Jon, awaiting his response. "I believe it is Brenda Simpson's car parked next to my apartment at Tybee Island."

"Perhaps these will clarify matters. Let's see—Exhibits 5, 6, 7, and 8." He held them up and slid them across. "Dr. Browning, please identify the individuals in these photos."

Jon lifted the first one for a closer look, while Davenport looked on over his shoulder. It was a shot of Brenda on the beach in front of his apartment. The second captured her in a towel at the door to his bedroom, and the third was a zoom of Jon and Brenda dancing at Fannies on the Beach. The final photo showed them embracing, next to her car. He turned to Davenport.

"Sam, I'm going to need a moment to confer with my client," Davenport said.

"As soon as he answers the question."

Davenport nodded to Jon.

"These are photos of Brenda Simpson and me—"

"Let the record show that Dr. Browning has identified himself and Miss Brenda Simpson in Exhibits 5 through 8," Hallworth said, standing. "Let us know when you're ready to resume." He led Beth and the court reporter out into the hallway.

"Jon, you never mentioned you were involved with someone else," Davenport said.

"It's not what it looks like. Brenda works with me. Those photographs were taken last week, and it's the only time I've been alone with her."

"What about your car at her townhouse?"

"I've never been there."

"But it was your car," Davenport said, not waiting for a response. "Who took the pictures?"

"There was a van following us. I caught a man watching my place Friday night, but he got away before I could find out who he was. And it was my car at her townhouse, only I don't know how it got there."

"Is there anything else I should know?"

"You tell me," Jon said, shaking his head.

Davenport stood up. "He's about to crucify you, so watch yourself."

"Are we ready?" Hallworth said after settling back into his chair.

The court reporter gave the okay sign.

"So, Dr. Browning, you've identified yourself and Miss Simpson in these last exhibits. Would you care to acknowledge that you were having an affair with Miss Simpson, or do you normally engage in these types of activities with associates?"

"Sam, I believe you know the purpose for those pictures—"

"Dr. Browning, were you having an affair with Brenda Simpson?" Hallworth interrupted.

"No."

"Then let's just call this a business meeting." Hallworth waved a hand over the pictures. "Could you please explain the code of conduct for employees at a prestigious firm, like Stone & Associates, when they engage in business at the beach? And under what circumstances do you deem it appropriate for a female employee to dress in attire such as bikinis and slinky dresses?"

"She drove out to deliver contracts."

"I see," Hallworth said, reaching across the table to gather up the exhibits. "Then perhaps you are suggesting the papers are concealed in the swimsuit . . . or maybe she's got them hidden under the towel. I dare say it would have been possible to squeeze them into that tight little dress. What do you think?"

"I'll tell you what I—"

"Dr. Browning, why don't you explain what's been going on between you and Miss Simpson?"

"I didn't have an affair with her, if that's what you're implying."

"So you're testifying that these pictures mean nothing. If I were you, I'd be prepared to prove that in a court of law," Hallworth said. "How can you possibly consider yourself a decent father to your children when you're carrying on like this?"

"It's not what you—"

"That's not for you to decide—"

"You know—"

Hallworth slammed a fist on the table. "Let's get one thing straight, Dr. Browning. This is the procedure. I ask the questions, and you answer them."

"Then move on and stop threatening him every time you don't like the answer," Davenport said. "You follow the process or I'll end this right now."

Hallworth looked up, smiling. "Very well, Bill." He turned to Jon. "You've identified your car in Exhibit 3."

"Yes."

"He already answered," Davenport said, fighting to stay in his chair.

"Dr. Browning, if you weren't having an affair with Miss Simpson, please explain the presence of your automobile at her residence. And I'll remind you, we've already observed what was going on at the beach," Hallworth said.

"I can't—"

"You can't . . . or you won't?"

"I didn't park it there."

"So you're suggesting it somehow drove itself to Miss Simpson's residence?"

Jon paused, studying the table. Then he looked up. "If you want the truth, then let's back up and start with the attempted break-in at my—"

"Thank you, Dr. Browning," Hallworth interrupted. He stood up and extended a hand across the table to Davenport. "That will be all for today."

Davenport shook Hallworth's hand and stepped back, leaning into Jon's ear. "What just happened?"

"I'll explain later." Jon turned for the door.

"Is there someplace you need to be?" Davenport said, perplexed.

"If you'd be kind enough to drop me at the Seafarer Mission, I need to arrange a trip to Charleston."

Chapter 38
Saturday, July 30th
8:15 A.M.

Sleepless in Savannah is a nocturnal condition remedied only by the dawn of a new day. Jon had returned home from the deposition on Friday afternoon, nursing his miseries with pizza and beer. But mostly beer. He lay in the Pawleys Island Hammock drinking until midnight, finally making a path from the porch to his air-conditioned bedroom. The mattress was no less a serpent, tossing him about in the night, like the Tybee back river during a summer storm. Early Saturday morning he sat up in bed and counted the number of telephone rings, cursing himself for forgetting to turn off the ringer. The need for a first cup of coffee finally got the better of him and he climbed out of the sheets and trudged into the kitchen. He hadn't bothered to check the clock, but was sure it was still morning as the phone went off again. Pulling a bag of coffee out of the cabinet he answered, but detected only silence on the other end of the line. He cradled the receiver on his shoulder as he filled a carafe in the sink, waiting.

"Jon, did I wake you?" Brenda finally said, but slowly.

"No, I'm up." Jon stared at a mosaic of photos on the refrigerator. "Did you need something?"

"Listen, I got a call from Chase yesterday."

"Chase?"

"The guy from the help desk . . . He said you asked him to call if he had any breakthroughs on your e-mail. Evidently, he lost your number, so he called the office."

Jon poured water into a Mr. Coffee and pressed brew. "Give me his contact information, and I'll return the call."

Brenda read it off, and then continued after an awkward pause. "Jon, I was hoping we could discuss what happened last week."

"Starting with the finer points of how to spy on your friends?"

"What?" Brenda said. "I want to apologize for my behavior last Friday night."

"Brenda, listen. I've just gone through one hell of a deposition. It's not a good time."

"It didn't go well?"

"Honestly, no." He opened the refrigerator door, and then slammed it shut. "Of course, I'm not telling you anything you don't already know."

"Me? . . . How would I . . . Did I miss something?"

Jon grabbed the carafe and poured until his mug overflowed. Then he jammed it back into the coffee maker. "Brenda, we should have this conversation, but later."

"I'm worried about you. Isn't there something—"

"After I check in with Chase, I've got to pick up the kids. Beth already cut me out of the first half of the weekend, so I will call you when I have time." Jon hung up and dialed Chase's number.

"This is Chase. May I have your name?"

"Hi Chase. It's Jon Browning. I'm returning your call."

"Jonathon, I'm glad you called back. You're going to think I'm a real dork when you hear this one."

"Then you'll be in good company," Jon said. "What do you have for me?"

"I hate to admit it, but I forgot to check the dial-in server the night you reported your problem. I think they call it a brain fart, and I apologize. The server was scheduled for routine maintenance last night, and then suddenly, *voilà* . . ."

"*Voilà*? What do you mean?"

"It hit me—check the remote dial-in server for activity. So I did, and there it was. A connection to your network from twelve-eighteen until one-ten."

"Who was it?"

"Well, that's the thing. I'm afraid your system doesn't capture that information. But whoever it was, they used your login and password." Chase paused as if awaiting a response. When there wasn't one, he continued. "Anyway, end of mystery. You may want to take a look at your security policy."

"I appreciate the revelation, but how am I supposed to find this person?"

"It's called sneakernet. If you can find the computer that originated the transaction, then you've got your culprit. That is, unless it's been deleted. I explained to Brenda about how to find deleted files, and even how to zap them permanently for security purposes."

"Permanently," Jon repeated. He dropped the telephone without hanging up and raced into the bedroom, streaming a trail of coffee in his wake.

Landing in his desk chair, Jon set the mug on the floor and shook coffee off his hand. He ejected his laptop from a docking station and flipped it over. Taped to the bottom was a yellow sticky note with his logon and password. He secured the computer back into place, knocking over the coffee with his foot.

As the system booted up, a display of icons appeared on the computer desktop. He clicked on the mail application and waited as it loaded. Selecting the sent folder, he sorted it by date, and then scrolled down the list of files, stopping on one.

"I need a beer," he said, taking a breath.

It was the e-mail Richard had read to him over the telephone from San Diego. Verbatim.

Chapter 39
Saturday, July 30th
10:40 A.M.

The kids' overnight bags sat on the front porch as Jon pulled into the driveway. Before he could ring the bell, Beth appeared at the door with Bailey and Carver circling at warp speed, ecstatic about their weekend adventure at the beach. Jon took in the scene, and when he started to speak, Beth's stare shuttered him, so he packed the kids into the car and headed off for Tybee Island, stopping en route to pick up a box of Krispy Kreme's.

Leaving their dad behind at the street, Bailey and Carver made a beeline up the stairs for the screen porch. By the time Jon reached the door, Carver was stretched out in the hammock with his hands folded behind his head. Bailey tried to jump aboard, and he poked her with his foot, reminding her of the sleeping arrangements. Jon had them unpack their bags, and then ordered pizza delivery, later hiking down to the beach for the afternoon.

A thundershower cut short their time at the beach, so Jon loaded up the Land Cruiser and headed out for Seaside Sisters to do a little souvenir shopping. Carver bought a shrunken head that had been carved out of a coconut, which he affectionately dubbed, "The Witch Doctor". Bailey took a softer approach and purchased a bracelet adorned with multicolored fish charms. The children refused to leave until Jon selected something for himself, so he chose a tropical frame that could be used to display a photo of their first weekend together at the beach.

Next, they visited Fort Pulaski, where the attraction turned out to be alligator spotting—from a safe distance of course. Jon took pictures as they patrolled the moat surrounding the massive brick walls. For dinner, they drove down a dusty road to The Crab Shack, yet another opportunity to be entertained by alligators, only on a much smaller scale.

As they walked up to the entrance, Carver perked up. "Dad, what does that say?" he said, pointing to a shingle dangling outside the dining area.

Jon looked up as a hostess greeted them and cheerfully responded. "It says: 'where the elite eat in their bare feet'." She collected three menus, pointing to a pile in the corner. "You can leave your shoes over there, if you like."

Bailey and Carver turned and gave Jon their "are we going to get away with this" look.

Sensing the excitement in their faces, he realized an argument was out of the question. "Okay, but there's one condition," he said, as both pairs of eyes grew wide. "I want you to keep a lookout for alligators. I have no intention of anyone leaving here without all of their toes."

Bailey let out an "eeww", and then both of them tossed their shoes on the mound. Jon shrugged at the hostess and took off his Topsiders, lobbing them over his shoulder.

Later that night, Jon's premonition about Carver's sleeping arrangement came true, although it was alligators, not sharks that spooked him out of the hammock. As the adventure began to unravel, he finally persuaded Carver to bunk with Bailey on the sleeper-sofa, a double victory since she seemed to welcome the company in the new surroundings.

* * *

Sunday, July 31st

Sunday morning began with donuts and cartoons on the sleeper sofa. Afterwards, they hiked to Fat Tire Bike Rental, and then pedaled their way to the Tybee Lighthouse, where Jon helped Carver count all one hundred and seventy-eight steps on their climb to the top. They took pictures at the caretaker's cottage before biking over to The Sugar Shack for an early lunch of cheeseburgers and fries.

The afternoon attractions included bike racing and sand castles. In the course of the day, only one question came up about the separation. Bailey wanted to know why the 'vorce meant they had to spend so much time at Grandmommy's house. Jon dodged the issue by promising them more trips to the beach house in the future.

For the day's grand finale, Jon convinced the kids to wade into the surf for a selfie, but only after considerable plea bargaining. It ended with a promised visit to the ice cream shop on their next weekend layover. Carver offered a final protest, joining Bailey in the water only after spouting, "Dad, we can't eat ice cream if we're dead."

Before leaving Tybee, Jon called Beth to let her know they were on the way. No one answered, but he headed out so they would arrive home on time. When they pulled into the driveway, he was surprised to see her standing on the front porch. Directing the children inside for a bath, she helped them with their bags and motioned for Jon to wait. A short time later, she stepped out and found Jon sitting at the top of the steps.

"Carver just told Bailey not to worry about alligators crawling into the bathtub," Beth said.

"It's a long story, but at least they're not worried about sharks anymore," Jon said. "Did you need to see me?"

She nodded, looking toward the neighbor's house. "Jon, I've been talking to Dr. Lowe about the counseling."

"Beth, listen I'm not up for another argument—"

"I've agreed to a joint session, the three of us," she interrupted. "He believes it's in our best interest to take a step forward, even if it's a small one. One of us has to do something to foster trust in the relationship."

"So you're ready to address the trust issue?" Jon said. He got up and retreated to a porch rail. "Is this your idea or Lowe's?"

"What difference does it make?" Beth eased over and placed a hand next to his on the rail. "The question is, what do you want?"

"What about the legal—"

"Don't complicate things," she snipped.

Jon watched as she withdrew her hand, clenching it into a fist before turning her back to him.

"Do I need to call Lowe?" Jon said.

"I've already scheduled an appointment for Tuesday morning. If it's important to you, I'm sure you'll make time, even on short notice."

Chapter 40
Monday, August 1ˢᵗ
9:10 P.M.

The secret to a successful stakeout is good food. Taming the more primitive impulses frees the mind to be more fully attuned to one's surroundings. At least that was Captain's philosophy.

The Oyster Bar was situated on the banks of the Cooper River, and by Lowcountry standards its charm occupied a rather narrow spectrum, somewhere between a dive and a shack. The distinction bore little significance since county officials were on the verge of closing down the establishment. Nevertheless, the locally owned restaurant was run by Captain's former galley-mate on the USS Wisconsin, serving up fried oyster po'boys, hushpuppies, and battered French fries that glistened beneath a fine layer of Crisco. The sweet iced tea conformed to strict Southern standards.

Paper sacks of food sat in Jon's lap, oozing pools of golden grease as they drove down a poorly lit street. Jon had just begun to pull entrées out of one of the bags as Captain hit the brakes.

"What are we supposed to do with a gallon of tea, sandwiched inside a Toyota Corolla?" Jon said. "And by the way, what's that smell?"

"In case you've forgotten, my clients aren't exactly predisposed to daily hygiene, at least not by investment banker standards," Captain said. He swung the Toyota over to the curb, checking a business card in his hand.

"I offered to drive the Land Cruiser."

"You're lucky I let you come along at all. I'm going against everything I learned in naval intelligence. I started to bring Sanky, but he doesn't need this kind of trouble." Captain yanked the parking brake as he eyed a crumbling building across the street. "Bless your own meal and do as I say." Captain turned off the ignition and bowed his head.

"What do you mean you agreed to let me come? I was the one who was attacked." Jon slapped a po'boy against Captain's chest. "I'm actually pretty good at research, and that's all this is. We call it due diligence in the business world. And while we're on the topic, you told me you were a boat captain."

"Amen," Captain said, cutting his eyes at Jon. "I worked in naval intelligence before I steered battleships." He began to unwrap his sandwich. "Boy, do you know where you are?"

"It may surprise you, but I have been to Charleston, a time or two."

"This ain't exactly the historic district. Now let me tell you something. If this fellow's done his homework, he'd, no doubt, recognize your car. It wouldn't do to be sitting in a marked vehicle at his place of business. I'm worried he'll come walking out and spot you, as it is, and blow the whole operation."

Jon gave Captain a smirk.

They ate in silence and watched the building. When he was finished, Captain got out of the car and crossed over to the opposite sidewalk, peering inside through a glass-paneled door. Overhead, paint was peeling off the shutters, half of them hang-

ing unevenly. He checked out an adjacent alley, and then returned to the car.

"It appears the address on the business card is upstairs," Captain said, pointing to the second floor. "There's a window visible
from the alley, but no lights are burning. Just to be safe, let's lay
low for a bit, and then we'll make our move. In the meantime,
how about an update on your legal situation?"

Jon spent the next twenty minutes recapping the most recent
events, while Captain listened intently. Afterwards, he waited
patiently as Captain picked at his teeth with a toothpick, until
finally he couldn't bear the silence any longer. "So what do you
think?"

"Any chance the van out at the beach had South Carolina
plates?" Captain said.

"I can't rule it out, but I wasn't close enough to tell."

"So we've got nothing to connect it to this place. And that e-
mail you found on your laptop, do you think it's got anything to
do with this?"

"Whoever sent it had access to my house out on Skidaway,
which definitely means Beth is involved. But I haven't figured out
how she knew about my argument with Michael, much less his e-
mail address."

"Maybe it's an inside job. Could she have been working with
someone at Stone & Associates?"

Jon shook his head. "I haven't thought about that, but then
again I was never in naval intelligence."

"That's real funny." Captain tossed his toothpick out the window and explained the plan before slipping out of the car. He
entered the front entrance of the building, but was back on the
sidewalk minutes later, motioning for Jon to join him.

Jon jumped out and lost sight of Captain as he slipped into
the alley across the street. Sprinting after him, he worked his way

deeper into the alley until it dead-ended at a dumpster. Captain stood waiting for him.

"A sign inside says he's been locked out of the office, at least until he pays three months of back rent. The landlord put a padlock on the door."

"What's plan B?"

"Right over your head, Boy," Captain said. "We'll climb up on the dumpster, and then shinny up the fire escape. I'll go first and you can take the flank." He pulled himself up onto the steel ladder and scaled a couple of rungs before looking down. "Hurry along, now."

Jon hesitated, listening as the fire escape creaked under Captain's weight. Then he mounted the dumpster and climbed up after him. When they reached the second floor landing, there were two windows within reach. To their surprise, one was raised a few inches, and Captain leaned over and lifted the sash. It squeaked, but put up little resistance. He turned back to Jon, whispering, "I'll crawl through first and get a bearing. You wait 'til I give you the signal."

Captain disappeared headfirst through the window, and Jon waited until he stuck an arm out, motioning him inside. He slid through the opening and stood up, waiting for his eyes to adjust. When he looked over, Captain was gesturing for him to draw the blinds. He took care of them, and then headed to the other side of the room, where Captain was motioning again.

Jon noticed a large metal desk pushed up against a wall. Captain panned a penlight across it, revealing a mound of folders and papers. The light continued up the wall, where a collection of photographs clung to a corkboard. A pair of file cabinets flanked the left side of the desk, and to the right another desk sat away from the wall in the middle of the room. The front door to the office was visible, just beyond it. Captain pointed the light back to the first desk, reaching out and turning on a small lamp.

"Listen up. We've got to move quickly." Captain looked around the room. "I'll check the desk, and you take a look in the file cabinets."

"What's that?" Jon said, gesturing next to the corkboard.

Captain followed his gaze, stopping at a frame on the wall. He dropped into the desk chair, rubbing a hand across his face. "It looks like a business permit."

"It expired two years ago."

"Not surprised," Captain said. "Let's get to work."

Jon walked over to the first cabinet and tugged on a drawer. It was locked, so he gave it a second try before returning to the desk. "Did you find any keys over here?"

Captain pulled out a drawer and tossed over a key ring. "Try these."

Jon worked the locks, eventually hitting on the right key. The top drawer opened with a squeal, revealing a batch of discolored files, like old newspaper clippings. He decided they weren't relevant and moved on to the next drawer. It contained alphabetized files beginning with the letter *F*, all too old to be relevant. The third and fourth drawers offered more of the same. He found a key to the second cabinet and started in.

The files were newer, but disorganized. He searched the top drawer, where he thought the *B's* might be located, but there was no Browning folder to be found. He closed the drawer, just as Captain called out.

"Take a look at this. My eyes aren't too good in this light, but that looks like your car to me."

Jon took the negative, holding it up to the desk lamp, able to make out an image of the Z4 parked in front of Brenda's townhouse. Captain handed over an envelope and instructed Jon to put it inside.

Back at the file cabinet, a scan of the top two drawers was unproductive, but about halfway through the third, Jon discovered a file labeled "South Coast". Pulling it out, he found copies of the photo exhibits used in Hallworth's deposition, as well as a few additional shots. He continued to rummage through the contents, finding receipts for film developing, gas, Wendy's, and a room at the Best Western in Savannah. When he took another look inside the drawer, he noticed a receipt sitting in the bottom. As he read it, his heart pounded. Walking over to the desk, he lowered his hand beneath the lamp for Captain to see.

"You hit the jackpot," Captain said. The words "Home Hardware" were printed across the top. A little further down, it had a description, "24 in. solid", and a price of "$8.99". The date matched perfectly.

"I found something else," Jon said. He returned to the file cabinet and retrieved a folder. "These documents prove he has been working for someone at South Coast." Jon rifled through more receipts and a series of handwritten invoices made out to the church.

As they mulled over the find, both suddenly froze as a floorboard creaked behind them. Captain turned the penlight on a door in the rear of the office. It parted slowly, and then swung open all at once.

"Who's there?" a man shouted. He stumbled out, wearing a wrinkled t-shirt and fatigues. His face was covered in stubble and he clung to a bottle of Thunderbird.

Captain motioned for Jon to stay put, and then slowly got up and approached the man. "Monday night cleaning crew, mate."

The man steadied himself, looking from Captain to Jon. "Hey, a cleaning crew? I don't have—"

"The landlord sent us." Captain grabbed him by the shoulders and spun him around.

"Son of a bitch is going to throw me out, is he?" The man swiped a hand across his mouth as Captain nudged him along. Then he stopped and twisted, pointing at Jon. "Hey—"

Captain shoved him into the back room. "You mustn't distract the workers." After closing the door, he returned to the desk. "That's our man, Mr. Jesse Franks. He has a rat's nest back there, but the good news is I don't think he'll be any more bother."

Jon resumed his search in the file cabinet, pulling out another folder and tucking it under his arm. In the last drawer, he found a Colt 38 snub nose. He called Captain over for a look, but they left it, undisturbed. Jon locked the cabinet and returned to the desk. "Are there any signs of my driver's license?"

"Afraid not, but I found this," Captain said, waving an invoice. Franks had handwritten "Elizabeth Browning" at the top, but there were no dates or amounts.

"It looks like he was in the process of setting up the Browning file. I found this, but no receipts were inside." Jon shook the folder, showing Captain it was empty. "Why do you think he would bill Beth and South Coast?"

Captain held the blank invoice up for a closer look. "Maybe he was working for both of them, or possibly there was confusion over who was going to pay? Of course, we don't know what else he intended to bill, but one thing's clear. He knows them both."

Jon looked at Captain and ran a hand through his hair. "Captain, does this bother you? Snooping around in a man's private records?"

"Do you really want to discuss this now?"

"It just seems a bit ironic that you're a preacher of sorts, and here you are breaking and entering."

"There's two sides to a coin, Boy. The way I see it, a person can be the devil, himself, or an angel. Now you're supposing Franks to be a devil. But I see it a bit differently. Did it ever occur to you he might be an angel?"

"Are you suggesting an angel attacked me?"

"I suspect they're not going to erect a monument to him down at that park of yours, but you have to admit he fell from heaven." Captain pointed up. "He dropped from the sky and left his calling card. Some might call that a holy hunch."

"What if it was meant for the police, not us?"

"You're the one who kept the card from the police, so if reconciliation is in order, I suggest you take it up with the Almighty."

"Touché," Jon said. "Did you check the other desk?"

"Nothing."

Jon turned to the door where Franks had appeared earlier. "I'm going to check the back room. Maybe he has my license in there."

"Careful not to rouse him," Captain said. "He seems pretty tame, but you never know. I'm going to take a look in the closet, and then we need to get out."

Grabbing the penlight, Jon crossed over to the door in back and slipped inside. Franks was fast asleep, snoring atop a foldout cot next to the wall. Jon searched through his pockets and found his wallet. Easing it out, he thumbed the contents. The driver's license was still inside, so he removed it and replaced the wallet. As he turned to leave, he noticed a bookshelf in the corner.

Jon moved closer, realizing the shelves were packed with shoeboxes. He pointed the penlight at the labels on the boxes, discovering they were alphabetized. Piles of cassette tapes spilled over the tops. He located the box labeled *S*, but found nothing. Then he tried *H* for Hallworth—nothing. On the top shelf, he found the *B*'s. As he dug into the box, he uncovered a tape labeled "Browning". Then beneath it, he found four more. After examining the labels, he stuffed all five into his jacket.

As he started for the door, Jon made a detour over to the cot where Franks was still sleeping. He removed some cash from his pocket and counted it out, dropping it on Franks's chest. "Two hundred a tape, like we agreed." He turned off the penlight and walked out, closing the door behind him.

"Any luck, Boy?"

"I found my license."

Chapter 41
Tuesday, August 2nd
10:30 A.M.

Jon paced in the waiting room with a cell phone to his ear, trying hard to calm his suspicions. An answering machine beeped over the line, and he flipped the phone shut, cutting his eyes at the closed receptionist window. Lowe had left him waiting for the past thirty minutes. Even stranger was the fact that Beth hadn't shown up. He stuffed the phone in his pocket and picked up a copy of *Psychology Today*. When he recognized the cover from his last visit, he tossed it in a chair.

The deposition photographs loomed in Jon's head, elevating an already heightened uneasiness about the appointment. With any luck, Hallworth's tactics would remain within the legal process, where they belonged, sparing him the prospect that today's counseling session was about to turn into an inquisition. The possibility gave him a bad feeling, especially since he had just learned that certain questions about South Coast would have to wait. According to voicemail, both David Stephens and Randall Phipps were out of town for the week, which meant a face-to-face meeting to get to the bottom of the church's connection to Jesse Franks was days away.

When the receptionist finally appeared, she escorted Jon into Lowe's office. Lowe sat in the center of the room, and next to him Beth was seated with a pile of tissues in her lap. A torrent of tears flowed down her cheeks.

"I'll just wait outside," Jon said, turning to leave.

"Jonathon, I'll be with you shortly," Lowe said over a shoulder.

As he returned to the hallway, Jon could already tell the situation wasn't good. His stomach felt queasy, and he closed his eyes, trying to hold back images playing in his mind.

He looked up as Lowe entered the hall.

"My apologies for the delay." Lowe folded his arms, propping himself against the door. "Jonathon, I'd like to clear the air about our last meeting. I realize it must have been difficult for you to set aside that experience in order to be here today, so for time's sake I'll lay my cards on the table. I need your help." He paused, looking somewhat weary. "Beth arrived in pretty bad shape this morning. We've had a long talk, and quite frankly, I've just prescribed medication for her."

"What brought this on?"

"Simply stated, she's having an anxiety attack. And unfortunately, they're rarely isolated incidents. She'll need to be treated for the foreseeable future," Lowe said. "But despite the setback, she wants to carry on with the session."

"If it's of any consolation, I've seen these bouts before."

"That wouldn't surprise me. Given all that has happened since our last meeting, may I ask what your expectations are for today?"

"I'm here at Beth's request."

"I'm glad to hear that," Lowe said. "I believe you can make a difference, if you are willing to listen to her. It just may be the catalyst we need for a breakthrough."

"I'll do everything in my power."

"That's all I ask." Lowe paused, as if wrestling with his thoughts. "If you don't mind, I'd like to keep this between us, but things have taken a bad turn for Beth since you moved out. I'm sensing she's somewhat overwhelmed by her newfound responsibilities, but mostly the prospect of single motherhood. The change has been too much, too fast for her."

"That may be true, but this started weeks ago."

"Nevertheless—"

"She brought it all upon herself. Are you saying she's changed her mind?"

"Yes and no." Lowe held out his hands. "I'm offering you both a chance for healing, but it will require time."

"And do you intend to get to the facts?"

"Without question," Lowe said, delving into Jon's eyes. "Today is the first step in saving your marriage." He placed a hand on Jon's shoulder and led him into the office.

As they entered, Beth remained seated with a box of tissues, avoiding eye contact. Lowe offered Jon the chair next to her and grabbed a pad from his desk. When he returned, Lowe pulled up a chair, facing them.

"I am encouraged that both of you have agreed to be here this morning. It is a very good sign. I would like to reassure you that all things are possible with God. By his grace, he will provide you with the strength to drive out these demons and begin healing this marriage."

Jon looked away, shifting in his seat.

"Jonathon, I sense a bit of apprehension, but that's normal as we get underway." Lowe paused to write on the pad. "If you will allow me a professional courtesy, I am sure your concerns will be addressed in due time. Now, Beth has come to the session with a heavy heart. Deep down, it is important for you both to release your emotions before we can honestly deal with the facts, leading us to our objective, which is reconciliation." He reached out to Beth, who was now staring at a crumpled tissue. "Beth, I would like for you to kick off the discussion. And please, take all the time you need."

Beth dabbed at the puffiness under her eyes. "I'm terrified about what's happening to my marriage." Tears welled up once again. "I've turned into little more than a bundle of nerves, especially when I'm around Jon. And I—"

"Every time I try to discuss—"

"Jonathon," Lowe interrupted.

"I don't think I can't do this," Beth said, shaking her head.

"I believe you can," Lowe reassured. "You're in a safe place now. Take your time."

She wrestled with the sniffles, but finally broke through. "It all started at my women's Bible study. We were discussing how each of us labors with burdens from our past, how we can be paralyzed by guilt feelings. When necessary, we are to seek forgiveness from those who may have been hurt."

"I understand," Lowe said.

"So I prayed, and after a period of time I was overcome with a mysterious presence. In my heart, the time had come to heal these personal indiscretions." She pressed a hand to her chest. "I made a decision to cast off the unhealthy yoke that had been laid upon my marriage."

Jon leaned forward in his chair and stared at the bookcase as Lowe shot him a look. "Go on, please."

"It was late, and we were alone in our bedroom. After I began to talk to him, Jon looked at me like . . ."

"Take a breath," Lowe said. He jotted on the pad.

"When I was a little girl, one night my mother admitted a terrible mistake to my daddy. She had overdrawn the bank account, and he became furious . . . He threw the checkbook at her. She was upset and called him a name. Then he slapped her."

"That's got nothing to do with this," Jon said.

"Beth, why do you think this particular incident came to mind?" Lowe asked.

"It was the look in Jon's eyes. I believe I saw what my mother must have seen. And I'm certain I had the same feelings." Beth's entire body suddenly shivered. "I'm shaking, just talking about it."

"What happened next?" Lowe said.

"It was the following week . . . Jon went crazy in our bedroom. That's the only way to describe it. He started throwing things, destroying our beautiful—"

"Beth."

Lowe placed a hand on Jon's arm to silence him.

"Continue."

"All I could think about was my dear children, and I ran down the hall with him screaming after me. I locked the door in one of their rooms, gathering my babies into my lap." Beth wrapped her arms around herself. "I couldn't bear for them to see what was happening."

"You're doing fine," Lowe said.

"Two days later, there was only silence between us. I knew we had unfinished business, so I sat down to talk to him. For some reason, he changed the confession and put words in my mouth. He told me I was promiscuous and accused me of sleeping around, even violating our marriage. But I never said any of that." Her body started shaking again as she slumped in the chair. "I tried to reassure him that he needed help, but he started making demands. When I refused, he got angry. He'd already destroyed our bedroom, but this time Jon went outside and trashed the pool. By God's grace, the children weren't within striking distance." She started to cry.

"We're going to need a moment," Lowe said to Jon.

Jon stepped out, and after a lengthy stint in the waiting room, he returned to find Beth calm once again. Lowe reconvened the session.

"Beth, is there anything else you would like to say?"

"At the time, I didn't understand his violent behavior. It wasn't the person I fell in love with, or the man I married. But then I began to remember." Beth played with a tissue. "Those memories prompted me to look into his family history. It was painful, but the process led me to something entirely unexpected. I know it's a fear that all women harbor at some point in their lives, but in my case it was real . . . she was real. And it's the reason I've retained Mr. Hallworth." Beth fumbled in her purse for a photo. "I'm talking about Brenda Simpson."

"I can't just sit here and take this anymore." Jon came out of his seat. "This is—"

"Somebody did this to her," Lowe snapped.

"It's all lies."

"I'm afraid . . . we'll have to end with that." Lowe cut his eyes at Jon, and then helped Beth out of her chair, shouldering her to the door.

When Lowe returned, Jon was standing next to the window.

"This is a total waste of time," Jon said.

"You didn't want to hear it earlier, but the pattern is obvious. There is the matter of your family history, an irregular MMPI—"

"So now it's irregular?"

"An irregular MMPI, suggesting pathology and abusive—"

"Let's be perfectly clear. I have never abused anyone."

"Jon, abuse takes many forms. Often it's physical, but not always. It can be mental as well."

"Then I'm the one being abused."

"We've already been through this. You don't seem to understand. It started in your childhood, and now you're repeating the pattern. Without treatment, you'll never escape the cycle. It's likely you'll even pass it on to your children." Lowe paced over to his desk. "Can't you hear her plea? And think of the children. The alternative isn't pretty."

"What alternative?"

"I'll recommend a complete separation from your family."

"You can't do that."

"Try me," Lowe said. "With the information I've collected, the Department of Family and Children's Services will file a restraining order. Beth won't have to lift a finger, so don't force me into this scenario. I'm fighting for you, Jonathon. If you don't trust me, Sam Hallworth is going to put you through a living hell."

Jon ran a hand through his hair. "You're leaving me with no options."

"I'm doing my best to help you. Sign the release . . . It will diffuse Beth's concerns, but more importantly, it will protect your children."

"Do you really believe the things she's saying?" Jon said.

"Counseling is give and take. If her story is fabricated, it will come out in the counseling. And I'll be honest, she's making associations that aren't particularly healthy."

"Then tell her."

"At the proper time. Between you and me, there's an obsession with material objects. One in particular."

"What do you mean?"

Lowe gave him a sideways look. "Your new car. What type of vehicle is it?"

"BMW."

"Right, she's fixated on it, just like this Brenda Simpson."

"That's ridiculous."

"She's made herself physically sick over some story about how the governor wants you to run his next campaign. Do you have any idea how inadequate she feels in comparison?"

"And that's my fault?"

"She needs your commitment. And I can help . . . South Coast can as well. But more importantly, the divorce suit will be dropped." Lowe walked over and placed a hand on Jon's shoulder. "We desperately need a win. That's why I'm unyielding on the release. It's a symbol of hope to Beth."

"Okay listen, there's clearly more going on here than I realized. This association problem . . . Is it something you can work on?"

"Making the diagnosis is half the solution."

Jon drew his hands down his face. "I guess you're right."

"All I need is your signature." Lowe reached into his desk and pulled out a prescription pad. "Now, allow me to offer a little something to help you get through this."

Chapter 42
Tuesday, August 2nd
10:00 P.M.

Jon sat back at the makeshift desk in his bedroom and popped the cork on a bottle of Wally's Hut. He poured wine into a glass and took a sip, spinning around to lift a briefcase-sized safe out of a dresser drawer. Dropping it onto the desktop, he thumbed a combination, and then lifted the lid. The wine tasted a little dry as he took another sip, removing five cassette tapes and a tan envelope. Turning the envelope on end, he shook out a cassette and a note, and then laid them next to the other tapes, ones he now thought of as the Charleston tapes.

He was no expert, but the handwriting on the tapes seemed to match the note from the Tybee Island Causeway. "Browning" was scribbled in large letters on all of them, along with dates that he assumed would pinpoint the sequence of events. Additional names had been written in parenthesis at the bottom of three, the remaining two being exceptions. One was labeled, "Genesis", and the other, "The Big Peach".

Much to his disbelief, the names were all familiar. Jon focused on the dates, noting they were recorded within the last few weeks. Studying the original tape from the causeway, he was confused as to why Franks had chosen to tease him with it, since it was clearly the second in a series. The memory of the initial tape drop on the night of the governor's reception momentarily distracted him, drawing images to mind that he preferred to forget. He set the cassette aside, consoling himself with another sip of wine.

He selected the oldest tape, which was the one with the "Genesis" label, and inserted it into a cassette player. The recording started with the sound of a closing door, followed by footsteps. They grew louder until a man's voice cut in.

"I was surprised you called," the man said, his tone a bit raspy.

"I've got a business proposition for you," a woman responded.

"I work for the preacher, but you know that." The man's voice faded, like he was moving about the room. "But I'm listening."

"You'll be happy to know I picked up a bottle of Thunderbird." There was a squeaky sound, like rusty springs. "Why don't you come over, and I'll explain the offer?"

"I don't get it," the man said.

"Shhhh . . ." she whispered.

"What is this . . . Some kind of—"

He was cut off mid-sentence as a skirmish broke out, finally ending in blasts of heavy breathing.

"Damn lady, what's the idea? I figured you for one of those, you know, 'til death do us part types."

Jon felt the hair on his neck stand up as the woman responded.

"Yeah, that's right, only in case, it's more of a short-term strategy."

After a period of extended silence, Jon ejected the tape. He wiped his forehead and paused to reflect. *Genesis . . . the beginning? What is Franks up to?* He dropped the cassette on the desktop and passed over the second tape, grabbing the third and inserting it into the player.

"Stein" was printed at the bottom of the label. It instantly produced vivid mental images as the recording started with playful bantering between Stein and a woman over cocktails. Jon recognized a metallic clanking in the background, the sound of a halyard striking a sailboat mast. The conversation waxed on over a second round of drinks that seemed to never end. Finally, Stein suggested they retire into the stateroom, but the woman declined, carrying on about the view of the night sky on deck.

There was shuffling before he heard the sound of a cushion that gave off a soft hiss.

"Now isn't that better?" the woman said.

There was rustling, interspersed with inflections of heavy breathing.

The woman giggled. "Stop, I'll spill my wine."

A motor started up in the distance, but quickly faded away.

"So tell me, why the sudden interest in Chatham Medical Devices?" Stein said. "Two hundred and fifty thousand is a lot of money, especially since our stock hasn't gone public."

"Are you suggesting it's a bad investment?"

"That depends on who you ask."

"I'm asking you."

"We have to be careful." Stein hesitated. "I'll put you in touch with a broker who can handle the transaction for you."

"That's the spirit . . . This calls for a celebration."

"Whoa . . . the Rolex never leaves my wrist," Stein said. "How about some music?"

A salsa beat struck up in the background.

"You're not going to make me dance alone, are you?"

"Leave me out of this. You're the entertainment tonight," Stein said, laughing.

Jon stopped the recording, running a hand through his hair. He rewound the tape and listened to most of it a second time. Afterwards, he grabbed the wine bottle and headed out to the porch for some fresh air. The wind and surf offered little comfort as he nursed another glass of wine before going back inside.

Inserting the "The Big Peach" tape, the recording started once again with the sound of a door closing. There was silence for the next few moments, not even footsteps. Then a voice broke in, but the quality was poor.

"May I say, time has certainly done you no harm, my dear," a man said.

"Aren't you the gentleman? It has been awhile."

"Well, no doubt about it, you were the belle of the ball last night. And I must say, that dress is intoxicating," the man said. Ice rattled inside a glass. "You'll have a drink with me?"

"In Savannah, a lady doesn't wear a dress in public twice."

"There're a lot of things a lady doesn't do."

"You're so bad," she teased.

"I just couldn't get the damn thing out of my mind. Any man who didn't take a second look is a fool."

"It's the least I could do, since you were kind enough to extend the invitation."

"How about a toast to Jonathon?"

"Don't you think that's taking things a bit too far?"

"My apologies. Now, if you'll excuse me, I need to step into the other room for a telephone call . . . and to remove the foot from my mouth. When I return, I'm hoping you'll still be here, looking as pretty as ever."

A door closed, and there was a series of wispy sounds, like pillows fluffing. The recording went silent for a time, interrupted only by an occasional rattling of ice.

When the man returned, he said, "You read my mind."

The tape continued without revealing the man's identity, although his voice was distinctly Southern. When it ended, Jon set it aside with the others.

From the start, the fifth tape troubled him the most. He studied the label, where the name "Porter" had been scribbled. Once he was only a few minutes into it, he realized he'd had enough of what was now turning into a familiar theme. Jon's attention drifted in and out of the conversation as his thoughts gravitated to another concern. *Were there copies of the tapes?* The realities were starting to hit home, revealing betrayals he was only beginning to fathom.

He emptied the wine bottle into his glass, and then retreated to the porch. Stretching out on the hammock, he wondered if he had done the right thing by keeping the tapes a secret from Captain. With everything he had just learned, he realized he would have to come up with a new plan. But one thing was certain. Jesse Franks knew everything.

Chapter 43
Wednesday, August 3rd
8:30 A.M.

How do you break into a church?

Jon had toyed with the idea for the past two days, ever since the visit to Jesse Franks's office. If the saints were watching over South Coast's three hundred and fifty thousand square feet of stucco and glass architecture, there was no telling what act of God he was setting himself up for.

Jon slid out of the Z4 and started across the parking lot, glancing at a row of white Lincolns parked snugly in their reserved spaces. As he passed by, he couldn't help but notice the Blackman Lincoln plates on the front of each, a local dealer who also happened to be a major contributor to South Coast's capital programs. He wondered who held the pink slips.

Jon left the palm-lined parking lot and headed up a walkway toward the executive offices. Over the rooftop he could see the bell tower rising up, facing the highway out front. The sound of rushing water stopped him as he peered over a hedge at a small pool drinking in the flow of a manmade stream. A winding path diverted him to the water's edge, where a bench was perched among shade trees, alive with the melody of singing birds. Next to the bench, he noticed a plaque designating the area as the

"Meditation Pond". A nearby speaker resembling a rock played an arrangement of heavenly music. He turned and headed for the entrance.

"Good morning, ladies," Jon said, greeting a pair of attractive receptionists as he entered. His eyes were drawn to a display of oil paintings on the wall behind them, the vibrant colors enhanced by lighting from the ceiling.

"Dr. Browning," one of the receptionists said. "Where on earth have you been keeping yourself?"

"The usual places, only I've just realized I'm running behind on a project for Randall. Is he in?"

"Was Brother Phipps expecting you?" she asked. "I'm afraid I have some disappointing news."

"He told me to drop by any time."

"Unfortunately, he's out of the office this week. Is there something you needed right away?"

"I'm afraid so. But I don't actually need to see Randall, just his project files. It's a banking matter, if you know what I mean."

"We're only supposed to answer the phones," she said, looking over at her associate.

"I understand. I don't want to get anyone in trouble." Jon paused, studying one of the paintings. Moses stood with his staff raised above the sea. The sky was filled with dark, ominous clouds. "Is it possible to reach him by phone?"

The receptionist hesitated. "Darlene, could you let Dr. Browning into Brother Phipps's office? I need to stay close to the phones. The Women's Council is supposed to call about a brunch for the Middle East Relief Fund, and you know how they are."

Darlene reached into her desk and pulled out a key ring. "I'll fix you right up, Dr. Browning." She jingled out of her seat and motioned for Jon to follow her into a hallway. Just past a second reception area, she unlocked an office and turned on the lights.

"Brother Phipps's assistant has the day off, so you'll have to see me if you need anything else."

"Thank you, Darlene." Jon was about to step inside, but had a second thought. "Randall mentioned that David Stephens has one of the files. Is it okay if I interrupt him?" He pointed to a nearby door with Stephens's name on it.

"Today just isn't your day. Brother Stephens is out as well. I can get you in his office, if you know what you're looking for."

"I'll be sure to lock up," Jon said. "Thanks again." He slipped into Randall's office.

Jon sat down and opened a credenza behind an oversized desk. He worked his way through the drawers, ultimately finding nothing. Afterwards, he checked the desk, but with the same result. Somewhat disappointed, he looked around the room and concluded there was no reason to waste any more time there, and then he hurried out the door, checking the reception area as he headed over to Stephens's office.

A search of Stephens's credenza and desk yielded no payoff, dampening his enthusiasm until he spotted a door on the far wall. Upon examination, it was locked. When a second trip to the desk failed to turn up any keys, he headed back over to rattle the hinges. With frustration mounting, an idea suddenly struck, and he reached for his wallet and pulled out a credit card.

To his surprise, the card slipped effortlessly into the door jam. With a click, he entered a storage room. A stack of boxes sat just beyond the door, and behind them, a table blocked access to a row of file cabinets against the back wall. He climbed over the table and squeezed into a tight spot in front of the first cabinet. Starting from the top, he worked his way through the drawers and then across to a second cabinet, both with no results. In the third, his luck changed, uncovering files labeled with names of various church members. He wasted no time zeroing in on a Browning folder.

There were handwritten notes, including Beth's request for church counseling. He scanned the pages, stopping often on phrases containing the word "abuse", double-underlined. Behind the notes was a lengthy history of the Browning's, liberally spinning the abuse theme like tar and feathers to his family tree. Lowe's words suddenly hit him, but he put them aside, knowing now wasn't the time. He flipped more pages, pulling out a record of current year contributions to the church. The statement displayed Jon's name at the top, but as he reviewed the transactions, he was surprised by his surprising generosity.

Jon dug a little further, accidentally spilling the contents of the folder on the floor, where he spotted several canceled checks made out to Jesse Franks. He cleaned up the mess and examined the checks closer, each written for a thousand dollars, with the phrase "Marital Counseling" printed in the memo section. In the back of the file, he found copies of Hallworth's photographs from the deposition. He closed the folder and headed back into the office, making a U-turn when he noticed a Rolodex sitting on the credenza. After flipping through it, he extracted Jesse Franks's business card.

"Dr. Browning." A head popped into the office. "Are you finding everything you need?" It was Darlene.

Jon froze as a man in uniform appeared next to her. "I was just working on Stephens's files." The security guard smiled as Jon fumbled to get out his next words. "Is there a copy machine nearby?"

"It's out here in the reception area," she said. "Anything else?"

"You're an angel, Darlene." Jon waited for the duo to depart, and then headed back into the storage room, dropping the folder on the table. Returning to the file cabinet, he scanned dozens of alphabetized files. A Blackman file caught his attention, and he peeked inside, finding notes and contribution records. After a bead of sweat hit the sheet in his hand, he decided to move along. Giving the last cabinet a tug, he realized it was locked. He ran a hand through his hair, and then reached for a letter opener on the table. It slipped easily enough into the lock, but no amount of jiggling seemed to do the trick. Just as he was about to move on, the copy machine beeped, giving him another idea.

A trip to the receptionist's desk produced a key ring, and within minutes, he was sorting through files once again. In the bottom drawer, he found one labeled, "Property Purchase–State of Georgia", and inside, a contract for thirty acres of land adjoining the church. He scanned the first page to confirm the seller. Two pages later, he found a sales price of thirty thousand dollars.

Jon bit his tongue and moved on, turning to the last page of the contract. At the bottom, David Stephens, Richard Stone, and John Edward Callahan had all signed, the date coinciding with the governor's last visit to Savannah. Jon headed for the copy machine.

After an extended period at the copier, he replaced the files and was ready to depart, when a thought struck him. Digging back into one of the cabinets, he uncovered a Callahan folder. He had skipped over it previously, but now it raised serious questions, especially since the governor wasn't a member at South Coast. A second pass through the bottom drawer produced a Stone file, which he carried out to the copier, along with the governor's. When finished, he started for Stephens's office, only to have Darlene surprise him again.

"Brother Stephens is on the phone and would like to speak to you. You can take it in his office." She smiled and headed back down the hallway.

Jon dropped the files on Stephens's desk and picked up the telephone. "This is Jonathon Browning."

"Why are you in my office?" Stephens said.

"The bank needs an update on Phase III—"

"Nonsense."

"Randall indicated you have the contract on the land purchase."

"Forget about the land. The bank isn't involved."

"I need the purchase price for my projections."

"Tell the bank it's immaterial."

"They have specifically requested the information."

"Get out," Stephens said. "I am instructing Darlene to lock up behind you."

"Maybe I should talk to Randall—"

"Leave Randall out of this," Stephens shouted. "He's got plenty to worry about without having to babysit a bean counter."

"As you wish, David." Jon hung up the phone.

Chapter 44
Wednesday, August 3rd
2:30 P.M.

Wednesday afternoon found Jon huddled in a corner at the Bull Street Library, focused on the task of sorting through the maze of documents he had uncovered in Stephens's office. He spent most of his time studying the documents in the Browning folder, advancing more quickly through the Stone and Callahan files, afterwards relocating to a library computer where he logged on to an electronic periodical database. A search on South Coast Church produced a list of articles on the church's involvement in the community, all from the *Savannah Press*, with the exception of an interview Randall did with a regional magazine. None mentioned the aggressive building program or the purchase of land from the state.

Jon conducted an additional search on the state government's website. Despite hundreds of references on land issues, he found nothing related to the option Stephens had secured from the governor, or South Coast taking title to state-owned property. Frustrated that he had turned up no new information, he packed up and left when the library closed.

Back on Tybee, Jon stopped off at MacElwee's Seafood House for dinner, opting for a corner seat at the bar. He ordered a Bass

Ale, hoping it would help wash away the lack of progress he had made that day. Even with the church files raising a myriad of questions, the library search had delivered nothing in the way of answers. Names, dates, and contracts turned over in his mind as he barely touched his dinner. After a second beer, he lost track of time and watched a performer set up his gear, afterwards feigning interest in a news broadcast on a television over the bar. When he noticed it was growing dark outside, he drained his mug and paid the bill.

Heading down Butler Avenue, he passed the DeSoto Beach Hotel and turned onto 7th Street, noting that the beach combers had vacated most of the curbside parking. As he neared the end of the street, his pulse quickened when he spotted the car. Even with daylight drifting away, he had no trouble recognizing the Lexus parked in front of the Baineses' house.

Climbing out of his car, he marched to the top of the boardwalk and scanned the beach in both directions. There were few people out, and none appeared to fit her profile. He headed back to the house and mounted the steps, slowing as he slipped inside the screen door. The door to the living area was slightly ajar, and a flashback of the recent attack coursed through his mind as he inched it open. His eyes were immediately drawn to the light over the stove. Crossing the room into the kitchen, he dropped his satchel on the counter next to an open bottle of wine.

As he turned back to the living room, he noticed a hat on the sofa. A designer purse peeked out beneath it. He passed them up and slipped out onto the porch, moving toward the bedroom. He proceeded slowly in the near darkness, holding his breath. As he approached the bedroom, he discovered that the door was open, but there was no light on inside. He grabbed a nearby lounge chair before reaching inside the door for the light switch. An amber dot glowed across the room, lighting up the blackness like a firefly. He flipped on the switch.

Their eyes instantly met, and then like the uncorking of a champagne bottle, Beth's manicured fingers removed a cigarette from her puckered lips, unleashing what looked like dragon's breath, spewing out of an abyss. Without blinking, she grasped the bedcovers, tucking a loose end under one arm.

"I like what you've done with the place," she said, lifting a wine glass off the nightstand.

Jon tossed aside the chair.

"What's with the, I'm not into you look."

"Beth, you broke into my apartment."

"Enough with the drama," she said. "How about a drink for old times' sake?"

"What are you doing here?"

"The Baines were kind enough to let me in." She set down the glass and folded her arms.

Jon backed up to the door, running a hand through his hair. A pair of jeans and blouse lay crumpled in his desk chair. "What do you want?"

"Did you and Brenda enjoy yourselves?" she said, patting the bed.

"Beth, we're not discussing anything related to that circus of a deposition you and Hallworth put on." Jon went down on a knee and checked under the bed, afterwards heading over to inspect behind the headboard. "You should leave."

"Looking for the boogieman, Darling?"

"I've learned my lesson about photographs and recordings." He crossed the room, retreating to the doorway.

"This is what you might call a distressed wife visit," she said, pressing the sheets tight against her.

"I can see you've recovered nicely since yesterday's session with Lowe."

"I didn't take the pictures, okay?" she snapped. "And what's this about recordings—of what?"

"Listen, I think it's best that you head on home."

"Very well," she said, her tone softening as she peeled back the covers to reveal an eyeful of lace and tanned curves. "I didn't come here to argue." Swinging her legs off of the bed, she slipped her toes into a pair of high heels and scooped up the wine glass, brushing against Jon as she squeezed out the door.

Jon's eyes tracked her out onto the porch, breaking his trance to duck into the kitchen for a much-needed beer. Still struggling for a bearing, he took the beer out to the porch, where Beth was now settling into the hammock, with the wine and cigarette in hand. She crossed her legs at the ankle, the tips of her red heels pointing up into the air. He raised the beer, trying his best not to stare.

Beth glanced his way. "Remember me?" She looked out toward the Atlantic, listening to the surf as it pierced the darkness.

Jon stepped over and took the cigarette, snuffing it out on the railing. She grabbed his shirt and tugged, throwing him off balance. He collapsed on top of her as she pressed her lips to his. Their drinks tipped and soaked them both, the dregs dripping to the floor. He lingered for a second, and then pulled back, crawling out and peeling the wet shirt from his skin. Beth reached up and started on the buttons.

Jon raised his hands in the air. "You can't be serious. So far you've sued me . . . stolen money . . . set me up—"

"Shhh . . ." Beth wiggled out of the hammock and steadied herself on the heels, returning to the buttons. "That's not what's on your mind."

"How did we wind up here?"

A button popped and rattled across the floor as she slipped the shirt off his shoulders.

"Nothing you've told me—"

"Jon," she said, pressing up against him. Her eyes leveled on his, letting go of the shirt. It landed in a soggy plop. "I'm here for you."

"Nice try," he said, looking into her eyes.

"Darling, we'll do things your way." She raised up on her toes and brushed his lips.

"Beth, there's no way—"

"I'm here to negotiate, surfer boy. I'm sacrificing body and soul." She kissed his shoulder. "You do remember how to close a deal?"

"Beth, I know about . . ." Jon closed his eyes as the words stuck in his throat.

"I'll tell you anything you want to know." She ran her hands down his chest. "I believe the first thing you taught me was to make yourself vulnerable." She kissed his chin. "What do you say?"

"Hallworth . . ."

She lifted his hand and kissed a finger. "That tastes good on you. What are you drinking?"

"It's . . . just a beer."

Pulling his hands around her back, she pressed them on her hips, stretching up on her toes until their lips touched. "Remember me?"

"Beth . . ." he whispered.

"I'm right here."

"I only want . . ."

She nibbled on his lip. "I know what you want."

"I only—"

"Shhh . . . Like I said . . . I'm here to negotiate."

Chapter 45
Thursday, August 4th
6:50 A.M.

Purgatory flared at sunup as Jon stirred between the sheets, waking from a deep fog. He rolled over and launched a hand across the nightstand, but came up with nothing. Abruptly, the ringing stopped. He was about to settle back into the pillow, when it started up again. Looking around, he wasn't quite sure where he had left his phone. When the caller rang a third time, he climbed out of bed and headed for the kitchen.

"Jon, Bill Davenport here." His voice was alert.

"Bill, what time is it?"

"Listen, I only have a second, but wanted to remind you about our hearing with Judge Green in two weeks."

"A hearing?"

A horn blew, followed by traffic sounds in the background. "Are you still there? My bad. I guess I forgot to call you," Davenport said. "After that circus of a deposition with Hallworth, I had a little tête-à-tête with the judge. I don't know if I mentioned it, but we're both members at the same club. Anyhow, he's agreed to a private hearing down at the courthouse. He'll put you and the wife up on the stand and give you a taste of what it's like to sit in the judgment seat. If Hallworth's got your wife thinking he's running the judicial system, she'll get the picture, pronto. Green doesn't play favorites, but he's fair."

"You want me to prepare for a hearing? Is that what you're telling me?"

"I've already got your financials. Ninety-eight percent of these cases come down to the clams." A car door slammed, and Davenport started huffing. "First rule—know your walk away position. What'd you decide about the children?"

"I want sole custody," Jon said, stepping out onto the porch.

"It takes one hell of a case for a judge to separate children from their momma. If you're going to take that route, we'll need to work on our strategy."

Jon paused, shifting the telephone to his other ear. "I'm prepared to do whatever it takes."

"Then the ball's in your court. I can't get together until the morning of the hearing."

Jon heard an echo, like heels against marble.

"Call the office and have Suzanne set up a meeting," Davenport said. "Bring anything that's pertinent to the case. You know the game. It's like show and tell."

"But shouldn't we meet before—"

"Sorry, I've got to go."

"Hold on, Bill. Dr. Lowe is pressing for the legal release. He claims he can avert the litigation, if I work with him."

"That's the shrink who's playing church with Hallworth? I've got three words for them—no, and hell no. You're living in the Bible Belt, son. Get yourself out of that pack of Pharisees and find another church. You sign that release and the pope won't be able to absolve you. You're bright, so don't go pissing in the wind. Call Suzanne." Davenport hung up.

* * *

The Ford F-250 bucked like a bronco on the washed-out ruts, kicking up dust in its wake. The road straightened out as the truck hit a mud hole and started to fishtail. Hallworth jerked the steering wheel and laughed as he glanced over at his passenger. He'd never seen the holy man in such a state of fear. It was a sight to see him off his A-game for once, almost worth foregoing a few billable hours. Stephens had requested an emergency meeting, and insisted that their offices were off-limits, especially when he heard about Rhodus.

"Why are you driving like this?" Stephens said, grabbing the dashboard and bracing himself for the next jolt.

"Gets the stress out," Hallworth said. "And in case you didn't know, I'm on the clock—billing the lovely Mrs. Browning for every second of this little adventure. Now tell me what this is all about."

"You're officially my attorney, so we're talking confidentially. Right?"

"Listen, we've been through this ad nauseam. We're ironclad, brother. Our relationship falls under the umbrella of attorney-client privilege. You're an officer of the church, shrouded by the entire separation clause bonanza, courtesy of Mr. Thomas Jefferson, himself. No sitting judge is going to force a Southern clergyman to testify against his parishioners. The Catholic Church screwed up with their little sex scandal, but that's in a whole other league."

"We're operating in the best interest of our parishioners, upholding the sanctity of God's covenants," Stephens fired back. "When it comes to our members, there's God and those he ordained. The world's going to hell faster than this truck, and I took an oath to uphold the sanctity of the church."

"Amen. And I'd ask you to preach on, but I need details."

"The serpent was in my office."

"Browning?" Hallworth said.

"That's right. He paid a visit while I was in Atlanta. I spoke to him on the telephone—he was probably sitting at my desk. He claimed he was looking for my records on the building program."

"Did he find anything?"

"I'm getting to that. I came home early to check things out, and the files were in order."

"Then what are you so worked up about?"

Stephens gazed out the window as a thicket of greenery zipped past. "Everything's there, but I can't be sure he didn't go through them."

"I've warned you to keep those files at my office. It's for your own protection," Hallworth said. "So what're we doing on the road to Sodom and Gomorrah, here?"

"Jesse Franks's business card disappeared from my Rolodex. It was there last time I contacted him, and now it's gone—after Browning's visit." Stephens clenched a fist. "So I called Franks and discovered someone broke into his office on Monday night."

"And?" Hallworth said.

"His office is a toxic waste dump, so he's clueless. But that business card ties me to Franks."

"What else was in your files?"

"The usual. But that moron, Franks, has upped the ante." Stephens pounded a fist on his knee. "I need to silence Browning, once and for all."

"What you need is that legal release on his counseling sessions."

"Exactly. But Lowe is wavering, so we have to come up with a backup plan, something solid. With the right leverage, we can threaten to drag him and the venerable Stone & Associates into a public scandal. Once that happens, he'll come begging, just like the others."

"I've told Lowe we need a little more fire and brimstone in this case." Hallworth locked the brakes, barely avoiding a ditch as the truck slid onto a side road.

"If he bucks, I'll force Richard Stone to move in and apply pressure," Stephens said. "We'll negotiate a settlement, like always."

"So you're looking for something to guarantee we can wrap this up on our terms," Hallworth said. "Hang on. We're turning in here."

The truck skidded to a stop amidst a cloud of dust that cleared quickly, revealing a house fifty feet in front of them. The structure was unpainted with piles of weathered lumber to one side, leaving the impression it was under construction. Stephens sank down in the seat, visibly unsettled by the scene. There were chickens in the front yard, scratching at a patchwork of dirt and weeds. He hadn't noticed at first, but a pack of dogs howled from behind the house, big ones from the sound of things. Noticing a barn to his left, a rooster crowed in the distance.

"Stay in the truck until I give the signal. You can feed him the finer points of the operation after I get the conversation started," Hallworth said. He opened the truck door.

"How do you . . . who is this guy?"

"This boy is a real hammerhead. He's so bad they've banned him from working on the shrimp boats. And I don't have to tell you, it's not a job that requires charm school credentials. He got himself mixed up in a little cocaine trafficking, but he's mostly known for snorting the stuff. The sheriff down here is trying to root out the dealers, so I did a little pro bono work for Rhodus. Let's just say he owes me."

"And what exactly do these credentials have to do with us?"

"Well, we've got a little quid pro quo arrangement. The man knows how to take care of business, and besides, I can bill him out as a consultant," Hallworth said. "Don't mention your profession. It might spook him. These people have a code that makes snake handling look civilized."

"Oh, that's just great," Stephens said, tossing his hands in the air.

"And take off the coat and tie." Hallworth hopped out of the truck and walked over to the barn, where a man emerged. After they talked for a while, Hallworth motioned to Stephens.

"Good afternoon," Stephens said.

The man tipped his hat. A NAPA Auto Parts advertisement was barely visible beneath the grease stains. Strings of hair hung like moss around the periphery. His bare rawhide chest glistened beneath a pair of denim overalls, the pants legs riding up inside a pair of unlaced boots.

"Rhodus, this is the man I was telling you about," Hallworth said.

As Stephens leaned against a pickup, a flurry of snarls and barking flared from cages mounted on the back. Hallworth and Stephens backed away.

"Shut up, you pack of fools," Rhodus yelled.

Stephens took another step, managing to position Hallworth between him and the dogs. He pointed at the cages. "What do you have in there, hunting dogs?"

"Them's hog dogs. That one's Winston, and that there's Churchill," Rhodus said, rather proudly. "They's both full-blooded pit bulls. Just doin' their duty." The animals hassled as they circled inside the cages.

"What's the story behind the names?" Hallworth said.

"My pa was right fond of Winston Churchill. He used to tell me stories from the Great War. They's what you might call a tribute to my old man."

"You like hunting hogs, Rhodus?" Hallworth said.

"Not my favorite kind of huntin'. I do it mostly for hire."

"People pay you to hunt hogs?" Stephens said.

"Hell yeah." Rhodus stuck both hands inside his overalls and scratched. "The islands are full of hogs. Developers'll hire you to get rid of 'em, seeing how they don't make good neighbors. Me and the boys, here, are goin' out to Skidaway this evenin'. Hogs are tearin' up their pretty little golf courses. City folk forget it was theirs to begin with."

"A lot of people live on that island. You're going to hunt right there in their backyards?" Hallworth said.

"Somebody's got to do it. Rich people don't mind hittin' them golf balls with a club, but they prefer to hire outsiders to beat their hogs."

"What do you mean?" Hallworth said.

"You boys know how to hunt a hog?"

Hallworth and Stephens shook their heads.

"That's what I thought. All it takes is a dog, a piece of rope, and a bat." Rhodus opened a box in the back of the truck and showed them the rope and a Louisville Slugger. "See you take the pit bulls and turn 'em loose. They stalk the hog, sending up a howl once they's hot on the trail. When they track him down, they grab onto his ear and drive 'em to the ground." Rhodus slammed a fist into his hand for effect. "After they's on the ground, the pit bull flips the hog over on his back and locks his jaws on him and waits for me."

"Those dogs are strong enough to flip a hog?" Stephens said.

"Them dogs can flip a Chevrolet, if they've a mind to," Rhodus said, looking at Stephens as if he didn't know anything. "So I

catch up to the dogs and the hog. And I take this . . ." He extended the rope between his hands. "I tie the hog's legs." He twirled
the rope, wrapping it around an imaginary hog. His eyes locked
onto the men to make sure they were following him. "Then I take
this . . ." Rhodus dropped the rope and pulled out the bat, shaking it a time or two. ". . . and I beat the dog off the hog."

"You do what?" Hallworth said.

"I have to get the dog off the hog." Rhodus hunched over and
swung the bat. "Otherwise, he'll tear into that hog like a bowl of
Jim Dandy. Hog ain't no good for eatin' if the dog gets into him."

"Oh, sweet Moses," Stephens said.

Rhodus looked dumbfounded, tugging at the bill of his cap.

"That's a compliment, Rhodus," Hallworth said. "You're a
man who knows how to deal with hogs."

"You boys got hog problems?" Rhodus said, spitting in the
dirt.

"Stephens, here, has a man that's charging at him like a wild
boar. I think you know what I mean."

Rhodus looked over at Stephens. "So what do you need from
me, mister?"

"It's like this. I need you to stalk and hog tie him, and then
deliver him to an address I'll provide. I don't think you'll need the
dogs, but it's up to you. Have you got a blindfold?"

"I can bag him like a sack of corn," Rhodus said, pulling a
burlap bag out of the truck. "This one's a real loser, huh?"

"The worst kind—abuses women and children," Stephens
said.

"Then why ain't you brought in the law?" Rhodus said, spitting again.

"They're afraid to call the police," Stephens said. "We want to
scare him a bit, at least until we can get more evidence."

"And he won't be no trouble? I ain't looking to tangle with no law, either," Rhodus said, directing the question at Hallworth.

"I've taken care of you before, haven't I?" Hallworth reached for Rhodus's shoulder, but then thought better.

"This guy's no match for you," Stephens said. "He's a suit—a banker."

"A banker? They's worse than a hog," Rhodus said, glancing over at the house. "I might need to teach this ol' boy a lesson."

"That's the idea," Hallworth said.

"Them bankers will take your stuff when you ain't at home," Rhodus said.

"That's right," Stephens said. "Like thieves in the night."

Chapter 46
Friday, August 5th
8:10 A.M.

Stephens stood in the doorway to Hallworth's office, hunched over from the weight of a box cradled in his arms. The previous day's adventure into Bryan County had raised sufficient issues to warrant a follow-up meeting, especially with Jon's recent activities hitting so close to home.

The windowless office had a damp cave-like feeling, reinforced by stacks of boxes in the corners and a mysterious odor that oozed out into the hallway. He noticed an oversized waste can behind the desk, the variety typically used by locals to wheel trash to the curb. A paper shredder had been mounted on the hinged lid, allowing pulverized documents to fall directly inside.

Stephens dropped the box on a conference table and pulled out a handkerchief, wiping his face. "It just occurred to me what they remind me of—burning tire rubber," he said, pointing to a cigar smoldering in the ashtray. "I think I'm going to heave."

"I'm trying to help you, choir boy," Hallworth said, sliding his shoes off the desktop.

"Then maybe you can give me a hand out at the car."

"Tricia," Hallworth yelled. He motioned for Stephens to sit. A middle-aged woman appeared at the door with a worried expression on her face. "Darling, how about going out to Mr. Stephens's car and retrieve his files." He glanced over at Stephens who was still staring at the doorway, even after Tricia had departed.

"I told Tim to expect our call this morning." Stephens walked over to the desk, fanning with the handkerchief as Hallworth punched speed dial.

"I'll try his cell phone, just in case he tries to weasel out on us." Hallworth picked up the cigar.

"This is Dr. Tim Lowe," the voice answered.

"Dr. Lowe, I believe you were anxiously awaiting our call," Hallworth said.

"Just a second," Lowe said. They heard a door close. "Can someone explain why I'm the one in the hot seat? A legal release should be a lawyer's responsibility."

"Are you saying you didn't contact him?" Stephens said.

"No one answered."

"Tim, the release has to come from you. I can't put the screws to him unless you want to incriminate us all," Hallworth said. He sucked on the cigar. "You're not supposed to breach client confidentiality, remember? That's part of your pledge of allegiance to the APA."

"I left a message, but he hasn't responded," Lowe said. "What's the backup plan?"

"We're working on it, but I have to tell you, you're looking more and more like an albatross," Stephens said. "It's not a good sign, any way you look at it. Call him back, and if he doesn't pick up, leave another message. Tell him you want the release by noon on Monday or Beth will expedite the divorce proceedings. But use a little psychology. Remind him of the progress you've made and how Beth views the release as a next step, a sign of commitment."

"Then you'll back off?" Lowe said.

"Just don't come whining to us when your cut of the payoff flies south for the winter," Hallworth said.

"Let us know if you hear anything." Stephens ended the call.

Tricia backed into the room, dragging a box into the corner. Then she disappeared, only to return minutes later with another. "Can't find 'em like that anymore," Hallworth said, winking at Stephens. Tricia grinned, and then left the room. "So I'll put Rhodus on standby for Monday night."

"Let's talk about the other half of the operation. I'm concerned about Franks," Stephens said.

"Those pictures he took were on the money."

"He's a sleaze and a drunkard." Stephens walked across the room and sat down. "When Beth and I met with him to discuss the park setup, I made it clear we only wanted to throw Jonathon off balance, shake him up a bit."

"You've worked with the guy plenty of times. That's why I trusted him—and you—for the deposition photos."

"We're not talking about an altar boy, okay. But he seems more desperate this time."

"Perhaps you'd like to clarify that for me." Hallworth leaned forward in his chair.

"He apparently interpreted my instructions to mean he was supposed to eliminate him in the park. Of course, Beth was talking to him when I left, so maybe she confused him. I don't know."

"As in . . . kill him?" Hallworth raised his eyebrows.

"I said to scare him, not murder him." Stephens shot Hallworth a look. "A sober person, especially someone in his trade, doesn't make that kind of mistake."

"Is that why he later showed up at Browning's apartment?"

"How should I know? But one thing is certain. The idiot attempted to plant a steel bar in his skull."

"You could have been an accessory to murder," Hallworth said, lighting the cigar again. "And in a public park."

"Beth said it was dark and isolated in the early morning, the perfect place to shake Jonathon off that arrogant perch of his. Quite honestly, I'm getting a little concerned about her. She's been acting a bit detached lately. Maybe I made a mistake by cutting her in, but it was the best way to make this work." Stephens stood up and began to pace.

"If she expedites the divorce, we'll be out of it sooner than planned. Hell, we may already be screwed. I think she's going to take the money and run."

"This is precisely why we have to exercise dominion over the flock. There's nothing more asinine than a depraved soul running around like she's got a free will." Stephens turned and pointed at Hallworth. "And it's the reason the holy law has been preserved and handed down to the church. So in case you haven't heard, death is an acceptable punishment for violating his covenant."

Hallworth chuckled. "Did they teach you that in seminary? What's the class called, Stoning 101?"

Stephens's face hardened. "Mock the church, if you like. We can arrange to have your membership probated for a season. Perhaps you've forgotten where you came from, that is, before you had the financial support of South Coast Church."

"Get a grip. This woman's done a number on you. I'm helping you solve the problem." Hallworth snubbed out the cigar. "Can't you laugh once in a while? I've got Rhodus lined up. What else do you want me to do?"

"There's no time to bring in a new player, so I'm afraid we're stuck with Franks," Stephens said. "Rhodus can take care of Browning, and Franks will deliver the girl to Tybee."

"No dice," Hallworth said, shaking his head. "It's no good at the beach house. We have to turn back time for this one."

Chapter 47
Saturday, August 6th
12:45 P.M.

The security system at Stone & Associates registered an entry at seven-thirty on Saturday morning. It recorded a departure at eleven-seventeen and a subsequent reentry at twelve-forty-five in the afternoon. The comings and goings were strictly by the book, bypassing a routine that would have activated the security cameras and identified both the employee and his guest. According to company security policy, all systems were normal.

A pair of Bass loafers plopped onto the desktop in Charlie's office as the hems of his Calvin Klein jeans rose up, revealing a pair of bare ankles. The navy stripes of his oxford Polo were pressed crisp and tucked snugly into his jeans.

"Next time you invite me to go drinking at lunch, remind me to run for my life," Charlie said. "I have to work this afternoon."

A cotton sundress sashayed around the desk, her bronzed legs moving heel-to-toe in airy sandals. "Beer under protest—get real, Charlie," Beth said, dropping a matching purse in a chair.

"Did I order another beer?" Charlie said, throwing his hands in the air.

"I can read your mind."

"Can you read it right now?"

"She leaned in close. "You're like a dog on a bone.""

"Beth, it's just you're so—"

"Hold that thought," she said, pressing a finger to his lips. "I love it when you drool over me. I need a favor." Tugging at the straps on her dress, she straightened up and retraced her steps.

"I'm your man," Charlie said.

She hesitated in front of a bookcase with her back to him. "If something doesn't give soon, this divorce is going to kill me."

"Tell me what you need."

"The pictures hit a nerve at the deposition, but I can see Jon's busy little mind, hard at work. He'll find a way to discredit them, and if he does, they're likely to call you as a witness. How do you feel about facing him in a courtroom?"

"No one can prove I moved the car. As for Brenda's behavior at the beach, I sent her out to Tybee on business, not to flirt with your husband."

"But you're the one who told her that Jon had more than a passing interest in her. And . . . you bought dinner."

"It's her word against mine." Charlie stood up and rounded the corner of the desk. "And I gave her cash, remember?"

"You're way too confident, Charlie," Beth said, looking away. "Sometimes I don't know if I'm going to get through this."

Charlie moved up behind her and massaged her shoulders. When she relaxed, he slid his hands down her arms. "We'll figure it out—together."

"Are you aware that he's going to make partner, if this Johnson-Medisys deal closes?"

"You're forgetting one thing. Our secret little e-mail has Richard rethinking everything. It was a stroke of genius, if I say so myself," Charlie said, puffing up again. "Did you delete it?"

"I took care of it a few nights ago," she said.

Charlie's hands settled on her hips as she turned toward him.

"I don't think it's enough to break the bond between them."

"Jon is jeopardizing Richard's deal with his old buddy, Bob Stein. And he stands to lose a lot of money, if it doesn't close."

"Don't you see it? Richard's trust in Jon runs deeper than that. That's the reason he hasn't fired him, and why we have to force his hand."

"Wait. You're saying you want me to kill the merger?" Charlie said. "If it tanks now, Richard will hold me responsible."

Beth reached around and picked up her purse. She took Charlie by the hand and led him down the hallway until they stopped in front of Jon's office. Rummaging inside the handbag, she pulled out a key and inserted it into the lock. The door swung open, and she closed it behind them. Walking over to the desk, she fingered through some files, and then proceeded to the window where she drew the curtains. Back at the desk, she turned on a lamp.

"This isn't a good idea."

"Shhh . . ." Beth seated Charlie at Jon's desk, and then wiggled around him and nestled onto a stack of papers on the desktop.

"Are you crazy? Jon could walk through that door any minute."

"You and I both know Richard's out of town, and Jon has been barred from the office." Beth leaned over and grabbed the arms of the chair, pulling it closer. "Now pay attention. What am I sitting on?"

Charlie crooked his neck, looking around her with raised eyebrows. "The desk?"

"Focus, Charlie."

"Papers . . . I don't know . . . The Johnson-Medisys contract?" Charlie said, taking a second look. "How did you know?"

"Correct me if I'm wrong. These are the originals?"

"True, but I created those documents."

"And Richard still requires Jon's approval. That's the reason you sent Brenda to Tybee."

"Did you not hear me? I'm in charge now."

Beth leaned forward and pinned Charlie's back against the chair. "Listen to me, and do yourself a favor. Who is ultimately responsible for signing off on the final contract?"

"Uh . . ." Charlie allowed his eyes to drift down Beth's legs. "Jon . . . He told Jon to sign them."

"And what if he altered the documents before signing them?"

"But he'll dispute—"

"It's your word against his. You told me, yourself, that if negotiations drag out much longer, Michael Johnson will be forced to lower his price. And let me reassure you, Bob Stein will reward you handsomely for taking care of business. His shareholders will make a fortune."

"It's too late. The papers are already signed."

Beth reached around and tapped a finger on Jon's computer. "You're forgetting about the power of modern technology. School kids are forging hundred dollar bills on cheap printers. Surely you're smarter than that." She lowered her shoulder and a strap slid off. "You just need a little inspiration."

"Beth, not here."

"Charlie, my darling, this is the perfect place. Take him down, and guess who's next in line for partner?"

"It doesn't matter . . . This isn't going to work. He's competitive as hell."

"Let's see," Beth said, leaning down, nose-to-nose with Charlie. "It didn't stop you in the ladies room at the governor's reception, did it?"

"Beth—"

"You've always wanted what's his. So take it."

Chapter 48
Sunday, August 7th
7:20 A.M.

The breeze drifted in from the Intracoastal Waterway like a sonnet as Jon stepped out of his car next to a faded block building. Beyond it, a million dollar view of salt tides and marsh set the stage for the R/V Savannah rocking back and forth in the current. As he popped the trunk, he spotted Captain's Toyota parked under a palm tree, and then hoisted a gym bag onto his shoulder. He paused to take in a parade of fluffy clouds marching in from the coast, and beneath them a flock of seagulls floating on the wind.

Jon inhaled the morning air like it was a fine wine, paying homage to the marsh's fragrance, an acquired appreciation since moving to the Lowcountry. As he approached the water's edge, he spotted a number of fishing boats downriver before his eyes returned to the R/V Savannah nestled securely to her mooring at the Skidaway Institute of Oceanography. The ship's hull reflected glossy gray hues off the water, its bow forming a sharp "V" that rose fifteen feet above the tide.

"Ahoy there," Captain called out from the bridge.

With a wave, Jon hurried over to a dock, meeting up with Captain at the base of a wooden gangway.

"Those who go down to the sea in ships . . ."

". . . have seen the works of the Lord," Jon responded.

Captain put an arm around Jon's shoulder, laughing. "Psalm one hundred and seven," he said. "Spoken like a true seaman."

The men stepped onto the ship's deck and headed toward the bridge, just as a sailor ducked out of the companionway. "Don't believe a word this man tells you," he said to Jon.

"Jon, this is Captain Ralph Sweeney," Captain said.

"Welcome aboard." Sweeney raised a thumb at Captain. "I spent twenty years with this one in the Navy."

"Twenty-two, and don't start with the lies," Captain said.

"Well now, what do we have here?" Sweeney cut his eyes over the starboard transom.

Jon turned for a look, and then hurried down the gangway. When he returned, he said, "Gentlemen, I'd like you to meet Brenda Simpson."

"It's a pleasure to have you aboard," Sweeney said, checking his watch. "Now if you don't mind, it's time to get underway." With a rolling motion of his hand, two deckhands sprang into action as Sweeney mounted the bridge. In a matter of minutes, the twin diesels powered them downriver.

Once the ship reached the main channel, Sweeney relieved himself of the helm and ushered his guests below deck to the galley. "We're not operating with a full crew on this run, so you'll have to serve yourself," Sweeney said, pouring a cup of coffee. After everyone sat down, he continued. "As you already know, we're making a run out to Gray's Reef to check buoys for the Institute. This means you boys, and girl, will be on the buddy system. While en route to our coordinates, feel free to roam about the deck or bunk in the cabins. Brenda, the master berth is up in the bow, and it's all yours."

"Sounds great," Brenda said.

Sweeney smiled and scratched his speckled beard, adjusting a cap that was embossed with a gold logo. "In case you're wondering, the Savannah is a research vessel, ninety-two feet in length. She was built in Jacksonville and can accommodate up to four crew and twenty passengers. She only draws eight feet, which makes her well-suited to the estuaries and rivers in the area. There's enough fuel and supplies aboard to stay afloat for ten or eleven days, that is, if you keep Captain out of the icebox. Of course, we're on a short run, so we won't need much in the way of supplies."

"Speak for yourself," Captain said.

Sweeney ignored the quip. "Anyway, the ship's outfitted with laboratories, a conference room, sleeping berths, and work areas. She's a wonderful ol' gal."

"Tell us about Gray's Reef," Jon said.

"Before we reach the coordinates, you'll want to go down to the dive room and select a wet suit. Once you're in the water, I'm counting on the three of you to stick together. Captain knows the routine—he's done this many a time." Sweeney got out of his chair and pointed to a coastal chart on the bulkhead. "The reef's eighteen miles off Sapelo Island and has a footprint of about seventeen square nautical miles. Unlike the sandy bottom we're used to around the beach, you're going to find that the reef is a limestone formation with plenty of nooks and crannies to explore. You'll be amazed at the marine life and quickly come to appreciate why it's now a national marine sanctuary. You've all dived before, right?" Jon and Brenda nodded as Sweeney retreated to the doorway. "All right, make yourselves at home. I've got to go steer this lady into the Atlantic."

They finished their coffee, and then headed to the dive room to pick out equipment. Afterwards, they stowed their bags and reconvened in the conference room.

Morning light squeezed in through a row of portholes, breathing life into an otherwise sterile room that was outfitted in industrial-style furnishings. Jon and Brenda pulled up chairs to a metal table, while Captain retrieved a coffee pot and mugs from the galley.

"Since we're all together, I actually had an ulterior motive for bringing us here today," Jon said.

"But we are going diving, right?" Brenda said.

"That much is true, but before we arrive at the reef, I wanted to thank you both for supporting me through the insanity that has somehow become my life. I have to confess—I haven't been the easiest person to deal with lately. But I have come to trust the two of you, and feel like you're both good sounding boards." Jon turned to Brenda. "Anyway, I'll forewarn you, I'm going to say some things that may be unsettling, but I need you to be honest with me."

Brenda looked at Captain, then into Jon's eyes. "I hope this isn't going to be embarrassing."

"Captain has already heard the Tybee story," Jon said. "So just relax."

"Jon told me how someone tried to set you up, and I know for a fact he doesn't want to jeopardize your wellbeing. Everything's above board with the three of us—we're mates." He held up the coffee pot and eyed Jon. "Anyway, I think it'd be a good idea to start from the beginning, when Franks tried to take you out with that iron pipe."

Brenda's face suddenly froze. "Wait—what? Does that mean what I think it does?"

"We don't exactly know what he was up to," Jon said.

"He nearly cracked your skull," Captain said. "And yes, it means exactly that, Brenda."

"When did this happen?" Brenda said.

Jon let out a breath. "Do you recall the day I came to the office, all roughed up?"

"You're talking about the morning your suit . . ." Brenda paused, pushing a strand of hair behind her ear. "Okay, you've got my attention."

"Captain's right. It all started a few weeks ago when a homeless guy, who later turned out to be a private investigator, took a swing at me in Factors Square."

"Jon," Brenda said, her eyes growing big. "Why didn't you say something? Iron pipes? A private investigator? Does this have something to do with your divorce?"

"Good question. I haven't quite figured out who hired the PI."

"Or why," Captain added.

"So far, we know he tried to break into my apartment and cashed checks using my driver's license. It's also clear that he's the one who photographed my car at your townhouse, not to mention the recent ones of us at Tybee."

"Why are there pictures of us?"

"They were used against me in the deposition. That's why I've been keeping a distance. I had to be sure you weren't involved," Jon said, his voice trailing off. "And now I need to apologize."

"Don't be silly. We were both set up—obviously," Brenda said. "Charlie is the one who sent me out to Tybee. In fact, he insisted I go."

"Did he say anything that might connect him to the guy who took the pictures?"

"Let's be careful not to jump to conclusions," Captain said.

"But you don't understand. If it hadn't been for Charlie, I never would have gone out to Jon's apartment in the first place. It was his idea that I spend the day at the beach. He said Jon would welcome the company. He even gave me money for dinner and picked the restaurant, one apparently suitable for photo-ops." She slid out of her chair and crossed the room to one of the portholes, then turned. She was blushing. "Charlie said he had noticed the way you looked at me, Jon. He went out of his way to explain how the separation had taken a toll on you. And I have to confess, he put a guilt trip on me, making me feel bad that I hadn't been there to help you." Brenda looked away. "In hindsight, it seems pretty foolish."

"Brenda, the pictures were taken by a private investigator from Charleston. They somehow wound up in the hands of Beth's attorney. Does any of this relate to what Charlie told you?"

"How do you know it was a private investigator?"

"Captain and I paid a visit to the PI's office. We found copies of the pictures. He also had photos of my car parked at your townhouse."

"Which we both know never happened," Brenda said, toying with her hair.

The three sat in silence, lulled by the rattling of diesel engines, until Jon finally came out of his chair and started pacing.

"What?" Captain said.

"Walker," Jon said, thinking out loud. "Charlie is Walker . . . I'll tell you about it later." He turned to Brenda. "Remember the morning I came to the office and you had taken Charlie to have his car detailed? Do you recall what you said?"

Brenda looked Jon in the eyes, responding with a question. "His car was filthy . . . like he had been to the beach?"

"Someone moved my car the night before. Only, I couldn't figure out how they got the key—until now." Jon hesitated. "I keep a spare in my office at the Skidaway house. That suggests, Beth is directly involved."

"Lawyers call that circumstantial evidence," Captain said. "How well does Beth know this Charlie fellow?"

"They grew up together," Jon said. "But the PI's invoices we found in Charleston were all paid by South Coast."

"You can prove that?"

"You don't want to know. Just think angel, Captain," Jon said, diverting his eyes. "Brenda, when you were looking for the e-mail to Michael Johnson, did anyone at the office know you were checking the computers?"

She nodded, looking confused. "Charlie sort of nosed around. But I didn't find it, even after I went back to search for deleted files."

"It recently turned up on my personal laptop." Jon walked back to the table and sat down. Brenda followed him. "If you think about it, Beth had access to the spare key and my computer. And Charlie was the one who knew about the blowup with Michael."

"You didn't tell me you found the e-mail," Brenda said.

"That's why I'm telling you now. What I don't get is—what does it have to do with Beth?"

"Ahem."

Jon cut his eyes at Captain.

"I hate to admit it, but the mounting evidence suggests Beth may have put Charlie up to all this, especially since we know the photographs found their way into her lawyer's hands. That's motive enough in my book. But I have to tell you, this South Coast connection is puzzling to me, seeing how they're supposed to be helping you reconcile. But one thing's for sure, I owe you an apology. I told you to trust Stephens."

"Wait. What about the PI attacking Jon in the park? Are you suggesting the church was involved in that too?"

"Stephens refers to the PI's activities as marital counseling," Jon said. "At least, according to church records. But I'm not convinced he would go as far as murder."

"Ahoy, landlubbers," Sweeney said, stepping into the room. "Sorry to interrupt, but we've got about forty-five minutes to touchdown. I suggest you all suit up for an equipment check."

Brenda walked barefooted up the starboard deck of the *R/V Savannah*, clinging to the rail. Her wet hair danced in the salt air, revealing a look of contentment on her face. As she approached the bow, her sweatshirt fluttered at the waist and she stopped to lean on the rail next to Jon. "That was awesome," she said. "Thanks for inviting me."

"It's hard to believe the reef is so close to home. Captain says a day on Gray's Reef is as good as going to church," Jon said, studying the blue-green swells over the transom.

"Did you see that beautiful orange coral?" Brenda stretched to see what Jon was staring at.

"I couldn't get close enough for a look. The barracuda were hanging around them."

"Barracuda? Why didn't somebody warn me?" Brenda's mouth dropped open.

"I've heard they're passive in open water, as long as you don't provoke them." Jon laughed as Brenda protested with a playful slap to his shoulder.

"You know, there's nothing like the scorn of a provoked woman," she teased. "Do that again, and you'll be dealing with this barracuda." She bared her teeth.

Jon smiled and adjusted his sunglasses. "Be careful. I have witnesses." He nodded toward the ship's bridge. "Captain said he was going to keep an eye on you, particularly after the way you scared the jellyfish."

"Touché," Brenda said. "I deserved that."

To starboard, a cruiser approached, but then veered off to port, heading toward the Wilmington River. It accelerated, kicking up a sizeable wake as it jetted upriver.

"Wow, what kind of boat is that?"

Jon studied the sleek torso, a sure sign she was built for speed. He pointed to the stern. "It's the Shiva, Bob Stein's boat."

"Shiva? That sounds pretty strange. Is that his wife's name?"

"Hardly. It's more like a mission statement . . . one that's about to backfire on him."

"And?" Brenda said, placing a hand on her hip. "You're not going to tell me what that means, are you?"

"Brenda, I need to ask you something." Jon's expression turned serious. "Have you received any strange telephone calls at the office?"

"How do you mean?"

"Hang ups? Anonymous callers?"

"Not that I recall."

"The night Richard confronted me about Michael's e-mail, I received a call. It was pretty odd, but definitely a warning. The person said to sign nothing. Naturally, I thought it was related to the acquisition, but in hindsight it doesn't make sense."

"What day was that?" she said.

"I'll have to check my calendar, but I'm thinking it may have something to do with Charlie."

She shook her head. "Maybe . . ."

Jon put a hand on the deck rail next to Brenda's. "I feel better now that the air's been cleared between us—"

The ship suddenly lurched, crashing into a wave that showered the deck with spray. The bow lifted, and they both dropped down, covering their heads.

"See what happens when you call me names," Brenda said, giggling. "The sea looks after her own."

"I really mean it."

"Jon," Brenda said, titling her head. "I'm sorry about what happened at Tybee. I hope you don't think I'm the sort to, well, come on to a guy. You must think I'm some kind of floozy."

"Are you?" he said, meeting her glance.

Brenda started to respond, and then scrunched her nose. "Okay, that's not fair. You're trying to confuse me."

"Such depth for a barracuda," Jon said. "But you didn't answer my question."

"Oh, no you don't." She poked him with a finger. "If I answer, I'll wind up flapping around on this deck, like a fish out of water, wondering which question I really answered. Let's see, did I acknowledge my embarrassment? Or maybe, I admitted to coming on to you? But wait, I might have confirmed that I'm a floozy." She poked him again. "If I'm not careful, I'll be guilty of all three. Next thing I know, you'll tell me you named your boat something weird that translates to 'Brenda is a floozy'."

"Brenda, I hate to rain on your parade, but I don't own a boat." Jon leaned his head against the rail. "Anyway, what I wanted to say is, I'd be honored if you'd let me take you out to dinner when this is all over. Only this time, it will be a date and . . ." He stopped mid-sentence as he caught the look in her eyes.

Brenda looked down, clasping her hands together. She sat silent for a moment, as if harboring a secret, and then looked out over the water, speaking softly. "You know, that's about the—"

"Am I in the doghouse?" Jon said.

Brenda shook her head and leaned over, pulling off his sunglasses. The green hues in his eyes played off the ocean. "I'd be delighted to."

Chapter 49
Monday, August 8th
3:15 P.M.

Stephens sneezed as he stepped into Hallworth's office, rummaging through his suit pockets and pulling out a handkerchief. "I don't know why I put up with this."

Hallworth reclined at his desk with his feet propped up, finishing up on a telephone call. He hung up, oblivious to the junkyard vibe in his office. "What is that you were saying, counselor?"

Stephens cut his eyes to a corner. "Do you intend to put my files in a safe place?"

"I'll get around to it. Nothing has ever disappeared from this operation on my watch."

Stephens stormed over to a chair and plopped down, still looking around in disbelief. "You can't possibly know that," he said, not waiting for a response. "Let's make this quick. I spoke to Tim at church yesterday and Jonathon hasn't responded. So there's progress on his front. How about you? What do you have?"

"So the weasel's going to leave us holding the bag."

"I'll take that as a no, which means we execute our fallback plan tonight. Call Rhodus with the orders, and I'll contact Franks."

"Are you sure you can trust him?" Hallworth said, unwrapping a cigar.

"If he screws up one more time, he's out. The same applies to Rhodus."

Hallworth tucked the cigar in his mouth. "Perhaps you'd like to deliver that ultimatum yourself."

"Just make sure he follows instructions. I'll schedule a follow-up with the elders," Stephens said, springing from the chair.

Hallworth ignored Stephens's overtures, choosing instead to sort through a desk drawer. "Why aren't those clowns tightening the screws? We've produced enough evidence in this case to bring on the second flood. With all that ordained power you keep preaching about, they should be throwing the book at him for adultery or insubordination—something."

Stephens leered at Hallworth as he lit the cigar and a gray cloud formed over the desk. "They're mostly figureheads. At least, that's what I use them for, other than PR work."

"Public relations?" Hallworth said.

"More like religious press leaks. When all else fails, elder committees are the perfect channel for shoveling confidential dirt."

"The big man complex, huh? What do they do, go home and tell their wives?"

"I suppose that's part of it. But mostly they solicit prayers for the lost souls. It sort of sanctifies the leak."

"So what's this pack of holy robes done for us lately?"

"I thought I just explained that. This afternoon they'll be briefed on how Jonathon has continued in his unrepentant behavior."

"For what purpose?" Hallworth challenged. "And don't look at me like that."

Stephens marched over to the door and clasped his hands behind his back. "I'm recommending a letter of excommunication. If we don't hear from him by the end of the week, we'll organize a church trial to have him removed from the membership."

"A worthless gesture, my friend. To hear Beth tell it, he doesn't fall for that kind of nonsense."

"You're forgetting the PR angle. Once word gets out that South Coast has kicked him out of the church, and it will, the entire city will be abuzz about the up-and-coming Dr. Browning." He watched Hallworth's eyes light up. "And that's where Richard Stone enters the picture. He's got a lot of skin in the game. I don't have to remind you of the humiliation this situation poses to him. How would it look if his handpicked protégé dumps his wife and kids? Take it from me. At this stage of the game, Richard has an aversion to scandals, like this." Stephens puffed up when he noticed Hallworth's expression of approval. "That's why we'll make sure he gets a sneak preview of coming attractions."

* * *

Jon finished a three mile run on the beach, taking in the ocean breeze as he jogged in place to cool down. Darkness was falling, and lights from the houses just across the sand dunes flickered like fireflies. In the distance, the silhouettes of ships at anchor in the mouth of the Savannah River floated like ghost ships, waiting to steam into port. He took a bearing and noticed the 7th Street boardwalk was within shouting distance, then closed his eyes and took a deep breath.

A wave of dizziness came over him, and suddenly Jon felt something tightening around his neck. Gasping for breath, he realized he was losing his balance as an arm flexed beneath his chin and began pulling him backwards. The assailant seemed to effortlessly drag him through the sand, the pressure on his throat now so tight he thought he was going to black out. Without warning, the attacker came to a stop and delivered a sharp jab to Jon's back. Shrouded in near darkness, they were surrounded by the dunes, making it impossible to draw anyone's attention.

"Put this on," a man said. He tossed a burlap bag across Jon's shoulder.

Jon reached up, taking it in his hand. "What do you want?"

He reacted with another jab. "Did I ask you a question?" The man adjusted his grip. "Shut up and follow orders."

Jon opened the bag and draped it down over his head. "Your voice sounds familiar."

"Shut up."

A noose was fitted around Jon's neck, and then pulled snug. A hand gripped his shoulder and forced him to his knees.

* * *

Brenda had just finished up with a late dinner, when the doorbell rang. Peeking through the peephole at her front entrance, she spied a delivery man hovering outside with a pizza box. She called through the door, "You've got the wrong address." But the man didn't hear, so she opened up. Like a wild animal, he pounced, slamming the door shut as he forced his way inside. A hand covered her mouth, and as she struggled for control, fear gripped her. In her mind, she was scolding herself for being so careless.

Moments later, the man shoved Brenda inside a vehicle—handcuffed, blindfolded, and gagged. She tried to remain calm, but realized she had already lost track of time. Had it been thirty seconds or thirty minutes since the attack? She wasn't sure, only that it seemed like an eternity. She took a deep breath, trying to get a grip. The engine started, and suddenly there were metallic sounds bouncing all around her as the vehicle rattled into motion. The interior filled with greasy fumes that smelled like the auto repair shop where she had her car serviced. With no means of communicating, she decided she needed to stay calm, no matter what came next.

* * *

Jon winced as his wrists were secured behind his back with a zip tie.

"You're with Stone & Associates, is that right?"

"You're cutting off the circulation," Jon said.

The man stopped abruptly, and Jon braced himself for retaliation.

"Are you Jonathon Browning?"

Jon leaned forward, trying to ease the pain. "Who wants to know?"

There was silence as the wind gusted, rustling the sea oats around them.

"Are you still there?" Jon said.

There was no response.

"I'll make you a deal," Jon said.

The man let out a chuckle. "I've definitely got the right man," he said. "Did you listen to the tape?"

"The tapes . . . You know about the tapes?"

"There's more than one?"

"What the hell's going on?" Jon said.

"Your presence has been requested at," the man paused, as if unsure of himself, "5755 Topsail Court on Skidaway Island."

"That's my address—my home."

"Then why was I was informed that you are living in the house just over this dune."

"My wife is divorcing me, but somehow I don't think that will come as a surprise to you."

"So there must be a lawyer involved."

"The sleaziest kind you can imagine," Jon said. When the man didn't respond, he realized he may have hit a nerve.

Without another word, the man began to free up Jon's wrists, afterwards loosening the noose. Then he said, "You can take off the sack."

Jon removed the burlap bag, rubbing his itchy eyes. As he looked up into the moonlight, there was a man towering over him.

"You just don't know when to give up, do you, Browning," Charles Rhodes said. "Didn't I tell you to forget about this case?"

* * *

Twenty minutes had passed, and Brenda had managed to settle down, even though on the inside she was still terrified. She tried to imagine she was at Gray's Reef, breathing in and out of the diving tank, listening to the soothing sound of percolating bubbles. The vehicle was traveling in fits and stops now, a sure sign they were moving through Savannah's maze of traffic signals and stop signs. It was a positive sign since it meant they were still in the city.

With a cooler head, Brenda began to take a virtual inventory. Among the lingering garage-like odors, she was certain she'd caught a wisp of alcohol, making her wonder if the man was sober. If not, maybe there was a chance the police would pull him over. From where she sat, it seemed likely the vehicle was probably a van, and the sounds behind her were some type of loose tools bouncing around in the back.

The man didn't speak again until announcing their arrival. An automatic garage opener buzzed, and once they came to a stop, she was wrestled out of the van into a building. Up a flight of stairs, the air quickly cooled down as she felt plush carpet under her bare feet.

Without warning, the man gave her a shove, throwing her off-balance. She screamed, but it came out muffled through the gag. With her hands tied behind her, she had no means of breaking the fall. As she landed facedown, the impact was not what she had expected. It was surprisingly soft. The smell of fresh linens engulfed her, followed by the sound of a door closing and more rattling. A switch flipped, and Brenda sensed light through the blindfold.

The man touched the back of her head. "All right, darling, I'm going to take off the blindfold." She felt a tug. "If you try anything stupid, like screaming, then it's no more Mr. Nice Guy. You understand?"

Brenda nodded, feeling her cheek brush against the satiny linens. As the blindfold dropped free, she immediately noticed she was on a floral comforter, the only thing in her periphery, as she dared not move. She felt the gag loosen, and a rush of cool air flowed down her throat, causing her to cough before laboring with the first few breaths.

The man grabbed a shoulder and rolled Brenda over on her back, lowering his face just above hers. "Now that's better. My, my—you're as pretty as a picture," he said, his alcohol-laced breath overpowering. "Are you going to be good?"

Brenda studied the man's eyes. "Where am I?" she said, grinding her teeth as her clinched fists lodged in the small of her back.

He recognized the look. "You do as I say, and I'll loosen them next." He slid off the bed and went to work on the floor.

Brenda scanned the room. The bed was distinctly feminine, decorated with lace and frilly pillows. The room had clearly been professionally decorated. Even the mats in the picture frames had been perfectly coordinated with the wall color and hues in the comforter. Well-appointed with lamps and accessories, the furniture looked expensive. She noticed the closed door where they had entered, and then another doorway leading into a bathroom. From the looks of things, her assailant was out of his element.

The metallic sound she had heard in the van returned, only this time it made her think of lounge chairs banging together. She looked down at the foot of the bed, where the man was busy tightening the legs of an aluminum tripod. He reached down and lifted a camera and attached it on top. Afterwards, he glanced at his watch and frowned before noticing how Brenda was studying him.

"Can you tell me why you brought me here?"

The man stared at her, as if he was seeing her for the first time. He smiled, exposing a row of yellow teeth, and then circled around the bed. "Right nice of you to ask," he said, sitting down next to her. "You're not going to be any trouble, are you?" A hand wandered down to her waist, touching the exposed skin between her jeans and t-shirt.

She recoiled, as if she had been poked with a branding iron. "Please, don't do that."

The man smirked and reached around his back, pulling a pistol out of his waistband. He shook it in the air. "I'm going to untie your hands now."

* * *

"I'm working undercover, so I had to make it all look real, just in case I was being tailed," Rhodes said, looking out toward the Atlantic. They were both seated on the screen porch at Jon's apartment.

"That's not what I asked you. I hired you to investigate my wife, and the next thing I know, you're attacking me. What do you know about the PI who dropped off the tape?"

Rhodes shook a beer bottle, checking to see if it was empty. "He's presently under investigation."

"When I hired you, you told me you were retired FBI. Did you lie to me?"

"I was retired, until that PI showed up on the Tybee Island Causeway," Rhodes said. "I spent the last five years of my career working on a case, only none of the victims wanted to talk for some reason. When the trail finally went cold, I hung up my badge without an arrest. Then along comes Jonathon Browning, and guess what happens? The players resurfaced, and I decided to come out of retirement and reopen the case. As a client, you were a conflict of interest, so I had to dump you."

"You might have warned me before you disappeared."

"I tried that night at Telfair Hall, but it was too risky to say much."

"For you or me?"

"Both," Rhodes said.

"What's with the outfit?"

"It's part of the cover. A couple of years ago, the Bryan County sheriff staged my arrest and came up with the Rhodus alias so I could investigate one of the suspects, a lawyer," Rhodes said. "The guy's a real scumbag. He showed up recently with, of all things, a preacher. Can you believe that?"

"What are their names?"

"I'm not at liberty to say."

"Then perhaps you'd like to tell me what's going on with my wife."

"Honestly, I wish I could. But that part I haven't nailed down. She somehow conned one of my suspects into getting involved in whatever game she's playing with you, but her activities don't exactly line up with the prior crime pattern."

"So you're saying she's not acting alone."

"To be quite honest, I'm not after her," Rhodes said, shifting in his seat.

"Well, you and I differ on that point," Jon said. "Based on what you know so far, do you suspect she's involved in a felony?"

"Could be—if someone intends to pursue the case. A little more evidence might make it compelling."

"How would murder factor into that equation?"

"Son-of-a . . ." Rhodes said, leveling his eyes on Jon. "What's a man got to do to retire in this town?"

* * *

The kidnapper tinkered with the camera, adjusting the height of the tripod as he checked the viewfinder. While he was busy, Brenda remembered how Jon had described the PI's photographs the day before. Her mouth fell open as it suddenly dawned on her that this was the private investigator. *What was his name? . . . Franks.* She rubbed her wrists, and then took a peek at the pistol tucked in his waistband. Franks checked his watch for a third time. Something wasn't going as scheduled.

"Are you the one who took the pictures at Tybee?" Brenda said.

Franks looked up. "How's that, darling?" Grinning, he looked at her anew and walked over, reaching out with his hand.

"No," she said, raising her fists.

"Nobody's going to hurt you." He pulled out the pistol, and with his free hand, felt the smoothness of her stomach. "It looks like it's just you and me. I'm going to take a few pictures, so I'll need you to ditch the outfit." He motioned for her to stand up.

Brenda examined the hollowness in Franks's eyes, and then eased to the floor beside him. He took a half-step back, waving the pistol in a rolling motion. She crossed her arms and grasped the hem of her t-shirt in both hands. Pulling it over her head, she focused on his eyes as she lifted the shirt high up in the air. The pistol hand relaxed, and a smile returned to his face. His eyes followed the shirt, and then slowly began to drift lower.

Before he had time to think, Brenda thrusted a knee forward and caught Franks in the groin. He gasped and grabbed the front of his khakis, dropping the gun to the floor. As the t-shirt slipped from her hands, she delivered a second blow. This time he lost his balance and fell against her. They both toppled, and Frank's forehead smacked the corner of a nightstand on the way down. Brenda hit the floor first, and then Franks landed with his full weight on top of her.

Franks let out a wheeze, and Brenda tried to shove him off of her, but he was too heavy. With no time to waste, she pushed again, this time using a knee to roll him to one side. Scrambling to her feet, she grabbed the pistol and aimed, but Franks lay motionless.

Brenda spun toward the door and crashed into the tripod, knocking it over. As she steadied herself, she caught her reflection in a picture frame. Turning back to the bed, she grabbed her t-shirt and raced out for the door.

Chapter 50
Tuesday, August 9th
1:15 A.M.

Brenda didn't slow down until she reached the street, struggling to pull the t-shirt over her head. Looking back, the house was barely visible now, and it seemed ominous, hiding behind a stand of moss-draped oaks. The night air felt like a sauna as she wiped perspiration from her forehead. There were no signs of life in the area, but she noticed a street number on the mailbox. She spun around to take off again and stubbed her toe on a rock, forcing her to hop for a couple of steps before coming to a stop in the middle of the road. The pain brought tears to her eyes, and she wanted to check the wound, but she knew it was best to move on.

At the first intersection, she looked back and realized she had been in a cul-de-sac. A light buzzed over a street sign, and she studied a deserted road running to her left and right. Not knowing which way to go, she decided to take a chance to the left, where she spotted a light in the distance.

As she limped on, Brenda began to notice a few driveways along the way in the shadows. She thought about making a detour up one for help, but chose instead to put more distance between her and Franks. Moments later, she had to stop briefly to rub her aching foot. Perching on one leg, she massaged the injury, suddenly freezing in place when the brush stirred next to the road. Four deer sauntered out, and then disappeared down a golf cart path. Looking ahead, she pressed on, favoring the good foot.

Halfway to the next light, Brenda paused for a look back at the sign she had seen on the corner. It was no longer visible, but the name, "Topsail", registered with her. *I've just escaped from Jon's house*, she thought. Shaking her head in confusion, she pushed ahead with lingering questions in her head. *Why was the PI in Jon's home? Where was Jon?* She wished he was with her right now.

At the next intersection, she set her sights on a light that had become visible further ahead. Picking up the pace, she had covered most of the distance, when the sound of an engine caught her attention. Looking back, a vehicle pulled into view, giving Brenda a first sign of hope. She stepped out into the middle of the street and started waving, just as the car eased around the corner. As it accelerated, her eyes locked onto the vehicle's dimensions in horror. It was a utility van.

Brenda bolted for the side of the road, wincing each time her bad foot hit the pavement. When the van was nearly on her, her instincts suddenly screamed, *dive*. As she landed in darkness, she continued to roll, feeling the sharp pricks of palmetto bushes as she came to rest. The van's tires screeched to a stop, and Franks hopped out, hitting the street running. Without thinking, Brenda was on her feet again, pushing deeper into the woods, gasping each time the brush slapped her in the face.

Somewhere behind her, Franks screamed. She could feel thorns tearing away at her jeans as she ran with her hands in front of her face. Seconds turned into what seemed like hours, but she finally broke through to another street. Stopping to get a bearing, she listened for sounds, but heard nothing. In the darkness, she could make out the glow of another street light around the next bend. On the brink of exhaustion, she refused to give up and pushed forward.

When she had made it to the bend, she heard a different sound—a squealing fan belt. It took a moment, but she was pretty sure it was the van, so she slipped into a roadside ditch as lights emerged from the darkness. The van blew past her, but came to a stop somewhere up ahead with the engine idling. Not wanting to lose time, Brenda clung to the ditch, advancing until she was able to spot the van sitting at a stop sign. Beyond it, she noticed an iron gate next to a tiny booth. *A neighborhood security gate.* She had heard Jon mention them many times. The fan belt squealed, drawing her attention back to the van as it turned and sped away.

Approaching the booth, Brenda could tell from a distance it was unmanned. There was a posted sign: *Closed from 9 P.M. until 7 A.M.* It directed drivers to the main entrance during off hours. She stepped around the corner and noticed a small box attached to the wall. Opening the cover, she almost cried as she reached inside and pulled out a telephone receiver. Without dialing, she heard a voice say, "Main gate."

Brenda waited next to the booth, feeling frantic. The security guard had agreed to call for a cab, and then drive down to assist her. She peered into the darkness, biting a fingernail. *What was it Jon had said about the island?* Unfortunately, it came to her. *A wildlife refuge.* He used to talk about spotting wild boars, vultures . . . alligators. She placed a hand over her mouth as she thought about her escape, conjuring up images of animals leering at her from the darkness.

Finally, she saw headlights approaching. When the security vehicle was near, the van suddenly appeared from a side street, flashing its lights. Brenda crouched behind the booth, peeking around the corner. A man in uniform rolled down his window to speak to Franks, pointing as he talked. The van's backup lights came on, and it turned around. She headed into the nearby brush with the palmettos stinging like bees, but this time she hardly noticed.

Both vehicles pulled up to the gate. The security officer got out first, waiting for Franks to join him.

"This is where she made the call," the officer said, looking around. "If it were my daughter, I'd contact the police."

"It's just a silly thing she does, running off like this," Franks said. "I'll take it from here."

As an afterthought, the guard flipped on a flashlight and pointed it at the van. "Sir, are you a resident of the island?"

"I'm a guest of the Browning's on Topsail Court."

"If you like, we can drive over to the main gate and see if she shows up."

Franks scratched his head, looking around like he was thinking. "You go, and I'll wait here, just in case she reappears. We can use the phone if either of us hears anything."

The guard puckered his lips and nodded. "Good idea." He wiggled his cap as he started for his vehicle. Halfway to the car, he yelled over his shoulder, "Do you want me to call the Browning residence and let them know what's going on?"

"They've got sleeping children."

"Ten-four," the guard said. He hopped in the car and drove away.

Brenda looked on as Franks took his time returning to the van. With his back to her, she managed to slip to a security fence that bordered the woods. Taking a second look in his direction, she pulled herself up and climbed over the fence. On the other side, the area was enveloped in blackness, alive with swampy insect sounds. All she could think about was alligators.

Franks crawled into the van and closed the door. He turned off the headlights and settled back in his seat. With just enough time for Brenda to have thoughts about hiking down the secluded road outside the gate, a pair of headlights appeared and turned into the entrance. A taxi pulled up to the gate, forcing her to give up the safety of her hiding place. She leaped out of the brush and scrambled over to the vehicle, fumbling with the rear door handle.

The driver lurched as Brenda jumped in and slammed the door. Before he could get a look at her, there was a shriek that drew his attention to the gate. Franks had jumped out of his van.

"Drive!" Brenda shouted.

"What?" the driver said, looking in the back seat.

"Drive-drive-drive!" she said, pounding the headrest.

"Okay, okay," he said, spinning the car around.

As they sped away, Franks's arms flailed between the bars of the gate. He was screaming at the top of his lungs.

* * *

The door flew open before Jon had time to knock. Brenda bolted through the doorway, looping her arms around his neck and squeezing as she began to cry into his shoulder.

"I'm here now," Jon said.

Fifteen minutes later, as they were speeding down Abercorn in the Z4, Jon looked over at Brenda. She was sitting with her feet perched on the edge of the seat, with her knees pulled up under her chin. The wind was tossing her hair about, all out of sorts.

"Did you pack a pair of shoes?" Jon said, looking down at her bare feet. They passed under a street light, illuminating the car's interior. For the first time, he realized he had never seen her when she wasn't picture-perfect. Somehow, in the midst of all the chaos, he found himself drawn to her. She didn't notice his stare, or even hear the question, as she focused intently out the windshield. Jon took another look and let it pass.

At the next traffic light, Brenda finally stirred from the trance, looking around. "Where are we going?"

"Someplace safe, at least until it's okay for you to go home," Jon said, checking her reaction. Looking down, he spotted a pistol in the waistband of her jeans and raised an eyebrow. "What's this?" he said, trying not to sound alarmed.

"I took it from the kidnapper."

"Did he hurt you?"

Brenda held out an arm, eyeing the patches of dried blood on her arms and legs before poking at a hole in her t-shirt. "No," she said, looking up. "Jon, the light's green."

He put the car in gear. The next time he glanced over, she was looking at him like one of her wounds.

"Do you want to talk about it?"

"I don't know . . . I think I'm in shock."

"You should be."

"Jon, it was the private investigator . . . it had to be." She snuggled her arms around her knees. "I was inside your house, and he was going to take my picture in your bedroom. Only, I think he was waiting for someone else to show up."

"That someone was me. They planned to kidnap me tonight as well."

"You? Why didn't you say something?" she said, reaching out and resting a hand on his shoulder.

"I was thinking on the way over that this is proof-positive of Beth's involvement. There's no doubt she provided access to the house."

"If she wants a divorce, why doesn't she just do it?" Brenda said. "This is insane."

"It was to be our picture."

"What?"

"You said Franks was going to take your picture." Jon downshifted, approaching another traffic light. "He intended to take our picture in that bed."

"So it's like the others, only this time caught in the act?"

"Exactly . . . A staged scene to make it look like we were involved before I moved out."

"But kidnapping?" Brenda studied Jon's face. "Either she hates you or she wants your money."

"Maybe both," Jon said. "But it's even harder to accept the fact that she's mixed up in attempted murder."

Jon pulled the car up to the rear entrance of the Mission, where Captain stepped out and shuffled Brenda up a stairway to a room next to his office. It was furnished with an assortment of dusty odds and ends, clearly set up for safety, not comfort. They all agreed that her living arrangements were not to be disclosed to anyone until they could find some answers.

Out on the Tybee Island Causeway, Jon juggled several thoughts that had been plaguing him since leaving downtown Savannah. Finally he gave in, flipping open his cell phone and dialing. Turning down the volume on the stereo, he checked the time. It was three-thirty in the morning. The voicemail system answered, prompted him through the options.

"David, I'm calling on behalf of your associate, Jesse Franks. You may be interested to know that he was unable to complete his counseling session tonight. I'll give you a word of advice . . . Back off . . . It's over." He flipped the phone shut and found solace in the growling engine as he topped the Lazaretto Creek

Bridge. Jon glanced over his shoulder at the Cockspur Lighthouse and floored the accelerator.

Chapter 51
Tuesday, August 9th
10:15 A.M.

Jon had been tailing Beth's Lexus since it left Skidaway Island. So far, she had dropped off Carver and Bailey at their grandparent's and visited a nail salon. At the moment, she was pulling into a Starbucks parking lot. The drive-thru was backed up like an amusement park attraction, giving him ample time to park his car and hop into the passenger seat as she waited in line.

"What do you think you're doing?" she said as her head snapped around. A pair of large, oval sunglasses glared at Jon, bug-like.

"I just wanted to do a little follow-up on your Tybee visit last week."

"In case you're thinking about getting stupid, I'm on the way to see my attorney."

"This won't take long," he said, as Beth inched the car up to the speaker. He gestured. "A Venti Mocha for me."

Beth ordered, then lifted her sunglasses and lit into him. "Get out."

"At least let me buy you a coffee." He handed her a fifty as she pulled up to the window. The barista passed out two cups.

Beth waved the money out the window. "Keep the change," she said, peeling around the corner of the store. Jon juggled with his coffee as she turned to him with a venomous smile.

"I have it on good authority that a crime took place out at Skidaway last night," Jon said.

Beth jerked the Lexus out into the flow of traffic, and Jon looked back to see his car fading in the distance.

"Listen, if you have anything to say, tell your lawyer to contact Sam Hallworth. You're not playing Mr. Dealmaker with me. I don't have to put up with your nonsense anymore."

"I have an offer for you."

"Nice try, but we're dealing on my terms, just in case you haven't figured it out." Beth's cell phone rang, cutting her tirade short. "Yeah," she snipped, listening intently before responding. "He's sitting in my car right now . . . Nail him, and there's a bonus in it for you." She hung up.

"Does the name, Jesse Franks, mean anything to you?" Jon said.

Beth slammed the steering wheel. "Screw you."

"Okay, just settle down. We'll play on your terms, but allow me to let you in on a little secret. Franks is going to do time. The bank has him on their security cameras, and as it turns out, the money was drawn on our New York account. That means the funds crossed state lines, making this a federal offense."

"You're wasting your breath, Darling. I'm afraid—"

"Care to tell me what you did with the hundred grand?" Jon said.

Beth looked out the side window in silence.

"That's what I thought. Perhaps I'll take the matter up directly with Franks. The man's for sale, you know. He can certainly shed some light on the photographs and last night's kidnapping fiasco, maybe even spill the beans on your love life."

"I tried to patch things up at your little beach shack, but apparently you're not interested in reconciling the marriage."

"Word on the street is—you're not either."

"Good bluff, Darling. But you forget. I know how you operate." Beth puckered her lips.

"Which makes this much easier. Of course, Franks may want to negotiate on his own when he finds out he's up for attempted murder." Jon shook his head. "That's the problem with men, you can love them, but you sure can't trust them, especially when you're messing with their minds."

"You're a psycho, and Dr. Lowe intends to prove it when he testifies in court. Maybe you and Jesse Franks can be roommates up at the penitentiary." Beth cut the wheels and steered the Lexus onto the Talmadge Bridge. "Now, you listen to me. You're going to give me everything. And while you're at it, sell the Beemer. When I'm done with you, you're going to be penniless. You're getting nothing, Sweetheart. We'll see who thinks you're wonderful when you lose everything." She jammed the brakes, and the car screeched to a stop. "Get the hell out of my car!"

Jon opened the door and stepped out, leaning back inside. "I'm available, if you want to talk."

Beth slammed the accelerator, almost taking off his head as the car sped forward. He eased over to the railing, looking down at the Savannah River two hundred feet below. Jumping off the Talmadge Bridge would be the easy way out.

Walking up to the rear entrance at Stone & Associates, Jon checked the alley for Charlie's car, and then headed inside. As he passed Brenda's door, she called out to him from her desk. He did an about-face.

"What're you doing here?" she said, getting up.

"I just hiked down from the Talmadge Bridge," Jon said, smoothing down his hair. "How are you this morning?"

"Thankful," she said, letting out a breath. "You'll be happy to know I started the morning with a plateful of grits." She frowned. "That thing you just said about the bridge, that's a joke. Right?"

Jon smiled, and then stepped into the hallway. "I need to see Charlie."

"Jon," Brenda said, lowering her voice. "He's on the telephone . . . and I think it's with Beth."

"Then my timing is perfect." Jon started down the hall with Brenda trailing behind. When he came to Charlie's office, he pushed the door open without breaking stride.

Brenda stopped in the hall, raising a hand to her mouth. The door closed.

"I'm on a call here," Charlie said, placing a hand over the mouthpiece.

Jon walked over and snatched the receiver away, holding it at arm's length. "He'll call you back, Darling," he said, and then slammed it down.

"Have you lost your mind?" Charlie stood up.

"I'm not in the mood, Charlie." Jon took a seat in front of the desk.

"What's the meaning of this?"

"Sit down. I'm not going to hit you, if that's what you're thinking."

"Buddy, what gives? I've known you for over ten years—"

"Save it."

"Jon, I'm here for . . ." Charlie stopped mid-sentence, easing nervously into his chair.

"At first, I refused to believe it," Jon said. "The e-mail was pretty slick, and it made Richard angry. I'll count that one as pure jealousy."

"Can I just say something? I'd like to—"

"I had someone trying to convince me a ghost was driving my car, but then I discovered you were at the beach on the night it found its way over to Brenda's townhouse. The parking spot was a little too perfect, you might say." Jon stood up and looked down at Charlie. "And then you sent Brenda out to Tybee for a little romance."

"You're forgetting, I've been doing my best to help you. I mean, you've already gone gorilla on Michael. And now you've botched the contract. Richard's pretty upset."

"The contract is final."

"Only problem is, you altered the terms right before you signed them." Charlie let out a sigh, and then chuckled. "Richard knows I'm the one who calmed Michael down, when he discovered the change. In fact, he told Richard to fire you." He put his feet up on the desk. "I wouldn't count on the big *P* if I were you. At least, not at Stone & Associates."

Jon stepped around the desk and stuffed his hands in his pockets. A smile appeared, lingering long enough for Charlie to squirm in his chair.

"Jesse Franks is going to talk," Jon said.

"Afraid not, Buddy. You're not winning this one."

"Judges don't much care for evidence tampering. And Franks isn't willing to take the fall. He'll finger you and Beth for the motive."

Charlie's forehead wrinkled, but then he grinned. "You had me there for a minute. But then again, you're negotiating, aren't you? I'll call your bluff. And I'd like to help, but the facts are stacking up against you. The judge isn't going to like what he sees, especially after Richard fires you. I guess that makes me the white knight."

"Don't count on it—"

"Of course, when it comes to Beth, I'm what you might call a knight in shining armor. You see, she thinks I'm wonderful." Charlie pressed his fingers into a tent. "Now, get out of my office."

Chapter 52
Wednesday, August 10th
8:25 P.M.

Spanky's Beachside was only a short walk from Jon's apartment, a convenient excuse to have a drink before Richard arrived. The sun hung low over the treetops, sinking to the west as a warm breeze swept in from the ocean over the restaurant's outdoor deck. He checked his watch and ordered a beer for himself and a chardonnay for Richard, deferring on the appetizers until the next round of drinks.

The meeting was long overdue, and Jon had good reason to be guarded. It had been a week since Stephens had caught him sneaking in at the church, but the discovery had yet to complete the loop to Richard via Randall, and of course, ultimately back to Jon. But there was also the certainty that the Johnson-Medisys deal was about to get tense, especially since Charlie had taken the bait. Today was a day of reckoning, and he didn't expect the conversation to be pleasant.

Jon cleared his thoughts as he spotted Richard in a seersucker suit approaching the table with an outstretched hand. "Thanks for agreeing to meet out here on my turf," he said, standing to greet Richard.

"I suppose it's my fault that you've chosen to show up for a meeting in a flowered shirt and shorts," Richard said. They sat down at the table beneath a neon beer sign.

"Let's give credit, where credit is due." Jon picked up his beer, tilting it toward Richard's wine glass. "Cheers."

"You look different," Richard said, sampling the wine. He shifted for a look at the Atlantic. "I trust that's a good thing."

"Let's not mince words, Richard. Why don't you tell me why you suddenly wanted to meet?"

"It's time we talk. In case you haven't noticed, we've got a situation on our hands."

"I'm listening."

"Sign nothing . . . Does it mean anything to you?"

Jon cut his eyes at Richard, speechless for a moment. "Perhaps you'd better explain yourself."

"Did you follow the advice?"

"That depends."

Richard toyed with his glass. "Ah, my friend, confession is good for the soul. A season is upon me, one that requires your understanding. Of course, you would have figured it out sooner or later. But I've had a change of heart, and it's best you hear it from me."

"Not to mention, you're running out of options," Jon said. "South Coast seems to have an interest in every wealthy person in Savannah, and then some."

"Who tipped you off?" Richard said, frowning.

"Richard, we're talking about blackmail."

"There's no getting past it," Richard said. He gave Jon a guarded look. "Twelve years ago, long before you joined the firm, Stone & Associates was the envy of every boutique investment bank in the Southeast. We closed a major acquisition for Savannah Gas and Light, winning instant notoriety in the business community. The deal earned us credibility and generated more press than money can buy. Business fell at our doorstep. I was landing accounts unheard of for a firm our size." He smiled. "It felt like a real Wall Street firm."

"What's this got to do with me?" Jon said.

Richard paused to finish off his wine, and then motioned for the waiter. "Wealth and influence came quickly for me. Much too quickly. I had no idea of how to handle money or publicity, for that matter."

"I would say you're well past that phase, now."

"That's true. But it might have turned out differently, had it not been for Donna. You see, she sought David Stephens's help when it all started to unravel. It's the reason why I'm ashamed to face you with the facts." Richard wiped his forehead with a handkerchief. "Jon, I had an affair on the heels of my success . . . and Donna found out. She couldn't deal with it alone, so she went to the church for counseling. They referred her to a psychologist, not this Dr. Lowe you're seeing, but it was a similar arrangement. At the time, I had recently joined the church board. Stephens took me to lunch one day and threatened to go public with the affair. It would have ruined what was left of our marriage and thrust Stone & Associates into a scandal. I don't have to tell you, this town simply isn't big enough. You can get past these sorts of things in New York, but not in Savannah. He blackmailed me, Jon. And to this day, Donna doesn't know. God bless her. I just couldn't drag her through it after what I'd done."

"So you paid him off," Jon said. "And now Stephens is after me?"

Richard sat silent while the waiter laid out plates and another glass of wine.

"I'm still paying him off. And yes, he's setting you up. That's why he wants the legal document."

"I didn't sign it."

"If you don't mind my asking, what's he got on you?"

"Photographs. They've staged evidence to make it look like I'm having an affair with Brenda. If that isn't enough, Charlie—"

"Our Brenda?" Richard interrupted.

"You look surprised."

"I had no idea," Richard said. "What's this about Charlie?"

"He modified the Johnson-Medisys contract to give Bob Stein more leverage. But it doesn't matter, the deal's dead."

Richard nodded, and then his eyes met Jon's, but quickly retreated. "Any idea about how they got to Charlie? . . . Never mind, it doesn't matter."

"So you allowed Stephens to come after me. Why haven't you done something to stop him?"

"I was hoping you would find a way to bring him down." Richard looked at Jon, his eyes heavy.

"And you think you have the right to risk my life?"

"Come now, let's not go overboard."

"Someone tried to kill me, Richard."

"Murder? You're saying Stephens wants you dead? That's preposterous."

"I didn't say it was Stephens."

"Hold on now," Richard said. "That's not the way it worked in my situation."

"Well, that's how it's going down for me. And thanks to you, I'm about to take one for the rest of you cowards."

"Jon, I tried to stall them. I contacted one of the church elders, who convinced Beth to accept the verbal agreement when you moved out. I had hoped it would derail their plans."

"Why are you telling me this now?" Jon said.

"I intend to meet with Randall."

"That's not advised."

"Why not?"

"Randall is up to his neck in all of this, not to mention the South Coast land deal. You met with the governor and witnessed the transfer of state property over to the church."

"That was simply a favor. Stephens worked for the governor, you know that."

"Come on, Richard. What do you take me for? Stephens purchased the land for thirty thousand dollars. It's worth two million. That's not exactly what you call separation of church and state."

"You think Stephens is blackmailing Callahan?" Richard sank down in his chair, reflecting. "He's blackmailing the governor."

"And you witnessed the payoff. Your signature, alone, should be good for another twenty years of silence."

"What's he got on the governor?"

"The governor can wait. Right now, I need to know if there's anything else you haven't told me."

"No, Jon. That's everything. I've scheduled a meeting with Randall on Friday. I'm going to get it all out in the open."

Jon slid his beer aside and stood up. "I could lose everything, including my children. Think about that." He started across the deck.

"I'm sorry," Richard called out.

Jon didn't look back.

Chapter 53
Thursday, August 11ᵗʰ
4:45 P.M.

Stephens's next salvo arrived by Federal Express, and although unsettling, appeared to be less toxic than his previous efforts. After reading the letter, Jon's thoughts turned to Richard, whose position on South Coast's board now brought into question his knowledge of Stephens's newest threat to expel him from the church. It certainly brought a new context to Richard's confession at Spanky's the previous evening. After all, Richard had personal considerations. A public humiliation for Jon would introduce the risk of reopening his old wounds. Weighing the options was one of Richard's strong suits. The question was, with the stakes now raised, which path offered him the greatest return.

As he pulled into the church parking lot, Jon mentally rehearsed, preparing to execute the first step in his plan. He moved through the reception area and down the hall, stopping at an assistant's desk.

"I need to see Randall," Jon said.

"He's in with David Stephens," she said. "Was he expecting you, Dr. Browning?"

"It'll only take a minute."

The assistant rose and walked over to Phipps's door. She knocked and entered. A moment later, she motioned for Jon.

"Thank you," he said, closing the door behind him.

The men stood up from a conference table, both very cordial. A set of blueprints lay in front of them.

"Jon," Randall said, offering his hand. "I hope nothing's wrong."

Jon slapped a letter on the table, and then turned without a word.

"What's the meaning of this?" Randall said, skimming the letter. "You're removing your membership?"

"I don't have time for an inquisition. Stephens will explain it to you."

Randall's brow furrowed as he took off his glasses, looking to Stephens.

Stephens cleared his throat, lowering his eyes. "I've been meaning to update you on the Browning marital case."

"Jon, have a seat and let's talk," Randall said.

"I'm afraid it's a bit late for that," Jon said, walking out.

The causeway twisted like a ribbon, bisecting the expanse of marsh grass between Savannah and Tybee Island as if it were floating on the salt creeks. With the tide retreating into the Atlantic, the sun was now headed toward the western horizon. Jon pulled the Z4 off the road to let down the top. He fastened his seatbelt and cranked up the stereo, peeling out as he steered the car toward home. The gears shifted effortlessly as the motor whined like a Stratocaster. At the next curve, he studied the car's shadow as it stretched off into the marsh, finding its way back to the blacktop at the next bend.

A glance at the speedometer confirmed he was clipping along at ninety miles per hour. He pressed harder on the accelerator, backing off only when he approached the next curve. The engine roared as he downshifted, and then accelerated coming out onto the straightaway. The road ahead was clear, so he checked the rearview mirror. He pushed until the needle dipped past one hundred. Anticipating the next curve, he took his foot off the gas and downshifted.

After looking down at the speedometer once again, his eyes locked on the Fort Pulaski entrance coming up. A blue van pulled out onto the highway, moving in his direction, but in the mainland-bound lane. Jon slowed, laying down on the horn. The van seemed unfazed, dodging oncoming traffic as it picked up its pace, just ahead of him. The driver zigzagged across both lanes, slowing just enough to squeeze Jon toward the shoulder.

Jon braked, but at his current speed he knew the Z4 would spin out of control if he steered it onto the grass. If he somehow missed the approaching Lazaretto Creek Bridge, the car would hydroplane across the wet marsh like driving on a sheet of ice.

The driver of the van now straddled the center line, managing to position the rear of the van to within inches of his bumper. Jon accelerated, figuring he had the advantage of getting past him. The van suddenly veered, blocking him from pulling ahead. As the bridge's guardrail clipped past on his right, Jon could think of only one option as he aimed the BMW directly at the van. His bumper crashed into the van's fender, unleashing an eerie sound of crumpling metal. It was followed by the pitch of squealing tires, and in a flash, Jon lost control of the steering as his car locked onto the van. The vehicles started up the arched bridge with the van's engine racing, inching him ever closer to the railing. Jon spun the wheel hard to the left, and the Pirellis finally gripped. The van broke loose, and then went into a spin as the back end slapped the Z4 on the driver's side. The two vehicles ricocheted off each other, sending the van racing into the oncoming lane as the BMW bounced off the guardrail in a shower of sparks.

Glancing over, Jon caught a glimpse of the driver just as the van slammed head-on into a steel support on the far side of the bridge, catapulting end over end into the tide below. His senses seemed to slow in the ensuing seconds as he crashed through the railing, taking to the air. Plunging fifteen feet, the car's front tires struck mud and plowed straight into the marsh. He heard silt and water tearing away at the Z4's body before it careened into a series of rolls. As he lost consciousness, the last thing Jon remembered was the look on Jesse Franks's face as his van plunged into the water.

Chapter 54
Friday, August 12th
6:00 P.M.

The bright light reminded Jon of a childhood dream—one where he was floating in the heavens and surrounded by an endless expanse of big puffy clouds. There was a sense that he should be worried about something, but he couldn't quite shake the feeling that he was in a good place, a safe place. As he did his best to untangle what it all meant, he opened his eyes and saw a blinding whiteness. Wincing, he wanted to shout out in pain, but instead was distracted by a pinging in the distance, slowly getting louder. It sounded like a submarine's sonar . . . coming toward him . . . or was it just getting louder?

A man's face appeared above him, followed by more blinding light. "Jonathon, can you hear me?"

Jon attempted to cover his face, but his hands didn't respond. Instead, he rolled his head to one side.

"Jonathon, this is Dr. Meadows."

"Where . . . am I?" Jon said, scarcely above a whisper. He rolled his eyes toward the voice.

"You've been in an accident," Meadows said. "But you're now in ICU at Memorial Hospital."

Jon squinted, and then opened and closed his eyes, struggling to focus. Standing over by a door, he spotted a blurry Captain and Brenda staring back at him.

"You've suffered a concussion." Meadows lifted one of Jon's arms. "See if you can move your fingers."

Jon managed to squeeze his fingers into a fist and pain shot up his arm, causing him to shut his eyes again.

"That's good," Meadows said. "Painful, I know, but good. I have been treating you with a mild narcotic to help you rest, but it's time to get you up and moving." The doctor prodded at each of Jon's legs, drawing similar reactions. "I'm afraid you're going to be sore for the next few days."

Jon looked around, searching for the source of the pinging. He traced a tube from his arm up to an IV. "Before you torture me any further, can you explain what I'm doing here?" He slowly raised a hand to his forehead.

"You flew your sports car off of the Lazaretto Creek Bridge and rolled it over several times, a hundred feet into the marsh. Lucky for you the tide was out. Otherwise you would have drowned. There was another fellow who wasn't so lucky."

Jon lowered his hand. "The, uh, van."

"That's right, Boy," Captain said, stepping closer. "It was Jesse Franks."

"He was trying to . . . force me off the road." Jon looked over at Captain, and then turned to Brenda.

"Hi," Brenda said, joining Captain at the bed.

"Jon, there's a policeman outside. Evidently, they're still trying to determine who to charge with the accident," Captain said.

"What do you mean? Franks tried to kill me."

"I'm convinced, but you were well over the speed limit," Captain said. "They're debating whether the accident could have been avoided."

"Bring him in, and I'll explain."

"Not so fast. We've called Bill Davenport. I suggest you wait until he arrives before making a statement. Franks is dead."

Jon closed his eyes.

"Richard stopped by earlier," Brenda said. "Once he found out you were okay, he had to leave for an appointment. But he said he would talk to you later." She reached out and touched his arm.

Dr. Meadows stepped away from the bed. "It will take a while for the medication to wear off, so I'll send in a physical therapist in the next hour or so."

Jon watched the doctor walk out, just as Davenport stuck his head in the door. He sat in on the police interview, which lasted until the physical therapist arrived. Afterwards, Davenport hung out in the hallway, making telephone calls. When he returned to the room, Jon was propped up in bed sipping water from a straw.

"I've got to run, but here's the lay of the land," Davenport said. "They're looking into who had the right-of-way. Best case, you'll be ticketed for speeding. Worst case, involuntary manslaughter."

"I already told you about Franks," Jon said. "He's the one who attacked me before. This time, he intended to finish the job."

"That's the guy from the park?" Davenport said.

"And the one who took the photos you saw at the deposition. We think he kidnapped Brenda," Jon said, gesturing toward the door. "Captain and Brenda will testify the man was a lunatic."

"That's great. Of course, the prosecution will use the same photographs as motive to prove you were trying to get revenge. But we'll get together at the office in a couple of weeks and hear them out. Now, you and I have a court date next Wednesday regarding your divorce. Given the circumstances, I could beg off with the judge."

"Not a chance," Jon said. He stirred too suddenly, and the pain soured his expression. "Let's get this thing over."

"I admire your spunk," Davenport said. "What's the decision on the children?"

"I'm going for custody."

"Then have a stiff drink before the proceedings. You're in for one helluva brawl. I'll put you on the stand, but I expect we'll argue with Hallworth until the matter is deferred to a jury trial."

"I'm willing to take my chances."

"Get some rest, and I'll see you next week." Davenport's cell phone rang, and he disappeared into the hallway.

Chapter 55
Saturday, August 13th
11:30 A.M.

Dr. Meadows released Jon from the hospital on Saturday morning with orders to walk as much as he could for the next few days. With the court date approaching, Jon was unwilling to give up his time with the Carver and Bailey, no matter how bruised up he was. He made arrangements with Captain to pick up the children for their weekend visit, while Brenda drove him out to Tybee. When they arrived, she helped him make the climb up the steps, a feat that felt like an ascent on Mount Everest. He plopped down on the porch as she began to open up the apartment.

"We'll wait for the others to join us before taking our first walk," Brenda said, flipping on a ceiling fan. "Do you want to stay out here or lie down on the bed?"

"Brenda, can I ask a favor before the kids arrive?" Jon shifted in the chair. "I need you to logon to my laptop and print a hard-copy of the e-mail sent to Michael for my court file."

"Not a problem. But after that, no more work for today." She walked over and put a hand on his shoulder. "And if you give me any flack, I'll call Sarge at the hospital."

"You say that like it should mean something."

"So you don't remember? Sarge was a nurse in ICU—she had that Mama Cass presence about her. You know the type, sumo wrestler with a touch of peach fuzz on the chin." Brenda laughed. "I think Dr. Meadows was afraid of her." She disappeared into the bedroom.

Jon scanned the beach, feeling better now that he was home once again. He watched an airplane fly by pulling a Fannies on the Beach marquee and smiled, remembering Brenda's last visit. He called out over his shoulder, "Is everything okay in there?"

Brenda stuck her head out. "Jon, the file isn't on the computer." She stood silent for a second, tugging on her bottom lip. "Hang on. I'm going to try something." She went back inside, and moments later, he heard Brenda talking to herself. Finally, she reappeared on the porch. "Someone deleted the file." She hitched a hand on her hip.

"What? I didn't do it. I'm the one who found it."

"Fortunately, I was able to recover it, thanks to Chase." Brenda stopped and leaned her head to one side, staring at Jon. "I don't like that look."

He diverted his eyes to the beach, and then glanced up at her. "I didn't tell you, but Beth was here."

Brenda spun around and started for the screen door.

"Wait, I don't mean now. It was last week. She . . ." Jon stopped mid-sentence.

Brenda was silent as she walked across the porch, looking out over the Atlantic.

"Nothing happened." Jon ran a hand through his hair. "Actually, that's only partially true. I found her inside . . . in the bed. She came on to me." He lowered his head. "And I probably should have thrown her out sooner than I did, but I thought I had a shot at ending all of this nonsense . . . I wanted you to know."

Brenda turned and lowered her eyes, smiling and hugging herself. A tear appeared before she could wipe it away. The emotion quickly dissipated as the sound of stomping feet started up the outside steps.

"Daddy!" Bailey shouted. She opened the door and barreled into Jon's lap.

Jon groaned, lifting her up into the air.

"How's my little Shamu?"

Bailey squeezed her arms tight around his neck.

"Hold it right there, sister. Didn't I tell you Dad was *insured*?" Carver said, marching onto the porch, stern-faced.

Brenda looked at Jon and mouthed, "What?" She smiled, wiping the tear from her cheek.

Jon glanced over at Captain, who was now at the top of the steps, and then turned back to Carver. "I was *injured*, but I'm going to be fine."

"Dad, I saw a picture in the newspaper. It was the Z4," Carver scolded. He planted both hands on his hips.

"Come over here," Jon said. Carver eased over with hands still in place. Jon gave him a hug. "So it's like this, I decided the alligators needed the car more than I did."

Bailey's eyes bulged as she slapped a hand over her mouth and giggled.

"It's not funny, Bailey," Carver said. "Alligators are serious business. Don't you remember the show on Animal Planet?" He shook his head. "Stupid girls."

"What's important is that we're all together. And we have two wonderful guests who are going to help me get better," Jon said.

"Dad, you can sleep with me on the porch tonight," Carver said. "I'll take care of you."

"Stupid boys," Bailey said, sticking her tongue out at Carver.

"That's enough. You guys help Captain with the bags."

Carver and Bailey scrambled to the door, where Captain struggled with an armload.

"Boy, I can already tell you're glad to be home," Captain said, dropping his load on the floor.

Bailey stopped and turned back to Jon. "Is he really a sea captain, Daddy?"

"You want to handle that one, Captain?"

"Come with me to the car, and I'll tell you a tale of the sea," Captain said. He opened the screen door, and they headed downstairs.

Jon cleared his throat. "Are you okay?" he said to Brenda.

"I'm fine," she said. "You're alive, and that's what's important. I guess it's a little soon for me to be putting on like that. I'm sorry."

"No apologies needed."

"Do you think Beth deleted the e-mail?"

Jon rubbed his leg. "The Baines let her in the apartment. I may have surprised her by showing up when I did. Her behavior could have been a diversion."

Brenda shook her head.

"What?" Jon said.

"She seems to have this crazy notion she can control you."

"Listen, I'm glad you know everything." Jon reached out and squeezed her hand. "And thanks for recovering the e-mail."

Brenda's mouth twisted into a smile. "Don't mention it."

"Daddy, Daddy, he is a real sea captain," Bailey shouted, nearly pulling the door off its hinges.

"And he's got a tattoo," Carver said, shuffling in behind Bailey. He was dragging a bag and a Spiderman pillow.

"Boy, what did I tell you?" Captain said.

Carver swung the pillow around and covered his face. "It's a secret," he said, the words all muffled.

Jon and Brenda looked at each other, and started laughing.

Bailey looked up to study their reaction, pasting a funny expression on her face. "Daddy, what's a tattoo?"

"Have Captain explain it to you," Jon said, still choked-up.

"You're gonna just throw me to the wolves?" Captain fired a look at Jon. "I know how to deal with winos . . ." He stopped mid-sentence, when he noticed Bailey hanging on his every word. "Never mind. I'll deal with it."

"Okay, everybody, it's time to take Daddy on a beach walk," Brenda announced.

"Yippee!" Bailey shouted.

Chapter 56
Sunday, August 14th
8:30 P.M.

Just before sunset, Brenda packed up and headed for home. With Jesse Franks out of the picture, she had quickly resolved to move out of the Mission and get her life back. Shortly afterwards, Captain shoved off with the kids and shuttled them back to Skidaway. Jon felt a newfound sadness as he waved goodbye, the emptiness providing motivation enough to focus his energy on the upcoming court date. Back inside, he switched on a lamp and retrieved the safe from his dresser, laying the contents out on the desk. Without realizing what he was doing, he handled the Charleston tapes loosely, like they were contaminated. It wasn't until he had wiped a hand on his shirt for a second time that he realized what he was doing, as the mental image of Franks's tragic death sent a shiver through his body.

Jon extracted the South Coast real estate contract and reviewed it from front to back, stopping when he got to a page with the governor's and Richard's signatures. He felt a knot growing in his stomach, but instead of surrendering, he pressed on, reaching over and arranging the cassettes in sequence by date. Selecting the one labeled, "The Big Peach", he slipped it into a cassette player, and then connected the player to his computer to make a copy. While it recorded, he listened to the tape in its entirety. Afterwards, he caught himself gazing out the double French doors, not sure of how long he had been sitting there. He dropped the tape on the desk and reached for his day planner, checking the dates on the cassette and contract. They matched.

Sinking back into the chair, Jon recalled Richard's confession from four days ago, now with a growing measure of distrust. He closed his eyes and focused. Richard wasn't one to shy away from conflict, a sure indicator that whatever Stephens had on him was pretty damning. It was possible he had come clean at Spanky's, but there was also a chance he was acting out of self-preservation. Jon opened his eyes, running a hand through his hair. It wasn't like Richard to deal in half-truths, especially with something as personal as the confession. Of course, he had always possessed the corporate instinct and knew how to negotiate. On many levels, he was one of Jon's mentors, and someone who had taught him valuable insights on business. If Richard was still hiding something, he wasn't acting with Jon's best interest in mind. But then again, why would he go to Randall, especially if it risked bringing everything out into the open?

Jon picked up his cell phone and dialed.

"Brenda, it's Jon."

"Hi, Jon."

"Listen, I have a question for you." He paused, sensing an awkward silence on the line. "Are you still there?"

"Funny me. I thought you were calling to see if I got home safely."

"Sorry. Is everything okay?"

"Don't patronize me."

Jon hesitated before responding. "I deserved that."

Brenda giggled. "I'm just kidding. What's on your mind?"

"Can you pinpoint the last time Richard met with the governor?"

"That's easy. It was the same day you were allegedly attacked by the wild boar. You had to cover for him on the conference call with Michael."

Jon glanced down at the date on the cassette tape, hesitating for a moment. Flipping in his day planner, he found the page matching the date. Even with "The Big Peach" still a mystery, he now understood why the tape haunted him. It was recorded on the day of the attack in Factors Square—the day after he had picked up the first tape. And it was the same evening he had drinks with Charlie and the others at the Moon River. He ran a finger down the page. There was a note scribbled at the bottom: *Break-in.*

"I called home that evening, and no one answered . . ." Jon's mind drifted to the sidewalk outside of the Moon River and the crowd crossing Bay Street. ". . . It was Beth."

"You lost me," Brenda said. "Weren't we talking about the governor?"

Jon had forgotten he was still on the phone. "Do you know where the governor was staying?"

"It was the Hyatt."

"I've got to go," Jon said. "Can I call you back, maybe tomorrow?"

"Sure. I mean, I'm just the one who's been caring for your children all weekend—"

"Brenda," Jon interrupted. "I will call you."

He hung up and flipped to the previous day in his planner. Next to eight o'clock, it read: *Governor's Reception.*

Chapter 57
Monday, August 15th
6:40 A.M.

A single red rose lay at the base of the cross as Jon sat on the bench in Factors Square with a sense of uneasiness. He was only beginning to grasp the magnitude of what was unfolding, wondering if he had somehow brought it all upon himself. The seven weeks since the attack had been like a dream. But then his fingertips touched the indentation on the bench, where Jesse Franks had struck the first blow, and his mind cleared. He knew at that moment his world was about to change.

Jon's cell phone rang, and he checked the display. "I'm on my way."

When he arrived at the office, Brenda met him at the back door, studying his eyes as he entered.

"Sorry to call so early, but Richard seemed anxious to meet with you. I've never seen him like this."

"Everything will be fine." Jon smiled.

Brenda feigned a response as he headed down the hallway.

Richard sat at his conference table, with the weight of a battleship reflecting in his countenance. "Jonathon, please come in. I'm glad you could make it." He gestured to the chair next to him.

"Richard, are you okay?"

"I met with Randall, as I told you I would." A cup and saucer rattled in Richard's hand as he set them down. "And as I suspected, the story was a complete shock to him."

"I find that rather hard to believe."

"He said he had no idea, and I believe him."

"What happened?"

Richard got out of his chair and strolled over to a window. "Randall called a special board meeting that went on for most of the weekend."

"I know it wasn't easy, but you've done the right thing. Confession is good for the soul—you said so yourself."

"And I was a fool." The intensity of Richard's response caught Jon off guard. "Jonathon, sometimes innocent people become casualties in these things. Of course, I don't have to tell you. You've closed enough deals to understand what can happen in negotiations."

"But that's business."

"You're a student of Dr. Freidman, so you understand market dynamics better than anyone—self-interest has the potential for both good and bad."

"Richard, you do understand we're talking about the church, not one of our clients."

"I appreciate your sensitivity, but I suspect your grasp of history is better than mine. We prefer not to admit it, but we both know the church suffers under the same human conditions as any other institution."

Jon nodded in agreement. "Go on."

"After I told Randall how Stephens blackmailed me, he called a meeting on Saturday morning to brief the board on the situation. The initial discussion was held without David Stephens present, for obvious reasons. Once he was brought in and confronted with the matter, he was offered the opportunity to defend himself. And he did. In fact, he denied everything."

Jon came out of his seat. "The evidence is in his office. I saw it with my own eyes."

"That's the embarrassing part." Richard raised a hand and squeezed his temples.

"You didn't find the files?"

Richard returned to the table, picking up his coffee. "We called in security to search the office, while we held Stephens in the boardroom. There wasn't a trace of anything related to you or me or anyone else, for that matter."

"He moved the files."

"After all this time, why would he do that?"

Jon cut his eyes at Richard.

"You know something you're not telling me?" Richard said. "Never mind, it doesn't matter now."

"You're certain there were no files in Stephens's office?"

"That's right."

"But he's in charge of counseling," Jon said.

"What's your point?"

"Don't you think that's odd?"

"Now that you put it that way . . . I don't know why it didn't occur to me."

"Stephens has no intention of taking a fall."

"You're probably right," Richard said. "After all was said and done, he refused to step down."

"There's one other interesting detail I may not have mentioned. Are you aware Stephens opened a separate set of bank accounts?"

"Of course, I do. They're for SCMI."

"Do Randall and the board have oversight?"

"Randall has his flaws, but on the balance, he's a man of principle. And regardless of Stephens's defiance, he accepted responsibility for his omission. That is, allowing Stephens to operate so freely." Richard paused as he looked Jon in the eyes. "But to answer your question, Randall turned in his resignation."

Jon showed no emotion. "So how is South Coast going to deal with Stephens?"

"I can't say."

"But they're going to, right?"

Richard raised his cup. "It's no longer my business. I also resigned from the board last night."

Chapter 58
Tuesday, August 16th
8:20 P.M.

Jon sat in the South Coast parking lot, trying to decide if Stephens was going to show. An earlier call to Darlene had confirmed a scheduled meeting with Tim Lowe and Sam Hallworth at eight o'clock, and now as he checked his watch, he realized they had been waiting inside for twenty minutes.

Jon had parked the Land Cruiser away from the building, next to an outdoor basketball court. As he waited, a group of middle-aged men shuffled up and down the asphalt in the grueling heat. He could almost smell the sweat dripping, prompting him to turn on the air conditioner.

Just as he was about to give up, Jon spotted a Lincoln turning in at the fountain out front. He tracked the white sedan as it pulled into a reserved spot near the meditation pond. Stephens hopped out, carrying a briefcase and Starbucks cup. Jon sank back in his seat and turned up the air, allowing Stephens time to settle into an agenda with his co-conspirators.

By the time Jon entered, the administrative wing was dark. He slipped down the hallway, noticing a cleaning crew moving between offices at the far end. At the reception area outside of

Stephens's office, he slipped across the carpet and stopped outside his door. In the quietness, he heard muffled sounds inside the office. Jon pressed closer, his heart pounding as he anticipated fireworks when he crashed the meeting. Sound bites came to him, fading in and out, like a bad telephone connection.

"It's . . . too far . . ."

"Sit down . . . Get a grip . . ."

". . . dead . . . you're . . . . illegal . . ."

Even with their elevated voices, Jon was unable to follow the conversation, only that the exchange had spiraled into a series of profanities. He backed away from the office as he heard a crash inside, and then more yelling. Someone jerked open the door, and Jon dipped behind a file cabinet. The door slammed, and Tim Lowe stormed past him, his heels pounding once they reached the tiled hallway.

Jon sprinted after him, slowing when he reached the hall. He called out his name, and Lowe spun around in his tracks, pointing with a folder that was in his hand.

"You . . ." He shook the folder. "Stay away from me or I'll call the police."

"Actually . . . It's a federal case, now." Jon flipped open his cell phone, keeping his eyes on Lowe. "Why don't we start with the FBI?"

"You're deranged." Lowe's neck was turning red. "And the diagnosis proves it."

Jon relaxed, letting his hand drop to his side. He lowered his voice, tempting Lowe with his coolness. "Let's see . . . The diagnosis . . . That would be severe psychosis."

"That's right—"

"Your actions are unconscionable."

"My credentials speak for themselves. Or have you forgotten? I deal with the likes of you every day in this miserable city." Lowe's voice snarled, like a cornered animal.

"Then you won't mind if I get a second opinion."

Lowe shrugged matter-of-factly, pausing to study a painting of *The Last Supper* on the wall. Then a smile appeared. "Professionally speaking, that's completely unnecessary."

Jon sensed Lowe's growing detachment, easing to within inches of him. Up close, his eyes were glassy.

"You're wrong, Tim. And do you want to know why?" Jon planted a finger in Lowe's chest. "I've already gotten a second opinion, and you know the diagnosis, don't you? It's not exactly what you professionals call inconclusive."

Lowe snapped to his senses. "Tell it to my attorney," he shouted, as he turned and disappeared down the hall.

Jon retraced his steps to the office and entered without knocking. Stephens and Hallworth looked rattled as he appeared in the doorway.

"Gentlemen," Jon said. "What do we have here?"

"We're in the middle of a private meeting," Stephens said. "What do you want?"

"I should be asking you that question."

"Leave, or I'll call security." Stephens reached for the telephone.

"I bumped into Tim in the hallway."

"You're crazy, Jonathon. You'd be well advised to do as I say."

"I didn't think you professionals used words like crazy, especially in front of a patient."

"Anything you say can be used in a court of law," Hallworth said.

"So now you want to read me my rights. That's what you've been trying to avoid all along, isn't it?"

"If you're smart, you'll shut up," Hallworth said.

"That's excellent advice. And quite generous, seeing how you're the opposing counsel." Jon sat down in a chair next to Hallworth. "Or perhaps, you're the opposition." Jon cut his eyes at Stephens. "I'm confused in my state of psychosis. Maybe you gentlemen would like to explain your little arrangement."

"How dare you barge into my office, threatening me," Stephens said. "In fact, you're no longer a member here. You're trespassing." He began to dial.

"I'm also a bit fuzzy on this ordained power you keep throwing around. It sounds a bit unorthodox to me."

"This is Reverend Stephens. I need assistance in my office at once," Stephens said, as he glared at Jon.

"Who serves in your kingdom? Lowe? Hallworth? Jesse Franks? I guess we can scratch Franks. He's made what you might call the ultimate sacrifice. But then there's Beth . . . Now she adds an interesting wrinkle."

"We're aware of your predicament, Jonathon. If you're suggesting we had anything to do with Franks's attempt to kill you, then you're wasting your time," Hallworth said. "You'll never prove it in a court of law."

"Shut up!" Stephens shouted, pointing at Jon. "You have nothing. Sam, get this down on paper. The man's making baseless accusations that could ruin my career."

"Next time you see me, you'll think differently." Jon slid out of the chair and turned to face a security guard standing in the doorway.

"You'd better pray Lady Justice is wearing her blindfold on your day in court," Stephens said. "Between the divorce and my defamation suit, you'll be lucky if she doesn't crucify you."

The security guard took Jon by the arm and led him out.

Hallworth got up and closed the door, reaching into his jacket for a cigar. "That's pretty cute. Defamation of character."

"You heard him."

"Only you're forgetting. I'm no good as a witness. I'm your attorney, so it's your word against his."

"That's your defense?" Stephens said.

"Do you think Beth Browning talked?"

"Forget about her. We have to nail Jonathon."

"I'll see him in court tomorrow."

"Do what you have to do . . . And don't smoke that cigar in my office."

Chapter 59
Wednesday, August 17ᵗʰ
10:35 A.M.

"The court has no interest in Mrs. Browning's former profession or her earnings potential, thereof." Judge Green wasted little time in cutting Jon off mid-sentence, without the faintest hope of rebuttal. "While your arguments are dutifully conceived, Dr. Browning, I can assure you that this line of testimony only confirms the obvious—the plaintiff has most recently been employed as a caregiver in the home. So let me make it perfectly clear. I do not wish to entertain further comments on the matter. Counselor, do you have further questions for the defendant?"

"No sir, Your Honor," Hallworth said, stepping away from the podium. As he retreated to a table where Beth was seated, the expression on his face blossomed into a smile. The essence of cheap cigar trailed him back to his seat, where Beth appeared rather amused with the exchange.

"Very well, Mr. Hallworth." The judge shifted his gaze across the aisle, where Bill Davenport had been busy preparing a defense. "Mr. Davenport, I believe you have the honor."

Davenport rose to his feet, buttoning a double-breasted jacket. He rounded the corner of the table, fine-tuning a pair of wire-rimmed spectacles perched on his nose. Deferring eye contact with his client, he contemplated whether Jon realized the judge had just delivered the first strike across the plate. Setting a folder on the podium, Davenport approached the witness stand and handed a document to Jon. "Judge Green, if it pleases the court, I would like to present defendant's Exhibit 1." He circled back to the podium as the judge shuffled papers.

"All right, you may proceed," Green said.

"Dr. Browning, as you are aware, the document before you contains an accounting of cash outlays for the Browning household over the past eight years. Now, I see there are several columns of figures on the report, but the last one is labeled child-rearing expenditures. Could you tell us what these numbers represent?"

"They are figures prepared by our personal accountants—"

"We'll get to that, Dr. Browning," Davenport interrupted. "Please explain the specifics of what is included in the report."

"It addresses everything—food, clothing, school supplies, medical costs, child care, tuition . . . even vacations," Jon said. "I have also highlighted what they refer to as household overhead."

"Can you explain what you mean by overhead?"

"Our accountants have determined that a portion of general expenditures are for the benefit of our children."

Davenport lowered his head and glanced over the top of his glasses. "And what would be included in this household overhead?"

"Things like mortgage payments, insurance, taxes, utilities, and automobile expenses."

"Dr. Browning, would you now tell the court who put together these figures?"

"As I started to say earlier, each month First Savannah provides an electronic report to our personal accountants."

"And who are your accountants?"

"Jones, Lockhart & Reed."

"Might this be the same group of CPAs I've read about in the *Atlanta Business Chronicle*—the ones who serve some of Georgia's most influential citizens, including sports and media celebrities?" Davenport said.

"Yes, it is. That's how I heard about them."

"You read about them in the *Business Chronicle*?"

"That is correct."

"I just wanted to make sure you weren't referring to the celebrities." Davenport paused as he detected a snicker from Beth. "Why do you and Mrs. Browning require such a service? Now don't be offended, 'cause you've done quite well for yourselves. But isn't this a bit much, Dr. Browning?"

"That depends. I've always had a goal of becoming financially independent, regardless of earning capacity. In fact, a modest income makes a game plan all the more important. And based on my experience, Jones, Lockhart & Reed has a solid track record in doing just that."

"I see . . . You're referring to a disciplined approach," Davenport said. "And from your recollection, did Mrs. Browning agree with your plans, and if so, how did she feel about them?"

Hallworth came out of his seat, preempting Jon's response. "Your Honor. At present, I believe we've heard enough about Dr. Browning's perspective on financial planning. If I'm not mistaken, Mr. Davenport agreed to limit the discussion to historical expenditures and the generous support both of these parents have provided to their dear children. In due time, I am sure we will address the assets and longer term implications of these proceedings. When we do, I am confident Mrs. Browning can provide a personal account of her objectives as they relate to financial matters. After all, she is an accomplished professional with a college degree."

"Mr. Davenport?" Green said, apparently undecided on the matter.

"Your Honor, the long term plans help clarify the cash outlays. Mrs. Browning is requesting a substantial settlement in this case. I am merely establishing the credibility of the information in the exhibit, and that it accurately represents this family's finances. The present and future are inseparable, if we are to understand the financial landscape in this case."

"Mr. Davenport, I'll go along, but Mr. Hallworth's objection is so noted. You'll both have an opportunity to be heard when we take up the issue of marital assets."

Davenport waited for Green's permission to proceed, which came with a wave of His Honor's glasses. "Dr. Browning, is Mrs. Browning aware of the bank services that are being used to provide visibility into the household finances?"

"Yes, she is. We've managed our finances this way for the past eight years. The report confirms this."

"Do you have confidence in these figures?" Davenport held up the exhibit.

"Our income taxes are filed using the same data, so the answer is yes."

Hallworth popped up a second time, "Your Honor, the defendant need not provide additional commentary to the court. The question called for a simple yes or no."

Davenport rephrased the question, "Do you have confidence that the figures are accurate and reliable?"

"Yes," Jon said.

"If called upon to do so, do you believe a representative from Jones, Lockhart & Reed would be available to come before this court and testify as to the credibility of the figures?" Davenport said.

"Objection," Hallworth shouted.

"I withdraw the question. Dr. Browning, do you believe these figures accurately represent what is required to generously support the children in the years ahead?"

"Unquestionably," Jon said.

Pleased with Jon's responses, Davenport continued, "Dr. Browning, based on the factual data your CPAs have professionally tracked over the past eight years, what observations can you make about Mrs. Browning's petition for financial support?"

"When compared to the accountants' report, I find her demands to be roughly double our historical spending levels. Mrs. Browning's request for support bears no resemblance to our current lifestyle."

Hallworth flinched, but then thought better of coming out of his seat again. Instead, he leaned over and whispered into Beth's ear. She nodded back at him.

Green stirred in the bench, and then peered over the top of his bifocals. "To Mr. Davenport's earlier point, I'd like to get to the specifics, Dr. Browning. What exactly are you saying is overstated in the plaintiff's affidavit?"

"Your Honor, if we start at the top, the disparities are numerous—"

"For example, the mortgage," Davenport interrupted. "The plaintiff's affidavit lists a house payment that is substantially more than the one on the current residence, which is conservatively valued at seven hundred and fifty thousand dollars. She's requesting that Dr. Browning support her charitable donations to the tune of four figures. My client has agreed to carry the children on his health insurance, but for some unknown reason there seems to be a need for another thousand dollars a month in medical expenses. From best I can tell, he's also being asked to fund the plaintiff's personal savings of twenty-four thousand a year. And I know we've agreed to talk about this later, but we must put matters into context. Dr. Browning has offered the plaintiff fifty percent of all financial assets, which alone provides Mrs. Browning with cash accounts in excess of three hundred thousand dollars. And despite that, my client has been petitioned to fund future college expenses, adding yet another four hundred and fifty thousand dollars of personal liability. I haven't even touched on the non-cash property she will receive. A quick review of Dr. Browning's financial affidavit clearly demonstrates he doesn't have the faintest hope of committing to such terms." Davenport closed his folder.

Green studied the report for a moment before continuing. "Mr. Davenport, do you have anything else?"

"No sir, Your Honor."

"Very well, Mr. Hallworth, you may proceed."

Hallworth pushed back his chair and stood in place. "Did Mrs. Browning agree to hire Jones, Lockhart & Reed? And if so, did she concede to their rather stringent method for controlling expenditures?"

"I question your choice of words—"

"Dr. Browning, you're not here to make enquiries," Hallworth interrupted. "I ask the questions, and you provide answers. In this particular case, I am once again asking for a simple yes or no—"

"Your Honor," Davenport called out over a shoulder, still en route to his seat. He turned. "Your Honor, Mr. Hallworth is attempting to impugn my client with his masterfully crafted questions. The opinions of the plaintiff's attorney have no place in this line of questioning."

"Mr. Hallworth, do you wish to modify or withdraw the question?"

"Your Honor, I'll modify. Dr. Browning, did Mrs. Browning agree to hire Jones, Lockhart & Reed and operate under this particular method of controlling expenditures?"

"Are you referring to now or when we originally made the decision?" Jon said.

"Yes, yes. Tell me everything," Hallworth said, exhaling.

"When we first married, she was one hundred percent in agreement with—"

"One hundred percent? Come on, Dr. Browning . . . a hundred percent?"

Davenport had just seated himself, when he sprang to his feet again. "Your Honor, I respectfully object to Mr. Hallworth's attempts to intimidate my client into modifying his statement. Does he want to hear from Dr. Browning or not?"

"Mr. Hallworth?" Green said.

Hallworth rephrased, "Dr. Browning, are you certain she was one hundred percent in agreement?"

"Yes, I am sure."

"And how long ago was that?"

"Almost eight years."

"Eight years . . . I see. And today?"

"It's obvious she has a different perspective."

"A different perspective," Hallworth repeated. "Are you suggesting she has changed, and you have remained totally committed to the original plan? Are you testifying that you have followed, to the letter of the law, each and every word of the original plan, as you call it? Are you suggesting that factors in your lives have not changed that might have an impact on her perspective today?" He reached inside his jacket and fingered a cigar as a sour expression formed on his face. "Have you followed through on all of the commitments the two of you made eight years ago?"

"Your Honor, must my client continue to endure this derogatory mode of interrogation? This is not *The People's Court.*" Davenport removed his glasses.

"Gentlemen, it's time for a little prayer meeting," Green said. "I'll see you both in my chambers." Without batting an eye, the judge rose and disappeared through a door behind the bench.

The two attorneys glared at one another before scrambling to an exit. The court reporter grabbed a pad and followed suit. Beth and Jon sat speechless, suddenly shrouded in silence as the morning sun drifted into the courtroom through a cathedral-like window.

In a hallway outside, the attorneys negotiated a series of twists and turns, pushed through a set of frosted doors, passed an assistant's station, and then entered Judge Green's office. The judge had already seated himself at a desk, flipping through an assortment of legal documents and phone memos. He looked up when the court reporter appeared in the doorway.

"If you don't mind," Green said, "this is a private matter."

* * *

"What in hell's name are you doing?" Beth said. She sat on the edge of her seat with her eyes glued to Jon on the witness stand. "That accident must have knocked something loose."

Jon responded by addressing a police officer in the back of the room. "Is it okay if I leave the stand?"

"Just remain in the courtroom." He hitched a hand on his holster, and then exited a door at the rear.

Jon stepped out of the stand. "We'll discuss the accident, as you call it, when the judge returns."

"Hey, just remember, you're no Boy Scout," she snickered. "And by the way, you're boring us all, Darling. That judge looks like he could pass out any minute. But that's about to change. We've enlarged a few of our photographs into glossy eight by tens, the perfect size for a half-blind judge."

"I would be disappointed, if you hadn't," Jon said, starting toward her table.

"Do you want to wager on whose story he buys? I'll bet he doesn't know a merger from an acquisition. You're out of your element." She raised a shoulder, looking directly into his eyes as a smile surfaced. "What's that look?"

"I came here to do the right thing. But I'll let you in on a little secret. I know more than you think about your arrangement with Franks."

"Nice try."

"And your involvement with the others," Jon said. "Shall I continue?"

Beth's demeanor cooled as she slid out of her seat and walked round the table, picking up a water pitcher. She filled a glass, clearly detached from the debate. "The officer locked the door on his way out," she said, plucking an ice cube from the water and touching it to her lips. Then she cut her eyes up at the judge's bench.

"Beth—"

"There's that Boy Scout look again." She eased closer and draped an arm over Jon's shoulder.

Chapter 60
Wednesday, August 17th
11:20 A.M.

Bill Davenport closed the door to Judge Green's office and joined Hallworth at a conference table. Both men sat in silence, trying to read the judge as he reclined behind his desk, studying his clasped hands.

Green spoke without looking up, "Sam, what's the meaning of these shenanigans. I'm trying to conduct a hearing, and here you are carrying on like a damn politician. I don't have to remind you. These antics don't set well in my courtroom. You keep it up, and you're going to find me on the defendant's side of the aisle."

"Judge, if you'll allow me. My client may wish to exercise her right to a jury in this case, but I'm still conferring with her on the matter. We're hopeful of reaching a resolution without the expense of a trial, but it's difficult, given the defendant's unwillingness to negotiate on reasonable terms." He glanced over at Davenport.

"Your Honor, I respectfully disagree," Davenport said. "Based on the plaintiff's current demands, my client has no choice but to petition the court for custody of the children."

The judge gave Davenport a tired look. "This is a sad state of affairs, gentlemen. You both know where I stand." Green pushed a button on his telephone. "Would you bring in the docket?"

The door opened, and a woman popped in, firing away rapid-fire. "Judge Green, the first opening is four weeks out—"

"What about the jury docket?" Green said.

"Let's see . . . twelve weeks."

"Sam, are you sure this is in your client's best interest?" Green waved the assistant out of the room. "While you're contemplating a response, let's have a look at your billing."

Hallworth hesitated.

"I know you brought it, just in case we reached a settlement. Let's have it."

Hallworth dug through a leather portfolio and produced a single sheet of paper. The judge took it, wrinkling his forehead after a quick review. Next, he secured Davenport's billing. When he was done, he laid them aside and removed his glasses.

"Sam, how long have you been working on this case?"

"It's been a few months—"

"Six weeks," Davenport interrupted.

"Based on these figures, I'd say you gentlemen are working on entirely different cases," Green said. "This doesn't look good, Sam. What's your defense?"

"There's the matter of an investigation into Dr. Browning's personal affairs. It may interest the court to know that we have recently determined that the defendant has been engaged in certain indiscretions."

"Go on," Green said.

"I believe a jury will find my client's demands to be quite reasonable, once they are presented with the evidence."

* * *

Jon removed Beth's arm from his shoulder, and she turned and worked her way around the witness stand and up a set of steps to the judge's bench. Up top, she found the judge's robe and draped it around her, dropping into his chair as she scooped up the gavel from its perch.

"My mother used to brag about how you had a gentle breeze in your sail," Beth said, eyeing the gavel. "But she never quite understood that corporate instinct of yours, did she? You and your little band of worshippers . . . They treat you like you're some kind of prophet. Even the governor thinks you're wonderful." She tested the gavel against her palm.

"Let's talk about a settlement," Jon said, looking up at the bench. "We should work out what's best for the children."

Beth slammed the gavel down on the bench. "So what do you have to offer, counselor?"

Jon raised his hands and paced a few steps up the aisle. As he turned to face her, the cavernous courtroom amplified his words. "For starters, you take the house—"

"The house," Beth mocked. "I'm touched, Darling."

"Let's be serious."

"What else, counselor?"

"The retirement accounts," Jon said. "And the Lexus—it's already paid off."

"Pay off . . . I like the way you think. Let's explore that train of thought a little further." Beth stood up, and the robe slid off her shoulders. She closed her eyes, fingering a button on her jacket. "Come here—"

"Beth, forget—"

"I said, come here."

"If you'll just be civil, I'm going to give you what you came for."

"Like you have a choice," She said, staring down at him.

"You can take the savings and investments."

"Well-well," Beth said. "That's raising the flag."

"With the house, you're looking at a settlement of one and a half million."

Beth fell back into the chair. "Your first love—all mine, Darling." Her expression sobered. "I want it in writing."

"Done."

"And the money wired into my account."

Jon wavered for a moment, and then casually approached the bench. "There's only one condition. I'll walk away from it all, but I need one thing."

Beth's eyes widened.

"I want the children," Jon said.

Beth tilted her head, lowering her gaze upon Jon. Her eyes were lonely, like a bottomless black hole. She lifted the gavel high above her head, allowing it to hover in the air for a few seconds. Then she thrust it down on the bench with a force that echoed across the courtroom.

"Sold!" she said.

Chapter 61
Thursday, August 18th
9:15 A.M.

Richard twisted a Mont Blanc pen, studying an inscription as if it held the meaning of life. "You've got to hear me out. I had no idea it would come to this."

There was a knock at the door, and Brenda entered with a folder. She set it on the conference table. "Bob Stein is on the phone. He says it's urgent." She turned to Jon. "And I need you to sign some paperwork after you're done, here."

"Tell him I'll call back," Richard said, waiting for Brenda to leave. "I officially dismissed Charlie this morning, and there's the matter of removing his signing authority from the operating accounts. As chief operating officer, you'll need to execute the documents." He dropped the pen on the table.

"Of course," Jon said. He noticed Richard staring at his woven shirt. "I know it's not policy, but I'm leaving as soon as we're done."

"Listen . . . Charlie is out of the picture, and he was next in line, behind you. We both know Terri isn't looking to take on more responsibility. This wasn't in the script, Jon."

"We both know Michael gave notice a month ago that he intended to terminate the agreement. Bob thought it was a bluff, but he was dead wrong."

"I need you to get Michael back at the table," Richard said, leaning forward in his chair. "This acquisition puts Stone & Associates back on top."

"I'll call one of the Merrill partners in Atlanta," Jon said. "I'm sure they can rustle up half a dozen resumes within the week."

"That won't revive the Johnson-Medisys negotiations."

"The deal is dead, Richard."

"But it's worth millions to the firm," Richard said. "Of course, you already know that."

"Of course."

"I'm offering to make you a partner, Jon."

Jon's eyes drifted over to the window. "Of course, you are."

Opening the folder, Richard dropped a contract on the table. "With the partnership, you will take thirty percent of the Johnson-Medisys fees in the form of equity. At our current capitalization, you will hold a minority ownership in the firm and receive fifteen percent of the profits from this point forward. It's all there."

"I appreciate the offer, but I'm leaving."

"I need you in this partnership. I'll concede I mishandled the South Coast situation, but that's behind us now. You have my word that nothing of this nature will ever happen again. Tell me what else I can do."

"How about the governor?"

"To my knowledge, he knows nothing of your circumstances. And if it's Stephens you're concerned about, I can't accuse the governor of being mixed up in blackmail. I have no evidence."

Jon stood up and walked over to the window, staring outside. "Stephens, now there's a name I would like to forget."

"Jon, you've been through hell. A divorce, alone, is enough to handicap anyone. And you've got all this South Coast nonsense on top of that. Don't jeopardize your future."

"I won't stand idle while this self-ordained hypocrite continues to control people with his so-called religion."

"How do you intend to bring him to justice, especially since he's hiding behind the church veil? And anyway, the records have all disappeared. We'll have to trust that Stephens will get his due, even if it's not until the hereafter."

"The courts won't touch him, once they discover that the church records contain confidential counseling information." Jon ran a hand through his hair as he walked back to the conference table. "Michael has offered me an interim CEO position at Johnson-Medisys . . . and I've accepted."

"But he's broke," Richard said. "He needs the Chatham deal more than Bob."

"You're forgetting. The patents have issued on his intellectual property."

"All the more reason to accept Chatham's original terms."

"Bob is the one who breached the agreement, and Michael called his hand. The problem is, Chatham can't hit their current growth projections without the merger, nor can they cover the breakup fee without outside capital. As it turns out, they've burned through their cash."

"That's exactly why Michael and Bob have to sit down and resolve their differences."

"Michael has signed a term sheet with a VC," Jon said. "Johnson-Medisys now has access to funding that will keep them and Chatham afloat."

"Venture capital? That's preposterous."

"The creditors are supporting Michael's offer to acquire Chatham Medical Devices."

"Bob and his investors will lose everything. You can't do this to me."

Jon cut his eyes at Richard.

"Richard, you did it to yourself."

"So you're just going to turn your back on me?"

"Once the merger is complete, I'll step down, and Michael will resume the reigns at Johnson-Medisys. After that, I'm planning to launch a venture fund focused on emerging biotech startups. A number of firms have already expressed an interest, and I'll allow you to participate as a passive investor under two conditions. One—not a nickel more of Stone & Associates' money goes to South Coast. Two—whatever Bob Stein's professional fate, you agree to sever your relationship with him. We'll put it in writing."

"Number one noted and accepted," Richard said. "As for your second condition, hasn't Bob paid a big enough price?"

"The matter is not up for debate, Richard."

Richard sat silent for a moment, toying with his pen. "Done," he said. "But hear me out on one point. South Coast is the exclusive beneficiary of Stone & Associates long-standing policy of giving back to the community. Once I cut them off, I'll be faced with some pretty bad publicity. Stephens will see to it."

"In my opinion, you should press charges," Jon said. "But in the interim, leave Stephens to me."

"Are you certain that's how you want to proceed?"

"Positive." Jon stood up.

"Perhaps we can have a drink at the club later and flush out more of the details?"

"Much later."

* * *

The Mission was dark as Jon climbed the stairs to Captain's office. Nearing the landing at the top, he heard Captain wrapping up a telephone call. By the time he made it to the doorway, he found Captain pouring a cup of coffee.

"I was hoping you would be in," Jon said.

"Out of purgatory, are you? You're looking cheery, considering yesterday's rumors."

"News travels fast in this town."

"A street preacher is half intelligence officer, remember?"

"How were the grits this morning?"

Captain gave him a bothered look. "A bit on the runny side. But you know the boys, there were no complaints."

"About the divorce settlement," Jon said. "I won, you know?"

"Coffee, Boy?" Not waiting for a response, Captain picked up a mug and blew inside of it. "Now there's a headline. Rich boy leaves country club lifestyle for beach shack. That is, if he can still afford it. Maybe we can get the *Savannah Press* to print a cover story."

"Now that you mention it, I'd like to speak to your friend at the *Press*. What was his name?"

"Talbot," Captain said.

"You're overlooking the fact that I got the kids."

"Now don't go shoving out to sea just yet," Captain said. "You'd do well to remember who you're dealing with."

"Bill Davenport drew up the final agreement, and I've already signed it. Once we wire the funds to Beth tomorrow morning, it will be official."

"Congratulations. Guess I've never seen a man so happy to lose it all. I can offer you room and board, if you like. But you'll have to work for it, seeing how I've got money problems of my own."

"What's going on with your sponsors?"

"Hurricanes, typhoons, mudslides—you name it." Captain tipped his cup. "Most of the businesses in Savannah are global players, now. They have to spread the charity around for publicity purposes. You can't blame them."

"Sorry about what happened at South Coast. I thought we had a shot at a partnership. Who knew Richard would step down from the board?"

"Now that crew, I hadn't counted on. So save your breath," Captain said.

"I have another idea, if you're up for it."

"You just let me deal with this."

"If that's the way you feel, I'll take it up at the Mission's next board meeting."

"You're a might bit sure of yourself this morning, aren't you?"

"After all is said and done, I'm still an investment banker. And don't you forget it."

Chapter 62
Friday, August 19ᵗʰ
8:00 A.M.

The Land Cruiser backed up the winding drive, stopping at a brick walkway. Jon hopped out and opened the tailgate, taking a moment to breathe in the sweetness of the marsh. The morning had yet to surrender to the sun, the breeze offering a lingering crispness. As he headed up the walk, a sonnet emerged from a canopy of moss-draped oaks. What had once been a manicured lawn, remained only in his memories as the front door opened and Beth appeared in an outfit fit for the cover of *Vogue*. Jon looked at the yard one last time. "Just walk away," he said to himself.

Beth stepped off the porch, with her high heels clicking on the brick steps. She stopped at the bottom, a little too close for Jon's comfort. "Did you say something?" Looking down, she smoothed her skirt as Jon backed away. Before he could respond, she continued, "Never mind. Listen, I've already got the children packed."

"How are they doing?"

"That's what I wanted to talk to you about. Until we're comfortable with the arrangements, I've told them they're going to have an extended visit with you—"

"Hold on. Whatever you're up to, I'm not going along with it. That's why I wanted to be here for—"

"They're children, dearest Jonathon. And regardless of your opinion on the matter, we shouldn't act in haste."

"We have to be honest with them, starting now."

"Is that how it works in your world of mergers and acquisitions? I don't think so."

"This is different." Jon started up the steps, and Beth cut him off. "Where are their things?"

"We'll do this my way, or I'll call Sam Hallworth," Beth said.

Jon pulled out his cell phone.

"I'm warning you," she said.

"Do I need to call Bill Davenport and stop the transfer?" Jon flipped the phone open.

"You're like the rest of them."

"I have no clue what that means."

Beth hitched a hand up on her hip and opened her mouth to vent, but hesitated when she looked into his eyes. Pushing a strand of hair behind an ear, she looked away. "Listen, my mother doesn't know about the settlement. She came over last night, and I couldn't trust Carver and Bailey not to blab. All hell is going to break loose when she finds out."

"You didn't answer my question."

"I need a little time . . . to think this through. Then I'll deal with it." The whites of her eyes turned red.

"I'll get the kids, so you can take care of whatever it is you need to do," Jon said.

"Their bags are beside the door."

"What about the rest of their things?"

"You got the children, not the rest of their stuff."

"That's how you want to play this?"

"They have a home here, too," Beth said, turning as the front door inched open and a nose stuck out. "Bailey, wait inside."

"But I want to see Daddy."

"Do as I say or you'll spend the weekend in your room." The door slammed, and Beth turned to face Jon. "How are you going to live in that beach shack with two children? You've got nothing. And I have it on good authority that Richard's cleaning house downtown, so you just might be out of a job." She looked away, proud of herself. "Then again, maybe you can live with that LBJ heathen. I hear street thugs make excellent playmates for children."

Jon stepped up on the porch and grabbed the overnight bags. Carver's Spiderman pillow was on top. "I'll put these in the car. Just send out the kids."

"I swear, if you try to tarnish me in the eyes of my children or anyone else—"

"You're doing just fine on your own, Beth."

"Who died and made you pope? Your career and that stupid PhD, they're worthless. We're about to find out who really thinks you're wonderful."

"Five," Jon said.

"Don't you dare threaten me."

"I have names."

"Good bluff, Darling."

"Five," Jon said, holding up his fingers. He stared into her eyes.

"You'd like people to believe that, wouldn't you?" Beth followed on his heels he carried the bags to the car. "If you think you can waltz around and play God, then you've got another thing coming."

"I'm doing no such thing. And if I were you, I wouldn't confuse God with the affairs of South Coast Ministries . . . Incorporated."

"You say that, like South Coast is the sign of the beast."

"It's a sign of something all right."

"You're losing your mind."

Jon tossed the bags in the car. "Does Stephens have any idea that you beat him at his own game?"

"Ever the negotiator, aren't you?" Beth said. Her confidence slipped as she noticed a smile forming at the corners of his mouth.

"Need I remind you, God knows everything?"

"And you know nothing."

"Time will tell."

"Jon, wait," Beth said, grabbing his forearm.

"Get the children, Beth." Jon removed her hand. "And go buy yourself a new outfit or something."

Chapter 63
Saturday, August 20th
6:30 A.M.

Jon had always loved the beach in the morning, hopelessly addicted to sunup. He brewed a pot of coffee, and then walked down to the surf to watch the big red ball leap out of the ocean. The children woke up around eight to the smell of bacon and banana pancakes. Brenda showed up in time to set the table on the porch, and later helped rearrange the apartment to keep the three of them from tripping over each other. The task was complete by mid-afternoon, down to a string of palm tree lights on the porch, Brenda's housewarming gift to the children.

Carver and Bailey couldn't wait to hit the beach, coaxing Brenda to take them for a walk, just as Captain showed up for a visit with Jon.

"Now ain't that a sight to tickle the soul," Captain said, studying the children as they scampered across the sand with Brenda chasing them. "I have to confess, you got the better end of the deal. Is everything final with the bloody lawyers?"

Jon sat on the porch next to Captain, nodding. "The settlement is fully executed. You're looking at a man who's poor in the wallet, but rich at heart."

"You know, the Good Book says there's nothing new under the sun. The way I see it, everything started and ended with your wallet, in more ways than one."

"Well, a wallet by any other name . . ." Jon leaned back in the chair with his hands cradled behind his head, cutting his eyes at Captain. The weariness seemed to be gone. "So give me the good news."

"Who says there's good news?"

Jon waited in silence.

"It appears that Richard Stone wants to stake out some holy ground of his own," Captain said.

"Go on."

"He gave me a check for ten grand and said it was a first installment."

Jon whistled. "That'll buy a lot of grits."

"A man never really knows when he's in the presence of an angel," Captain said. "And now that I think about it, I prefer my angel theory better than that holy rock approach of yours down at Factors Square." He took one last look at the Atlantic and popped out of his chair. "It's time for me to ship out."

"Do you mind if I bring the kids down to the Mission in the morning?"

"While you're at it, send them over next Friday to work the breakfast line," Captain said, heading for the screen door. "By the way, Sanky sends his greetings."

"I hope you don't mind, but I contacted a friend at SCAD, who just may be interested in taking on a restoration project at the Mission."

"Savannah College of Art and Design? Now, that'll make a statement. I like it," Captain said as he started down the stairs. "Blessings to you, Boy."

Jon looked out at the beach, where Brenda was playing Ring-Around-the-Rosy with the kids. Heading in to the bedroom, he pulled out the safe and dumped the cassettes on his desk, selecting the original from the Tybee Island Causeway. He found an oversized envelope and a slip of paper, and then copied an address onto the envelope, underlining "Attention: Aaron Talbot, Editor, *The Savannah Press*. Holding up the cassette, he said, "Stephens, I would like to introduce you to Aaron Talbot," and dropped it into the envelope.

Looking across the desk, Jon's eyes settled on a photo in the tropical frame from Carver and Bailey's first weekend visit to Tybee. The three of them stood with their arms locked in the edge of the surf.

Carefully placing the remaining tapes back in the safe, Jon paused at the one labeled, "The Big Peach". He dropped it in with the others and returned the safe to the drawer.

Slipping on his swimsuit and sunglasses, Jon descended the stairs, stopping off at the mailbox. He lifted the flag and slid the envelope inside, and then hurried across the boardwalk to the beach, joining Brenda and the children in the edge of the surf.

"Hey, you bunch of guppies."

"Dad, I'm not a guppy," Carver protested. "I'm a shark."

"And I'm the Little Mermaid," Bailey squealed as she studied the tide washing over her feet.

"And Brenda's a barracuda," Jon said, bracing himself for a slap on the arm.

"What are you, Daddy?" Carver said.

"I am the beast from the deep blue sea." Jon grabbed Bailey and swung her in a circle before snuggling her close.

"Those beasts don't live around here," Carver said, looking to his dad for reassurance.

"They can only be found in the Caribbean."

Carver looked out at the waves. "Anyhow, sharks and beasts are friends, right?"

"Only if the shark agrees to eat his vegetables," Jon said.

"Sharks don't eat vegetables. They eat people," Carver said.

"Eeww," Bailey screeched.

"Say, why don't we head down to the pier for corndogs and ice cream?" Jon said.

"Yippee!" Brenda shouted, letting out a giggle.

Just as the kids began to hop about in the surf, Jon's cell phone rang. He checked to see who was calling, and then flipped it open.

"Richard, you're about to miss a beautiful sunset." Jon paused, listening for a moment. "I see . . . That makes me feel better . . . Yes." He nodded. "That's great. So you and the governor have an understanding. He told you what? . . . He still wants me to spearhead the campaign? Well, the timing's not good for me. When you speak to him again, perhaps you can deliver a message? Tell him I've just put away a little something for his reelection in a safe place . . . That's right . . . to help get the word out to the people next fall. And I'm sure he'll appreciate this later, but tell him it's from me and Beth." Jon paused. "Glad to hear it. Give my best to Donna."

The children ran ahead as Brenda turned to him, her eyes hidden behind a pair of sunglasses.

"Is everything okay?"

"Couldn't be better."

"I thought you and Beth were, well, sort of done."

"Sometimes confession is good for the soul. But there are other times when patience is the best policy." Jon rested a hand on her shoulder. "Trust me."

"So, is that your new philosophy?"

"Actually, it's not new."

Brenda wrapped an arm around Jon's waist and squeezed. "I don't exactly know what that means, but I always knew you were going to be all right. Now, about that dinner you promised me. I was thinking about Fannies on the Beach and dancing."

"That's not exactly my cup of tea. Anyway, we've got the little palm tree lights on the porch. How about grilled lobster, a nice Joseph Phelps cabernet, Johnny Mercer on the stereo and . . ."

"And . . ." Brenda said, waiting. She lifted her sunglasses, opening her eyes wide. "A little blue dress?"

Jon smiled, and then looked up ahead. "Guys, wait up," he called out, dragging Brenda along.

They caught up to Carver and Bailey, who were playing leap frog over a tidal pool. When they got closer to the pier, the smell of French fries sent the kids into a frenzy. Inside the pavilion, a band was drawing a crowd.

"Hey, that's *Light In Your Eyes*," Brenda said, singing along. She started up the stairs, taking Bailey by the hand.

Jon felt a tug on his arm and stopped to look down at Carver, who stood frozen in place. Staring up, with the wheels turning inside his head, Carver placed a hand on his hip.

"Something you need to say?" Jon said.

"Dad, can I have a tattoo?"

Dennis Carr lives in Atlanta where he and his wife, Cheryl, enjoy sailing in their spare time. His writing delves into the private lives of corporate executives, where egos and bottom lines make for great mystery. His second novel, *Corporate Rules*, is a global biotech thriller.

Follow Dennis on Facebook

www.ingramcontent.com/pod-product-compliance
Lightning Source LLC
Chambersburg PA
CBHW020819180626
46814CB00001B/33